PLANETARY DESTRUCTION IS IMMINENT AND ALL I GOT IS THIS STAT MENU

J. J. ACKERKNECHT

This one's for me, and for you, too.

PREVIOUSLY, IN "HOMICIDAL ALIENS ARE INVADING AND ALL I GOT IS THIS STAT MENU"

The Engineers sent the Accumulated Universal Knowledge Archive Project (or just "The Archive," if you're in a hurry) to Earth, and ruined everybody's weekend. Anya Nowicki was already having a tough time, as she'd just quit her job as a barista and was wondering how she was going to make rent, when the Archive—and its Artificial Intelligence assistant, Felix—crashed into her shitty apartment in Brooklyn and integrated with her. Felix informed Arya that the Archive had been sent to Earth as a defensive measure against some invading aliens that were due in a month. Hearing such news, Anya did what any reasonable person would do in the same situation: assumed she had gone insane and went to bed.

However, Anya's best friend Tori confirmed the next day that Anya was not insane (to her mild relief), and that it seemed like aliens really were on their way (to her extreme disappointment). Since it was obvious that things were only going to get worse, Anya decided to get superpowers. Using the Archive and its nigh-limitless ability to grant skills and abilities, Anya granted herself super strength (which did wonders for her height and metabolism), the ability to summon the fiery power of the Flame Dominion, and regenerate from any damage, as well as a few other things.

Following her power-up, Anya was contacted by the Engineers themselves, specifically an Initiate named Red-507. Red-507 informed Anya and Tori that the aliens, known as gnosiphages or "knowledge eaters," were due within hours, not weeks. Also, Anya wasn't the only host for the Archive, but one of thousands all over the globe. Tori left to go inform the police, while Anya hurried to meet with Earl, a nearby host, along with a pair of reporters: Jennifer and Angel. All four encountered the alien in the center of the park, where it made quick work of killing Earl, and several police officers. Anya managed to save Jennifer and Angel as well as one of the officers before she barely managed to kill the alien.

Anya fled the park after the fight and returned to Tori's apartment to recover. Her fight with the alien had increased Anya's Archive level significantly, allowing her to level up and acquire her first class: Phoenix Monk. After leveling up, Anya decided it was time to meet with somebody official, and sat down to breakfast with Christian Riley of the FBI to discuss the invasion. Things didn't go as smoothly as either of them would have liked, and Anya excused herself after committing some light assault on several other federal agents.

Deciding that finding other hosts was the priority, Anya and Tori took off for the nearest host signal, located in Virginia. There, they encountered a pangolin named Pan who had become super intelligent (well, for a pangolin) and capable of speaking. But almost immediately after finding Pan, they were attacked by a gnosiphage, a special type known as an overseer that addressed Anya as "Thief," and adapted to her attacks during the fight. Anya nearly died, but managed to chase the overseer away thanks to some assistance from Tori and the United States Air Force.

The Air Force escorted Anya, Tori, and Pan to a base nearby, where Anya spoke with President Hanover, and Director Suzanne MacDougal of the FBI. After some discussion (not all of it nice), they all agreed that Anya would assist the government in finding other hosts along with the aliens, and that Agent Riley would accompany her.

Just as soon as she had some food and a nap first.

Anya slept, and as she did, found herself within the Flame Dominion itself, and confronted by its incarnation: a small, glowing sparrow that had quite a mouth on it. The bird told Anya that she had a natural connection to the Dominion, as she shared its own desire to both harm their enemies, and nurture their allies.

Anya dropped Tori back off in New York, then traveled across America with Riley and Pan in search of other hosts. Their search eventually led them to Chicago, where they met Samaira, her cat Chandrali, and Gary. Samaira wielded powerful, transformative magic known as the aether, while Gary built robots out of literal garbage.

Samaira and Gary had tracked another alien to a local shopping center, where it was using crowds as cover. With Riley's help, they managed to peacefully evacuate the shopping center, then move in together and kill the alien. Every time an alien died, it released a data transmission that Felix could decode, and relay to Anya. The latest data transmission showed that most of the hosts on Earth had been killed, and the gnosiphages were very adept at hunting them down.

The next day, Anya, Samaira, and Pan agreed to go with Riley and meet Director MacDougal in person to discuss their next moves. MacDougal and Hanover agreed to form a new organization to focus on combating the alien threat: the Department of Extraterrestrial Research and Defense (DERD), which Anya and the other hosts were strongly encouraged to join. Samaira was for it, but Anya had reservations about becoming a government pawn. For the moment, all the DERD wanted them to do was what they had already been doing: patrol America and keep an eye out for hosts or aliens.

However, after days spent searching the country and still not finding any sign of either, Anya spoke with the Flame Dominion again. With the bird's help, Anya formed a plan to bring other hosts to her: have Jennifer, the reporter Anya saved, broadcast a message that other hosts would be able to interpret and find her.

While Jennifer set-up the broadcast, Anya and Tori met with Samaira to discuss an idea they had. It wasn't clear if ordinary people could learn the supernatural skills of the Archive, and Anya proposed that Samaira teach Tori how to use the aether, since it was relatively safe. Samaira agreed, but wanted to keep it a secret for the moment.

Following Jennifer's broadcast, Anya traveled to the meeting location she had designated in Greenland. Soon enough, she was joined by a wide array of hosts from across the globe. Among them were Renn, a psychic from France; Mona, a necromancer from the UK; Brody, a transformed orca whale from Australia; Esmeralda, another psychic from California; and Dr. Arvo Immonen, a healer from Finland, along with many others. The host meeting was crashed by robots from the New Allied Territories (NAT): a rogue nation set up in the ruins of Bengaluru following an alien attack. The robots were controlled by Chancellor Vastukar, and joined by other hosts from the NAT: Zixin the sniper, Asmund the berserker, and Ursula the polar bear.

Arvo was able to calm everybody down, and the meeting ended peacefully, with Vastukar leaving an open invitation for any hosts to come to the NAT and join him in creating a new world. Anya returned to America with Arvo, Gary, Samaira, and Pan.

Hanover was preparing to announce the alien invasion to the public, as mysterious events and attacks had begun to escalate. At Samaira's request, and after some bargaining with MacDougal, Anya agreed to join the DERD, along with Pan and Arvo. Gary abstained.

However, before Hanover could make his public announcement, the gnosiphages struck. Several of the aliens, including the overseer from before, assaulted the White House. The battle left the White House in ruins, but the overseer and its fellow aliens were reduced to ash and dust.

A message from the Engineers confirmed that the death of one overseer was positive, but there were still plenty of aliens still scattered across the globe, including two more overseers, each stronger than the first. However, the Engineers stated that they could help somewhat, and scrambled the Archive signal of each host, making them almost impossible for the gnosiphages to locate.

After things had calmed down, Anya and her friends celebrated their victory and survival with dinner together. She and other DERD members would be sent to a new outpost, located in Alaska, while Gary would head to Antarctica and set-up a huge, robot-producing factory. Anya managed to find a quiet moment to ask Samaira out on a date once they were settled in Alaska, and she agreed.

The invasion was ongoing, but perhaps things were finally looking up.

PART ONE
HUNTER & HUNTED

FROM EARTH #6

From *The San Diego Union-Tribune*
DISAPPEARANCES REPORTED IN COASTAL TOWN, 17 MISSING

Seventeen people have been declared missing from the coastal town of Carlsbad, California. All seventeen people were last reported as going to or being at Tamarack Surf Beach between the hours of five and seven in the morning. According to the Carlsbad Police Department, there were no signs of violence anywhere along the beach, though they did report that several items had been found abandoned. The abandoned items included three surfboards, a radio, several pairs of shoes, an expensive watch, and more. In addition, two dogs were found wandering the beach, with leashes attached. Both dogs and the abandoned items recovered by police were identified as having belonged to the missing persons by friends and relatives.

"From what we can tell, there's nothing to link the missing people, other than that they were at the beach somewhere near the area of Tower 37, between the hours of five and seven in the morning," said Captain Delonzo.

One of the missing, Tyson Becking, 46, was a regular at the beach.

"He went jogging there every morning, before the crowds came," his wife, Theresa, said. "The only time he wouldn't was if there was a storm or something like that. He loved to run on the beach, but he'd never go near the water if the weather was bad."

Another of the missing, Michelle Davies, 22, was an avid surfer, and winner of several competitions. Her parents stated she was always safe, and well-trained at both surfing and swimming.

"She never would've gone into the water if she didn't know it was safe. She was a daredevil, but she wasn't stupid," her mother said.

Others who reported their friends and loved-ones missing had similar statements. All were either familiar with the area, or had arrived in groups of two or more. None of the residents along Carlsbad Boulevard, which runs parallel to the beach, reported hearing any disturbances or witnessing anything out of the ordinary.

"It was just another regular morning in Cali," said one resident. "Well, except for all the alien stuff on the news."

———

From *Rutherford News Network*

INDIAN GOVERNMENT IN EXILE, NEW ALLIED TERRITORIES CLAIMS CONTROL OF SUBCONTINENT

There has been no word from any leading member of the Indian government since an enormous, non-nuclear explosion of unknown origin destroyed much of the city of Bengaluru. Since that day, the self-proclaimed New Allied Territories (NAT) has stated that India is now under their leadership. Its leader, Chancellor Vastukar, has made only brief statements regarding the country, and many world leaders have dubbed him a terrorist leading a rogue state.

Now, weeks after the destruction of Bengaluru, President Chatterjee has reappeared along with most of the members of the Indian government. President Chatterjee and others were found in front of the UN Headquarters in Geneva with their families. All were unharmed, but stated they had been taken there against their will.

President Chatterjee has since been sequestered at the Indian embassy in Geneva, where he regularly meets with representatives of the UN, and speaks with world leaders about returning India to control of its duly elected officials.

"We have been kidnapped and forcibly removed by nothing less than a terrorist," Chatterjee said in a statement last night. "The man calling himself Vastukar is not a leader, but a despot, no matter what he might claim. He is responsible for the destruction of Bengaluru and the deaths of countless people. India does not belong to one man, but to all her people, and we will continue to lead her until we take back the country we were elected to lead. With the help of our allies, we will succeed."

Attempts to contact any representative of the NAT have been met with silence. However, following Chaterjee's statement yesterday, the NAT did issue a response via the internet. A video was posted to several social media and news websites, featuring an Indian man identifying himself as Vastukar.

Most notable among the statement provided is the following quote:

"Former President Chatterjee had his opportunity to lead this country and her people, and he failed. He spent his time in office enriching himself, rather than the nation he should have been serving. This is not an uncommon problem. All nations suffer this weakness in leadership. But that time is ending, and something better awaits us all. Not just in India, but the world over. The otherworldly intruders that have come here are a temporary distraction, and the real work of building a better future will begin when they are gone."

A brief statement from InterPol confirmed the identity of the man in the video as genuine. When asked how India's allies would be assisting President Chatterjee in reclaiming control of the country, President Hanover of the United States replied that, "We're looking at all possibilities."

UPDATE: The neighboring countries of Sri Lanka and Nepal have gone silent, and any air traffic into those countries has been diverted. Attempts to contact members of their governments have failed.

———

From Oni-Chan (鬼ちゃん), an online message and image board, sub-board /VG/ (Vidya-Geimu)

Anon-01: World of Guildcraft servers are down AGAIN

Anon-02: This was never an issue a couple months ago

Anon-01: There wasnt aliens a couple months ago

Anon-03: WTF that gotta do with anything? Aliens settin up a rival MMO and taking down the competition. Top kek

Anon-04: They fuck up signals. It's why everybody's cell signals were jacked in January. That's when they landed.

Anon-01: But aren't all the aliens dead now or something??? That tall chick set one on fire at the White House, game over

Anon-04: That was ONE alien. There's a shitload of them.

Anon-02: Define "shitload"

Anon-04: a load of shit

Anon-01: lol, lmao even

Anon-02: Alright but if there's so many, where'd they all go? Shit's been quiet for weeks now. Every day in February some wild shit was going down but now it's total crickets

Anon-03: Yeah seems like they fucked off. But if they didn't, there's gotta be less of em now right? So even if they fuck up signals or whatever, there's fewer, so it should be all good

Anon-02: Do servers work like that? Sending cell signals or something kinda the same? I don't think they do.

Anon-04: Fuck if I know

Anon-03: mr expert here

Anon-01: I dont give a shit if its your moms ham-looking head blocking the signals I just wanna play duuuuuude I havent looked at my elf clerics shapely ass in days

Anon-03: Imagine the smell

Anon-03: brrrrrrrrt

Anon-02: Begone, brap poster

Anon-04: I dunno why but I haven't been playing games as much since everything went batshit. Wonder why that is?

Anon-05: Because the dull paste

Of your life now has flavor

Amidst the chaos

Anon-02: Is that a haiku?

Anon-01: Who let you off the anime board you absolute weeb

Anon-04: roses are red, violets are blue, your poem was shit, and so are you

———

Transcript From *Rutherford News Network: Special Broadcast*

JENNIFER CHANG: Good evening, I'm Jennifer Chang. Nearly three weeks ago, the White House came under attack by hostile extraterrestrial lifeforms. It was an attack that was echoed all across the world, and has been declared by many world governments as an invasion. However, the invasion did not start three weeks ago, but rather, well before that.

The first known contact of the invading alien forces with people happened here, just outside New York City at a small park in Brooklyn. I know because I was there, along with my cameraman, and the woman who saved us from a creature that killed two civilians and several brave members of the Brooklyn Police.

That same woman was at the White House when it was attacked, and helped others like her drive the assault back and save President Hanover.

And tonight, she's here, with us. Hello, and thank you for joining us. Has the DERD settled on your call sign yet? What should we call you?

ARDENT: They're calling me "Ardent," which isn't what I would've chosen, but I guess it could've been worse.

JENNIFER: Well, I guess the big question everybody is asking since the press conference in the Rose Garden—or what was left of it—is "How did this happen?" There's a lot of video of you online during the fight at the White House: most of it shows you on fire, and flying.

ARDENT: The DERD won't let me go into detail about everything, but I can say the basics. I'm a human, born on Earth, in the States. Everything was normal until the aliens showed up back in January.

JENNIFER: And you got your abilities then?

ARDENT: Yup.

JENNIFER: How?

ARDENT: [Laughs] I can't say.

JENNIFER: Can you tell us what your abilities are, specifically? Fire-related, I'm guessing, based on what's been recorded and what I've seen in-person.

ARDENT: I can't give specifics, but you're right. I've got a pretty good handle on making fire do what I want, and flying around to a lesser degree. I'm also very strong.

JENNIFER: No hiding that last one. And tall, too. Is your height and build the result of getting your abilities, or—?

ARDENT: I can't say. Sorry.

JENNIFER: Can you tell us about the aliens?

ARDENT: We don't know why exactly they're here, but they're extremely dangerous and hostile. They usually appear like normal, everyday things: refrigerators, toilets, a stop light, a rug, and so on. But there's always something wrong with them. They'll have eyes where they shouldn't, or hair, or something else. If anybody sees anything like that, run, and call the cops or the DERD hotline.

They also tend to be more active at night, but they can still move around whenever they like. Beyond that, I can't say much else. We're doing all we can to stop them, though.

JENNIFER: How many have you personally stopped so far?

ARDENT: Quite a few, thankfully.

JENNIFER: And the most recent altercation was at the White House?

ARDENT: Correct.

JENNIFER: So no alien contact in three weeks? Is the invasion over?

ARDENT: No, it isn't. The aliens are still here, and we're still looking for them. The DERD is still a new government organization, but we're working together with other countries to form a coalition, share resources, information, and help each other out in emergencies. That way, something like the attack at the White House will never happen again. Hopefully.

JENNIFER: Will this coalition be responding to problems involving other people with abilities like yours?

ARDENT: Uh, what do you mean?

JENNIFER: I mean like Vastukar, in India. Reports say he and a number of other hosts are expanding their control over the subcontinent. Will the DERD and this new coalition be countering acts of aggression like that?

ARDENT: I... don't know. That's above my pay grade. I can say that I'm willing to stop anything that might be a threat to innocent people. Alien or otherwise.

JENNIFER: I see. Thank you, Ardent. When we come back, we'll be speaking with a much-requested guest who's had quite a lot of followers online since his reveal: Pan the Pangolin.

ARDENT: Are we clear? Cause I'm fucking hungry and you said there'd be a buffet or—

1

The blizzard lashed the land and air alike with countless whirling barbs of ice. It turned what should have been a calm, if cold, day into an inhospitable gauntlet of the elements. Even in the light of mid-afternoon, visibility was cut to a few yards in every direction by shifting walls of gray and white. It was a death sentence to the unprepared and the foolish, a promise of quick death at the fangs of winter.

Anya Nowicki, of the planet Earth, United States, Alaska, Nunivak Island, Department of Extraterrestrial Research and Development Outpost #1, Dormitory A, Room 1-3 (next to the supply closet), stood outside in the center of the howling winds in a t-shirt, shorts, and flip-flops.

"C'mon," she muttered. Another attack would come at any moment. She had barely dodged the last one.

A lance of glittering blue light shot out from the snowy void and sped toward Anya's chest. She grunted and jumped to one side, but the lance curved in mid-air and struck her in the ribs.

The blow would have punched a hole in concrete, but Anya's kinetic dispersal skill softened it.

It still hurt like a son of a bitch.

The lance broke into a dozen finger-sized darts after it struck her, and all of them arced around her into a small hail of energy shards.

Anya brought her heavily muscled arms up in front of her as she flew backwards into the sky with a push of her Singularity's Grasp artifact. Most of the smaller blue darts sailed past her, but several connected and struck her arms, stomach, and legs. They blossomed into crystalline growths that spread over the points of impact and began sapping the heat from her Sun's Heart.

"That's fighting dirty!" Anya shouted into the storm, but couldn't keep the edge of a laugh out of her voice. The Sun's Heart flared in her chest, evaporating all the snow and ice around her for a dozen yards, and causing the crystal growths to overheat and shatter.

Laughter echoed back at Anya, playful and feminine. It swirled around her with the winds, coming from everywhere and nowhere.

Anya focused her heat sense, trying to pin down the source of the attacks, but the swirling cold was getting in her way. She caught a glimpse of something, her heat sense picking up the candle-like glow of a living creature, before it vanished back into the frigid curtains of ice.

"Rrrrrnnnn!" a voice bellowed beside her. A section of the earth rose up and formed itself into the rough shape of a human: broad-shouldered and lumbering. Hands of frozen dirt and rock sprang from the ground and seized her ankles as the shambling earthen figure swung a granite fist at her.

Anya condensed an immense amount of fire at her feet, crushing it into a tiny white-hot sphere, and then released it in a sudden explosion. The golem and grasping hands were blown into clods of lifeless dirt as she used the momentum of the explosion to propel herself away and toward where she had spotted the heat signature. She sensed it again, a flicker of light and warmth, and she propelled herself toward it.

"Gotcha!" she shouted, and reached for her opponent.

She was met by a gaping mouth full of silver fangs.

Anya jerked her arm away as the mouth chomped down, missing her by inches. The mouth belonged to an enormous tiger, longer than a pickup truck and almost as tall. The tiger's white hair made it almost invisible in the snow, the black stripes shifting over powerful muscles as it stalked toward Anya. Silver battle armor, sleek and elegant, flowed with the tiger's movements and shielded the head, back, and sides.

"Good kitty," Anya said. The tiger roared at her, further exposing saber-like fangs and sprang forward. Anya's Xhama Thul and combat cognition skills made quick work of analyzing both the huge cat and her armor. The armor was light, favoring mobility over heavy defense, and offered the least coverage on the tiger's belly.

Anya caught the tiger's huge paws in her own powerful hands. It was like wrestling with a living tank. One of the paws slipped free of Anya's grasp and whapped her hard on the side of the head. Kinetic dispersal took some of the impact away, but even the reduced force of the blow would have decapitated a normal human.

Anya's neck popped and she grit her teeth. She seized the offending paw and yanked the tiger back with her into a throw. She planted her feet against the under-protected belly and kicked up, her flip-flops slapping against the armor-clad underside as the tiger grunted and went flying. Anya added a moderate gravitational shove to fling the tiger even farther, and sent it yowling in protest into the storm.

"Brute!" the feminine voice called out from the storm. Before Anya could respond, the earth shook around her and rose up in a wave of several tons' worth of frozen dirt, rock, and mud. She was buried at once with only her hand remaining free. Another one of the blue lances of energy struck her exposed hand, and the freezing crystals started to grow again.

She could have gotten out, but this had just gotten gross.

Besides, they were going to be late for dinner.

Anya used her free arm to shove hard against the shuddering ground and roll out from under the smothering hill of undulating earth just enough to get her head out.

"All right! You got me!" she shouted.

No sooner had she said the words than the earth slid off her, the cold crystals on her hand vanished in a flash of blue sparks, and the blizzard blew itself away into a clear, sunny March sky.

"Are you okay? I didn't hurt you?" a small, shy voice asked beside Anya.

Pan the Pangolin emerged from a hole in the ground with the ease of a swimmer coming out of a pool. He was frequently mistaken for some kind of mega-armadillo by new residents of Outpost #1, but his foreclaws were much larger, his tail wider and longer, and his scales significantly thicker and more intricately layered. Especially since he had upgraded himself with the Archive.

He was a rotund, bulky figure. He only came up to Anya's thigh, but that still made him more than twice as big as any other giant ground pangolin. He wore a puffy green jacket and thick black snow pants, along with a little modified ushanka atop his narrow head that was secured under his chin. His wet nose twitched as he sniffed at Anya, and his wide, dark eyes glittered, as if he were on the verge of tears.

"I'm fine, buddy. You did get some mud up my nose, but that's no big deal. You did real good," Anya said as she sat up. Pan hopped out of his hole, waddled to her side and gave her a hug, which she returned.

"I'm going inside now. It's cold!" Pan said, then waved a claw at her as he awkwardly waddled away in his thick winter attire, like an ambulatory potato.

A short, slender Indian woman jogged over. She had glowing midnight hair that sparkled with inner starlight, wore a flowing outfit of rich blues and pure whites, and a silver tiara with a sapphire at its center around her head. The tiger followed behind her, ears slicked back, sulking.

"Not hurt?" Samaira asked.

"Yeah. You broke like, three of my ribs," Anya said, then laughed at the look of horror on Samaira's face. "I'm kidding, I'm all right. Even if you had, they'd be healed by now."

Samaira scowled at her, but couldn't quite stop the corner of her mouth from quirking.

"Brute," she said again. "Don't joke about that. Can't risk anything serious while Dr. Immonen's still away."

"I gotcha. How's Chandrali?"

The giant tiger looked between Anya and Samaira with her luminescent blue eyes, then fell onto her side, exposing her tummy. Samaira scoffed and tapped a gem around a silver collar Chandrali wore, and her armor vanished in a flash of light. With the tiger's tummy now fully exposed, Samaira began rubbing. Chandrali purred. It sounded like a race car revving its engine.

"How the hell did you whip up that blizzard?" Anya asked.

"Placed some arrows in a perimeter around the exercise field and gave them a weather conversion function. There's a cold front moving in from the south, maybe a light storm. Definitely couldn't have done it somewhere warmer," Samaira said.

"How big was it? I was jumping all over the field and it felt like it was everywhere."

The exercise field of Outpost #1 was an expansive plain of snow-covered grass surrounded by a wide track for running. Big enough to hold any number of games on it at the same time, if the weather ever allowed for it.

"It only looked big because I moved it around with you. It was actually pretty small. If I used the aether to create a localized blizzard big enough to cover the field... geez. I dunno if I'd be able to pull enough aether in to do that for long. Even with just the little movable storm I did make, the aether around the base is gonna be a bit sparse for a while. Although..."

Samaira looked up and over Anya's shoulder at the invisible currents of the ever-changing magical energy known as the aether.

"Although?" Anya asked. Samaira blinked and focused back on Anya and shook her head. Her hair danced around her face and shoulders with the movement, and the starlight within it glittered.

"Nothing. Just thinking. Boo? Any changes?" Samaira asked the empty air. A tiny figure appeared next to her a shade of dark, translucent blue. They had the form and rough size of a chubby baby, except their arms and legs ended in rounded points rather than hands or feet. Their head was shrouded by what appeared to be hair at first glance, but was really the long, elegant branches and leaves of a weeping willow.

"Noooooo. I'm sorry. I was hoping it would work out," Boo, the

Artificial Intelligence for Samaira's Archive, said. They sounded as pitiful and woe-be-gone as always.

"Hmm," Samaira said and brought her menu up. Anya stood beside her and looked it over as well.

SAMAIRA UPADHYAY: LEVEL 39 AETHERIC RANGER
Statistics

- Awareness-9
- Dexterity-25
- Fortitude-28
- Intelligence- 32
- Strength-5
- Willpower-8

Skills

- Aetheric Manipulation-36
- Aetheric Channeling-36
- Aetheric Theory-21
- Archery (Oella Mandai)-23
- Combat Acrobatics -15
- Bestial Affinity (Feline)-18

"Yeah, still the exact same as it has been since the attack on the White House," Samaira said, and clicked her tongue. "It doesn't make sense at all."

"Why not? We didn't get any experience or anything from fighting with Vastukar's robots in Greenland," Anya replied. She still wasn't sure how to feel about that. On the one hand, it was a bummer that they couldn't level up and get more points from the Archive just by sparring and training with each other. On the other, it meant there was no incentive for the hosts to fight anything but the gnosiphages, so going after each other just for a level-up was off the table.

People had enough reasons to fight amongst themselves well before the Archive arrived. Anya was glad that the Engineers hadn't given them another.

"Right, the internal logic of the Archive is consistent, but it still doesn't make sense. If each number is representative of the correlating mastery of a skill, then it should go up, regardless. That thing I did with the blizzard, moving it around? I learned how to do that on my own. That didn't come with the skill increases like most of my other knowledge did."

"So?" Anya blinked, feeling a bit stupid. Samaira had been enrolled in some kind of Master's program at the University of Chicago. Anya had tried college for exactly half a semester, and then bailed for the city and to work in a shitty coffee shop.

True, there had been other, personal reasons for her move, but...

She batted the thoughts away and focused on Samaira, who had already been talking for several seconds.

"—should account for natural increases in the host's learning. It already does this during our fights with the aliens, but only them. There's no natural skill increase for organic learning done outside of alien combat," Samaira said and gestured at the exercise field where she had created her storm. "That was a cool blizzard! I want points for that, darn it!"

Anya grinned. She suspected Samaira had been one of those students that thrived on getting stickers on their tests when they did a good job.

"What?" Samaira asked as she caught Anya grinning at her. "What're you smiling at?"

"You," Anya replied. "You want the extra credit."

"There was nothing 'extra' about that! I did a good job, I learned something, and this silly Archive with its arbitrary and opaque rules for rewarding its users is asinine!"

"Isn't learning its own reward, though?"

"Yes, but—oh. You're teasing me."

Anya's grin widened, and she crinkled her nose at Samaira.

"Lil bit," she admitted.

"What about your skills?" Samaira asked as she smiled back at Anya.

"No change."

"Did you check it?"

"No. Why would I?"

"Consistency in information gathering. Double check everything."

"Fine. Bring up my menu, Felix."

Another AI hologram, with the same body-type as Boo but with a rose for a head and colored orange, appeared between Anya and Samaira along with Anya's glowing orange menu screen.

"Hello! Great fight, but everything's exactly the same!" Felix said. Anya had learned from day one that Felix could make getting polio sound as if it were cause for celebration.

"See?" Anya said as she gestured at her menu.

ANYA NOWICKI: LEVEL 41 PHOENIX MONK
  Statistics

- Awareness-10
- Dexterity-21
- Fortitude-43
- Intelligence-10
- Strength-23
- Willpower-10

Skills

- Flame Dominion-43 (+5 from Artifact)
- Kinetic Dispersal-21
- Combat Cognition-18
- Regeneration-37
- Xhama Thul-16
- Gravity Dominion-23 (+5 from Artifact)

"I just like checking. Nothing wrong with being thorough," Samaira replied as she studied Anya's menu. "I'm a little bummed out

I didn't hit the level 40 mark. The bonuses you get every ten levels aren't bad."

"I'm looking forward to that second class. That's gonna be another game changer."

"Nine more levels to go until that happens. But I'm excited too!" Felix said. "What're you gonna get? Another combat class? A support class?"

"I dunno. Nine levels seems a long way off, especially with how quiet things have been. Mostly."

Samaira sighed as she closed her menu screen and dismissed Boo, and Anya did the same with her screen and Felix.

"Right now, the only barometer for a normal human learning alien skills is Tori. How's her practice with the aether been going?" Samaira asked.

"She said she managed to manifest some physical objects last time I visited. Got a glass made of the aether to hold water for a minute before it vanished and soaked her. She should be here in another hour or two if you wanna ask her yourself," Anya said, and cricked her neck to the side.

While she and Tori exchanged texts and calls almost every night, they definitely did not discuss her practicing the aether. Anya didn't want to risk anybody with the government overhearing or looking through her texts, even Riley.

"Maybe, if I can make sure MacDougal won't overhear us. But that's really impressive! Materialization for a solid minute is tough. I think that'd be equivalent to an Archive skill level of three or four, at least," Samaira replied. "And speaking of impressive, I'm surprised you took as many hits as you did. I obviously wasn't going hard or anything, but I wasn't really pulling my shots either."

Anya rubbed her side. Her regeneration skill had mostly healed everything back up to normal, but there was a lingering soreness, like a bruise. If she had been wearing her armor, the Regalia of St. Llothec, she wouldn't even have had that. However, the purpose of their little bout was to practice her raw abilities, no help from gear or items from the RAC shop.

"Hm," Samaira pursed her lips and narrowed her eyes at Anya's side. "You're sure I didn't hurt you?"

"Sam, I'm fine, honestly. I got worse hits rough-housing with my brothers when I was a kid."

"Speaking of…"

"No. Before you even ask."

"You still haven't told your family? It's been nearly two months since the Archives hit!"

"Look, I have a very specific plan for how I'll tell my family, okay?"

Samaira arched an eyebrow at Anya and asked, "Which is?"

"I won't," Anya shrugged her huge shoulders.

Samaira sighed, but didn't push.

"If you wanna talk about it, I'm here, okay?"

"Thanks, Sam. Now c'mon. We still gotta get ready before the big dinner starts."

Samaira reached out and took Anya's hand in hers as they strode across the exercise field and toward the main buildings of Outpost #1.

The outpost consisted of six long dormitory buildings, an administration building, a radio and air-traffic control tower, recreation building, a few hangars for aircraft of varying sizes, a pair of long runways, the exercise field, and some other assorted buildings and guard towers. It was purely utilitarian in its construction, often reminding Anya of a child's toy blocks all piled together.

Outpost #1 sat on the southern shore of Nunivak Island, off the western coast of Alaska. The only other sign of habitation on the island was the tiny town of Mekoryuk, on the northern side. It would have been a phenomenally boring place to be stuck under normal circumstances.

Anya looked down at Samaira's small, slender fingers intertwined with her own and smiled.

In the month since they had all come to Nunivak to assist with its rapid construction, Anya and Samaira had been on precisely two dates. Not much, but it was all they had been able to find time for given the schedule of meetings, planning, more meetings, assisting with the outpost's construction with their skills, and on a couple of occasions, being dispatched to deal with potential (but false) alien sightings on the mainland.

They had been, without a doubt, the best two dates Anya had ever been on.

Almost perfect.

Their first had been a couple of weeks after the attack on the White House. They had flown to Anchorage for dinner, and wound up staying out all night talking. The second had been a week ago, when Samaira had packed a dinner for them and they had flown to a mountain peak in Denali National Park to watch the northern lights.

They had finished their meal and stared up at the slowly shifting curtains of light above them, and then at each other.

Samaira had bitten her lip as Anya leaned in, her eyelids lowered…

And then their communication discs had gone off.

It had been Riley, requesting that they return to Outpost #1 to greet some government dignitaries from Canada and their hosts who had arrived ahead-of-schedule.

Samaira had giggled at the interruption, but backed away.

Almost perfect.

Since then, things had been too busy for another date. More meetings with heads of state and foreign hosts, locating and talking with stray American hosts who were on the fence about joining the DERD, press-briefings and news conferences, and intelligence reports.

They had spent some evenings together in the dormitory common room, playing games or cuddled on the couch together to watch TV. It was a common room, however, and other agents and personnel were coming and going, and Pan was usually there with them. Anya had invited Samaira back to her room to watch a movie on a couple of occasions, but she had always gotten flustered and promised to do it another time.

Anya hadn't wanted to push.

So, for now, hand-holding was as far as they had made it.

Both women strolled past a few agents and interns who had assembled at the edges of the field to watch them spar, and other agents-in-training as they jogged around the outpost's many walkways in formation. Hundreds of heat signatures glowed around the outpost, all of them visible to the heat sense Anya's Sun's Heart granted.

It made her think of seeing candlelight through a frosted window.

Samaira pressed a button beside the reinforced metal door of Dormitory A when they arrived. A black sphere emerged from above the door and shone a light on Samaira, then Anya.

"Upadhyay, Samaira. Nowicki, Anya. Identities confirmed and logged. Welcome back," a robotic voice intoned, and the heavy door slid open.

"Still can't believe Gary helped them build all this shit," Anya said as they entered the dorm building. It was two stories tall, painted an inoffensive shade of off-white with black trim, and had thirty one-bedroom dorms plus an additional ten multi-bedroom dorms.

While they were all referred to as dorms, the rooms were more like apartments. Anya's dorm was actually a significant upgrade in every way from her old place in Brooklyn. Each one had their own kitchen, bathroom, living room, bedroom, and a spacious closet. Not luxurious by any means, but very cozy.

"What're you gonna wear to the big fancy dinner?" Samaira asked as they entered the building and waved hello to the agent at the security desk in the wide, black-tiled foyer.

Anya looked down at her t-shirt, shorts and flip-flops and gestured at herself. Samaira laughed and rolled her eyes.

"Be serious! MacDougal's gonna be there, probably some press, and at least one Prime Minister. Maybe three."

"What're you wearing?" Anya asked.

"It's a surprise."

"Well then, so is mine."

"Just please tell me you're not actually wearing that," Samaira said and pointed at Anya's dirt-covered clothes.

"What? I think I look good in this, except for the dirt," Anya replied, and flexed. Samaira studied her, her eyes lingering in a few places before sliding up to Anya's face.

"You do, but you're also going to look very silly if you're the only one dressed like that. Which you will be. Riley's wearing a tux, I hear."

"I figured he'd been born in his fed suit. And fine, I'm not wearing this. I'm wearing something moderately appropriate for the occasion."

Samaira nodded and turned away as they reached a fork in the hallway. Anya was in room 1-3, while Samaira was up the stairs in room 2-4. She paused on her way up the stairs to look back at her.

"See you at the dinner, then," she said, and walked away. Anya stayed where she was, watching as Samaira left, then glanced at a clock on the wall nearby.

"Ah, shit," she muttered. She had to get ready for Tori's arrival, as well as make sure Pan was good to go. The little guy was cute as hell, but he needed the same amount of upkeep and supervision as a toddler. Anya hurried to go find Pan, muttering to herself about "stuffy-ass dinners," as she went.

2

The dinner that night was in the main dining hall in the center of Outpost #1, next to the recreation building. Outpost personnel decked out the hall with decorative lights, fluttering flags from America, Japan, the UK, EU, and Canada, and even a red carpet lining the otherwise plain sidewalk leading inside.

The inside had gotten a makeover as well: elegant flower displays sat at each dining table, a live band played unobtrusive music in the far corner, and the usual plain white fluorescent lights had been replaced with softer mood lighting.

Representatives from five different governments were present, and seated on an elevated stage at one end of the hall. Prime Minister Miura from Japan, and Prime Minister Tremblay, from Canada were probably the most notable. Prime Minister Stark from the UK, and Presidents Bisset and Hanover (from France and America, respectively), were in a meeting with other members of the EU somewhere in Germany. MacDougal stood in for Hanover, while other high-ranking members of the UK and French governments represented their absentee leaders. All of them sat beneath a sign that bore the flags of their respective countries, as well as the seals of the Department of Extraterrestrial Research and Defense and its foreign equivalents.

The seal for the DERD showed an open book behind a shield, both surrounded by a laurel wreath. Beneath both was the phrase, "Ex intellectu, victoria."

From understanding, victory.

The paperwork had gone through last night between the DERD and other countries to form an international joint task force that shared resources and intelligence. Together, they would track the gnosiphages across much of the northern hemisphere, and bring hosts together.

Given all the chaos, confusion, death, and revelations that had happened since January, the need to celebrate something was understandable. And despite her protestations at the stuffy ceremony of it all, Anya wasn't too upset. She hadn't gotten dressed up and gone to a party since...

"Oh my god," she said to herself as she stood just inside the dining hall entryway.

"What is it?" Tori asked beside her. She had spent much of the time since her arrival at Outpost #1 helping Anya with her hair and make-up, and was currently trying to smooth out a single wrinkled edge of her own black evening gown.

"I haven't been to a fancy dress-up party since my high school prom."

"Your prom is your measuring stick for a fancy dress-up party?" Tori asked.

"Yes?"

"So you've never been to a fancy party, period."

"I guess not."

"What's a prom?" Pan asked from Anya's other side.

"A dance where a buncha awkward teenagers get tanked and shuffle around each other until they go to the real party afterwards," a voice tinged with a Bostonian accent said from behind.

A man of average height and build, with short black hair and an easy-going face smiled up at her as she turned to face him.

He wore a sleek tuxedo, which seemed out of place on him, somehow. Anya had only ever seen Christian Riley in blue or gray suits and ties. He looked about as comfortable in his tux as a fish in the desert.

"Yeah, the after-parties in Clemson weren't much to write home about. Especially since home was also in Clemson," she said as she smirked down at Riley. "Nice tux."

"Very dashing," Tori agreed.

"Ah, knock it off. It's a rental. And I feel like fifty pounds of shit stuffed in a ten-pound bag. Also, I'd like to arrest whoever invented bow ties," Riley replied as he tugged at his collar.

"I dunno. It's weird seeing you without the usual suit, but it's nice," Anya said.

"Well, whatever it is, it'll have to do. You three, on the other hand…" Riley gave her, Tori, and Pan a quick up-and-down look, and nodded in approval.

Pan wore a kind of long black coat trimmed with gold that split halfway down the back to allow his tail through, and crisp gray slacks. MacDougal had had somebody make them especially for Pan just for tonight. It was considered a waste for him to spend his RAC, the Reward Allocation Currency the Archive distributed, on something as mundane as clothes.

MacDougal insisted he still needed some clothing to wear because first, Pan needed them in the colder climate; and second, because she didn't want anybody mistaking him for a wild animal.

Tori wore a simple, but elegant, black evening gown that accentuated her slender frame. Her blond hair was a curtain of pale strands that flowed over her neck and shoulders, with a few strands braided together along the sides and pulled back.

Anya's outfit was a bit more elaborate.

Despite what she had indicated to Samaira earlier, she had put some thought into her clothes for the evening. She had picked it with Tori's help from a store on Fifth Avenue in New York a week ago, bought with her significant DERD agent salary.

It was somewhere between a gown and a robe, made of a deep, rich red, with heels to match. Its cut and the way the folds had been arranged made it resemble something a Roman noblewoman might have worn ages ago. It left Anya's shoulders and arms bare, save for a wide gold bangle Tori had selected to fit around Anya's right bicep. Anya had actually been forced to heat the gold and widen it so it fit around her muscle.

Her hair, already short, had been done in tight braids that wrapped around her temples like a wreath and piled upward, leaving her neck bare.

Anya had allowed herself a moment in front of her bathroom mirror before she had left her apartment. Tori had looked on in approval.

"I do good work," she had said.

"Fuck yeah you do," Anya agreed, before floating herself out of her room with Gravity Dominion rather than bother running in heels like a drunk ostrich. She had floated Tori along as well, sparing her having to traverse the icy paths of Outpost #1 in her stilettos. They had met with Pan and helped him with his clothes, which he didn't seem to mind, and then made for the dining hall.

"You look good," Riley said as he studied all of them once more. "I definitely think somebody'll appreciate it."

"MacDougal better. I mean, getting dressed up is nice and all, but if she expects me to do this sort of thing regularly—"

"I'm sure the boss lady appreciates it plenty. But I was referring to our favorite magical archer. Where is she, by the way?"

"Shocked she isn't here already."

"Can we eat now?" Pan asked at her side, and tapped Anya's legs with his long claws.

"You go ahead, buddy. I think MacDougal said they'd have some ants for you at one of the side tables. Tori, would you mind?"

"Nah. C'mon Pan, you can be my date for the night," she said.

"Yay!" Pan said and waddled away with Tori, his wide tail thumping against the floor as they made for one of the tables.

"Oh," Riley said, and his eyebrows rose up as he looked past Anya. She turned to follow his stare just as Samaira entered the dining hall.

She wore a sari made of overlapping curtains of translucent blue silk and trimmed with delicate silver designs. The shade of blue was as pale as a clear winter sky, and contrasted beautifully against the dark brown of her skin. A silver anklet bounced just above her foot as she walked, tiny crystalline beads releasing subtle music with every movement. She had similar pieces of jewelry on her wrists and dangling from her ears. Samaira had not infused herself with the aether, as she did when she fought, so her hair was its usual glossy shade of black, tied in a single braid of interweaving strands that fell down the length of her back.

She stopped as she saw Anya, and Anya couldn't stop but feel a moment of satisfaction as Samaira's mouth dropped open a little as she did.

"Wow," Samaira said as she looked Anya up and down.

"Same."

"I thought you were just gonna show up in… I dunno, maybe your regalia?"

"I like my regalia, but I also like being fancy every now and again."

She neglected to mention it had been the better part of a decade since she'd had the opportunity. Both women continued to stare at each other for several long moments until Riley cleared his throat.

"You should go check in with MacDougal before you settle in to dinner," he said. "And her various counterparts, too. Especially the PMs."

"Right. Shall we?" Anya asked. Samaira smiled up at her, and the two walked toward the elevated stage at the far end of the dining hall where MacDougal and other guests of honor sat. Anya was keenly aware of both of them drawing stares the entire way.

"Agent Nowicki, Agent Upadhyay," MacDougal said as the two approached the long dining table on the stage. Suzanne MacDougal had chosen a simple dress of navy blue and a matching bolero jacket. She was probably the oldest person in the dining hall, or maybe even the outpost itself, but the few wrinkles that did appear on her dark skin did not convey age or frailty. The wrinkles in her brow and beside her thin mouth had the appearance of being chiseled into her, rather than some weakness of her flesh. Her gray hair had been collected into a bun at the base of her skull, more like a lump of iron than anything else.

She showed no indication of surprise at how radiant (in Anya's own opinion) Anya and Samaira looked, only gestured to the men sitting on either side of her.

"Allow me to introduce you to the DERD's newest allies,"

MacDougal said, and introduced the Prime Ministers of Japan and Canada first, then the Secretary of State for Defense from the UK, and finally the Minister for Europe and Foreign Affairs from France.

"And their respective hosts, who I believe you have already met, unofficially," MacDougal said of a rather diverse group of individuals seated beside the members of their own countries.

A woman with light tan skin and sharp, lovely Eurasian features sat beside the UK's Secretary of State. She had short, punkish hair dyed (or colored naturally through the Archive) an almost neon shade of cyan. Anya had last seen her in ornate, gothic plate armor and a purple cloak, but tonight she wore a high-collared black gown with a slit up the side that almost reached her hip.

"Mona De Rozario," MacDougal said, "and her counterpart in the EU, Renn."

The French host was absent his trademark gold-and-white helmet, and he looked like a disheveled vagrant somebody had stuffed into a tuxedo. His brown hair was unkempt and pointed in every direction it could, and his gaze was almost sleepy, until he actually made eye contact. Anya could feel the weight of Renn's gaze as he studied her. His smile was amiable, almost charming.

Almost.

There was something about the mixture of easy-going grin and the gaze that went from sleepy to intense as soon as it fell on her. It made her think of a crocodile, lying motionless for hours to the point it could be mistaken for a floating hunk of wood. But, sooner or later, it turned into a flurry of lethal, thrashing movement.

"Jiro Yamada from Japan," MacDougal continued down the row of seated attendants. Even among the small crowd of unusual guests, Jiro stood out. He was tall—taller than Anya—which put him somewhere around eight feet in height, and wider than a refrigerator. He also wore a tuxedo, but it was obvious he was wearing armor underneath. Unlike Renn, he had not dispensed with his helmet, and the tactical headgear with the mirrored visor was an absurd contrast with his formal attire. Jiro rotated his head to look at Anya and Samaira, nodded once, and said nothing.

"And our neighbor from the north, Harrison Evans," MacDougal finished with the young man at the far end of the table. He looked mostly normal: dark hair slicked back to expose a pale brow, average features, and a fit but not too muscular frame under his tux. But his eyes were red, and a pair of glossy black horns sprouted from just below his hairline and curved upwards. He grinned at Anya, exposing a pair of vampiric fangs.

What a fucking edgelord, Anya thought, and had to make a conscious effort to not roll her eyes at him. Anya had fought beside all the hosts at the table and several others back in February, when they had all met in Greenland.

Harrison's powers involved a lot of demon-summoning. The creatures he commanded (and that, according to the DERD intel reports, were lurking within his shadow or the folds of his cape this very moment) weren't actual demons. They were not spiritual emissaries of a punitive afterlife, but rather, transdimensional creatures of flesh and blood from somewhere known as the Infernal Plane. The few Anya had seen certainly looked demonic: red skin, cloven feet, black horns, the whole deal.

"Yeah, haven't seen you guys in-person since back in Greenland," Anya said.

"And what a delightful time that was," Renn said. His French accent was evident, but his sarcasm was more ambiguous.

"I certainly had fun," Mona added. Jiro focused his attention elsewhere, and Harrison ignored all of them in favor of staring into his wine glass.

With the introductions made, Anya and Samaira took their seats at the other end of the table, sitting beside Riley. There was some polite conversation among MacDougal and the other representatives, but Anya tuned it out after a few minutes.

"Y'know, I would've killed to be at one of these types of things a few years ago. Now, all I can think of is how much this tux is pinching at the waistline," Riley whispered to Anya, and she snorted back a laugh.

"It's kinda nice, though I'm starting to feel like a bit of a show horse," she said, and tried to ignore all the people in the hall casting glances—some subtle and some very obvious—at her and Samaira and the others. "So, the others won't be joining us?"

"Nah, Esmeralda and Grant are at Outpost Two, holding down the fort."

"I've told you how it's bullshit that the newbies get the cushy posting, right?"

"Not in the last five minutes, no."

Anya huffed and tried not to dwell on it. Esmeralda Gomez had been one of the hosts back at Greenland: a shy Mexican-American girl about Anya's age. Some kind of psychic. She and Grant, a new host who had come in after the attack on the White House, had been stationed at Outpost #2.

Which was near Guam.

On a tropical island.

Anya had let MacDougal know, frequently, how unfair this decision was. Her literally saving the President should have counted for a better posting, but MacDougal had said all outpost assignments were final. They might rotate the hosts' positions in the future. Maybe.

"The Doc's gonna swing by there after he's done making his medical rounds in South America," Riley added. "I heard he's not in a rush to get back to anywhere Hanover has control over, though."

"Hanover pissed off Arvo?" Anya asked. Arvo Immonen was probably the closest thing to a living saint as could be. He'd joined the DERD with Anya, Pan, and Samaira under the condition that he would be free to continue his work of curing every single ailment and malady across the planet. The idea of the man being anything but calmly accepting and warm was borderline absurd.

"I'm not up on all the details, but sounds that way, yeah. Oh. Uh-oh. Boss lady," Riley nodded towards MacDougal, who had caught his eye. The director regarded Anya in silence, then cast a meaningful glance at one of the Canadian officials beside her, then tapped her watch and tilted her head to the side.

Give me a few minutes to finish here and we'll talk, the pantomime said. Anya didn't know what that was about, but she just gave an accepting shrug, and then looked down at the empty plate in front of her.

"Well, while I wait for MacDougal to wrap it up, where can I get some food? Is there a menu or what?" she asked.

"Buffet style," Samaira said as she scanned the room and spotted a long table in the corner laden with heavy metal tureens and uniformed servers. "I think they actually did that just for you."

"They did not."

"They did," Riley confirmed. "Decided it was more cost-effective than single-plate dining."

Samaira giggled.

"Better get the DERD's money's worth, then," Anya said and went to the tables, picking up five plates on the way and making them float beside her.

"Anya, look!" Pan said beside her as he approached her in the line for food. He had a large porcelain bowl clutched between his claws. It was full of tiny black and red specks that Anya recognized as dead ants. "They got a bunch of ants just for me!"

"Do not spill those, please," Anya said as she grimaced at the bowl. Pan extended his long tongue and slurped up a couple dozen of the dead insects.

"Do you want any?"

"Pan, I appreciate the offer, but as always, no thank you. Humans do not generally like to eat those. At least not without flavoring," she said. She knew some people ate insects, but they usually cooked or spiced them somehow.

"Flavoring?"

"Yeah, like salt or honey or something. It's not for me, but I guess some people like it."

"I can make ants taste even better than *this*?"

"Well, I dunno. That stuff might be bad for pangolins. Even special ones like you."

"Flavoring…" Pan said and began to waddle away, his black eyes sparkling with the possibility of ants, but better. Anya considered following him, but let him go. He'd eaten weird stuff before and been fine.

Anya got several plates of food and tried to eat them as delicately as she could. A few photographers were present to document the evening for press release and historical purposes, and one of them usually had their camera pointed at Anya. The last thing she wanted was to appear in some official White House press release with her cheeks stuffed out like a chipmunk with an eating disorder.

However, the sparring she had engaged in that afternoon had given her a bit of an appetite. She compromised and only took great bites of food when she was sure no cameras were pointed at her.

MacDougal was still chatting with the representatives at the table, and Anya decided to indulge herself and have a fifth steak. Maybe even try to put one of the salmon fillets between two steaks and make a surf-and-turf sandwich. But she'd look like an absolute pig if someone caught her eating that, and Samaira might be grossed out... or would she be impressed?

Her internal struggle was interrupted by a presence at her side. Renn stood there, looking up at her with something like amusement, but in a way that made Anya feel like she was the butt of some secret joke.

"Need something?" she asked, and looked down at him.

"Oui. I have decided to assault my palette with one of those salmon fillets that has been drowned in cheap butter," he said, and pointed a finger at one of the bright slabs of fish meat. It floated up and settled onto his plate when his finger twitched. "Also, I wanted to ask you what you think of... all this."

Renn gestured back towards the table of assembled government representatives, and the many flags hanging above them.

"Politics isn't my thing, but countries getting along with each other is usually good, right? And us all communicating means we'll be better prepped to attack the aliens, whenever they show up again."

"I would agree, but countries making alliances is the first step to them making enemies. Already they collect us like we're the new toys. You see them staring at you, not as a person, but as their new arms. That's what this is. It's the same old routine, but instead of nuclear weapons, it's hosts."

"That's..." Anya started to say pessimistic, but she couldn't disagree. President Hanover's first request upon their first meeting was for access to Anya's RAC store and the alien technology within.

"Look, I get it. But there has to be somebody making sure some host isn't just running wild."

"And you think it's them?" Renn jerked his head at the people assembled at the front of the room. "Why? Why are they more equipped to handle the Archive than us? No, they're slow, mired in their political games.

"Those people up there, our 'leaders,' their only power is to make you think you have none. Even now with the Archive at our fingertips, they lie and tell you that you need them, that they know best. Like a parent to a child."

"So, what? Just tell 'em to fuck off and make our own country, like the NAT?"

"No. Not yet, at least. But even something like the NAT is just the same old thing. Somebody at the top, running the show for everybody else. Somebody controlling who goes where, who knows what, and when, and keeping everybody else in the dark at their convenience. Tell me: has anybody mentioned the disappearances to you? The people that have vanished?"

"I saw a report about some people missing in California, if that's what you mean."

"There's that. Also somewhere in Canada, and Japan as well. Prime Minister Miura was talking about it earlier. But there's also Kan. Remember him?"

Anya rummaged through her memory and just barely recalled a tall, broad-shouldered man dressed in red leather armor and with a red hood that obscured his face. He had been part of Renn's group in Greenland, along with Mona and Harrison.

"He's missing?" Anya asked, and brought up her list of contacts. She had shaken Kan's hand and added him to her list, but as she glanced through it, his name wasn't there. "Felix? You were supposed to tell me if anything about my list changed."

"Uh, well, yes," Felix said, "but the thing is, I wasn't aware of the change either. I set an alert to notify me—and you—if anybody removed themselves from your contact list or died. Neither of those happened. His data just... went."

"What the hell does that mean?"

"It means I'm still registering that his data is present, I just can't access it. His removal from your contacts list appears to be a function of the Archive itself, rather than Kan choosing to remove it or him dying. I can't track his location or message him at the moment, but can confirm he's alive and on Earth."

"I found out yesterday, notified President Bisset, who notified Hanover, and who—I imagine—notified your Director MacDougal. She hasn't told you?" Renn asked, faux surprise on his face.

Anya looked between Renn and the table on the stage with MacDougal and the others. MacDougal caught her eye and glanced between her and Renn, then turned back to speak with the Canadian director.

"What's your point?" Anya said.

"How long did this merger between our countries take to arrange? Two weeks? That's considered pretty fast, in terms of politics. And since the gnosiphages haven't been going on as many murder sprees, maybe that's not so bad. But think about it: it took two weeks before our governments started truly sharing intelligence. Maybe that's two weeks where we could've found one of the gnosiphages, or other hosts. And still, they do not share everything, even within their organizations."

Anya glowered, trying not to look over at MacDougal. She focused on Renn instead, setting her plate down and crossing her arms over her chest.

"And lemme guess: you think you can do better?"

"No, but I know that *we* can. Your meeting in Greenland, that took mere hours to set up. Did you coordinate that with your government, or do it on your own?"

Anya opened her mouth to reply, but shut it again. She'd had Jennifer Chang helping her, but it had been all under the table. She had been pretty sure if MacDougal had known, she'd have shut her down.

Renn smirked at her and nodded.

"All right, fine. The government's slow as fuck, but they've got the network to do shit we can't. Sure, your devil pal up there can summon demons or whatever, and I can blow shit up, and you can float a fish fillet onto a plate. Neither of us can coordinate a multi-layered emergency response to evacuate a city, or respond to disasters in multiple places at once."

"You're right. For now. But this merger is between countries that mostly like each other. What happens when a not-so-friendly country starts setting up their own host alliances? Or if we kill all the gnosiphages, and then what? Everybody starts collecting hosts, and then it's only a matter of time before the inevitable happens," Renn shrugged. "I don't think either of us wants that."

"Is he bothering you?" a sultry voice asked behind Anya. Mona sashayed around her and ran her fingers along Renn's arm. Like the first time Anya had met the woman, her body temperature was inhumanly low. She radiated a subtle chill around her, but her skin had the healthy glow of warmed bronze. "Why are you pestering other guests when there's a perfectly good dance floor over there, hmm?"

"Ah, apologies. We were just discussing the merger," Renn replied, and kissed Mona's hand. "If you'll excuse me, I think my date requires some attention. Think about what I said, though."

Renn set his plate down on a nearby table with a look of mild disgust, then walked arm-in-arm with Mona to the dance floor. Anya stared after them for a moment before MacDougal caught her eye.

The older woman stood up as Anya approached, then said just loud enough to be heard, "Excuse me, gentlemen. I need the ladies' room for a moment," then gave Anya a subtle nod as she made for the restroom. Anya looked down at her plate, grumbled, but followed after MacDougal.

The director stood at a sink, her back to the mirror, and nodded at the door behind Anya when she entered. Anya rolled her eyes, but locked it.

"We alone?" MacDougal asked. Anya didn't sense any heat signatures in the stalls, or anywhere else but out in the main dining area.

"Yeah. What's going on? Also, why am I hearing about missing hosts from Frenchie out there?"

"I was going to tell you after tonight, during tomorrow's briefing. I heard about it from Hanover this morning, and since we had the dinner to prepare for, there wasn't time to set up a formal meeting," MacDougal said. "What did Renn tell you?"

"That Kan's been missing. Felix confirmed it, but said he's also gone missing from my contacts list, but not like he died or removed himself. That's it."

"He didn't say anything else?"

"Yeah, he said government's slow as hell and he doesn't trust you guys to get shit done efficiently."

"How original."

"I also heard Hanover pissed off Arvo, somehow. Mind telling me what that's about, or was that going to wait until tomorrow, too?"

"That's why I wanted a few minutes of your time. Dr. Immonen's been visiting Hendricks in his lab down south more and more frequently during his humanitarian excursions. Hanover got it in his head that the two of them are working on something dangerous, like a biological weapon. The good doctor didn't take well to this accusation and said he would be considering leaving the DERD."

"I can't blame him. Arvo would rather die than make any kind of weapon, biological or otherwise."

"I agree, which is what I told the President this afternoon when this little exchange occurred. Dr. Immonen's been ignoring our calls, and this is—quite literally—the first free moment I've had all day and wanted to ask you, personally, if he's made contact with you."

"No. I haven't heard from him in a few days. Last I knew he was in Argentina or something."

"Then tomorrow morning, I'd like you to get in touch with him. Just make sure he's doing all right. If he's at Gary's, maybe take the day to go for a visit. It's been a while since you've been down there, right?"

"A bit. But why me? I don't mind, but Sam seems more like the type to smooth things over."

"That's exactly why I'm not asking Upadhyay. She'd try to be a diplomat, and I don't need that right now. I need somebody to tell the doctor that he was right to be angry and Hanover is a stupid asshole. That seems like something that's in your wheelhouse."

Anya raised her eyebrows and MacDougal smiled at her.

"Leadership carries a lot of privileges, but burdens to match. One of the latter is that I'm often restricted from officially speaking my mind outside of my home, or women's restrooms. But it's important we maintain cohesion right now. Those people out there," MacDougal jerked her chin at the restroom door, "they're all nervous. Scared. A bunch of murderous aliens almost killed the President of the United States a month ago, and as far as they know, any one of them could be next. We need to look like we've got our shit together and everybody is on board.

"I know governments can be slow, Nowicki. I get it. Christ, I'm a black woman in her sixties. You think I haven't been frustrated as hell at how slowly progress happens sometimes? Sometimes haste is essential, but sometimes it's also deadly. Us rushing ahead without securing some basic alliances first could lead to disaster later on. So right now, I'm asking you to help with that. Can you do that?"

"Yeah. I'll talk to Arvo tomorrow, maybe pay Gary a visit too," Anya said.

"Thank you. Now, go on and try to enjoy the party. Shouldn't be too hard given how Upadhyay looks," MacDougal said, and left the restroom. Anya smirked to herself and followed a few moments later.

She found Samaira, Tori, Pan, and Riley by the bar together. Samaira, Tori and Riley looked up as she approached, while Pan remained engrossed in his food.

"What was that about?" Samaira asked.

Anya gave them the short version, careful to make sure nobody else was listening.

"So I might be gone to Antarctica tomorrow, but we'll see. In the meantime, you wanna maybe dance?" Samaira smiled up at her and took her hand.

"You guys don't mind if we take a few songs, do you?" Samaira asked Tori and Riley.

"If you think I'm gonna try dancing in these stilettos, you're either drunk or you've never worn stilettos," Tori replied, and sipped at a martini.

"You have fun. Watching all the pretty gals dance while I stand next to the drinks is weirdly nostalgic," Riley said.

The live band in the corner of the dining hall began to play something slow, and Anya and Samaira began to sway to the music together, along with a dozen or so other guests. Since Samaira was nearly two full feet shorter than Anya, she had to be careful with her movements, but they made it work.

Anya caught sight of Renn and Mona, back at the dining table on the stage. Renn met her gaze and gave her a smile and a nod. Mona fluttered her eyelashes mockingly.

"I don't think I like them very much," Anya muttered.

"Hey," Samaira said as she brushed Anya's neck with her fingers. "I'm down here."

"Sorry. It's just…"

"I know. That's for tomorrow. You know… I've been thinking about our last date."

"Yeah?"

"Yeah. Wishing Riley had called a few minutes later. And that I'm sorry if I'm going too slow."

Anya shook her head. "I wish he'd called later too. But Sam, it's fine. It's not a race. Things are crazy, and I can't blame you if you want to be careful."

"I just… I've dated a bit, mostly as an undergrad. My last girlfriend and I split up because I got too into my Master's program, didn't make time for her. I don't want to do that again."

"Okay. So, when's our next date?"

Samaira laughed.

"You make it sound easy. Like we don't have meetings and you're not going to be flying across the globe tomorrow, and more meetings, and more flying around."

"Easy or not, I'm willing to make the time if you are. This Friday? I'll clear it with MacDougal. I think she might owe me one after this."

Samaira turned her head to the side as she thought, and Anya could almost hear the gears in her head turning over the music. She was probably going over their entire schedule of briefings, patrols, and more for the week.

"Hey," Anya said, and brushed her fingers against Samaira's hip. "I'm up here."

Samaira chuckled at that, a dainty sound that made Anya want to tell the band to quiet down for a moment.

"Sorry, I was just thinking about if we were free or not, then."

"If we're not, then we'll make it so we are."

"Yeah. Yeah, okay. Friday," Samaira said.

"It's a date," Anya replied, and held Samaira closer as they continued to dance.

3

The night had finished with Anya escorting Samaira to her dorm, and getting a soft, lingering kiss on the cheek. She had literally floated back to her dorm, wishing Tori, Riley, and Pan a goodnight. MacDougal still had things to attend to, but Anya was done socializing.

She retreated to her room, changed into her pajamas, and crashed into her mattress. She dreamed of her and Samaira dancing across a mountaintop. They passed Renn and Mona, MacDougal and stacks of paperwork, President Hanover, and others.

Then, Anya's ear beeped.

"Anya?" a voice asked from within her head. Felix.

The beeping and Felix's voice were almost a relief. The dream had not descended into a nightmare, but Anya felt it might have if it had gone on much longer. She didn't want her memory of dancing with Samaira tainted by the subconscious stew of dreamland.

Reality had been sweet enough.

"Mmf," Anya mumbled and sat up. She wore a baggy sweater and flannel pants, more for the feel of comfort than a need for warmth. She glanced at her bedside clock.

04:30

It was still pitch black outside, but for the soft glow of the lampposts.

Felix waking her up and her ear beeping meant Archive news, and if it was happening at this hour, the news was probably bad.

"Felix? What's wrong?" Anya asked.

"I've been keeping an eye on your contacts list since we found out about Kan. Whatever happened with him just happened again, but with two more hosts."

Anya's stomach sank.

"Who?" she asked.

"Grant Wilkins and Jiro Yamada. Both were at Outpost #2 until a few moments ago."

Anya had only met Grant in-person a couple of times. He'd joined up a week after the attack on the White House, paranoid about aliens kidnapping him. Like Anya, he had taken fire powers, but gone with pyromancy instead of the Flame Dominion. Grant's skills lent themselves to ranged attacks, but were dependent on his magic staff and a few other enchanted items.

Anya was glad she'd taken the Dominion.

As for Jiro, he had been at the dinner less than six hours ago. He'd stayed at Outpost #2 quite a lot in the lead-up to last night's official gathering. Japan had agreed to "loan" Jiro out to the US and help patrol the Pacific region and share any other resources.

"Bring up my map," Anya said as she hopped out of bed and began to change into her usual attire: jeans, sneakers, a black t-shirt, and a heavy leather jacket. She also attached a thick leather strap around her left wrist, which had a marble-sized chunk of polished red stone set into its center, surrounded by a band of gold.

She studied her map as she dressed and frowned as Felix zoomed in on Outpost #2. The map showed the basic information of an area: outlines of an island, country, the streets of a city, that sort of thing. It was not a complete satellite image of whatever it showed, and the only active movement came from the dots representing people on Anya's contacts list.

Currently, there was only one.

Esmeralda Gomez, a psychic Anya had first met in Greenland. She was in her early twenties, though her round face and wide, dark eyes made her look a bit younger. Her signal shone bright and steady on Anya's map, exactly where Outpost #2 was.

"What about the other two?" Anya asked.

"Disappeared, just like Kan. They're alive, or at least the Archive is telling me they're alive, but I can't track them or find their contact data," Felix replied.

"Fuck. Okay, I gotta tell MacDougal, make sure nothing's happened to Outpost #2. If Esmi's still there…" Anya said and pressed Esmeralda's name on her list. The connection beeped, indicating it was going through, but nobody answered. Anya tapped her foot and stared at her screen as she waited.

After two minutes of nobody answering, Anya disconnected and hurried out of her room. She stopped by the DERD agent on night duty in the main foyer. He was scrolling through the news on his phone, and fumbled it when he saw Anya.

"Uh, Agent Ardent," he said, and Anya winced. It wasn't a terrible codename, or call sign or whatever, but it was still weird.

"Anya is fine, Frank," she said. "I need MacDougal. Just buzz her and tell her I'm on my way, and it's important. Then tell the people in communications to get a hold of anybody at Outpost #2."

"R-right," Frank stuttered, and picked up the nearby phone as Anya left. She soared across Outpost #1 to the administration building, where MacDougal, Riley, and some other senior agents had their rooms. The door opened as soon as Anya landed and she strode inside. MacDougal was already out in the hallway, clad in a gray silk robe and with a matching silk cap covering her hair. Despite her casual appearance, her face was as stern and solid as ever, though—for the first time —it did show some signs of her age and fatigue.

"Nowicki. What's happened?" MacDougal asked, and held her door open as Anya stepped inside the Director's room.

Despite her elevated position within the DERD, MacDougal's quarters weren't much larger than Anya's. They were much more utilitarian, though. Everything was standard: off-white walls, plain gray furniture, no television to speak of. The only sign that somebody actually lived there was a collection of photos on the wall in the living room. The photos showed a family with two children, and MacDougal standing with an older man, and a few pictures of all of them together.

"Jiro and Grant are missing, and Esmeralda isn't answering my calls through the Archive," Anya replied. MacDougal's eyes widened and her nostrils flared as she took a subtle inhale, and then her face hardened. "I had Frank tell the people in communications to try to get a hold of anybody else at Outpost #2, right before I came here."

"Good," MacDougal said and picked up a phone in the kitchen, and pressed a few buttons. She waited for barely a second before somebody answered. "MacDougal. Nowicki asked... Uh-huh. Yes. Mm. All right. Call Riley, and have him get to my room, then contact the office in DC. They'll get in touch with the White House. I'm with Nowicki now. Go."

MacDougal hung up the phone and let out a sigh.

"Bad news, I take it?" Anya asked.

"No response from Outpost Two."

"Shit."

"How long ago did you notice this happened?"

"Minutes. Felix woke me as soon as they saw I'd lost Jiro's and Grant's contact data. Felix, can you come out here and confirm?"

"I sure can!" Felix said and popped up beside MacDougal, who glared at the hologram until they floated back toward Anya. "Uh, anyway, what Anya said is true. I detected the same irregularity that I found with Kan's missing contact data occur approximately seven minutes ago, which is when I woke Anya."

There was a knock at MacDougal's door, and Anya opened it to reveal Riley, his hair askew and his eyes bleary from sleep.

"What's going on? I just got a call..."

Anya relayed everything to Riley while MacDougal sat at the kitchen counter and began rapidly typing out texts on her phone.

"Are they dead? Jiro and Grant?" Riley asked.

"No, I don't believe so. In addition to still seeing that their signal is active, I'm not detecting any declines in global host numbers," Felix said. While they didn't have the exact location of any hosts Anya hadn't made contact with, they and the other AIs did have a somewhat accurate running count of how many host signals remained on Earth.

"We know Esmeralda isn't. If she wasn't, I wouldn't have her signal," Anya said.

"But she could still be hurt or injured," MacDougal said. "Try calling her again."

Anya tapped Esmeralda's contact window and waited. The picture flashed and beeped, but nobody answered.

"Can't her AI answer?" Riley asked.

"Not unless they've been instructed to," Felix said. "If Esmeralda is unconscious or otherwise unable to communicate, she won't be able to tell her AI to respond. Furthermore, AIs are not permitted access to Archive functions without host confirmation."

"So even if Esmeralda told her AI in advance to call for help if she were unconscious, they couldn't?" Anya asked.

"Correct. The AI can search the Archive, but it cannot perform any action without immediate host confirmation."

"Shit," Anya chewed her fingernail. "Okay. I'm going down there."

"Contact Hendricks before you leave. See if he can send some of whatever he's been fiddling with down there to help you. I've been texting one of my contacts in DC, and we'll send some of the Pacific fleet to that area as back-up."

"What about Sam? She's plenty of back-up," Anya asked and MacDougal shook her head.

"We need somebody with fighting skills down there in case the worst-case scenario happens and there are still hostiles present. I'm going to ask Upadhyay and Pan to stay here, in case we also come under attack. I've alerted the staff on-duty, and they're at battle-ready positions. Defensive counter-measures are prepped. Once you take off in the Shadow Ray, we'll activate the force field Hendricks installed."

"Right. Better get a move on, then," Anya said. She emerged onto the snowy field where she found Riley waiting for her minutes later. Riley had changed out of his sweats and into a set of tactical gear Gary had provided the DERD agents with.

The gear consisted of upgraded body armor that could take an anti-tank round and keep its wearer alive. There were some kinetic displacement plates and lesser, impact-activated force fields. The gear was defense-only, though, nothing that could be weaponized. Riley had his handgun strapped to his thigh and a rifle over his shoulder, along with a trio of grenades at his belt.

"You coming with?" Anya asked.

"Yup," Riley nodded.

"Probably dangerous."

"Probably. Guess you're lucky I'm coming along, huh?"

Anya snorted and rolled her eyes as she and Riley strode along the heated walkways toward the hangar, where her Shadow Ray waited.

"You know, it's ballsy for you to come and all, but you're probably gonna be in the way if there's a fight," Anya said.

"Maybe. That's why I'm gonna leave the fighting to you and do my job."

"Which is?"

"Poking around the outpost for anything we don't want left behind."

"Sneaky G-Man shit. Gotcha."

"Whoa, hey. Very above-board G-Man shit. No sneakiness."

Anya grunted at Riley and paused as they came upon the hangar. Samaira was there, along with Pan and Chandrali. Pan had bundled himself up in his coat and was standing beside a small heating post that had risen from the ground. Samaira was in a robe and long coat, her hair tied back in a loose bun.

"Hey, Sam," Anya said as she approached, then smiled down. "Heya, Pan. Chandrali."

Pan hugged Anya's leg while Chandrali didn't even bother to glance away from licking herself. Samaira took Anya's hand and gave it a squeeze.

"I heard," Samaira said. "I guess I'm staying here with Pan while you go down and do… whatever."

"Hopefully find out it's all just a power failure and a series of improbable accidents," Anya replied, and gave a weak smile. Samaira didn't return it.

"Don't be too crazy or anything, okay?"

Anya blinked. "What do you mean?"

"I mean, it's been a couple months since you got to cut loose. And I can see you've been antsy and just... look. it's nothing, and time matters. Just be careful."

"I will," Anya said, and gave Samaira a gentle hug. She returned it, her arms just managing to reach around Anya's back. Anya knelt down and patted Pan's head.

"I came out even though it's cold," Pan said and Anya grinned at him.

"Means a lot, buddy. Thank you," she said.

"I don't understand what's happening, but Samaira says we have to guard the outpost while you're out working? Something like that."

"Very important stuff. I'm counting on you," Anya said and waved at him, Samaira, and Chandrali (who continued to lick herself in a display of very obvious disinterest), and then joined Riley in the Shadow Ray.

The sleek, black craft hummed to life, rose into the air, and drifted through the hangar's retracting ceiling.

"Here's hoping it's nothing serious," Riley said from the passenger seat behind Anya.

"Here's hoping," Anya said. But she knew otherwise. She tapped a few buttons on the Ray's console, and it shot off toward the horizon across a still-dark sky.

———

SHE SPOKE with Gary on the way to Outpost #2 to give him an update and get a read on things. Arvo was there and said he'd meet her at Outpost #2 as well. He was traveling in his chrome, egg-shaped vehicle alongside four of Gary's newest Guardian robots. They were still a few hours away from the outpost, having left Gary's factory in Antarctica around the same time Anya left Outpost #1 in Alaska.

It had been about a half-hour since Felix had woken her.

"Satellite images don't tell us much," Gary said as Anya leaned back in her pilot's chair. Gary leaned aside to allow Anya to see a screen behind him on her floating communication window. The screen showed an aerial view of what looked like an exact duplicate of Outpost #1, except it was surrounded by dense foliage on most sides except for one, which had a picturesque beach stretching away from it. Outpost #2 was unmarked in any way that Anya could tell. It appeared to be in perfect condition.

"No life signs," Arvo said from a second communication window. "That doesn't necessarily mean there isn't anybody alive down there, just that Gary's satellite cannot find them."

"My equipment's pretty sensitive, Doc. But yeah, if anybody made it to the underground shelters, they'd be shielded from my scans."

"I don't get it," Anya said. "I thought the outposts had some pretty solid defensive measures."

"They do," Gary grunted. "I gave the DERD some of my best stuff, so long as they couldn't co-opt it into weapons systems or something. It's just like Outpost One: super reinforced concrete and alien alloys, early warning systems, retractable armor plating, and emergency forcefields that cover the whole place."

"So whatever did that," Anya pointed at the screen showing the ruins behind Gary, "was strong enough to get through all your upgrades."

"Doesn't look like it. None of the buildings have any damage. Looks like none of the defenses were even activated."

"Whatever happened, it happened quickly," Arvo said. "We all had the hosts in our contact lists. Easy enough for them to call for help at the first sign of trouble. Also true for the DERD agents, who likely have access to any number of emergency lines. But none called."

Anya chewed her lip and folded her arms over her chest.

"He's right," Riley said behind her. "The outposts check in with each other pretty regularly. The last time was at midnight. The next scheduled check-in was at 0500 hours. Outpost One has the same set of emergency warnings as Outpost #2, thanks to Gary. Somebody should have been able to press a button or something, but nothing like that happened."

"So whatever happened must have taken place in minutes, maybe seconds, or else somebody would've sounded an alarm," Anya said.

"Looks that way," Gary said. "And I can't tell much from the satellite scans. We'll have to wait until we actually all get there."

"Nothing for it, then," Anya said and leaned back in her chair to wait until she arrived at Outpost #2.

———

THE SHADOW RAY did a fly-by of Outpost #2 when they arrived. It appeared intact from the air, but quiet. No people milling around, and no radio contact. Anya stood up as the autopilot began the landing process near the beach and Outpost #2's docks, and looked at Riley.

"Gonna get ready real quick," she said.

"Do I need to cover my eyes or anything?" Riley asked, and Anya smirked and shook her head.

"Nah. Just a little flash of light and then I'm good."

With that, Anya touched the red stone embedded in the leather wristband. There was a flash of light, and then her normal clothes had been replaced by her Regalia of St. Llothec. She'd made the purchase of the quick-change armband off the RAC store a couple weeks ago, at Samaira's prompting. It was a basic enchanted item that stored her regalia in a tiny pocket dimension, no bigger than a typical drawer. When pressed, it swapped whatever she was wearing for the regalia, allowing her to be battle-ready in about a second.

The Regalia of St. Llothec resembled something a warrior monk might wear: a sleeveless dark red tunic and black pants. The former had gold trim, while the latter had a golden, three-pronged insignia on the right leg. It had bracers that covered her forearms up to the elbow, and boots that went up to her knees, both with intricately etched bronze-gold plating over them. It was incredibly light, but Anya knew from experience that it could take a significant amount of punishment and not be damaged. Plus, there were all the runes and upgrades she had applied.

She brought up her menu to double-check her stats and make sure she was as ready as she could be.

ANYA NOWICKI: LEVEL 41 PHOENIX MONK
Statistics

- Awareness-10
- Dexterity-21 (+13 from gear)
- Fortitude-43 (+16 from gear)
- Intelligence-10
- Strength-23 (+6 from gear)
- Willpower-10

Skills

- Flame Dominion-43 (+17 from gear)(+5 from Artifact)
- Kinetic Dispersal-21 (+11 from gear)
- Combat Cognition-18
- Regeneration-37 (+18 from gear)
- Xhama Thul-16 (+6 from gear)
- Gravity Dominion-23 (+10 from gear)(+5 from Artifact)

Equipped Items & Artifacts

- Shard of the Everstar (x2): A fragment of the shattered Everstar, which can still hold vast amounts of heat energy that may be drawn upon in times of need.
- Alchemical Tincture of Restoration (x2): A potent mixture of ruby sage, blessed powdered cinnabar, akontolthweek, and other assorted restorative substances. Apply to any major wound or ingest orally in case of internal damage only or multiple smaller injuries.
- Sun's Heart (Superior): Grants access to higher level of Flame Dominion skill. (+15% efficiency when using this artifact)(+5 to related skill for this quality)
- Singularity's Grasp (Superior): Grants access to higher level of Gravity Dominion skill. (+15% efficiency when using this artifact) (+5 to skill for this quality)
- Regalia of St. Llothec, the Ever-Burning (Excellent): Provides protection from any and all heat-based hazards, as well as kinetic damage. Also boosts the wearer's innate heat-producing abilities and endurance. (This Excellent quality

item has a current cap of five lesser-quality runes and three equal quality runes) (+8 to Flame Dominion skill, +4 to Kinetic Dispersal skill, +3 to Fortitude statistic)

- Rune of the Shield (Refined): Provides dual enhancements to quality and defense of imbued item. (+100% to item durability parameters and +100% defensive bonus) (+3 to Kinetic Dispersal skill)
- Rune of the Shield's Embrace (Excellent): Provides additional defensive covering beyond the standard coverage of imbued item. (+100% of item's base defensive capabilities to any uncovered body parts, additional +25% defensive capabilities to covered areas)
- Rune of the Maiden (Refined): Provides dual enhancements to healing and stamina of the wearer of imbued item. (+6 to Regeneration skill and +3 to Fortitude statistic)
- Rune of the Warrior (Refined): Provides dual enhancements to strength and agility of the wearer of the imbued item. (+3 to Strength and Dexterity statistics)
- Rune of the Stallion (Refined): Provides dual enhancements to speed and stamina of the wearer of the imbued item. (+4 to Fortitude and Dexterity statistics)
- Rune of the Mender (Excellent): Repairs damage done to imbued item, provided the item remains above 10% of total durability. Item requires at least thirty minutes to repair per 10% of damage done.
- Rune of the Comet (Excellent): Provides dual enhancements to the gravitational and heat abilities of the wearer. (+6 to Gravity and Flame Dominions)
- Rune of Force (Refined): Provides dual enhancements to the gravitational and kinetic abilities of the wearer. (+4 to Gravity Dominion and Kinetic Dispersal)
- Mantle of the Gale (Refined): Imbues the wearer with additional speed as well as a light deflective wind-shield. (this Refined quality item has a current cap of five lesser-quality runes or three equal-quality runes) (+3 to Dexterity statistic)

- Rune of the Vortex (Refined): Provides dual enhancements to any wind-based abilities of the item and speed of the wearer. (+6 to wind-based air skills inherent to item, +3 to Dexterity statistic)
- Rune of the Greater Salamander (Refined): Imbued item is granted resistance from fire and wearer's fire-based abilities are enhanced. (+100% to heat and fire resistance for item, +3 to Flame Dominion)
- Rune of the Brute (Refined): Provides dual enhancements to the power and hand-to-hand fighting ability of the wearer of the imbued item. (+3 to Strength statistic and +6 to Xhama Thul skill)
- Sacred Orichalcum Chestguard (Charmed)(Excellent): Grants bonuses to protection and healing abilities of the wearer. Provides excellent defense for the covered area. (+4 to Fortitude statistic and +8 to Regeneration skill) (Bonus +2 to Fortitude statistic and +4 to Regeneration skill due to similar bonuses on worn items)

After the fight at the White House, Anya had had over 1.3 million Reward Allocation Currency. But after upgrading almost everything, and giving herself a second Shard of the Everstar and a couple of healing potions, she'd lost about a million, and was down to 335,531 RAC. She kept hoping she'd be able to save up for a cool spaceship or something else, but her survivability came first. She couldn't spend her RAC if she was dead.

There was a familiar, dizzying rush of power as her regalia and runes increased all of her stats and skills. It was like a natural high whenever she first put her gear on, but it settled into normalcy after a few seconds.

"Quick question," Riley said.

"Shoot," Anya replied.

"Those Everstar shard things and those healing potions, why don't you buy more of 'em? Just keep charging and healing yourself so you never run out of energy and never get hurt?"

"I thought about it, but after running some tests with Arvo, he said not to waste my RAC. The Shards of the Everstar do recharge me, but have diminishing returns. After the first two times I do it, the energy I can process starts getting a lot lower. Rest and food are about the only thing that can get me fully topped up again.

"As for the healing potions, it's like any other medicine. Too much of it can kill you. Or in my case, my regeneration skill will start recognizing the potions as toxins, and stop them from working. Two in a day is about my max."

"What do they taste like?"

"The potions? Like… cinnamon fruit punch and whiskey? Kinda?"

"That actually doesn't sound too bad."

Anya nodded in agreement as the Shadow Ray touched down near the docks. She approached the rear hatch and stepped outside, fists at the ready. The sun was just coming up now, and it looked to be the start of a beautiful, tropical day. The only thing to indicate that something was wrong was the presence of several large naval vessels dotting the distant horizon. They were black barbs along the surface of the otherwise tranquil azure of the sea, unnatural geometry interrupting the organic line of the water.

"Stay behind me," Anya said as she and Riley left the Shadow Ray and moved up the beach. They went up just enough to get a view of the remains of the outpost, and it looked much as Gary's satellite and their quick fly-by had showed it: a collection of drab buildings standing tall and sturdy amongst the emerald of the island and the pale gold of its beaches.

Outpost #2 appeared to be untouched, gleaming new and pristine as the day it was constructed.

"Weird," Anya said as she studied the buildings.

"Yeah," Riley agreed, then added, "Company."

Anya looked up as a great whooshing sound filled the air, and Arvo's chrome egg descended from the sky, along with four of Gary's Guardian mk-3 robots.

The Guardians were a significant step up from Gary's previous robotic servants. He had been forced to make those out of literal trash and scrap, but the Guardians were the result of his factory and the rare alloys and other materials he produced.

The Guardian series had long lower bodies with four mechanical legs, each ending in a claw. Their upper torsos rose out of the front of the lower body, with four mechanical arms extending from the sides. The robots were topped with a cylindrical "head," perched between their two upper arms, with a circle of glowing red eyes allowing the machines to view in all directions at once. From top to bottom, the Guardians were plated with thick, black armor with silver highlights, and the occasional glow of internal red light. They reminded Anya of some kind of techno-centaurs.

Each one was also twelve feet tall.

The Guardians took up a defensive position in front of Anya and Riley as Arvo's flying chrome egg settled onto the sand beside the Shadow Ray. Arvo Immonen emerged from the egg-shaped vehicle and gave Anya and Riley a quick wave as he hurried over.

The doctor was tall, athletic, handsome, and just shy of middle-aged. His long blond hair was pulled back in a messy ponytail that swayed as he ran towards Anya and Riley, and a pair of scratched glasses perched on the end of a somewhat crooked nose. As usual, the doctor was in a perpetual state of scruffiness, with a beard the color of hay lining his angular jaw, and his clothes rumpled and just off-center from each other.

"Hello!" Arvo called out as he approached.

"Good timing," Anya said and looked from Arvo and up at the Guardians. "So, these are the new models, huh?"

"Yes. Gary redesigned them after your sparring match a couple of weeks ago. I can certainly attest to their speed. My little egg had quite a time keeping up with them."

"I guess we send these big fellas in first?" Riley asked.

"You got it," Gary's rough voice, with a strong hint of a Chicago accent, echoed from speakers set into the Guardians. "My boys will go in, make sure there's no obvious trouble, and then the rest of you can follow. I'll leave one of the Guardians with Riley for defense."

"Appreciate it," Riley said as three of the four Guardians stomped forward and into the empty outpost ahead.

Anya brought up the Archive's map, which showed her the immediate area and Esmeralda's glowing signal. Wherever and whatever the woman's condition was, she was nearby and alive. She kept her eyes darting between her map and the surrounding area as the Guardians did a sweep of the outpost and its perimeter. She scanned for any heat sources, any shifts in gravity fields, but there was nothing of note.

For as far as Anya could sense in every direction, she and Riley and Arvo were alone. If not for the Archive map and her link with Esmeralda, she'd have no idea the other woman was there. The map showed her at somewhere on the far end of the base, well beyond the range of Anya's heat sense.

"Looks like you're clear. Nothing's jumping out at me," Gary said from the robot that loomed over them.

"Literally or figuratively?" Arvo asked as the three of them and the Guardian strode toward the outpost.

"Both. No signs of aliens or any other hostiles, and no signs of what happened. The outpost is all in one piece. Not so much as a bullet hole or a burn mark," Gary said.

Anya flew ahead of the rest of the group, trying to get close enough to Esmeralda's signal so she could lock onto her heat signature. She was on the far side of the outpost, according to Anya's map.

"Some life signs that way, maybe two stories underground," Gary said from a nearby Guardian, the towering robot gesturing with an arm nearly as long as Anya was tall. "Hard to say for sure how many. The downside of all my reinforced concrete and shielding is that it's pretty difficult to scan through. The outpost's power grid is out, so internal scans aren't working."

"Gotcha. I'm going in," Anya said as she approached the doorway to one of the dormitory buildings. The Guardians were much too big to follow, but took up defensive positions outside.

The dormitory was just like hers back in Alaska, so she knew the layout already. If the life sign was coming from underground, it meant the emergency bunker. Esmeralda must have made it down there when whatever happened had happened.

Anya threw the door to the dormitory open and rushed inside, fists up and ignited.

Nothing.

"Easy, kid. Let the little guy take the lead," Gary said, not from the Guardian this time, but from a small drone that flew out of its arm compartment. The drone was bulky and roughly ovoid, with a pair of oblong hover-discs extending from its back. A flashlight shone from its front end, illuminating the darkened dormitory's entrance hall. Pale green rays of light emitted from the sides of the drone, sweeping over the room in quick, yet methodical patterns.

"No sense in you sticking your neck out first," Gary said.

"So long as we don't waste too much time," Anya said, and followed the drone toward the back of the dorm. She checked her Archive map, and it showed Esmeralda was within a couple dozen yards of her, well within the range of Anya's heat sense.

Gary's reinforced building materials were likely blocking the signature. There could be a bonfire in the bunkers below Anya, and she still wouldn't have been able to sense it. Anya sighed and continued after the drone as it floated ahead of her, its lights sweeping along the halls.

As they walked, the silence began to weigh on Anya. She was so used to hearing the sounds of other people in her own dorm. The quiet pressed on her, and made every step, every breath, seem a hundred times louder than it actually was. The signs of absence were everywhere: an abandoned cup of coffee, a partially open bathroom door, a single shoe in the middle of the hall. Anya's eyes swept over everything, her combat cognition alerting her of potential ambush sites and any stray movement.

The group crept along the hall, wary of every corner and shadow, until they came to the door to the bunker area. The door was solid metal and more than a foot thick. Anya tugged on it and grunted. It was shut tight and locked from the other side. An indicator light next to the door glowed a bright red.

On the one hand, Anya was happy to see some sign of resistance. It meant Esmeralda and anybody else who was on the other side might be okay. However, it also meant Anya was going to have a lot of trouble opening that door.

It would take ages to melt, even longer to tear it out. She'd have to basically demolish the whole building, or get the Guardians to—

"Gary Hendricks. Emergency override. Password: Pretzel dog,"

Gary said. The armored door thunked loudly, then swung inward as the indicator light switched to green. Anya blinked at it, then at the little drone hovering ahead of her.

"Pretzel dog?" she asked.

"I was hungry when I came up with the passwords for this outpost," Gary replied. "Sue me."

"That works even though the power's out?" Anya asked as the drone descended a flight of stairs and she followed after it.

"The bunkers and emergency quarters under the outpost have their own secure power grid. Whatever happened to the primary grid wouldn't affect the stuff down here."

"Any clue what happened to the primary grid?"

"Not yet. Riley and some other drones are inspecting it now. Looks like somebody manually disconnected stuff, manually threw a few switches. Dunno why, though. The aliens would've just smashed it, and nobody else would have known how to do it except the base staff."

"Weird," Anya muttered. The stairwell leading down was lit by emergency red lights from the ceiling that cast the stairs and hallway ahead in a surreal ruby glow.

When Anya reached the bottom of the stairs, she finally picked up Esmeralda's heat signature. She stepped forward, but Gary's drone darted in front of her.

"Drone first," Gary insisted.

"Move your metal ass, then," Anya said. She didn't want to keep Esmeralda and any other survivors waiting. She knew Gary was only being cautious, but there was such a thing as being a little too careful. Especially when people needed help.

The drone passed several doors, until it and Anya came to the end of the hall, to the last one. Anya tried the door, found it locked, and didn't bother waiting for Gary to say whatever food-related passcode he needed. The door was much thinner and less reinforced than the one upstairs, and Anya tore it right off its hinges.

"Hello?" she asked as she entered the dark room, her whole body covered in a small layer of flame and chasing away the darkness.

Something made a rustling noise, and Anya and Gary's drone

turned toward the noise.

Anya's firelight and the drone's flashlight shone on Esmeralda, who sat on the floor, cross-legged, her head turned up and eyes rolled back in her head. Her eyelids twitched as if she were in REM sleep, and her lips closed and parted as she whispered nonsense.

"I'm contacting the doc," Gary said, and Anya nodded as she approached Esmeralda. She took a few hesitant steps forward, slow and easy, as if approaching a skittish animal.

"Esmeralda? Hello? It's me, Anya. Remember? We met a few times," she said as she approached. The other woman continued to whisper gibberish to herself, eyes blank and staring beyond the confines of the room.

"Anya?" a voice asked from behind her, and Arvo appeared in the doorway with Riley close behind.

"Hey. Esmeralda doesn't look hurt, but she's like, asleep or in a trance or something," Anya said. Arvo knelt next to Anya, his eyes focused on Esmeralda for a moment.

"She's mostly all right, physically. She's on the verge of exhaustion, and she's dehydrated. Her brainwaves are strange, like she's having a nightmare, but she's not asleep."

"Can you do anything?"

"I can try," Arvo said, and touched Esmeralda's hand. A pulse of invisible force filled the room and Anya fell back against the far wall. It was more out of surprise than any actual force. The pulse was less a shove and more of a shock of sensation. Fear, panic, anxiety, anger, all hit her in a tidal wave of emotion she hadn't been prepared for.

Anya had been focused and alert one second, and the next her whole body had been screaming at her that she was under attack, that she was about to die, that danger was everywhere. Her stomach knotted, her body became slick with sweat, her heart rate jumped, and the metallic and acidic tangs of bile and blood surged up into her throat.

Her view of the red room spun and began to fade. She had a brief glimpse of the dark silhouettes of Arvo and Esmeralda stretching and deforming, of becoming something nightmarish.

The dim emergency light faded, and Anya fell down into the shadows that converged on her.

4

"Awake. Ah, speak of the devil. Hello, Anya. How are you feeling?" a familiar voice asked. Anya cracked one eye open, wincing as she did and sunlight jabbed into her skull. She hissed, squinched her eyes shut, and took note of where she was.

She was on her back, on something soft and tickly. Probably a lawn outside, given the sound and salty smell of the ocean nearby, along with the balmy tropical breeze ruffling her hair. Three heat sources stood or sat around her, and Anya did a quick tally of who she knew to be on the island: Riley, Arvo, Esmeralda. Three. That checked out.

The voice above her belonged to Arvo, and Anya tried to open her eyes again, and was relieved to discover that the terror had receded.

"What the fuck happened?" she asked. "What was that shit in the bunker?"

"Sorry," a shy voice said from nearby. Anya propped herself up on her elbows, and spotted Esmeralda sitting on a bench. Riley stood some distance away, chatting on his cell phone, while Arvo knelt beside Anya, his hand on her bare shoulder.

"Sorry for what? Also, I assume you fixed whatever was wrong with me. Thank you," Anya said to Arvo, who gave her shoulder a pat.

"I kinda screwed up some stuff," Esmeralda said.

"Did you do whatever happened here?" Anya asked, and Esmeralda shook her head so hard that her black ponytail lashed her face.

"No way! It was the other ones."

"Other ones?"

"I woke up when I felt some kind of weird pulse from outside," Esmeralda said. "My skills, they're all psychic, and I can read people and things. Among other stuff."

"It's been a while since I've seen your skills," Anya said, and Esmeralda brought up her menu.

ESMERALDA GOMEZ: LEVEL 32 PSIONIC ARCHITECT
Statistics

- Awareness-19 (+8 from gear)
- Dexterity-8
- Fortitude-9
- Intelligence-27 (+12 from gear)
- Strength-5
- Willpower-32 (+15 from gear)

Skills

- Psionics-37 (+13 from gear) (+5 from Artifact)
- Psychic Materialization-41 (+12 from gear)
- Empathic Enhancement-18 (+6 from gear)
- Imagery Architect-17
- Psychic Bulwark-19 (+10 from gear)

"Psionics plus the empathic skill lets me read people. I can tell when people are lying, and stuff like that, but it's not telepathy. More like seeing somebody's aura, except you're feeling it. Sort of. It's hard to explain," Esmeralda said.

"We get the basic idea," Gary said from the drone hovering over Anya's shoulder. He'd had the decency to space his towering Guardians away from the clearly frazzled and nervous Esmeralda, each of them standing at an edge of the outpost and scanning the horizons.

"You felt a pulse?" Anya prompted.

"Pulse. Right. See, during the day, everybody's emotions are just kinda white noise. Kinda soothing, in a way. At night, all that emotional background sound goes way down though and it gets quiet. But then, around ten at night or so, there was this big pulse of something outside the outpost, out to sea.

"People's emotions, they all feel different. Even when it's the same emotion, it feels different from different people. But this thing, whatever it was, it didn't feel like anything. It felt like nothing."

"What do you mean?" Anya asked.

"Like it was negative emotion. Not sadness or anger or anything, but an emotional pit. A hole that wasn't just empty space but full of emptiness."

"Ah," Arvo said, and his already fair skin paled under the tropical sun.

"Arvo?" Anya asked. The doctor glanced down at her and cleared his throat.

"I think I felt something similar when I touched the aliens at the White House. Especially the snake one, the boss. How do I say this? Not a passive absence of something, but an active presence of nothing. Does that make sense?"

"No," Anya frowned, feeling quite stupid even as Esmeralda nodded emphatically and pointed at Arvo while she snapped her fingers.

"I don't get it either, kid," Gary whispered from the drone and Anya gave him a thankful smile.

"All right, too metaphysical for me. But you felt something weird, right?" she asked.

"Yeah. So I got up, figured I'd go let the guy on night duty at the front desk know and he could call the outpost director, or whatever. I went out there and told him, and he notified the outpost director and I figured I'd go outside and wait, try and get a better lead on whatever was out there. That's when I kinda lost the signal, so to speak. I knew it was still out there, but it went from this one big pulse out in the ocean to all these little ones scattered around.

"I went to go see Mr. Yamada, since he was staying here, only he wasn't in his room. Neither was Grant. Neither were a few people I knew. That's when I saw some people wandering around outside, walking toward the ocean. Except, they didn't have any of that white thought noise coming off them. They were just like radios with the volume turned off.

"I called out to them and they turned to look at me, then wandered away. That was when I started to get scared. I figured I'd better call somebody, so I brought my Archive up, except it wasn't working. My AI said everything was on the fritz, and there was no calling, no using the RAC store, nothing."

Anya's skin prickled, and she exchanged a look with Arvo and Gary's little drone.

The only time their Archives had failed to work had been in the presence of the snake alien, what the Engineers had referred to as an overseer. There were, supposedly, two left on Earth.

"I ran back to my dorm, and when I got inside…" her voice cracked and she had to take a breath before she continued.

"There was another host standing over him. I don't know who he was. A tallish guy wearing some kind of red armor, with a hood. I couldn't see his face. The agent at the desk had his head cut off, and this guy was like… pulling the blood out of him somehow, making it disappear into his hand."

Esmeralda took a long, shaking breath.

"I got scared. I only fought a few aliens, and it was always in groups where I was just support. I didn't know if the man in red was an alien, or a crazy host, or what, so I just ran. I'm not—I'm not a fighter. I know maybe I should have, but I was scared."

"Hey, it's okay," Arvo said as Esmeralda began to sniffle. "I am not much of a fighter either, so you're in good company. What happened next?"

"I started yelling for help, and that's when I saw Grant and Mr.

Yamada. Grant was kind of a jerk, but he was normal, and Mr. Yamada was always quiet, but he seemed nice. So I ran over screaming at them to help, but they were quiet, too. Like the people from before: no noise. Just radio silence. Then they both turned toward me and attacked. Grant started shooting lasers from his staff, or whatever it was. Mr. Yamada ran right at me. I'd seen him fight in practice before and I knew if he grabbed me, I was dead.

"So I ran. I threw up as many defensive manifestations as I could and I fled down into the bunker. Then I used all my fear and confusion and made a kind of psychic minefield around myself, except I was in such a panic I made it a little too well. Wound up locking myself in a kind of feedback loop of being terrified and running away from it and using my fear to throw up another barrier, but then getting scared of that and throwing up another one and so on," Esmeralda said and sniffled, wiped her nose, and gave Arvo a weak smile.

"If it wasn't for you, I'd probably be stuck down there forever."

"Ah, I can't take all the credit. Anya and Gary led the way, and Riley and the Navy had our backs," Arvo replied.

"So that weird, scary shit I saw before I passed out, that was just your psychic minefield?" Anya asked, and Esmeralda nodded.

"Normally I'd be able to control it better, but I panicked, used the panic to set up my minefield, and got stuck in my own trap. I knew that everybody in the base was gone already, figured I was about to die," Esmeralda shrugged and looked aside. It was a dismissive gesture, brushing aside her own mortality, but Anya didn't buy it.

Esmeralda's heart slammed in her chest, pushing her hot blood through her veins and raising her temperature. She was sweating and shaking from residual adrenaline.

Anya wanted to snap at Esmeralda, tell her she should have fought instead of hid, should have tried to save the people at the outpost. Any reprimands she had died on her lips whenever she looked down at the other woman, her frustration withering away into silent resignation.

Yelling at Esmeralda wasn't going to solve anything. It was maybe only because she had hidden that they had any clue as to what might have happened anyway.

"Can you bring up your map? Get your AI to show us the time when you came out here and saw Grant and Jiro?" Anya asked.

"Poco?" Esmeralda said, and a pale, purple AI with a tower of lavender blossoms for a head appeared alongside her map screen. The clock in the upper corner rewound to the previous evening.

Arvo, Anya, and Gary's drone all leaned in to stare as the map showed Esmeralda's dot, but instead of the clear dots that should have represented Grant and Jiro, there were just a pair of wide, hazy circles. A third circle, even larger and more difficult to see, was somewhere behind Esmeralda's dot.

"The recording isn't corrupted?" Arvo asked. "I thought Esmeralda said she couldn't use the Archive around this time?"

"It's like when we fought the snake in DC. It fucks with the Archive when it's around, but when it's gone, it goes back to normal. The Archive records all the data. You just can't access it until the interference is taken care of," Anya replied. In their case, it had meant killing the snake.

"No alien signals?" Anya muttered. "Poco, can you zoom out?"

"If Esmi asks me to," the AI said.

"Poco, zoom out, try to pin down any alien signals," Esmeralda said, and Poco complied. The map zoomed out to show the entire island and much of the sea around it. A hazy red circle appeared at the far right edge of the map, pale and indistinct.

"There! That means an alien was nearby. Right?" Anya asked.

"Yeah, but it could've been anywhere in a hundred miles or more with a range like that," Gary said as his drone scanned the map and took pictures with a series of rapid clicks.

"So Jiro and Grant just… attacked you?" Anya asked.

"Yeah, except it was them, but not them. Same as the guy in red. Something changed them, made them not themselves. Just like the DERD agents I saw walking away."

"Was it mind-control? Something like that?"

"Mind control doesn't work like that. You can't just psychically dominate somebody into doing whatever you want. You'd fry their brain and kill them before you even got them to walk two feet. Plus, it would take a ton of concentration."

"But something messed with their minds," Anya said. "And the only one that wasn't affected was you, the only psychic."

Esmeralda shrugged. "It could've been some other psychic thing. But just straight mind control? No way. I'd have sensed their minds fighting back, at the very least."

"A shame I wasn't here to scan them," Arvo said.

"Wow, everybody sounds so cheerful. I'm sure it's gotta be good news, right? Definitely nothing bad?" Riley asked from off to the side as he hung up his phone.

"Peachy," Anya said, and filled him in.

"Christ," Riley sighed when she was done and then crossed himself. "We're going with the assumption that these hosts have been taken over by the gnosiphages?"

"It sounds that way. If it's not them, it's another host," Anya said.

"They're hostile, regardless," Gary added.

"And what about the normal folks at the outpost? Where the hell did they go?" Riley asked, and Esmeralda shook her head.

"No idea. The whole place felt like it had gone into a deeper sleep than normal. Even when people are asleep, they feel a little when they dream. But it was just like everybody got turned off. Not dead, just... out."

"Creepy," Riley muttered. "What about that dead guard you mentioned?"

"A little blood, but that's it. No body. Drones scanned the whole place," Gary said. "We gotta let people know. Anybody getting approached by a host they don't already have listed in their contacts is a potential threat."

"I'll let MacDougal know, and she'll alert Outpost One and the Canadian folks," Riley said.

"I will contact Renn and the European team," Arvo said. "They can get in touch with their government handlers and spread the word."

Anya wanted to call Samaira, wanted to hear her voice and tell her personally to be careful, to stay safe. However, other hosts had to know as soon as possible. Riley was already calling MacDougal, and she would make sure Samaira and Pan were ready.

"I'll call Brody and Cooper, since they're closest," Anya said and tapped the Australian orca whale's name on her contacts list. He and his non-host friend, Cooper, were maybe only a few hours away, or less depending on how fast a given host could travel, and would be in the most potential danger. Plus, the two of them were both unrepentant stoners and would be slow on the uptake on the best of days.

She was relieved to see that Brody was still there, but fidgeted while the line beeped until he finally picked up.

"Oi! How ya goin'?" Brody asked when he appeared in the communication window. He'd taken some sort of environmental adaptation skill, and as a result, his body changed whenever he was on land, making it somewhat more human. He still had the rounded, broad features of an orca, but they were humanized somewhat. He was sitting outside on the beach somewhere, smoking an over-sized joint and drinking from a bottle of whiskey.

"Brody, hey. Remember me? We've spoken a few times since Greenland?" Anya asked.

"Oh sure. Fiery chick. Lotsa muscles. Coop says he hopes you're single."

"Dickhead!" Cooper yelled from off-camera and Brody guffawed.

"What's goin' on? You wanna tell Coop to fuck off, or you just wanna come down and get high?"

"No, sorry, this is business. Something, probably aliens, attacked the American outpost near Guam. You know the one?"

"Uh, think so. Coop and I went there with what's his name? Australia's boss or something?"

"Prime Minister," Cooper said and leaned into frame. He was a younger man, twenty-something, with a mop of shaggy blond hair and tan skin, and a lithe, athletic frame from time spent swimming and surfing. "H'lo. And yeah, fish-breath here and me went with the PM to the outpost a couple weeks back. Met some other hosts."

"I was here for that," Esmeralda said.

"So, aliens blew the place up? Fucking bad luck, eh?" Brody asked and puffed on his joint.

"No. Not sure about the extent of what happened, but it's bad. You guys are close, and we wanted to warn you in case any weird hosts show up," Anya said. "Their signals are disappearing from our contacts lists, and we think it might be some kinda psychic thing. Making hosts and regular people behave strangely. Just hunker down and let your government people know what's up. The DERD should have all the information in a few minutes."

"All right. If something happened up there, it could get here pretty fast. What's the convertible's speed at, Coop?"

"Well, for us it'd be about ten or fifteen minutes to get there from here, but for aliens or other hosts? I don't have a damn clue," Cooper said.

"All right. We'll call the boss, I guess. Though I could do with a bit of a fight, to be honest. What're you gonna do?" Brody asked.

Anya thought for a moment and said, "Go down my contacts list and make sure as many people know as I can."

"Right-o. Well, if you do—eed—el—" Brody's voice became erratic as his picture began to crackle and break up.

"Oh shit," Anya said just as her screen vanished. Felix appeared when it did, waving their tiny arms, face animated with alarm.

"Anya! The Archive!" Felix said.

"Yeah, I got it."

"Mine too," Arvo said.

"Ma'am? It looks like their Archives just shut down," Riley said on the phone. "Uh-huh. Ma'am? Ma'am? Shit. Cell reception's toast too."

"Oh God," Esmeralda said.

"Get ready, kid," Gary said from one of the Guardians towering over her. The giant robot and its fellows all shifted form slightly, guns and missile launchers emerging from underneath their heavy armor. Arvo all but vanished as he activated his living shadow skill and slipped away.

Anya ignited herself, her eyes glowing a bright, sunshine yellow. Flames burst from and crawled over her fists and feet. She popped her knuckles and cricked her neck to one side, then the other. She brought her fists up and faced outward, toward the sea and whatever was coming.

"All right, you fuckers. C'mon. I've been waiting a month for this."

5

They came from above.

The sky was vacant of everything but clouds one moment, then dominated by a rippling red orb the next. The orb burst out from behind one of the clouds and plummeted down to the edge of the beach in a streak of crimson like a bloody tear across a cheek. Anya grabbed Riley and Esmeralda under her arms and flew away as quickly as she could, just as the orb slammed into the edge of the beach.

"Damn!" Riley shouted as Anya skidded to a stop several dozen yards away and set the agent and Esmeralda down. The orb's exterior was made of some kind of rippling ruby liquid. It had partially splattered across the sands, but drew back toward the large orb as it began to collapse inward. The red liquid had to be blood: its color was too vibrant and primal to be anything else. The orb dissipated into countless flowing strands of it, all pulled toward the gauntleted hand of a broad-shouldered, hooded figure in red.

Kan.

Two others stood beside him.

The most noticeable was the hulking tower of muscle and armor that was Jiro Yamada. Anya had last seen him in an ill-fitting tuxedo, which had made him look borderline comical. Nothing about him now was even remotely amusing, however. His armor was matte black and thick, and it covered him from head-to-toe. The helmet covering his head was sleek, and had a pair of narrow, mirrored lenses over the eyes that looked somewhat insectile.

The third figure was much shorter and thinner than Jiro or Kan, with short blond hair and a narrow face, and wore flowing robes over loose clothes. He carried a staff of ivory tipped with a ruby the size of a baseball. Fire flickered within the ruby, and caused ruddy crimson light to illuminate the man's waxen countenance. Anya recognized him, too. Grant.

All of them had the same odd posture. It was as if somebody had replaced their spines with metal poles, and attached all their joints to unseen marionette wires. As they stepped forward, the movements looked almost mechanical.

Anya didn't even have time to make an attempt at talking to them. All three of them darted in different directions as if they'd practiced the move beforehand. Jiro rushed the nearest Guardian, Grant soared up and away from them into the air, while Kan summoned a pair of long sabers made of shining blood. Their movements were still off, still awkward, but there was no denying their speed.

"Whoa!" Anya shouted as she brought up a heavy field of g-force in front of her. The sudden swell of increased gravity made Kan slam into the ground. "Stay d—"

Anya didn't get to finish before the man swept both of his blades at her ankles and she was forced to leap backward to avoid them. She tried to increase the gravity on him and keep him pinned but he was slippery, somehow. She could feel the heavy force around him, pressing in on his weight, magnifying his own mass and using it against him, but then it lessened somehow and he was on his feet again.

His erratic movements and variation in personal gravity kept throwing Anya off, and Kan managed to slice her several times. Each one would have been fatal if not for her regeneration ability, and her armor. He managed to slice her on the side of the neck, and on the underside of each of her upper arms, all near veins. He tried for her legs and wrists, but her armor was reinforced there, and turned the glittering ruby edge of the blood swords away.

Anya's blood sprayed out in sudden arterial bursts, but quickly sealed. It was enough to cover the sand around her in blood, though, and when Anya thought she had finally managed to pin Kan to a single spot, he simply dropped out of sight into one of the bloody patches.

"Fuck!" Anya snapped and looked around frantically for Kan. He'd simply vanished into the bloody sand around her. She was forced to back away as Gary's Guardians charged past her and engaged their own target.

The towering mechanical constructs opened fire on the armored figure of Jiro, lasers and bullets and missiles slamming into him in a furious salvo of light and explosions. They broke against him like a gentle tide against a mountain. The weapons did not so much as cause the man to break stride. He swung a shovel-sized fist at the nearest Guardian and the sound of the impact made the air shudder.

A bright forcefield expanded between the Guardian and Jiro's fist at the point of impact. The protective lattice of light shielded the Guardian's body from the brunt of the impact, but not all of its momentum. A gale of wind rushed past from the passage of the attack, and Jiro followed through with his swing. The Guardian was thrown up into the air and over Outpost #2, little else but an over-sized base-ball slammed away in a home run.

"Look out!" Esmeralda shouted at Anya as she prepared to charge Jiro and back-up the Guardians. A thin beam of light, blazing hot, shot down from the sky and directly at Anya. The laser came from the gem atop Grant's staff, the whole of it glowing with orange and red runes along its length. It hit Anya between her eyes, and the heat of it could have turned a steel beam to slag in an instant.

Anya snorted and rubbed at the unmarked spot on her forehead.

"Kid shit," she said and rocketed herself into the sky at Grant. He fired more lasers at her, but none were any more effective than the first. She soaked them in, drank their heat into the eagerly pulsing center of her Sun's Heart, and pulled Grant to her with Singularity's Grasp.

It should have been easy. She had gripped all sorts of things—from cars to robots to struggling aliens—within the gravitational claws she commanded. Grant froze for a moment, then drew some sort of glowing rune in the air that made Anya's hand twinge, cramp, and then her claw attack faded and Grant was free of her grip.

He fired another salvo of lasers at her, along with orbs of white fire, and crackling motes of light that exploded when she drew near, but none of them were any danger to her. Against anybody who couldn't absorb heat, the attack would have been lethal in the extreme. But they barely tickled Anya, and made sure her Sun's Heart was constantly at capacity.

Anya didn't like wasting her energy on ranged attacks. Chucking fireballs looked cool, but for her, it was an inefficient use of the Flame Dominion. However, since Grant was being so charitable with his flame-based attacks, and her Gravity Dominion wasn't doing the trick, she decided to indulge.

Anya summoned wave after wave of heat into her palm, her Sun's Heart channeling the deadly energy from her center and into her hand. She condensed the heat down with Singularity's Grasp, turning the fireball from the size of a melon into a grape, and then shoving more heat into it. She repeated this several times as she absorbed more of Grant's attacks, refilling her internal well until she was ready.

She focused the now baseball-sized orb of condensed fire and explosive energy at Grant's staff. She would slingshot it at the staff with opposing gravitational forces, directing it as best she could. While Grant's fire wasn't an issue for her, the same wasn't true for everyone else on the beach, particularly Riley.

Anya released the orb and it shot from her hand faster than a bullet. It streaked across the distance between her and Grant, seeking his staff as if it had a mind of its own. It was moments away from impact when Anya exerted control over it and forced it away from the staff and Grant and caused it to land in the ocean with an explosion of water and steam.

The fireball probably would have hit Grant's staff without an issue, maybe destroyed it entirely.

It also would have hit Grant. Not directly, but he was holding the staff, and Anya wasn't entirely sure how well he was protected from fire. He had to have some protection, but it was impossible to be sure.

Anya glanced behind her to see Esmeralda and the Guardians struggling to pin Jiro, while Riley's heat signature hid off in the trees, with Arvo's signature not too far off. Esmeralda had to be exhausted, and Riley was next to useless, and the doc wasn't built for combat at all.

If Anya and Gary weren't able to stop Jiro, Grant, and Kan from… whatever had made them act like this, somebody was going to die.

Anya had never really entertained the idea of killing somebody before. She had only ever resorted to violence when her back had been against the wall. She glanced at Grant, at the vacant expression on his face. She didn't know what was wrong with him, but he was a danger: to her, to Esmeralda, Riley, Arvo, and anybody else if he managed to get past them.

And if whatever had happened to these three hosts happened to Anya and the others, they'd hurt more people down the line.

"Fuck," Anya growled. "I'm sorry, man."

She flew straight at Grant and rocketed right into his mid-section. She got him in a sort of modified clothesline: her upper arm slamming into his gut while her forearm bent around and secured his back. Anya also made an effort to blunt some of the impact with her kinetic dispersal skill, but that didn't do much.

Grant let out a rasp of air and coughed up blood as Anya slammed into his stomach and both plummeted to Earth. She adjusted her grip as they fell so she was behind him, arms under his armpits, a classic full nelson.

Anya hit the beach with her shoulder, taking the brunt of the impact. It hurt, but she could deal with it. Grant probably couldn't. He had gone limp in her grasp, but the steady, warm beating of his heart told her he still lived.

"Gary! I need help holding this one!" Anya said from the sandy crater she had created. One of the Guardians landed on the beach beside her a moment later and leveled a huge cannon down at Anya and Grant. "Don't kill him!"

"Relax, kid, I got a kind of cement sludge that would keep a rhino on steroids locked down. He'll be fine if—kid!" Gary said from the Guardian's speakers, the last word shouted in obvious alarm.

Anya had a split second to look down at Grant, specifically at the back of his neck.

It was squirming.

Grant's skin boiled and undulated as if it had turned into a liquid, and it was bone-deep, primal revulsion that made Anya shove him away more than anything else.

No sooner had she shoved Grant than the back of his neck and the lower half of his skull exploded outward in a spray of blood, skin, and bone fragments. Anya shouted in shock and no small amount of disgust as some repulsive, squirming horror emerged.

It was smaller than the palm of her hand and only half as thick. It was a slimy blackish-gray and had a smooth diamond shape. A long, whip-like tail extended from the bottom of it, and all along its pale underside and the tail were rows of hair-thin, twitching insectile legs.

The tail of the creature burst from Grant's back, along the curvature of his spine, the countless tiny legs detaching themselves from his vertebrae and bits of his nervous system. The writhing thing flew at Anya's face with blinding speed, faster than she could get her hands up, faster than she could dodge.

But not faster than she could ignite the air in front of her.

The volume of air in front of her face and chest, between her and the horrific wriggling nightmare that exploded from Grant, went from warm and balmy to hellishly hot just as the creature reached for Anya's neck with its multitude of needling limbs.

It burst into flame, its wet, fleshy body turning dry and brittle in moments. It curled in upon itself like a dying spider, managing only a final thrash of its tail before it was still. From living grotesquery to lump of charcoal before it even hit the ground, at which point it crumbled to black dust.

"Holy fucking... what?" Anya breathed as she stared at the charred lump at her feet. She'd also turned clumps of sand in a two-foot radius around her to glass. She looked from the thing, over to Grant.

He was very dead.

The base of his skull, neck, and upper back were a gory mess of burst skin, torn muscle, and exposed bone. Anya had a moment to take note of a small hole in the base of Grant's skull, before Gary's voice drew her back to the here-and-now.

"Kid! Are you okay?" he asked.

"I-I'm fine," Anya said, then spun around. "The others!"

"Alive but Jiro's trashed one Guardian and two more are in rough shape, and the third guy just vanished somewhere. It was good you kept that fire guy busy but we could use some help."

"On it!" Anya said and flew away from the beach and towards the ongoing fight. Thoughts of Grant and the thing inside him pricked at her mind, but she shoved them away. She could examine them later. At least she sort of knew what was going on now: Jiro and Kan had those disgusting squiggling things inside them. If they got the opportunity, they'd put them in Anya, Esmeralda, Arvo, and maybe even Riley.

Just ahead, Esmeralda was backing up the Guardians as they fought Jiro. She had summoned some sort of psychic constructs, one of which was a giant teddy bear three times as tall as she was, along with a unicorn, and a stag beetle bigger than a van. She had also covered herself in plate armor and wielded a long spear.

All of it glowed a soft pink, and looked to be made of partially translucent crystalline material. The teddy bear and the beetle both focused on protecting Esmeralda and striking at Jiro when he got too close to Esmeralda, while Esmeralda herself rode the unicorn and tried to jab at the man's exposed back if he turned on the constructs or the Guardians. Anya noted that none of her strikes appeared to be going for lethal areas, but only his legs and arms.

The host followed a fairly basic pattern: slash, thrust, vanish and reappear elsewhere, then repeat. The teddy bear and the stag beetle were both covered in slashes, bleeding some ephemeral pink, pale substance, but kept up their defense.

Just as Anya flew over to help subdue Jiro, a red figure emerged from a pool of blood right behind Esmeralda, twin swords angled in a scissor-like position to snip her head off her shoulders.

Anya called out a warning as she flew to her, landing with a thunderous boom of impact between her and Kan. The dual-wielding host registered no surprise at Anya's appearance, and the black depths of his hood offered no insight. Anya snagged Esmeralda in her gravity claw and yanked her down as she flew over her, burning fist aimed straight at Kan's hooded head. The red-clad figure altered the swords in his hands to a pair of shields, the crimson liquid changing shape faster than blinking. Anya's attack skittered off the shields—harder than any armor she had encountered before—and sprouted wicked little barbs that snagged at Anya's skin as her fist passed.

She snarled in surprise and pain and drew her fist back as she healed. Her blood flowed outward, coaxed beyond the natural limits by whatever skills Kan had. Her skin sealed around the cuts, stemming the flow, but not before it had created more bloody sand and Kan vanished into it once again.

Anya whirled around, trying to catch sight of him, when her heat sense alerted her.

"Behind you!" Esmeralda cried and the giant teddy bear swung one of its ponderous arms over Anya's head as a pair of gleaming red blades scissored towards either side of Anya's neck. She crouched and braced herself against the ground as the bear's punch passed over her like a small airplane. For as cuddly as the bear looked, the thing sure could hit.

It connected with something out of Anya's line of sight, but not her heat sense. It slammed into a warm, human-shaped mass and sent it flying down the beach. The stag beetle flew after it with a flutter of its pink, gossamer wings, and the teddy stomped after.

"Did he get you?" Esmeralda asked as she galloped over on her unicorn, and Anya shook her head.

"No, I'm fine," she replied and absently touched her fingers to her neck. Her regeneration skill had helped her bounce back from a broken spine, slashed arteries, getting impaled, acid burns, and a lot more. She wasn't sure if she could survive getting decapitated, however. She'd asked Felix about the limits of the skill, but her AI had only said it was largely dependent on her internal well of energy, supplemented by her Sun's Heart.

She wasn't eager to see if it was possible to come back from getting her head sliced off, or letting Kan try again.

"They've got things in them," Anya said to Esmeralda. Her psychic constructs were keeping the swordsman busy while Gary's Guardians had managed to slow Jiro down. They had covered him in some cement-like gel, and were trying to shove him down while continuously spraying him with it. It worked better than shooting him, but the man was still fighting back.

"Things?" Esmeralda asked.

"Some kinda fucked up parasite thing or something. It looked like it's attached to the skull and spine, from what I saw of Grant before it killed him. Damn near got me, too."

"Gary said something like that," Arvo's voice floated out of the air from a few feet away and Esmeralda shrieked and nearly fell off the unicorn. "Sorry."

Arvo's form remained indistinct, hazy, like a heat shimmer or a mirage, with only a faint dark shadow—almost invisible in the sunlight—to give away his exact position.

"I have an idea, but it will require precise timing and cooperation," Arvo continued.

"Go on, but make it quick," Anya said and glanced back at the fight. Jiro had one arm free and had ripped the nearest Guardian in half with it, leaving just two left. Kan had lopped off the teddy bear's arm, but the stag beetle kept him on his toes with quick rushing attacks.

"If I can touch either one of the hosts, I will have access to their nervous system and anything controlling it. The one that was in Grant, it knew Grant was lost and so it ejected itself, killing him on the way out. But if I can touch them first, I can paralyze them both: host and parasite, then extract the latter and get Gary to contain it for study later," Arvo said.

"Right. Just gotta get your hands on them," Anya said and looked at the two hosts. Jiro was covered head-to-toe in armor, no gaps for skin-to-skin contact. Kan was quick, and also covered from top to bottom.

"No problem," Anya sighed. "I'll figure something out."

"I know it's not an easy job, but I think we can do it. I'll be close by, but hidden, and will take any opening I see," the doctor replied, and then his wavering silhouette was gone.

A crash and a screech drew Anya and Esmeralda's attention. Jiro had dispatched the last two Guardians with a series of rapid punches that freed his arms, while Kan had managed to bisect the beetle lengthwise and decapitate the teddy bear.

"I've got seven more Guardians on the way," Gary said from a tiny drone not far away.

"Uh-huh, and how long until they get here?" Anya asked.

"Two hours, ninety minutes, minimum. Maybe it's time to run, kid."

"They might catch up to us over the ocean, or worse, a city. Plus, they're still alive in there, aren't they Esmi?"

Esmeralda nodded, her eyes wide and terrified. "Y-yeah. I can feel them. It's all kinda messed up, but I recognize how Jiro feels. It's him, he's alive."

"Then we stay, and we hope the Doc's right," Anya said, and then rushed forward to meet the two possessed hosts head-on once more.

6

Kan was the first to move. His fight with Esmeralda's psychic constructs hadn't slowed him down at all, and he vanished once more into a patch of blood-stained sand. Anya thought he might be teleporting or something, but Felix, Gary, and the Archive itself had told her there was no such skill or technology that would permit that sort of thing.

However, she'd learned her lesson, and didn't bother trying to track Kan via sight. Her heat sense told her exactly where he was.

"Got ya!" Anya said and summoned an intense gravitational vortex a foot behind her. Kan sprang up right next to the vortex, sword lunging at Anya as he rose from the bloodied sands. The sword entered the invisible well of gravity tip-first, and was immediately brought smashing to the beach by its exponentially increased weight. Anya spun around, her leg extended in a whirling, flaming roundhouse.

She connected with the side of the man's leather-armor, and grinned as she felt a satisfying crunch under her heel. That wouldn't kill him, she had pulled most of the kick's force, but it would slow him down. Anya used her own momentum to spin and bring her other foot up and around, weighting it with localized gravity and turning her boot into a tiny comet of force and fire.

Her second kick slammed into the center of Kan's chest piece, which erupted in a sudden torrent of blood, almost like a bomb. Anya was actually blown back by the sudden explosion, and had to take a moment as a literal rain of blood showered around her.

"Holy shit," she said, horrified for an instant that she had killed Kan. The hooded man appeared fine, but dazed. He was on his back, his armor in ruins, and losing some its deep red color, fading to a muddy brown.

One of his swords lost its physical stability, and collapsed into a puddle. Kan faltered, trying to stand and maintain the stability of his other sword. Pink, psychic chains appeared around Kan's wrists, bringing him down and keeping him in place. Anya readied to rush him and keep him still long enough to let the doc handle him, when a shadow moved behind her.

"Look out!" Esmeralda shouted. A towering pink knight, a paladin from an older fantasy game Anya recognized, dropped a kite shield in front of her and blocked a blow from Jiro's massive fists. The black-armored host had come up on Anya's side while she'd been occupied with Kan.

That was when she noticed that Jiro's armor hid his heat signature. It encased him so fully that nothing got in or out, not even his body heat.

The paladin, another one of Esmeralda's psychic constructs, struggled under Jiro's blow, its crystalline shield cracking along the top and side.

"Thanks for the cover!" Anya said and then darted out from under the paladin's side, and flipped behind Jiro. She grabbed his arm in a lock, using her own height and Singularity's Grasp to force the man's arm back and away, hyperextending it. If she had to break it, so be it. She only needed a minute to incapacitate Jiro, but he was stronger than he looked, and he looked plenty strong to begin with.

Despite Anya's superior hold on him, despite the literal tons he must have weighed underneath her gravitational assault, despite human bodies not being designed to withstand the sort of pressure she was putting his under, Jiro resisted.

It was nothing but brute strength, inhuman and unreal.

"C'mon!" Anya said and cursed as the man began to lift her up. The paladin hit Jiro several times with its shining pink mace, but it might as well have been bopping him with a balloon. The beach had cratered under the two of them, their combined weight literally in the tons based on the amount of gravity Anya was using to pull on Jiro.

He turned his helmeted head to regard her, and then reared it back and bashed her in the face.

Anya's nose didn't just break, it shattered, along with her cheekbones, most of her teeth, and her jaw. The pain was instant and immense, blinding. She fell back, her focus on Singularity's Grasp wavering and then breaking. She fell just outside of the crater she and Jiro had created under their weight, and let out a garbled howl of pain.

"Anya! Anya! Oh, oh no, no no no," Esmeralda babbled somewhere off to Anya's side. Anya was already beginning to heal, but it was too slow. She couldn't even see properly, but she could hear Jiro knock the psychic paladin away behind her, shatter it with a sound like a chandelier bashing against a cliff.

Anya's regeneration wasn't healing her fast enough. Ordinarily she would have just dodged for a few moments to let herself heal naturally, or since Arvo was here, go let him take care of it. However with both of the hostile hosts near, and the almost certainty of an alien overseer still lurking somewhere, Anya didn't dare risk it: either taking the time, or forcing Arvo to reveal himself in order to heal her.

She reached into the pouch at her side and withdrew the powerful healing potion she had purchased weeks ago, and poured its contents into her open mouth. Her bones cracked and popped as they began to reshape at once, doing in a few heartbeats what would have taken regeneration several minutes.

Her vision cleared just as Jiro took a swing at her. Anya ducked backward, the sheer force of wind from the the man's fists unbalancing her and throwing up a wall of sand in its wake.

"Anya! I'm having trouble holding the other one!" Esmeralda shouted. Her numerous pink chains and shackles around Kan flickered and cracked. He was currently spinning and lashing around like a bladed cyclone at the chains, slashing one and then another with a new pair of swords.

"God dammit!" Anya snarled and ducked, then rolled, then flipped over another series of attacks from Jiro. He was slower than her, no doubt, but he was relentless, and whatever he—or his armor—was made of was so dense and carried so much momentum, that Anya's typical gravity shoves weren't doing enough to deflect them.

"I'm getting… a headache," Esmeralda said, and blood trickled from her nose and ears. Anya started to wonder how she could be tired after such a short fight, but then recalled she had been in a fight last night, and then been in some sort of defensive stasis for hours after, with no sleep, or food, or drink.

It was no wonder the woman was starting to falter. The bright rose hues of her psychic chains continued to fade as Anya watched, becoming less solid by the moment.

And while Anya herself had not used up too much of her energy, and still had a lot of extra juice stored up in her Shards of the Everstar, she was also starting to feel drained. She couldn't keep fighting the two hosts at this level until Gary's backup robots arrived. She'd be tapped out long before then.

"Incoming!" A loud voice echoed above her just as something blotted out the sun.

The something was a kind of flying muscle car convertible, painted a cherry red and gleaming as if freshly waxed. The voice came from a hulking figure that looked like a cross between an orca whale and a man. Brody the orca slammed down onto the beach, a lit joint sticking out between his teeth, and an entire keg of beer gripped in one enormous hand.

Another figure soared down from the sky as the flying convertible sped by overhead, this one some kind of humanoid robot. However, the blank faceplate slid aside to reveal a very human face. Cooper looked between Anya, Esmeralda, and the two mind-controlled hosts, then began to back away from Brody.

"These two are being mind-controlled or some shit but they're alive! Esmi will fill you in on the rest. You take this big guy and I'll get the other one!" Anya said, not bothering to shout a greeting as she leaped away from Jiro and toward Kan just as he broke the last of Esmeralda's psychic chains.

"G'day, big wheels," Brody said to Jiro, with an enormous, toothy grin. "I've wanted to dance with you for a while now. Catch!"

Brody emptied the keg into his mouth, then threw it at Jiro's head. It crashed against him like a paper cup against a tank, and then both hosts closed on each other with the echoing boom of a pair of mountains slamming together.

"Uh, looks like y'got this one big guy," Cooper said and continued to back away from Brody and Jiro as they began to trade blows that caused the air around them to shudder from the impacts. He turned to face Kan as a series of bloody spurs extended from all over his body. "You got this one?"

"Just look after Esmi for now!" Anya snapped at him and tried to keep Kan's attention on her. She and the hooded man danced around each other, his slashes and thrusts coming far closer to Anya than she would've liked, and her punches and kicks missing more often than not.

It should have been easy to take him down, but that would have meant killing him.

Too soft… a smooth, familiar voice said from inside her head. Anya didn't have time to respond at the moment, and refocused her attention on the swordsman. Yet again, Kan did that bloody sand vanishing trick, and Anya couldn't help but roll her eyes. Whatever was controlling the hosts, it wasn't terribly original. She followed the heat signature just like before, following it underneath her as it moved between the bloodied areas of the beach, and this time met Kan head on as he leaped out and descended on her, his weapons aimed at her skull.

Unlike before, Anya didn't magnify the gravity around the swordsman, but did the opposite: she made him lighter than air, dodged to one side, and delivered a quick series of jabs to his ribs.

Kan grunted and floated up and away, like a feather on a gentle breeze. His feet kicked at nothing, his arms grasped at the sky. It didn't matter how fast he was if there was no solid matter for him to push off against, and he couldn't hide under the sand and blood if he wasn't touching it.

Anya favored a quick look behind her and saw Jiro was still thoroughly occupied with Brody. Anya wasn't entirely sure what the orca's skillset was, but it had something to do with adaptation. Brody took several hard hits to the face and body, and grunted in pain as he did. However, the next few hits appeared to slide off him, or only made his blubbery whale-hide ripple.

"You trying to tickle me?" Brody laughed and bit Jiro's head. Jiro reached forward and began to strangle the whale, and Brody was forced to spit him out and back away as he gasped for air. Some blood spouted out of his blowhole near the back of his skull, and it was obvious he'd been hurt bad.

Brody was buying her time, but she didn't think he could last forever, not without being forced to kill Jiro.

One problem at a time, little ember. You have a fight of your own, still, the voice whispered to her.

She refocused on Kan as he continued to float away, flailing in the air, but starting to come down now.

"Hey Doc! If you can hear me, I'll have this one ready for you soon!" Anya shouted over the din of the fight, hoping Arvo heard her.

"I can still... help," Esmeralda said as she hobbled over, leaning against Cooper. She had wiped the blood from under her nose and beside her ears, but she still looked like hell. She was noticeably paler than she had been a few moments before, her hands shook as she raised them, and her eyes were unfocused.

"Just stay safe and get out of here. Don't need to be saving your ass and fighting these guys. Go with Cooper and find Riley if you can," Anya said and flew at Kan at full speed, not waiting to hear Esmeralda's reply.

Kan saw Anya coming just as he was about to land, and extended his blades at her, ready to slice her in half. Anya got close, then cranked up the gravity around the both of them and sent them slamming to the ground. The sudden shift threw the man's timing off, and he crashed into the beach without having time to brace himself for the impact.

Anya also landed straight on top of him, her elbow driving into the small of his back. She kept the man pressed there, flat against the beach and crushed under her magnified weight. The armor and reinforced clothing Kan wore covered most of his figure from head-to-toe, until Anya reached up and yanked his hood back.

"Doc!" Anya shouted, and no sooner had she finished the syllable than the air shimmered beside her, and Arvo appeared, hand outstretched. She decreased the gravity field around the swordsman just enough so it wouldn't flatten Arvo, but almost crushed him when she saw the back of Kan's neck begin to stretch out, away from his spine.

The swordsman screamed, then froze as Arvo's fingers touched his cheek. The moment had seemed to last for several minutes, but it had barely been a single second. Kan's neck returned to normal, and he became limp and lifeless beneath Anya.

His swords turned to harmless blood and soaked into the sand around him. Anya wasn't taking any chances, and kept him pinned.

"Thank you, but he should be down for quite some time. The same goes for whatever…thing is inside of him. I will do my best to extract it when I am able, but for now, this is the best I can do," Arvo said.

"I'll go help Brody with the big fella," Anya said and glanced at where Jiro was struggling with Brody as the whale had actually absorbed one of Jiro's fists into his gut, trapping it in place and trying to bite through his armor. Brody's flesh around Jiro's arm had started to take on the same metallic look as his armor.

Gravity hadn't worked, but fire might, just not how she usually used it. Jiro's metal armor should be a pretty good conductor of heat, after all. If she could heat part of it just enough, it might be possible to force an opening in it that Arvo could reach through.

But heating metal armor to that degree would be pure torture for whoever was wearing it. Anya winced at the idea, but then glanced over at Esmeralda and Cooper as they hurried away to find Riley.

If she kept playing with kid gloves, they could all die.

Or worse, become more puppets for those things.

"Sorry, Jiro," Anya muttered, then flew straight at Jiro's back. She didn't waste time trying to be clever with him. He was too strong for that.

"Oi! Whaff's goink om?" Brody muttered around Jiro's other fist. Blood pooled out of his mouth, and what appeared to be at least a few dozen of his teeth were littered around the beach. Jiro turned to look at Anya over his broad shoulder, and began to wrestle even harder with Brody.

"Just hold him and keep him off me for as long as you can!" Anya said and began to transfer the immense heat from her Sun's Heart to Jiro's armored back.

The more Anya thought about it and the longer she had watched him fight, she'd come to the conclusion that Jiro had simply specialized in a very limited number of skills and nothing else. He hadn't displayed any movement abilities, no projectiles or obvious magic. He and the others had arrived via Kan's abilities, with Jiro merely providing brute force and damage absorption.

Anya did as she had done with the snake in DC: she gripped Jiro to her in a powerful bear hug, keeping them glued together with a powerful gravitational pull between his back and her front. The term "Death Spooning," popped into her head out of nowhere and she had to try not to laugh at the absurdity.

Instead she turned herself into a miniature sun, just as she had with the snake. Except this time, there was no magical ability that sapped the ambient heat from the air. Anya's skin began to glow, her veins like trails of liquid gold beneath.

"Ow! Hot! Ow, ow!" Brody said and started to back away.

"Fuck! Sorry!" Anya called out. She had forgotten that the heat would transfer to Brody as well. Whatever adaptation skills he had, she hoped they'd help him adjust. The orca lost his grip on Jiro briefly, but then grabbed him again. He winced as his skin let out a loud hiss as it made contact with Jiro's armor, but then grinned.

"No worries, girly! I gotcha now, big 'un!" he laughed and continued to grapple the huge man.

Jiro struggled, and both Anya and Brody were taken along for the ride. She didn't bother trying to hold him down or stop his movements, just hang on and avoid any damage to herself. Her Xhama Thul skill was suited for this: it told her how to grip, how to shift her weight, and feel how Jiro moved to anticipate sudden changes and avoid being grabbed or injured.

His armor began to glow.

Red.

Orange.

Yellow.

Anya gritted her teeth and tried not to think about what she was doing to the man inside. She just needed to get some of the armor off, just a little. At last, she felt the hard metal against her chest start to soften.

She focused all of the heat on the leg, drawing the blazing temperatures away from the other parts of the armor as it naturally spread. The rapid heating, and then cooling made the metal creak and crack in places.

At last she felt the armor around Jiro's knee weaken enough, and become something like very firm clay. Anya brought her foot up, weighted it with as much gravity as she could, and slammed it down against the back of Jiro's knee.

His armor didn't break, but it did smear against his leg and the joint weakened. She kicked again, diverting more and more heat to that single spot, all while Jiro pummeled poor Brody and bucked and shook as much as he could to get Anya off him.

At last the armor weakened, the heat enough to convert it to something approaching a liquid. A chunk of armor splattered away from the point of Anya's kick, hissing as it smeared across the wet beach. Jiro's knee snapped with it, and he collapsed forward onto his hands and knees falling atop Brody as he did. The whale let out a howl of pain, but he held on, and Anya with him. He rolled over and crushed her beneath him, but she clung to him like an obsessed lover, and continued to transfer the blazing heat.

"Weaken it around his fuckin' arms!" Brody yelled.

Anya was running low on energy, the burning nova of her Sun's Heart dimming to a warm glow. The Shards of the Everstar that hung on a heat-proof necklace under her armor, against her sternum, flared as she used the tactile contact to draw on its reserves. Her heart regained its fiery inner glow, and she moved the punishing heat to both of Jiro's shoulders.

The armor glowed and began to melt, seeping onto the sand in thick globs. Brody got one hand free of Jiro's crushing grip, grabbed his wrist, then twisted it around. The weakened shoulder joint lost whatever reinforcement it granted, and Jiro's shoulder dislocated with a jerk. Jiro scrabbled at Brody with his remaining arm, but the orca caught that, and repeated the process with another sickening yank.

"Gotcha!" Brody said above her. Anya grabbed the melted armor around Jiro's shoulders and pulled the liquid metal away as best she could, leaving his skin beneath exposed.

What the missing armor revealed was ugly, red and raw, charred black in places, and bloody from where the armor tore away in others. The smell was of burned steak and hot metal, and Anya had to force herself not to vomit, not just at the sight and smell, but the idea of what she had done to somebody.

The whole beach around them was glass and bits of slagged metal. Brody himself was burned in several places, though his skin was healing.

"Get him to the doc!" Anya said and pointed down the beach where Arvo waved a hand, his other still pressed tightly to Kan. Anya flew toward him and the still-unconscious host.

Jiro struggled within the orca's grip, but whatever his powers were, regeneration wasn't one of them. Two dislocated shoulders and a shattered knee would make moving difficult for anybody, regardless of what they were feeling. Anya consoled herself that Arvo could heal him back, better-than-new, in a few seconds.

Esmeralda, Cooper, and Riley emerged from the treeline nearby, the former still looking like she needed a week's worth of sleep, and the other two appearing very relieved. Riley was also on his phone again, which Anya took as a good sign. She brought her Archive window up and sighed as she saw that it had returned to normal.

The overseer, wherever it had been, had retreated.

A thump sounded from beside Anya, as Jiro had used his remaining leg to kick off the beach hard enough to leave an impact crater, and launch himself and Brody through the air. The movement, and the surprise of it, had been just enough for Jiro to break free and towards where Arvo currently knelt over Kan.

"Shit!" Brody cried.

Everything slowed down as Anya's combat cognition kicked in. Brody had been flung backward by the force of the leap, and the velocity Jiro was traveling at—coupled with his still mostly-armored mass and immense size—would kill the doctor on impact. Esmeralda was exhausted, Riley wasn't equipped to handle anything, and Cooper was moving into a position to protect the other two.

Arvo's eyes widened as he looked up and saw the human missile that was Jiro hurtling at him. He turned shadowy and darted backwards, his hand leaving Kan's exposed skin for a moment.

But that was all the thing controlling the host needed. Kan spasmed, and the parasitic creature inside of him burst out of his skull and back the same as it had from Grant. It unzipped the flesh along the poor man's back as its long tail whipped out and lashed forward at the doctor.

Arvo was about to die, or be taken over by that thing, which was really just a death sentence anyway. He was the only one that could freeze the things, and if he got taken over, they'd have no choice but to put him down. That, or Jiro's death tackle would turn him into a smear on the beach.

Anya blasted herself at Jiro's side with as much force as she could, creating a powerful explosion beneath her feet that rocketed her forward. She knew she likely couldn't grab Jiro and carry him, but she was praying she could at least turn him, just a fraction.

She could.

Her shoulder slammed into the armored man's side, and she shoved with all her strength, just enough to turn the torpedo he had become a few inches away from Arvo.

As she just managed to alter Jiro's course, she seized the doctor with her Singularity's Grasp and yanked him toward her. It was a bit harder to find him visually when he went all shadowy, but his heat signature was still there.

Arvo reappeared as Anya yanked him to her, saw the exposed flesh on Jiro's shoulders, and pushed his hand against the burned flesh.

Anya roasted the parasite when it was inches away from Arvo's face, creating a localized flash-fire that turned it to ash.

Time sped back up as Anya's combat cognition switched off, crisis averted.

Jiro fell forward onto the sand with a heavy thud, Anya and Arvo atop him. Brody fell with a loud grunt several yards away from them, and Riley had just withdrawn his pistol as he stood behind Cooper.

"Is he down?" Anya asked and looked at Arvo. His eyes were wide, a slack expression of shock and confusion on his face, but he understood and nodded.

"Y-yes. Mr. Yamada and the creature inside of him are under my control," Arvo said.

"Holy shit," Anya said and sat back with a sigh.

"What the hell was that?" Cooper asked.

"Is he okay?" Gary asked from a small, hovering drone that emerged from behind Riley and Esmeralda.

"I think so," Anya said. The burn marks that had covered Jiro's exposed flesh began to heal as Arvo kept his hand on him, once Anya had reabsorbed the heat from the armor. She looked at the doctor and smiled her thanks, unable to keep her eyes from drifting back to Jiro's charred skin.

"You did very well," Arvo said and smiled. "And I'm sure once we get this thing out of Mr. Yamada, he will tell you the same."

"I hope so. Speaking of that, what now? I mean, the other two are..." Anya's voice trailed off as she looked at the gory remains of Kan and Grant. Their blood and brains were scattered across the beach, along with fragments of their spinal columns. She gagged and turned away.

"I am sorry to say, but it will not be so easy. I think we should wait for Gary's robots to arrive, preferably with some sort of containment device?" Arvo asked.

"It's on the way," Gary said as he, Esmeralda, Cooper, and Riley approached, but kept their distance from Jiro.

"I must remain here until they arrive, then," Arvo said.

"I'll keep an eye out for shit. You too, Coop! What'd you even do during the fight? I was getting my ass kicked, the gal here roasted me fuckin' good, and I lost my joint! Swallowed it, I think," Brody said.

"You had it under control, mate. I was lookin' after these two," Cooper cocked a thumb at Esmeralda and Riley. "Did a good job, if I say so myself. Nobody died! Uh, except for those two, I guess. Fuck."

"Just help me keep an eye out while that doctor fella does his thing," Brody grunted, gave Cooper a friendly shove, and then limped toward the beach with him to scan the ocean.

"Thank you, both of you," Anya said to them as they left.

"You're buying beers next time," Brody said, to which Anya laughed and nodded.

"I need to lie down," Esmeralda said, and hobbled over to the edge of the grass, stretched out, and started to snore as soon as her head was down.

"You okay in case anything else shows up?" Riley asked Anya and she nodded.

"I'm recharged. I feel like I could eat a whole grocery store out of business though."

"Hey, great. I'm feeling useless anyway. I'll go hit the mess hall and bring you back some stuff."

"You're a saint."

"I'll keep you company," Gary's drone said, and followed behind Riley. Anya suspected it was just to keep an eye on the agent, though whether out of suspicion or a genuine concern for his safety—or both—Anya couldn't say.

"Anya, come here," Arvo said and extended a hand to her.

"I'm not injured, Doc, don't worry about me," she said.

"No, but even if you have recharged your Sun's Heart, your body is already experiencing fatigue. I can't refresh you entirely, but I can help."

Anya smiled and gave Arvo her hand, and a second later, she felt more awake, more alert. Not quite as good as before the fight started, but definitely better.

"Thank you," she said and Arvo nodded.

"Now, if you will excuse me, I'm going to focus on Mr. Yamada and his unwanted passenger, so I may deduce how best to extract it."

Anya nodded and flew up into the air to survey the land around her. This had the unfortunate side-effect of giving her a bird's eye view of Grant and Kan's corpses.

You didn't kill anybody today, little ember, the Flame Dominion said. *But, the day is coming when you may have to.*

"Got no problem killing aliens," Anya said.

You know that isn't what I mean. You took a little too long using the kid gloves down there.

"Well excuse me for not immediately wanting to murder somebody."

What if Samaira had been here? Or Tori? How long would you have waited?

Anya bit her lip and looked out at the turquoise waters.

The Flame Dominion remained quiet.

Somehow, that was worse than its questions.

7

Anya kept an eye out for the next hour or so while they waited for Gary's robots to arrive. Arvo remained by Jiro's side, hand on his shoulder at all times. He only diverted his attention briefly to heal Brody with his other hand. Anya had suggested she remove the rest of his armor, but the doctor said it wasn't necessary.

"It's less armor and more a kind of organic metal fused with his skin," the doctor said. "Removing it would be a difficult—and painful —process. I'm not sure how he, or the thing inside him, would react to any kind of damage or disturbance. Right now he's under, and I think it's best to not risk that."

"Wait, so I was melting his skin?" Anya asked and her stomach turned.

"Not entirely. If I had to compare it to something, I'd say it was closer to fingernails, or maybe Pan's scales. It's organic components are minimal, and me touching it wouldn't have had any effect. What you did was necessary, Anya. It saved his life, and ours. Any damage you did to him has already been repaired, and won't even leave a scar."

"That's a relief," Anya let out a sigh. "Y'know, I was coming to see you anyways, before this all happened."

"Oh?" he asked.

"Yeah, heard Hanover pissed you off."

Arvo frowned, an unusual expression for him.

"I mean no disrespect to your country, but the man can be very... difficult."

"None taken. And yeah, he can be a dick. Don't let him get to you though."

"I'll try. And if MacDougal is worried about me leaving, you can tell her to relax. My concern for the safety and well-being of others outweighs my irritation with any politician."

"Thanks, Doc. I'll let you do your thing," she said.

She spent most of the time after that in the air munching on some sandwiches Riley had brought. She hovered directly above Arvo, keeping an eye on the sea and the clouds. Gary's drone zipped around the island, scanning all the while. Brody and Cooper had brought their flying convertible car down to the beach, and had set up folding chairs near Arvo and proceeded to drink and smoke while they waited. Esmeralda continued sleeping in the shade nearby, Riley standing over her and chatting with various government officials on the phone as the minutes ticked by.

Anya glanced to the side and her body ignited when an echoing boom sounded across the sky some time later. Seven black dots emerged from a cloud miles away and were getting closer.

"Relax, it's just my boys," Gary said from his little drone as it flew up to be near Anya.

"Just about gave me a heart attack," she said and extinguished her fire.

"You should head back to Alaska after this, get some rest."

"Hell no. I'm not letting Jiro and that thing inside him out of my sight until they're locked down and Arvo and everybody else is safe."

Gary was quiet for a moment and then the drone turned to face her.

"It ain't your fault."

"If you're talking about Grant and the other host, I know it's—"

"Them, but the folks from the outpost that have gone missing, and the ones that got killed at the White House last month. And those cops that died in Brooklyn when this all started. You put too much on your-self, kid. It's a war. People die. It's not on you. Take it from somebody who's been there."

Anya folded her arms over her chest and stared down at the empty blocks of Outpost #2 far below her. Outpost #1 had close to 200 people living and working at it at a given time. Outpost #2 was the same, and now those people were just… gone. Nothing left of them but whatever was in their rooms.

They were dead.

It was a small island and all of the boats and aircraft used for trans-port off-site were all present and accounted for. So while there weren't any bodies, and no obvious signs of mass violence, Anya was certain that looking for survivors was a fool's errand. The place had felt like a tomb as soon as they had arrived.

"How'd you know I was still upset about the cops from Brooklyn?" Anya asked.

The drone was silent for a moment before Gary sighed and said, "Sam told me. Said you mentioned it a while ago. That you were having trouble sleeping."

Anya clicked her tongue and huffed.

"She's worried about you. I also hear you're taking training a bit too seriously," Gary added.

"Well, what else should I have been doing? Patrolling is next to useless and there's been fuck all else to do but sit on my ass!"

"That's what I mean. You've done all you can. Sometimes the cards you've been dealt just stink. Not every hand's a winner, and the best you can do is ride it out until something better comes along. Point being: not your fault. Not today, not last month, none of it. You've done everything you can, and I'm not gonna stand for anybody saying otherwise, yourself included."

Anya gave Gary's drone a non-committal nod as the squadron of Guardian robots approached, then landed on the beach. Anya flew down to stand next to Arvo, followed by the drone as the Guardians loomed over them. Brody and Cooper craned their heads around to watch as the centaurian robots landed on the beach nearby.

"Hey, those are nice!" Cooper said. He walked up to one, his own robotic suit clanking and whirring with his movements. "I been studying what makes my armor tick and it's pretty wild. These babies look a fair bit sturdier though."

Anya glanced at Cooper as she landed along with Gary's drone and asked, "You understand robotics?"

"I graduated from MIT. Just been taking the last year off to relax after four years of getting my head kicked in and enjoy being home. Didja think I was just some fuckin' stoner?"

"Uh," Anya said.

"Nah, it's fair. I am a fuckin' stoner, just one that likes machines and shit too."

"You could come down to the lab sometime if you like. That suit Brody bought for you off the store, I wouldn't mind looking at it. Some of the components look interesting," Gary said from his drone.

"Gentlemen, I hate to interrupt, but I still require assistance," Arvo said.

"Sorry, Doc. What's the plan?" Gary asked and the Guardians spread out in a defensive perimeter. Anya noticed that some of the Guardians had small cargo containers attached to their sides, and these opened to allow smaller droids out of them. Each droid was fairly basic, just a matte gray shoebox-sized rectangle with scuttling legs. Several sensory antennae emerged from their fronts as they approached Arvo and the fallen Jiro.

"I've managed to slowly peel the parasite off Jiro's spinal column and detach it—mostly—from his central nervous system. I can now remove it without killing him, and while keeping it unconscious. I need something to contain it in that will be secure, and preferably to keep it alive for further study," Arvo said.

"Yeah, I gotcha. The droids here have reinforced internal storage compartments, and we can put the little freak inside a stasis field to boot. If it tries to escape, the droid'll go boom and take it out."

"Perfect," Arvo said. "Please have this stasis field ready."

Some kind of mechanical mandibles emerged from the lower-half of the droids, like dozens of tiny, clicking metallic fingers. Light emerged from them as they each started to scuttle around in a pattern and assemble a long tube of steel and glass, just the right size to hold the parasite. They were spitting out some kind of thread or metallic wire, layering it to create the tube, like a caterpillar spinning a cocoon. The top of the tube remained open, and several of the droids expelled some thick, clear gel into the containment capsule.

"What the hell is that?" Anya asked.

"What I'm very bluntly calling 'stasis gel.' Stronger than cement, and goes from a liquid to a solid when you put a small electrical current through it. Think of how somebody's muscles tense up when you shock them. The gel is also oxygenated, so no risk of suffocation," Gary said. "I wouldn't trust it to hold Jiro after watching that fight, but those little parasite things? No problem. I'm having the droids install an external forcefield unit as well. The battery won't last long, but it'll be enough to get it to my labs and into something more secure."

"That will do. Are you ready?" Arvo asked.

"Looks like they're done," Gary's drone said as it flew over the cylindrical containment unit. The box droids had constructed a pair of gleaming metal spheres on either end, as well as some kind of battery casing along the side that one of them inserted a pair of flat silver discs into. When it did, the whole length of the tube hummed, and the gel inside emitted a faint glow. "Ready when you are, Doc."

"All right, here we go. Anya, please be ready to roast this thing if it twitches. Do not worry about me, I can recover from any fire damage."

"You got it," she replied and raised a finger, and had a tightly condensed, glowing ball of fire no bigger than a marble appear at its tip.

"We'll just… stay back here," Riley called from the treeline, while Esmeralda continued to snore. Cooper backed up to be near them, while Brody just turned his beach chair around and continued smoking as he watched.

Arvo took a deep breath, and then let his fingers sink into the flesh of Jiro's neck. It was like watching somebody stick their hand in firm pudding. Anya shuddered. The doctor withdrew his hand a moment later, and Jiro's skin parted bloodlessly around what he removed.

The parasite was slick and repulsive. It made Anya feel the same way as when she saw a cockroach in her apartment. There was instant, almost instinctive, revulsion at the sight of its gleaming, wet, gray-black body. It had countless hair-thin legs along its paler, ashen underside, and the long tail-like appendage that hung limply below it.

The parasite made a sucking noise as it parted from Jiro's flesh and Anya had to stop herself from gagging. She caught sight of Jiro's skull and spine for a moment. The skull had a small, clean hole near the base, about as big around as her pinky finger. The skull repaired itself as the skin closed up, Arvo's second hand on Jiro's other shoulder.

"I'm going to put it in the capsule there, but I will have to let go eventually. There will be perhaps a second at most to activate the stasis gel, and then the parasite will have regained full control of its functionality," Arvo said.

"I'm ready. Gimme to a count of three and I'll seal it up," Gary said.

"Do we go on the number three, or after the number three?"

"The first one."

"Right. Okay," Arvo took another breath and lowered the parasite into the capsule, and submerged it in the clear gel. Anya kept her finger trained on the foul little creature.

"I'm letting go in one, two," Arvo paused and then said, "three!" and jerked his hand back.

It wasn't even a second before the parasite twitched, thrashed its tail, and then froze in place. The humming around the capsule intensified for a moment, and then lowered. The gel now glowed a soft blue, and the silver orbs at either end crackled to life and encased the cylinder in a field of light.

The box droids swarmed over the capsule, their legs and metallic carapaces fusing together to create an armored shell around it. When it was done, the nearest Guardian picked the capsule up, and placed it inside the armored shipping container at its side.

"One alien freak, successfully in the can," Gary said. Arvo let out a sigh of relief and Anya extinguished the ball of fire at her fingertip.

"That is quite the relief," Arvo said and grinned. Anya patted his shoulder and helped him stand.

"Nice work, Doc. Now what about him?" Anya asked and nodded down at Jiro.

"He'll live, but I think he should be kept under secure observation for at least a couple of days so we can be sure he's back to normal. I've healed the damage done to him by the parasite, but my abilities extend only to the physical, not the psychological."

"I've got a containment area we can keep him in. Even as tough as he is, he won't be getting out," Gary said. "Would appreciate some help, though. Doc, kid, you mind joining me down south for a bit?"

"I was planning on escorting that alien freak anyway, just in case it tried anything," Anya said.

"And I would like to continue to monitor Mr. Yamada," Arvo added.

"You mind company?" Riley asked. Gary's drone turned to look at the agent, and Anya could almost see the old man frowning to himself.

"Trying to get some of my tech for your bosses?" Gary asked.

"Wouldn't dream of it. But Anya's got the fast ride, and I am supposed to accompany her when she's off-base. Plus, I admit to some personal curiosity at seeing your factory myself."

Gary grunted.

"Riley's cool, Gary," Anya said.

"Well, I wouldn't go that far," the agent replied and smirked. "But I'm not gonna try and smuggle anything out or take secret photos. Though I will probably get grilled by MacDougal once I'm back."

"I figured. If Anya says you're okay, then okay. But what about the other young lady there?" Gary's drone turned and nodded at the sleeping and still loudly snoring figure of Esmeralda.

"I would actually like her to come with us," Arvo said and everybody turned to look at him. "The parasite, it was engaged in some sort of mind control. Ms. Gomez's psychic talents may come in handy."

"I got plenty of room in the Shadow Ray for Riley and her," Anya said and Arvo smiled at her.

"Thank you. My vehicle is a bit cramped," he said.

"You wanna come too? Sounds like it's gonna be a party," Gary asked as his drone turned toward Cooper and Brody.

"No thanks. I'm a bit tired after getting the shit kicked out of me.

Gonna go back, have a nap, maybe go harass some whale-watching tourists for a laugh," Brody replied and began throwing the beach chairs and empty kegs into the back of the flying convertible.

"Uh, where's this factory?" Cooper asked.

"Antarctica," Gary said.

Cooper gave the drone a pair of finger guns and a wink and said, "Fuck that," and hopped into the convertible. "Maybe some other time, though."

"Give my best to that little ant-nibbler when ya see him!" Brody said as he got behind the wheel of the convertible, and then honked the horn several times in an annoying farewell as he and Cooper soared away.

Anya shook her head, then carried Esmeralda into the Shadow Ray, laid her out on one of the rows of seats, and strapped her in. Gary's Guardians took off with Arvo and his flying egg, as well as Jiro, who had been loaded into a secure containment unit and encased in stasis gel. That left Anya and Riley alone on the beach for a moment, with only the sound of the waves and the caw of seagulls.

"What's up?" Riley asked as he stood near the hatch of the Shadow Ray. Anya stared up the length of the beach, unable to look away from the ruined bodies of Grant and Kan.

"What about them?" she asked. "We just gonna leave them here, let the tide wash them away?"

"No. I've informed MacDougal, and she's probably talking to the relevant fleet Admiral," Riley said and nodded at the distant, dark dots of the US Navy ships on the horizon. "They'll send somebody to collect them, notify any family, and do a sweep and clean-up of the outpost."

Anya grunted, but couldn't look away. Eventually her eyes drifted to the outpost itself. Less than twenty-four hours ago it had been full of people living their lives. Now it was just empty, except for whatever material remnants had been left behind by the people who had been there.

"Anya. We should catch up to the others," Riley said. His tone was gentle, however.

"Yeah," Anya said and forced herself to look away and take her seat in the Ray's pilot chair. "Yeah."

She set the Ray's autopilot to fly to Gary's factory, and then leaned back as it began to take-off. She couldn't help but glance out the cockpit window one last time as Outpost #2 receded into the distance. Within seconds, it was gone.

8

The Shadow Ray's top speed was Mach 2.5, which meant the trip from the remains of Outpost #2 to Gary's factory in Antarctica took Anya, Riley, and Esmeralda another three hours. Esmeralda woke up a little while after they had taken off and began babbling and flailing against the seat harness before Riley calmed her down and explained everything. She nodded a sleepy assent and returned to snoring.

Neither Anya nor Riley spoke much during the trip, and she was grateful for the older man's silence. She wasn't really in the mood to discuss things, but knew she should call Samaira at the very least and update her. She let Felix know, and the comms window appeared in front of Anya and beeped once before the call was answered.

When Samaira's face appeared in the screen, dark eyes clearly wide with worry, and then Tori and Pan leaned into frame, Anya almost lost it. Her eyes stung and her throat tightened and she pretended to clear her throat. If Brody and Cooper hadn't arrived, if Arvo had made any mistakes, if Esmeralda hadn't pushed herself, it could have all gone very badly, very quickly.

She'd been close to dying several times since the invasion started, so she didn't know why now was so different. Maybe because it had been a month since her last brush with death. Maybe because she'd gotten used to being with Samaira. Maybe because things seemed to be going well for once, and now it had all turned upside down again.

"Anya!" Pan said and raised his claws in a wave.

"Hey you," Tori said.

"Is everything all right?" Samaira asked.

"I'm good, sorry. Just got distracted by the uh, the Ray's panel here," she muttered and cleared her throat again. She filled the three of them in on what had happened. They gasped or made appropriate expressions of horror or sympathy as Anya outlined the basics of the encounter. She didn't have it in her to get into all the details so soon afterward.

"Get some rest," Samaira said. "You've got another couple hours to Gary's. Once things are set up there, just try to take it easy for a bit. We'll hold the fort down here."

"The overseer, if it was there, got away. Whatever took out Outpost Two and is making those parasite things, it's still out there," Anya replied. "And if it had access to Jiro and Grant and their Archives, that could mean it has the location of every host on their contact list, which means you and Pan and I. That means Outpost One may be next. Not sure about that, though."

"We'll figure it out. MacDougal's had the place on red alert since Riley's first call. Harrison's on his way from Toronto right now. And as soon as we hang up, I'm going to contact every host on my list and make sure they know, if they don't already. No more surprises like this."

"Thank you, Sam," Anya said. She knew back in her head she needed to spread the word to Renn, the NAT hosts, and others, but it had been exhausting to think about. She just wanted to let her mind go blank and maybe follow Esmeralda's example. Even with Arvo's little energy boost, a nap sounded pretty good.

Samaira smiled at her.

"Just glad you're okay."

"Are bad guys coming here now?" Pan asked.

"If they do, I'll handle them," Samaira replied.

"You and me can hide in the bunker together and play cards," Tori added and gave Pan a soft pat on the head.

"I'm getting pretty good at Old Maid," he said, then stuck his long snout directly towards the screen and asked, "Can we play when you get back, Anya?"

"Sure thing, little guy. By the way, Brody says hello."

"Yay! I'll text him and say hello too."

"Get some rest," Samaira said. "I'm getting a notification from MacDougal. All hands on deck kinda thing. We'll talk more later? If you're up for it?"

"Always," Anya said and winked. Tori made a show of fanning herself in the background and Anya rolled her eyes. Samaira laughed and waved before she closed the screen.

"MacDougal'll make sure we don't get caught with our pants down twice. They'll be fine," Riley said from behind her.

"Maybe," Anya sighed, then leaned back in her seat. "Wake me if anything horrible happens."

"Will do," the agent replied. Anya let her mind wander away from the horrors of the morning's battle, and into the hazy darkness of sleep.

———

SHE AWOKE to a weight on her shoulder. Riley had his hand there, applying gentle pressure so as not to startle her.

"Hey," Anya said a bit too sharply as she sat up. "Sorry. I'm awake. Are we—?"

"We're closing in. Your console thingy beeped a few seconds ago," Riley said and gestured at the Shadow Ray's main screen. It showed the central dot of the Ray closing in on the dot that Anya had marked as their destination, smack in the middle of nowhere, Antarctica.

Gary's factory was located at almost the exact center of the icy continent, at the very bottom of the world. There was no indication of any installation for miles. Nothing but ice and snow as far as the eye could see. If one were to look very closely at certain places in the ice, they might see well-concealed vents, or maybe an enigmatic metallic circle whose purpose was unclear. But these were so well-hidden that somebody would've had to know to go looking for them.

When the Ray was within a dozen miles of Gary's factory, Anya brought its speed down and dropped her altitude with the help of the craft's built-in autopilot. No sooner had she done so than her ear beeped.

"Gary's calling," Felix informed her.

"Hey, old man," Anya said as she brought her communication window up, and Gary's face appeared before her.

"Heya, kid. Elevator shaft 26 should be opening up ahead of you right about now," Gary said. As soon as he did, Anya craned her neck to peer out the windshield of the Shadow Ray. A huge square hole opened in the ice beneath her, and flashing red lights popped up out of the snow at its edges. A solid metal platform emerged from the depths of a deep, cavernous elevator shaft that was almost the size of a city block, and stopped when it reached the surface.

"I got it," Anya said. She tapped a couple buttons on the console before her, and directed the autopilot to land. When it had, she swiveled around in her chair and tapped Esmeralda on the elbow.

"No, Mama. Necessito dos minutos mas," she mumbled and snored again. Riley chuckled and Anya rolled her eyes. Normally she would have let the woman sleep, but Arvo said he needed her psychic abilities. Anya tried again, and this time gave her a gentle shake for good measure.

"Huh! What!" Esmeralda said and bolted upright, eyes blinking unevenly, and glowing pink shields of light popping up around her.

"Easy! Easy there," Anya said. "You're okay. We're just at Gary's factory."

"Gary? Who's Gary?" Esmeralda mumbled and wiped her eyes. Her miniature psychic shields blinked out of sight as she yawned.

"The old guy with the robots."

"Me," Gary said from the screen floating behind Anya.

"Ooooh yeah. Gary. He has a factory?" Esmeralda asked, still sounding like she were half-asleep.

"This should have been in the briefing you got a few weeks ago. He's the guy who helped build Outpost Two," Riley said, arching an eyebrow at Esmeralda. She rubbed her temples and yawned again. "Gave the DERD a bunch of armor for the agents, a couple of non-combat armored hover-carriers. Which we'll definitely need to retrieve ASAP from Outpost Two, by the way."

"Sorry. Yeah. I'm just out of it. Head gets a bit scrambled after I use a lot of energy like that. You got any headache meds in your factory, Gary?"

"Yeah, and if that doesn't work, the doc can take another look at you," he said, then focused on Anya. "We're both in the main hub, by the way. A tram should be waiting for you by the time the elevator hits the bottom."

"See you then, Gary," Anya said and closed the window.

The elevator platform descended below the ice, and heavy rein-forced armored doors closed above her with echoing bangs. Every hundred feet or so, another set of security doors would close shut above the Shadow Ray. The elevator shaft probably had at least a couple dozen such doors in each of its entry points, be they horizontal or vertical.

The number "26" had been painted within each partitioned segment of the elevator shaft, and soft yellow lights flashed along the sides as Anya, Riley, and Esmeralda descended further and further beneath the ice.

When Gary had worked with Pan and the DERD to assemble Outpost #1 and Outpost #2 within a couple of weeks, Anya had been impressed. But that had been nothing compared to the factory that he had put together in just over a month.

It took ten minutes for the elevator to reach the bottom. It wasn't slow either; the platform hummed with speed, and only began to ease its descent near the bottom. Another set of security doors banged shut high above Anya, leaving her and the others in a wide open, mostly barren concrete room.

Several large metal doors lined three of the four walls. The fourth wall was thick glass, and a green light switched on as a sleek, elegant tram of brushed gray metal slid to a stop on the other side of it.

"Is this place really big enough that it needs its own tram system?" Riley asked as he left the Shadow Ray.

"Oh yeah," Anya said. It was her third visit to the factory. She knew that her Shadow Ray would be moved to one of the hangars, and ready for her whenever she left. Riley and Esmeralda both craned their heads around as they entered the simple but comfortable interior of the tram.

It was clinical white inside, with padded benches beside the windows. It resembled an upscale subway car, but smaller. The tram hummed to life as the door slid closed, and accelerated with a subtle surge that belied the speed at which it left the arrival platform. They sped along the dark tram tunnel for a few moments before emerging onto one of the primary factory floors.

Gary's factory made Anya think of what it might look like if Willy Wonka had been really into mechanical engineering and robotics rather than candy.

"Mother Mary and Joseph," Riley said as he stared out the window and crossed himself.

"Holy shit, dude," Esmeralda breathed.

The factory floor was something like an enormous, multi-tiered stadium. It had layers of assembly machines stacked on top of each other, the white lights above reflecting off countless metallic and coated concrete surfaces. Sparks flew in miniature firework displays from thousands of machines. Catwalks and conveyor belts formed neat, angular pathways between the machines and various levels.

Robotic drones flew through the air, each one with its own unique function. Many of them carried equipment loads, raw materials, or scrap metal. Others appeared to monitor different areas of the factory, while others repaired anything that looked broken or in need of attention.

Long transparent tunnels lined the walls, and trains carrying tanks of liquid or compressed gas zipped along them. They would stop at designated locations, unload their contents and accept new cargo, and then zoom off to their next destination.

The air itself vibrated with the noise and motion of it all. Anya heard the mechanical chorus of assembly even through the insulated walls of the tram. The tram itself had to be going at least sixty miles per hour, and it still took them almost two minutes to cross the factory floor. Perhaps most impressive was the implication of the huge number "4" painted on the walls of the factory at regular intervals.

There were seven factory floors in total. Those did not include the primary and secondary hangars, armories, storage facilities, labs, power plants, testing ranges, material refinement areas, waste-disposal zones, loading docks, or surplus depots. Gary had also added some people-friendly areas, such as basic dormitories, dining areas, and recreation rooms.

Anya didn't think she'd ever get used to seeing it. Just thinking about the scale of it set her mind spinning.

"How big is this place?" Riley asked as they entered another tunnel and the view of factory four was sliced off by the concrete walls.

"I'm not exactly sure. But there's six more factories like that one," Anya said. She wondered if she should tell Riley anything, but Gary wasn't stupid. If he'd invited the agent in, it's because he knew it didn't matter what he discovered.

"Six more?" Esmeralda gasped. "What the hell is he building?"

"An army?" Riley asked and Anya shook her head.

"He *is* building stuff like the Guardians, but they're not the majority of his work. He can tell you about the rest, if he wants," Anya said. Gary had mentioned some of the larger scale plans he had for his factory, and it had made her head spin. Riley just grunted and didn't push any further.

The tram eventually came to a stop several minutes later. It slowed and then hissed as it settled down onto its magnetic rail, and the doors opened onto a chamber a few stories high and almost as long as a football field.

The walls were smooth, pale stone decorated with recessed arches that had intricate geometric designs carved into them. Grecian columns lined each of the entrances and exits of the chamber, stretching high above Anya and the others as they passed between them. Planters lined the center of the room, each filled with small flowering bushes, and flanked a huge holographic screen that displayed a basic map of the entire factory: the seven enormous circles of the numbered factories surrounding the central area Anya and the others found themselves in. Other exits led away to different trams and rails, all of it neatly signposted.

The high ceiling was a delicate curve of glass and criss-crossing steel that gave the impression of sunlight filtering through, but Anya knew it was only artificial. They were almost a mile or more below the surface, and surrounded on all sides by multiple layers of reinforced armor plating, stone, and ice.

Gary had told her on her first visit that the arched chamber was a modified version of Union Station in Chicago. Anya had jokingly referred to it as GUS, or Gary's Union Station, and the nickname had stuck. GUS was at the center of the factory, and a short walk away from its beating heart: the hub.

Anya, Riley, and Esmeralda passed through an archway at the far end of the station, up a short flight of stairs, and into the hub itself.

Anya thought it resembled a small planetarium: a circular, domed room with a galaxy of display screens flitting across the ceiling, each one showing some aspect of the factory at work. Gary himself sat in the center of it all, resting in a comically out-of-place armchair. It was the sort of overstuffed, tacky piece of furniture you'd find in any middle-class family's living room. A small wooden table sat beside the chair, an open can of beer resting at hand and sweating condensation. Floating display screens hovered around Gary, not dissimilar to the Archive's pop-up holographic windows, and Gary tapped on them with a speed that bordered on inhuman.

"Heya, be with you folks in a minute," Gary said and tapped at several more screens.

"Everything okay?" Anya asked.

"Minor malfunction in Factory 3. Decrease in productivity on the pulse engine line."

"Pulse engine?" Riley asked. Gary swiveled the reclining armchair around and regarded Riley from behind his glasses.

"Yeah. Pulse engines. For my asteroid mining drones. Standard rockets are inefficient and wasteful. They consume too much fuel and take too much effort to reuse. My pulse engines use a magnetic pulse to accelerate and push themselves forward."

"Asteroid mining drones?" Esmeralda asked and Gary sighed.

"I'll explain if you gotta finish stuff," Anya said, and Gary waved a hand at her and then turned back to his screens. "Gary needs a lot of raw materials for everything he's working on. But most of the stuff on Earth is already spoken for. He didn't want to invade some country for their iron or gold or whatever, and he didn't want to tear up the Earth more than the rest of humanity already has. Thankfully there's a shit-load of raw materials just floating around up there."

Anya pointed towards the ceiling.

"Gary told me last time I was here. The asteroid belt is pretty far away, and so is everything floating around Saturn, but he's picked up something like 40,000 comets, asteroids and meteorites close to Earth. He sends his drones up into space, waits a week or two, and they come back with everything he needs."

"Smart," Esmeralda said.

"Mm," Riley said, a small smirk on his face. Gary noticed it and cocked an eyebrow at the agent.

"Something funny?" Gary asked.

"Yeah. The thought of all the big-wigs on Capitol Hill shitting themselves out of a combination of fear and greed with what I've seen and heard since we landed," Riley replied. Gary chuckled.

"I mean, we figured you'd built yourself up a nice little nest down here, but nobody had any idea..." Riley trailed away as he looked at all the holographic factory displays. While many of them only had indecipherable charts and lists of numbers and equations, many more acted as security monitors and showed aspects of the factory floors themselves.

A loader-bot carried an enormous container full of raw ore toward a giant smelter. A long assembly line of partially constructed flying machines whirred along with mechanical precision and efficiency. A drill bigger than a cargo plane chewed through solid rock to expand the boundaries of the factory even further. And across dozens of displays, robots of all shapes, sizes, and functions were being built: robots with wings, robots with scanners, robots with drills, and not a few robots with guns, missiles, and other weapons.

"Gonna take over the world?" Riley asked, his smirk still in place, but his tone becoming more serious.

"Hell no. Pain in the ass. No desire to run the place, but I do aim to clean it up a little. Keep it from getting any worse, maybe. Those," Gary said and pointed at a screen that showed tubular robots made of segmented, reinforced plastic. "Are my second version of ocean sweepers. I assume nobody will have any complaints if I get rid of all that plastic shit in the water?"

"Seriously?" Esmeralda asked. "You're gonna clean up the oceans?"

"Already am. Putting it all to good use, too. Breaking it down and recycling it into something better."

"Like what?"

Gary grinned and held up his beer.

Esmeralda and Riley exchanged a look.

"You're drinking plastic beer?" Riley asked and made a face.

"I'm drinking beer made from carbon I've extracted from plastics, along with a few other things. Carbon is just the base building block. For beer, for steak, salad, ice cream, you name it," Gary said. "Got a little matter materializer thingy prototype. It'll make just about anything if you shove the raw materials into it."

"Eeeeew," Esmeralda said.

"Don't knock it. I had a few dozen hamburgers from the thing last time I was here. Tasted great," Anya said.

"Still. Ew," Esmeralda repeated and made a face.

"I'll stick to the normal stuff for now," Riley said.

Gary closed all of the screens with a clap of his hands, leaving the domed hub a blank, featureless chamber. He stood up from the chair and approached the group as he rubbed his hands together.

"So, I take it you'll be reporting back to the bureaucrats about what you've seen?" he asked.

"You know I have to," Riley said. Gary grunted.

"Yeah. Tell them I'm happy to share some of the non-violent stuff if they ask nice."

"I'll let them know. MacDougal's been very happy with the armor and the armored carriers. Hanover would still like some guns, but MacDougal's keeping him at bay."

Gary grunted, then turned to Anya and smiled.

"Have a good trip, kid?"

"As best as I could. How's Doc doing? And Jiro?" she asked.

"Doc's still making sure Jiro's not gonna go apeshit in here. The big guy's still asleep, as far as I know. The little freak he had inside of him is under heavy guard in lab 8. Still in stasis."

"Is bringing that thing down here a good idea? What if it can tell the aliens where it is?" Esmeralda asked as Gary led them out of the hub and back into the station. He approached the platform for another tram and pressed a button, and an orange light began to flash.

"If that thing is capable of communicating right now—and I doubt it while it's in stasis—it won't make much difference. I've got this place armored up a hundred times over, with enough defenses and traps to melt anything I don't like within a hundred miles. Hell, part of me's hoping that thing *is* calling for help. If the aliens came to me, we could have this whole invasion thing sorted in a few days."

The flashing yellow light continued to blink overhead as another tram approached and glided up to the platform. It switched to green when the tram stopped and opened its doors. Everybody climbed aboard and the tram whooshed away as soon as the doors shut.

Despite the speed of the tram, there was hardly any jolt or feeling of movement. Esmeralda leaned against one of the side windows as they sped through another factory while Anya sat in one of the plush seats.

"No offense," Riley said as he glanced out the window, then back back at Gary, "but I saw your Guardians getting pretty thoroughly trashed on the beach not a few hours ago. You really think you could take on however many hundreds of aliens are left?"

"Since the Guardians were fighting people, they were also using non-lethal methods, and at half-efficiency. I didn't want to kill Jiro and the others unless I absolutely had to," Gary said, then looked at Anya. His brow creased with worry as he added, "It was a near thing."

"I'm fine, Gare," Anya said. He only sighed and nodded.

"Anyway, if it was aliens, screw 'em. Full lethality, full power. I've also got about a hundred Guardians on call around the factory. And they're only one type of combat bot. That also doesn't account for stationary defenses like automated turrets, mines, and some other fun tricks."

"Oh?" Riley asked.

"Yeah, and no, those I'm not sharing. A guy's gotta have a couple aces up his sleeve when shit hits the fan."

"So, we're going to see Dr. Immonen?" Esmeralda asked, and Gary nodded.

"Jiro should be secured by now," he said and tapped the side of his glasses. His eyes followed something in the lenses only he could see, and he grunted. "Doc's too nice for his own damn good."

"What?" Anya asked.

"I told him to wait until we got there to start checking on Jiro, but he's already giving him the once-over."

"Is he—?"

"He's fine. That exam room had plenty of defenses too, so even if Jiro went nuts, he'd be okay. Probably. Still stupid to not wait another few minutes."

"That's Doc for you," Anya said. She was grateful for Arvo—he'd saved her life at least twice—but she did worry that his eagerness to help was going to get him turned into another casualty. She just hoped today wouldn't be the day.

9

By the time the tram stopped at the research wing of the factory and they all entered the exam room, Jiro was sitting up on the side of an examination table watching Arvo examine him.

Jiro was back in his armor from head-to-toe, nothing melted or missing. He turned to face Anya and the others as they entered, his faceplate reflecting the room around him and hiding his face.

"And there they are now," Arvo said as he looked away from Jiro. The other man only inclined his head as he saw them. As Anya approached, she realized just how big Jiro was. At just about seven feet, she was tall. But Jiro loomed over her by a head and more, and he was at least twice as broad. Each of his arms was almost bigger around than Esmeralda's entire torso.

"How you feeling?" Anya asked, and tried not to focus on the mental image of his burned flesh. Jiro responded from inside his helmet, in muffled Japanese. A moment later, some sort of translator built into his armor spat out a flat, monotone reply.

"I am fine now. Thank you for your assistance. My apologies for endangering you all and not being prepared. It will not happen again," he said.

"I haven't had time to question him too much about what happened, but I can confirm that he's in excellent physical condition," Arvo said.

"Good. Sorry for the uh... burning and stuff," Anya said, and rubbed at the back of her neck.

"You did what was necessary. Thank you," Jiro said.

"Do you remember anything from what happened?" Gary asked, and Jiro nodded.

"Yes," he said, then turned to look at Esmeralda. He knelt on one knee, almost bringing his head to her eye level. "Little Esmi. I cannot apologize to you enough. I almost..."

"You had me pretty scared, too. But we're okay, and it wasn't your fault," she replied, and put her tiny hand over his enormous one. "I'm just glad you're okay now."

"I don't mean to interrupt the reunion, truly, but maybe you could fill us in on what happened so I can report the details to our mutual boss?" Riley asked, and cleared his throat.

"Of course. What has Little—Ms. Gomez told you?" Jiro asked.

"Everything up to when you and Grant came after me and I ran," she said.

Jiro sighed.

"I do not recall much. I was asleep. I felt a horrible pain, and then my mind was a mess. Images, feelings, and then only sleep again, but uneasy sleep. I will not sleep outside of my armor again."

"Anything else? Anything about aliens?" Riley asked.

"Was it an overseer? Like that black snake monster from DC?" Anya added. Pictures and a detailed sketch of the snake overseer had been distributed among all hosts, along with details of its ability to block Archive access. Jiro only shook his head.

"No, I saw nothing. No aliens. But I did feel something," he said. "It was like there was a string in the back of my head, and something was connected to it. Far away. And the string would... vibrate. I think it was the creature inside me talking to whatever was on the other end of that string."

"Psychic connection," Esmeralda said. "That's what it sounds like anyway."

"So it was mind-control?" Gary asked and Esmeralda shook her head.

"Probably not how you're thinking. Making somebody do something you want, turning them against their own desires, it's basically impossible. Their brain would short-out and they'd have a stroke or die. However, putting somebody's conscious mind to sleep and then manually controlling the electrical impulses that cause physical movement, that's possible. The effort for me to do it isn't worth it: I'd exhaust myself keeping somebody asleep and controlling their body, and it'd be stupid anyway. Just like playing puppeteer. But if you specifically made something to do that for you, and if that thing could do it more efficiently…"

"So that parasite attached to Jiro's skull and spine was basically just driving him like a car?" Anya asked and Esmeralda nodded.

"That's what it sounds like."

"Based on how I felt the parasites connected to the length of the central nervous system, that does seem to fit the bill," Arvo added.

"I remember flashes of sensation. My limbs jerking, or the sensation of falling. It was… unpleasant," Jiro said.

"Well, it's a bit of a relief to know the aliens can't just psychically reach out and control somebody at a whim. Gotta stick one of those parasites in 'em first," Riley said. "Though I gotta wonder why they left Gomez alone if they knew where she was. The bastards got Jiro, Grant, and Kan, probably everyone else on base too."

"My defensive field, probably," Esmeralda said. "If whatever is controlling those parasites tried to force their way to me, it could have disrupted the signal long enough to allow Jiro and the others to break free, or maybe just kill them. Probably why they came back when Anya arrived, too. Ever since the Engineers scrambled our signals, we've been hidden from the gnosiphages. Once the parasite controller —or whatever it is—found the outpost, it must have hid somewhere, using me as bait and hoping more would show up. Which you did. When my defensive field went down, it rolled in."

"So you could disrupt that 'string' Jiro mentioned?" Gary asked.

"I might? Hard to say."

"Mr. Yamada, could you feel anything at the end of this string?" Arvo asked.

"I do not have the proper words for the sensation. Something big was pulling on it, but not in a physical sense," Jiro replied, and Arvo nodded.

"It's like what I felt when I touched the snake overseer outside the White House. A presence communicating across a distance down some kind of pathway," Arvo said. "What I felt was sort of like a string, but one that went all over the planet and back up into space. That's where I lost sense of it."

"I recall something similar as well," Jiro nodded. "There was myself, but others too. Smaller strings. I think two of them were Grant and the other one, and I also felt it when their strings broke."

Anya frowned.

"Do you know how many other strings you felt?" Riley asked and Jiro sighed and shrugged his enormous shoulders.

"Maybe ten, maybe twenty. Plus a large central one. That one did not go to space, though. It was nearby."

"If the alien controlling the parasites was an overseer, that would match up," Anya said. "Our Archives went haywire right as you and the other controlled hosts got to the beach."

"But if there were ten or twenty other strings of psychic connection, how come we only saw three hosts?" Esmeralda asked.

"The others could've been farther away?" Anya shrugged. "Can you psychically communicate with someone if they're really far away?"

"Yeah, to a point. The farther you go, the more tension the string comes under. Stretch it too far, and it snaps."

"What then?" Gary asked. "If a host with one of these controller parasites in them lost its connection with the overseer communicating with it, would the host turn back to normal?"

Esmeralda shook her head.

"I have no idea! I'm not an expert on these things! Heck, I didn't even know they existed until this morning," she said.

"Easy, Ms. Gomez. We know this is all new to you. But since you're the only psychic we have at the moment, could you hazard a guess?"

Esmeralda frowned and knit her eyebrows together.

"If it works like my skills, no, a loss of communication wouldn't mean the host is back to normal. They'd still have that psychic parasite in them. It just wouldn't be getting any new messages from the over-seer. So it could, potentially, tell a bunch of hosts to, I dunno, fly some-where then meet it somewhere else the next day. They'd lose communication for the day, but if they knew where to go later, they'd get it right back."

"Mm," Gary grunted.

"That's just me totally guessing though," Esmeralda added and held up her hands. "I really can't stress enough how little I know about whatever the heck those things are."

"Fair enough. Thank you, Ms. Gomez," Riley said.

"I was about to leave Mr. Yamada to recover and go and check on our other 'guest,'" Arvo said.

"It's in one of the labs. We can walk there," Gary said.

"I would like to rest, if you do not need me any further," Jiro said as he laid back on the exam table. Esmeralda approached him as the others moved to leave. Anya could tell she wanted a moment alone with him, and she stepped outside with Gary and the others to give them some privacy.

"We sure he's, y'know, normal?" Riley whispered when they were outside and the door had slid closed behind them.

"His vitals and his brain activity are as normal as anybody's. There's also no sign of foreign material—biological or artificial—anywhere in him," Arvo said.

"That don't account for psychic stuff though, does it?"

Arvo sighed and shook his head. "No, it doesn't."

"Esmi should be able to tell though, right?" Anya asked.

"Figured that's what she was staying behind to do. Let's see," Gary said and tapped the side of his glasses. His eyes narrowed at a screen only he could see, then he grunted.

"Yeah, they're fine. Talking. Normal stuff."

"You're sure?" Riley asked.

"I'm not gonna invade on their privacy too much, but yeah. Like an uncle talking to his favorite niece. How long those two known each other?"

"He'd stop by pretty regularly, stay a few nights at a time, help with patrols and that sorta thing. Been going on for two or three weeks," Riley said.

"Long enough to form an attachment. I'm giving them their privacy, but if security picks up anything weird, it'll let me know."

"Well, I'd like Ms. Gomez's help with something, so I'm afraid their reunion may have to wait, loathe as I am to interrupt them," Arvo said and knocked on the door. Esmeralda emerged a moment later, her eyes red, as if she'd been crying or just about to.

"Y-yes?" she asked and sniffled.

"Doc says he needs your help with the little psychic freak we caught," Anya said.

"Right! Just, uh," Esmeralda turned around to face Jiro, who nodded at her.

"Maybe we could move him to the dorms if he's feeling all right?" Gary asked Arvo.

"That seems like it would be fine," he replied.

"What do you need me to do with the alien? Or whatever it is?" Esmeralda asked as they entered another examination room. This one looked less like a doctor's office, and more like something from a sci-fi movie. Strange mechanical arms emerged from the ceiling, glowing screens emerged from the walls, and long counters full of automated testing equipment—centrifuges, scales, ovens, pumps, and specimen tanks—lined the outer walls.

The center of the room was taken up by a cage of glass and glowing blue light. It was flanked by two hulking robots, more brutish and boxy then the centaurian Guardians, roughly the size and shape of gorillas, but made of armored plates and strong but flexible metallic cords. While the robots didn't display any obvious weaponry, it was clear that they were guarding the cage and more than capable of violence if the situation called for it. A cylinder of transparent gel sat in the center of the cage, inside of which the black-and-gray parasite was frozen in stasis.

Anya shuddered as she looked at it. Something about it, maybe the thought of all those little, hair-thin legs clamping around her, gave her the creeps. It was a decidedly unclean looking creature.

"That thing's so nasty," Esmeralda said, and Anya wondered if she was picking up on her thoughts. "It's not like the other aliens, though."

"What do you mean?" Riley asked.

"The other aliens I've seen were all trying to disguise themselves as something else. I fought a weird TV and a bush. I think Anya said she fought a fridge and a puppet?"

"Yeah. And a toilet, a stop light, a copy machine, and a fire hydrant. Plus the snake, but that was an overseer, and everything about them seems pretty different," Anya said.

"Right. But this thing, it just looks like a gross little alien monster. Same with the other two that, uh, came out of Grant and Kan."

"Felix?" Anya asked.

"Yes?" The AI responded as they blinked into view next to her.

"Are you getting an alien signal from this thing?"

"Hmm. Nope! Zero!"

"You're sure?"

"100%! We're standing right in front of it. Even if the gnosiphages figured out how to block their signals more effectively, I'd still be able to pick something up. But that thing isn't giving off any kind of signal."

"Can you bring up the map data from when we were fighting?"

"Sure can!" Felix said and made an orange-tinted window appear that showed a simple map of the beach outside Outpost #2 from earlier that morning. It clearly displayed Anya's location dot, along with Esmeralda's, Jiro's, Grant's, Arvo's, and Kan's. There was also the edge of a large opaque red circle coming from somewhere beyond the beach, in the ocean.

"Fast-forward to when Grant died and his parasite emerged," Anya said, and the dots on the map moved around at rapid speed until Grant's dot vanished. "Zoom out."

The map zoomed out to display the whole of the island. The reddish circle covered an area of ocean several times larger than the island itself. However, it was the only one in the area.

"That's an alien, for sure," Anya said and pointed at the red circle. "Somewhere in there. An overseer."

"We kinda figured that already," Riley said.

"Right. It sent the parasites, but they're not showing up," Anya pointed at the map, at the exact spot Grant's dot had vanished from. "If that thing is an alien, there should be another red dot or circle right here."

Gary frowned and stroked at his beard.

"Kid: ask your AI to show the fight from the night in Chicago. I'd ask mine to do it, but you were closer to the alien at the time, probably got a more precise read on it," he said.

"Felix?" Anya asked and her AI nodded and brought up a second screen. This one showed a map of Chicago from several weeks ago, the night Anya had met Samaira and Gary. They had fought a refrigerator inside a department store and it…

"Oh!" Anya said and locked eyes with Gary, who nodded.

"What is it?" Arvo asked.

"Felix! Fast-forward to when those little roach things came out!"

"You got it!" Felix said.

"There!" Anya pointed at the map. It showed her dot and Samaira's, as well as the alien's. "This is when we got separated during the fight, and the fridge alien was shooting out these eggs that hatched and turned into weird mini-monsters."

"They're… not on the map," Riley said.

"Right! The only things that emit signals are the gnosiphages. So if a gnosiphage alters itself to spawn some kind of monsters, those aren't gnosiphages. They're just… trash mobs."

"Trash mobs?" Gary, Riley, and Arvo asked at the exact same time. Esmeralda nodded with understanding.

"Unimportant enemies, for lack of a better term," Esmeralda said.

"So how does that help us?" Riley asked.

"It doesn't. At least, not now," Gary said and frowned. "The bastards really are getting smarter, aren't they?"

"Maybe it's my lack of battle experience, but I'm not sure I understand?" Arvo asked.

"Whenever we kill an alien, they release a data stream to the others.

Our AIs intercept the stream, decode it, and give it to us. The data shows the exact location of all the gnosiphages on the planet at the time of that alien's death. We also get experience, which helps us level up, and get stronger," Anya explained.

"But if this overseer is sending out parasites like this guy, and fighting through controlling other hosts, then killing them doesn't give us any bonuses. No data stream. No level-ups. They're taking away our allies while protecting themselves, their location, and stopping us from getting stronger."

"Damn," Riley sighed. "That's unnervingly smart."

"All the more reason to perform some tests on our little friend," Arvo said and approached the cage that held the creature.

"Are we sure it's safe?" Anya asked as a section of the glowing cage dimmed and slid aside. The opening was no more than a few inches wide: just enough for Arvo to get his hand through if he kept it flat.

"As much as we can be," Gary replied. "That thing is still surrounded by stasis gel. I'm going to soften it just enough for Doc to get his fingers in and touch the critter. If it twitches, the gel will re-solidify, and it'll get a powerful shock."

"I should add I've made some modifications to my arm, just in case," Arvo said. When Anya arched an eyebrow at him, he continued, "I've restructured the bone and muscle and connective tissues a bit. Think of it like a lizard's tail: if the creature becomes hostile or tries to take me over via my arm, I'll simply detach it, and grow another one later."

"Eeeew," Anya and Esmeralda said together, and made a face. Riley had a similar expression. The doctor laughed and Gary shook his head.

"Better safe than sorry, I guess," he said. "Ready, Doc?"

Arvo nodded and slid his hand through the opening, where his fingers immediately bumped against the surface of the gel. There was a pulse of light from the glass cage, the gel rippled, and Arvo was able to push his fingers through it. He grunted as he continued to push his fingers through the hard gel, and finally brushed one of them against the parasite's slick body.

"There we are," Arvo sighed. "Good so far. Confirms the obvious: it has to be inside of you to control you."

"Figured as much, but nice to know for sure," Gary replied.

"Hmm," Arvo said and pursed his lips.

"What is it?" Anya asked.

"I feel… something. Maybe it's the 'string,' Ms. Gomez mentioned. How to describe it? The creature, it's awake and aware but… passive. Its brain is very rudimentary. I don't think it can do much without guidance from the thing giving it orders."

"Can you locate it? Follow the string back to the source?" Riley asked and Arvo shook his head.

"The snake overseer was very powerful. It was directly connected, capable of sending and receiving. This thing, it's much simpler, much weaker, and the connection is faint. Of course, I'm also not a psychic," Arvo said and looked at Esmeralda. "But maybe with Ms. Gomez's help, we could figure something out."

Arvo extended his other hand toward Esmeralda. Anya looked at Arvo, trying to see if the parasite had somehow subtly managed to take control of him. It didn't look like it. Plus, Jiro, Grant, and Kan had all been silent. Conversational skills hadn't been among their abilities when they'd been under the sway of the parasites.

"It's okay," Esmeralda said as she caught Anya's suspicious look at the cage. "Dr. Immonen's still himself. And the parasite, it's in some kinda fugue state or something. Awake, but out of it."

"What's holding Doc's hand gonna do?" Riley asked.

"I'll essentially be acting as a go-between. Right now, as I understand it, Ms. Gomez can sense the basic psychic string of the parasite, but no details. Whereas I have more complete knowledge, but lack the psychic abilities to complete my understanding.

"If Ms. Gomez takes my hand, I'm hoping that will increase her psychic connection to the parasite. Further, whatever physical components within the parasite allow it to have a psychic connection with the overseer can be adjusted by me to better attempt to find it, with Ms. Gomez's help, of course."

"Kinda like tuning a radio dial and finding where the signal is," Esmi said, and Arvo nodded. She stepped forward and took his hand, bracing as though she might get a jolt for doing so. When nothing happened, her eyes widened.

"Wow, that's a lot clearer," she said.

"It's working?" Anya asked, and Esmeralda nodded.

"I can practically see the string now. It stretches to... a few dozen miles, maybe a little farther. But then it just stops. It's kind of swinging around, searching for a signal. Nothing nearby, though."

"You're telling me this bastard has a psychic range of at least thirty-six miles or more?" Gary asked, and Esmeralda nodded.

"Pretty much. That's the range it can start to pick up signals from the overseer. Then—and this is a guess—it'd be like a game of hot and cold. Not precise, but enough to help it hone in to get close enough for a more direct signal," she said.

"It would have to be within a mile or two, I'm guessing," Anya said. "The map Felix showed us put the overseer at something like that distance. So if it wants to issue new, direct commands, it needs to be close."

"But we know the overseer got the hell outta Dodge for now, and it's probably not gonna come back for this thing," Riley said.

"I wouldn't bet on it," Gary said, but he was grinning.

"What's got you so happy?" Anya asked.

"We've been looking for these aliens for a month now, chasing our tails or sitting on our asses. And the dumb bastards drop a genuine, bonafide alien detector right in our damn laps," Gary said and jerked a thumb at the parasite.

"You want to use that thing to find the overseer?" Anya asked, and Gary nodded. Esmeralda tilted her head to one side, then her eyes lit up and she nodded along with Gary.

"If you could just take its brain out while still keeping it functional, you could make it portable!" she said.

"Everything about these fuckers is so gross, damn," Anya said and both she and Riley made another shared expression of disgust. "Hauling around an alien parasite brain?"

"I wasn't just gonna throw it in a plastic baggy or anything, but yeah, pretty much. I'll need Doc's help, and Esmi's, to work on a containment unit and user interface to translate the psychic signals, but yeah, I could do something like that," Gary said.

"It's... better than the nothing we've had," Anya admitted. Even if the parasite had a range of a hundred miles, that was still tiny compared to the entire planet. And it was only for one alien. Still, if they could track that one down and kill it, they could find out what the rest were up to.

It was something.

Maybe now, they could be the ones on the hunt.

10

Arvo and Esmeralda had a lot of work ahead of them, and Anya left them to it. Gary left to go prep another lab with any equipment that might help with the construction of their new psychic alien locater device, leaving Riley, Anya, and Felix to their own devices.

Anya's stomach dictated they head for the dining area in the living quarters of the factory, and they boarded the nearest tram. Anya had a whole table of food in front of her not long after, and began scarfing it all down with abandon while Riley sat with a cup of coffee and a donut. He regarded both with skepticism, as if both had some nefarious purpose in mind.

"It tastes fine," Anya said as she ate her third tray of recycled sushi. "I had my doubts at first, but honestly, I'd kill to have one of these in my room at Outpost One."

"It smells like coffee. But I dunno, Nowicki," Riley said and looked across the table at Anya. "I keep hearing Hendricks telling me it's ocean junk, and just... blegh." He shuddered and Anya smirked.

"I thought the feds were supposed to be tough?"

"Tough, not stupid. Just cause a Marine like Gary would eat a box of nails and call it lunch doesn't mean I want to."

"You know how much I eat. You think I'd be digging into this stuff if it tasted like shit?"

"It's not just the taste. What're the side-effects of eating what used to be plastic and other stuff?"

"Doc checked it all out. It's legit. Besides, Gary's been living off the stuff for weeks and getting regular scans from his own lab equipment and Arvo. No side-effects."

Riley sighed. "But… oh, what the hell. Down the hatch."

He took a sip of coffee, smacked his lips, then raised his eyebrows at the cup.

"That's… good."

"See?" Anya asked.

"Well excuse me for not wanting to take unnecessary risks with my health, Miss Regenerative Powers," Riley replied, then bit into his donut and all but groaned with satisfaction. "Damn, that's good. God save me, Hendricks would rule Boston if he sold this stuff up there."

Anya laughed.

"Give him enough time and he'll probably start setting up his replicators for free."

"If he sets one up in my house, he has my blessing," Riley said as he took another sip of coffee.

Anya smiled at him, then looked down at her food. She had a couple of steaks in front of her, almost cartoonishly oversized t-bones, and the smell of them was amazing: savory and smokey.

Unbidden, the memory of Jiro's burning flesh sprang to mind, the phantom smell of him cooking in his armor wafting into her nose. Anya shut her eyes and shoved her plate away.

"Nowicki?" Riley asked.

"I'm fine," she said. "Just… lost my appetite."

"That sounds like the opposite of fine for you. What's up?"

Anya knit her fingers together and bit her lip. She stared down at them as she asked. "How long were you with the FBI? Before you switched to the DERD, I mean."

"About ten years."

"You ever have to… kill anybody?"

Riley didn't respond for several moments. Anya looked up from her hands to see him staring into his coffee cup.

Finally he said, "Yeah," and took a long drink of coffee. When Anya didn't say anything for several moments he continued, "It was my second year. I was part of a task force that was after some domestic terrorist ring. After a year of legwork, we were given the green light to move onto some warehouse they were using as a base and training ground. It was us, the Boston PD, and some guys from the ATF. It was a pretty big deal, especially to me."

"What happened?" Anya asked, and Riley sighed.

"It was all going well enough, at first. We were setting up a perimeter, and had air support on stand-by. Figured we'd close in, then rush 'em all at once from every direction before they could organize. The goal was to get the bad guys in cuffs, not body bags. We didn't want another Waco."

Riley set his empty cup aside and folded his hands together, an uneasy mirror of Anya's.

"No plan survives contact with the enemy. Our undercover guy had confirmed everybody was present in the warehouse. He missed one. One guy had dipped out to go get some takeout. We caught him on the way back before he made it to the warehouse, but the little shit got a shot off. Alerted the whole gang. Instead of catching a bunch of terrorists with their pants down, they had enough time to arm-up and get in defensive positions.

"Long-story short, a stand-off ended with us breaching the warehouse. The agents I was with got cornered. One died. The guy that did it turned to look at me, and that was it. I took him down."

Riley shrugged and looked across the table at Anya.

"I got called a hero and a bunch of other nice things. Didn't feel like it though. The guy I shot, he was twenty-two. Barely outta high school. Felt like I'd failed the agent next to me who got shot, failed the kid I shot for not seeing him sooner and tackling him before he could open fire. Felt guilty for not getting shot myself."

"I'm sorry, Riley. I shouldn't have asked," Anya said. Riley waved a hand at her.

"Nothing to apologize for, Nowicki. You've been through the shit and haven't even had the training for it. Unless the Archive gives you some kinda psychological adaptation to fighting and stuff?"

"Not really, no. I mean, I'm sure there's something in there for that, but I haven't taken any specific skills for it. I've taken a combat strategy skill, but not one that deals with the after-effects. When I was fighting Jiro earlier, it really occurred to me that I might have to kill him. That if I died, Esmi, and you, and Arvo would be next."

She decided not to mention the Flame Dominion to Riley. Tori was still the only one that knew about it.

"Mm," Riley nodded. "Look, there's no easy answer to this. I think, if you're any kind of decent person, taking another life is never a good thing. It might be necessary, but never good. Do you think you could have killed Jiro, if you had to?"

Anya clenched her hands together. "Probably. I don't like knowing that about myself, but if there was no other way to stop Jiro before he killed somebody else? Yeah, I guess. I mean, I've killed the aliens, but that's different. They're not people, and there's no chance of reasoning with them."

Riley nodded and unclenched his hands.

"It's not wrong to protect people, Nowicki. That's what you did today, and thankfully, you didn't have to kill anybody to do it. The hosts that didn't make it, that's on the aliens. They picked this fight, not us. As for whether or not you might have to do something as awful as kill somebody… I hope not. But you and the other hosts have an awful lot of power, and you need to decide how to use it. If you ever need help, I'm here, and I know Upadhyay, Pan, Hendricks, and a lot of others would be happy to listen."

"Yeah," Anya said and picked up her remaining food and took it to the recycler in the corner. "Thank you, Riley. I'm gonna go say good-bye to Gary and the others, and then I guess we should head back. You'll be ready?"

"Might try and smuggle some more of this coffee and donuts outta here, but I'll be set."

Anya said her good-byes to Arvo, Esmeralda, and Jiro. Jiro and Arvo were staying behind to run more tests and keep the former under observation. Esmeralda was staying to be with Jiro, but also because she didn't have anywhere else to go at the moment since Outpost #2 had been attacked.

Anya swung by the hub on her way to the hangar to see Gary one last time. He was back in his out-of-place recliner, glancing at a few dozen different screens every second.

"Taking off?" he asked as she entered.

"Yeah. We should get back to Outpost One, fill MacDougal in officially, see what needs to be done," Anya said.

"You did real good today, kid."

"Thanks, Gare."

Gary turned just a fraction in his chair, flicking his gaze away from the flashing screens and towards her. He opened his mouth to say something, closed it, and looked away.

"You know I'm always here, if you ever wanna visit," was all he said.

"Uh, yeah. I'll come back again soon, no worries."

"Mm."

Anya left the hub, feeling as though she had missed something, and returned to the Shadow Ray.

IT WAS a long flight back to Alaska.

Comparatively.

What would have taken at least a full day of non-stop air travel now only took several hours, but it was still more time than Anya cared to spend just sitting in the Ray's pilot seat.

All the coffee Riley had had didn't seem to affect his ability to sleep. He'd leaned back into the seats once they had taken off and began snoring almost at once. He'd managed to secure a very large jug of coffee and a box of donuts from Gary's factory, both of which sat on the seat beside him.

Anya was tired, but not sleepy.

And there was one other "person" she wanted to talk to about the day's events.

In addition to her fighting practice with Samaira and Pan, Anya had privately been training herself to do something else.

Anya leaned back into the pilot's chair, placed her hands on her legs, took a deep breath, and closed her eyes. She leaned back, not with her body, but her mind. A conscious effort of falling back into herself, away from the sights and sounds of the Shadow Ray, away from Riley's snoring and the aroma of bioengineered donuts.

Back, back, back, and down, down, down.

Into the Flame Dominion.

Anya opened her eyes after several moments, and found herself in an endless void of swirling colors: the deep reds of sunset, soothing oranges of a campfire, and cheery yellows of summer afternoons. All of them wove together in curtains of light that extended into forever, and she floated among them, toasty and warm.

After weeks spent meditating and focusing on her Sun's Heart, Anya could finally access the Flame Dominion at will. The Flame Dominion was a place, but it was also a cosmic force, and also a living thing, and also her, and also none of these.

She still didn't get the metaphysical stuff, but she knew enough to make it work.

A bird that looked like a cross between an enormous eagle and a peacock stood before her. It was made of bright, yellow light and nothing else. Sparks flew up from its body whenever it ruffled its feathers or flapped its wings.

"Hello, little ember," it said as Anya sat before it, its voice smooth and deep.

"Hey," Anya sighed and stretched out in the void. She let the warmth of the Flame Dominion seep through her, easing tense muscles and flowing through her.

"Long day?"

"God, yes."

"Well, this isn't your personal spa," the bird said and flapped over, sat next to Anya and pecked her on the forehead.

"Ow! Dick!"

"You can't just show up here whenever you like and take a nap."

"I came here for advice! Just gimme a sec! Damn," Anya huffed and waved the bird away. It avoided her clumsy swats and strutted away, its long tail feathers swaying behind it.

"All right. Whatcha need?"

Anya scoffed. "What don't I need? I seriously hurt another person today, and you flat-out told me I might have to kill somebody soon."

Anya trailed off and put her hands over her face.

"Jiro will be fine, primarily because you were willing to roast his ass a little to get him out of that armor. Nice work, by the way. And as for you killing somebody, well, yeah, you might. It's a war. People dying tends to happen during those. You got lucky as hell today. If those two Aussie chuckleheads hadn't shown up, you'd be dead or mind-controlled by now, or others would be.

"I doubt you're gonna get that lucky again. Let's do some hypothetical thinking. Imagine every fight you've been in with aliens, except instead of a gnosiphage, it's a human host threatening people. You taking them down for good?"

"If they were as obviously deadly and incapable of listening to reason as the gnosiphages?" Anya asked, then paused. During the fight on the beach, she had been the one the possessed hosts had been focusing on. She knew she could take a fatal hit and bounce back from it with regeneration. But if Kan or Jiro or Grant had targeted Riley first? Or if Tori had been there? Somebody totally incapable of defending themselves?

"Yeah, absolutely," she said. "I'm taking them down."

"Good."

"Is it, though? I don't want to kill anybody, but knowing that I might have it in me..."

The bird shook its head.

"You're only a killer if that's what you devote yourself to. If a father spends his entire life being the world's best dad—taking his kids on vacation, going to their plays, supporting them and nurturing them—but then kills one bad guy trying to hurt one of his children, does that make him a murderer? Or just somebody who had to kill? Is Riley a murderer? Gary might've had to kill people in Vietnam, so what about him? What about President Hanover? He's probably had people killed on his orders, but never actually pulled the trigger himself."

Anya didn't answer.

"I told you before, the reason I like you is because you like—and are capable of—both: the campfire and the flamethrower. The thing that your friends gather around, and the thing your enemy falls in front of. You're thinking that if you cross this line, it'll mean you're stuck being the flamethrower, but that's bullshit. You don't just have to be one thing. Picking up the flamethrower doesn't mean you can never sit back down by the campfire. But the worst thing you can do sometimes is be uncertain. Especially with what's coming."

Anya blinked at the bird and asked, "What's coming?"

"Oh, c'mon. I only know it because you do too: war. And not the war you're in with the aliens. I mean what comes after, if you win against the gnosiphages."

"What? War with people?"

"Of course! Humanity's spent pretty much its entire history at war. Why would that change now? The NAT's already started one, sort of. Kicked the Indian government to the curb and now they're eyeing their neighbors. People aren't just gonna stand by during that. And once the aliens are gone, it's gonna get worse. People are gonna get a god complex and megalomaniacal delusions of grandeur."

Anya sighed.

"Yeah. Probably. Christ, that's depressing," she said.

"Doesn't have to be. Maybe all-out war won't be necessary if you can help bring people together, now. You've already started that. Or maybe you decide it's impossible to play nice and nuke the first would-be dictator that tries to start some shit. But just waiting around and hoping for some magical solution that means you don't have to make a tough choice isn't realistic."

"Cool. Just some minor decision making," Anya brought her knees up to her chest and rested her head on them.

"Well, to bring the scale back a bit, I do have another suggestion you might like."

"Oh?"

"Yeah. Today was rough. Leverage that against MacDougal and ask for a few days off. With Samaira."

"We were talking about going on another date soon…"

"Good. Because she looked really good at the party the other night, and we got real close to first base last time."

Anya laughed.

"She did look amazing."

"I mean, we," the bird said and gestured between itself and Anya with a wing, "looked great, but she looked awesome. That wasn't just for the party. That was for you. Us."

"Me," Anya said. "She doesn't know about you."

"Yet. We both know you're not entirely comfortable keeping secrets from her."

"Yeah, yeah. When I'm ready and I don't have to also think about the probably impending super-powered conflicts in the future. One war at a time, please."

"No promises. Also, eat one of Riley's donuts. They smell fucking divine and he's asleep," the bird said, then pecked Anya on the foot.

She opened her eyes to the cockpit of the Shadow Ray and the near-silent hum of its magnetic engines. Sure enough, Riley was snoring behind her, and she managed to sneak a maple bar.

Riley was right. Forget Boston, Gary could rule the whole world just with these. Maybe that's what she could do: world peace through delicious baked goods.

Anya sat in the cockpit and chewed as she rolled her thoughts over in her mind. Her consciousness swung between all the possible scenarios her mind could conjure, and by the time the Shadow Ray landed at Outpost #1, she was mentally exhausted. She didn't have any solid answers, save one: whatever happened—tomorrow, next month, after the aliens were gone—she'd do whatever she had to to keep herself and her friends safe.

PART TWO
ALPHA & OMEGA

FROM EARTH #7

From the *New York Times*:

JOINT GLOBAL TASK-FORCE UNDER THE UN GETS GREEN LIGHT

President Hanover confirmed during a press conference yesterday that the Unites States has joined a cooperative effort consisting of several countries and their hosts to combat the extraterrestrial presence on Earth. Other nations include Japan, Canada, France, the United Kingdom, and Finland. Additional countries are still in negotiations to join, with Australia, Brazil, South Africa, and South Korea among them.

The task-force, currently known as the United Planetary Response Cooperative (UPRC), is currently overseen by the UN and its leading members. While each country maintains control of their own hosts, any joint efforts must receive unanimous approval from all members of the UPRC.

While details about the scope of the Cooperative's duties aren't yet clear, President Hanover made some additional statements yesterday regarding what the UPRC may be used for in a post-invasion world.

"I think the big concern on peoples' minds right now is that once we beat these alien freaks—and we will beat them—is what are all the hosts going to do? I'm working in conjunction with the UN and members of the UPRC to clearly define what hosts may—and may not —do, to guarantee a safe, productive future for everyone."

When asked if he had intentions to incorporate the American hosts —such as Agent Ardent—into the standard military, Hanover was emphatic.

"Absolutely not. No hosts in the military. And I'll say it now: we have no intention of using hosts as weapons against our neighbors, or any other country… unless they intend to use theirs to threaten the peace and security we're all working towards."

When asked if that meant he had plans to send hosts to combat the New Allied Territories following their expanding area of influence, Hanover stated that he was "Considering all options."

———

From Oni-Chan (鬼ちゃん), an online message and image board, sub-board /CoT/ (Conspiracy Theories)

Anon-01: I'm in Newport, OR and just got a notification from the local PD that there's an advisory to stay away forrm the beach after 7:00 PM and before 8:00 AM. Called a friend down in Florence and they got the same thing. Anybody know what this shit's about?

Anon-02: Am in Venice Beach, CA. Also got advisory warning. People are saying they might enforce a curfew. Coastal towns only.

Anon-03: Srsly? Fuck. I had a date then. We were gonna go down to the beach

Anon-02: Nobody cares about your normie date anon

Anon-01: Prolly gonna date one of the manatees or something

Anon-03: No u. Also no manatees here, I'm in Corpus Cristi.

Anon-04: Stay home and plow your manatee of a mom lmao

Anon-03: Fuck off

Anon-01: Seething

Anon-04: Anon-03 confirmed for manatee mom love

Anon-02: I'm looking up the advisory. Looks like it's west coast only. You are free to go on your normie date anon

Anon-04: So… what? This the aliens or some shit?

Anon-01: This board's gone downhill since the fucking aliens showed up. The answer to everything isn't "It was the aliens." That's just fucking lazy. Governments and secret societies and shit can still do plenty of shady stuff without the aliens being involved. I'm still not convinced this whole alien thing isn't just one big false-flag

Anon-02: Okay... but it's probably aliens.

Anon-03: As long as they're not gonna turn my town into a ruin or something idgaf

Anon-04: lol its corpus cristi who would even notice if they did

Anon-03: fuck you

Anon-04: exactly what an incestuous manatee-lover would say

Anon-01: Based and manatee-pilled

———

From the *Rutherford News Network*:

NASA CONFIRMS ASTEROID TO PASS CLOSE TO EARTH

Much attention has been rightfully focused on the otherworldly presence on our own planet over the last month, but organizations like NASA and SETI still have their eyes on the sky. Researchers at NASA stated that a large asteroid, approximately the size of Australia, would be passing between Earth and Mars in the coming weeks, but would miss Earth by quite some distance.

In the time since their initial statement, NASA released the following update:

"The asteroid will be passing by a bit closer to Earth. We initially predicted its trajectory would have it passing closer to Mars, but now we can see that it will be nearer to our planet. However, this is not a cause for panic. It will, at its closest point, come no nearer to Earth than approximately eighty-five million miles. We had recognized this earlier as a possibility, though unlikely. However, now we have confirmed, and run several models backing-up, the asteroid's path."

The asteroid has had its path confirmed by other international agencies such as the British National Space Center (BNSC), and the Japan Aerospace Exploration Agency (JAXA), among others.

11

The debriefing following the incident at Outpost #2 was anything but brief. All Anya wanted to do was go to her room and sleep for the next day or two, but MacDougal insisted on a full, in-person meeting while it was still as fresh as could be.

President Hanover attended via video call, along with the Joint Chiefs of Staff, and the President of France—Lionel Bisset—for some reason. Anya was curious about the latter, but ignored him as she went over everything that happened, including the proposed idea for finding the alien. Riley filled in a few blank spots, and also gave a bit more detail about Gary's factory. Samaira and Pan were there, but sat quietly along with MacDougal. Pan eventually curled up in his chair and fell asleep.

"...so now we're just waiting on Hendricks and Dr. Immonen to do something with that alien bug thing they got," Riley said. "At least, that's where we left it. Director MacDougal ordered us back here ASAP."

"Don't much like the idea of Hendricks having all that tech to himself. And now some kinda psychic alien too? No, that won't do," President Hanover grumbled. Anya frowned. She suspected that it wasn't so much that Gary had all the cool toys, but that he wasn't sharing.

Anytime Gary's tech or access to the Archive's Reward Allocation Currency store came up, Hanover got a hungry gleam in his eye.

"If he wants to play nursemaid to a mind-controlling alien, let him. He can spend the money and time taking care of it," MacDougal said. Anya hid a smirk. MacDougal knew not to push against Hanover's desire for all the advanced gadgets he wanted. Far better to refocus him to the problems he didn't.

Hanover just raised his eyebrows and nodded.

"And this Gary Hendricks can be trusted with the dangerous alien?" President Bisset spoke up for the first time, his French accent as thick and smooth as butter. He was a thin man, just past middle-aged, with a slender nose and short blond hair going white. He made Anya think of a stork.

"So far," Hanover replied.

"Hendricks was key to defending the White House last month, and has cooperated with us to the extent he is comfortable with," MacDougal added.

"And what is he comfortable with?" Bisset asked.

"Pretty much anything except distributing weaponry."

"Which is the one thing we keep asking him for," Hanover muttered.

The one thing you're stupid enough to keep asking for, Anya thought. Samaira looked at her, then at Hanover, and rolled her eyes and gave Anya a wink. Anya had to suppress a grin.

"He, and the other hosts like Ms. Nowicki and Ms. Upadhyay, have all done a lot for us," Hanover added. "I'm sure you can understand having to extend some trust to the various hosts, President Bisset?"

"Quite, quite," Bisset nodded. "On that subject, as you said this alien is psychic, correct? I would like to send my own representative to inspect the creature. He may be of some assistance."

The camera on Bisset's end panned to the side to reveal a man of average height standing just to the side. He wore a long white coat, lined with deep purple, and a white helmet with a reflective gold faceplate.

Renn bowed his head slightly and waved a white-gloved hand.

"Good afternoon," he said, his French accent apparent, but not nearly as thick as Bisset's. He also sounded like he had just woken up from a nap, or was extremely bored. "I would be happy to lend my expertise, if I am welcome in Mssr. Hendricks's factory?"

"I can ask," Anya said. "We've got our own psychic working on it, though. Don't wanna trouble you."

"No trouble at all! Many hands make light work. Or many minds, in this case."

"I think a joint operation would look mighty fine. No need to divulge the details, but the US and the EU working together would make for some appealing headlines, eh MacDougal?" Hanover said.

"Of course, Mr. President," she replied.

"Your psychic, I believe we last met at the impromptu gathering in Greenland. Madmoiselle Gomez?" Renn asked. "I do not believe she was at the dinner recently."

"That's her. But she's been through a lot. Maybe give her a few days to recover?" Anya asked and looked rather pointedly at MacDougal.

"Well, I'd say we need to get the ball rolling on this one," Hanover said, a strained smile stretching the corners of his mouth.

"If she has exerted herself in battle, I think some recovery might be necessary. As a fellow psychic, I am familiar with the strain it can cause. Forcing her to do anything right away might cause other problems," Renn said. "It wouldn't be good to announce a joint operation only to have it stall right away."

Hanover grunted at that.

"Very well. As a fellow psychic, what do you think is the soonest you two could meet-up and start working on... whatever it is you need to?" the President asked and waved his hand in a circular motion.

"A few days should be enough."

"President Bisset?" Hanover asked, and his French counterpart glanced at Renn and nodded.

"We will be ready in three days," Bisset said.

There were a few other details exchanged about the day's events and the plan moving forward, but most of it seemed like aimless bureaucratic nonsense and Anya tuned it out. When MacDougal finally ended the call, she took a moment to stare ahead at the now empty screen against the far wall of the meeting room.

She looked beyond exhaustion. The director of the DERD was by no means a young woman, but she looked at least a decade older than her sixty-some years in that moment.

"Gary's already pretty much on-board. He doesn't care about the politics. If it's about finding the aliens, he's in," Anya said, before MacDougal could even ask her about it. She nodded and sighed.

"Nothing to do for now but wait, then," the director said. "That's usually the worst part."

"I dunno, ma'am. I could do with a day off or two," Riley said.

"We're sure these mind-control alien things couldn't access the host maps and find our locations?" MacDougal asked.

"Felix?" Anya asked.

"Boo?" Samaira added.

Both of their AIs appeared and faced MacDougal.

"I'm 100% sure!" Felix said. "The Archive can only be accessed via conscious command, either tactile or verbal, or some other method the host may agree to with the helper AI if neither of those is possible."

"I know I make a lot of mistakes but I'm sure about this," Boo added. "If the mind-control aliens put their victims into a coma-like state to better manipulate their nervous system, the Archive wouldn't respond."

"So we're still hidden. Thank God for that much," MacDougal sighed. "You all go on. I've got a few more calls to make. Dismissed."

Riley, Samaira, and Pan all got up to leave, but Anya stayed behind. Samaira gave her a look, but left when Anya winked at her.

"Nowicki? If you're staying behind to grouse about Hanover—" MacDougal started to say before Anya shook her head.

"No, ma'am, nothing like that," she said.

"Oh? 'Ma'am,' is it? You must want something. My grandchildren always seem to remember their manners when they have a favor to ask of their Granny."

"A small favor," Anya replied and MacDougal waved at her to

continue. "I'd like a couple days off base. Since we have to wait for things anyway, I figured now would be as good a time as any."

"Your fight with Yamada and the other hosts: was that your first time fighting another person? For real, I mean. Not some barroom brawl or schoolyard scuffle."

"Yeah. Yes, ma'am."

"Riley mentioned you'd had a talk about it. Never easy, looking another person in the face and knowing you might have to take them down. I'll check my schedule and security reports. If nothing pops up, granted. Though I'll insist you be on-call for the entire period you're away. And don't fly too far in case things go sideways."

"I'd like Samaira to have the days off as well," Anya said. MacDougal raised her eyebrows and tapped her nail on the table.

"You two looked like you were enjoying yourselves at the dinner the other night."

Anya blushed a little but said nothing.

"We don't really have a policy regarding fraternization when it comes to hosts."

Anya waited for MacDougal to put her foot down. She'd say it was too risky to have hosts get their emotional health entangled with each other during the invasion, or it would be a distraction, or—

"So, until somebody tells me otherwise—or you or Upadhyay gives me a reason to—I don't see why I need to bother myself with the personal lives of you or anyone. Upadhyay can have time off-base as well, but same deal: on-call, night or day, and don't go too far."

Anya let out a sigh of relief.

"Thank you, ma'am."

"Don't make me regret it. And Nowicki? When you're done, mandatory psych eval." Anya started to protest but MacDougal shook her head. "No arguing. It's standard. Go on, now. Blow off some steam. Not literally."

Anya left the conference room with a bit of a bounce in her step. She found Samaira waiting in the hall outside, and she looked up as Anya approached.

"What was that about?" she asked.

"Just securing the next couple days off for us. You feel like going on a date?" Anya asked, unable to hide her grin. It only got wider as Samaira smiled back.

———

THEY WASTED no time in clearing their schedules and making sure Pan would be okay without either of them for a little while. Anya felt a bit bad about ditching the little guy, but he assured her he'd be fine.

"Me and Riley can hang out! And Chandrali," Pan had said. Samaira had asked him to catsit while they were away. "I can teach her to find better sand to dig in besides that weird smelly stuff in Samaira's house."

"Probably better to let her have her kitty litter," Samaira replied. Pan didn't seem to think this was a good idea, but relented.

Then they were off.

Anya felt like she was being let out for summer break. It had only been a week or two since she'd been away from Outpost #1 for recreation, but it felt a lot longer. She was glad for the engine upgrade Gary had installed: it meant they could leave the outpost and its assorted problems behind all the faster.

They were only a few minutes away when Anya's phone buzzed. She cursed at it and considered ignoring it until she saw it was from Tori.

ANYA: What's up?
TORI: Just got back into the NY office after swinging by DC. How'd the meeting and stuff go?
ANYA: Long story.
TORI: You wanna talk about it?
ANYA: Actually on a date with Sam right now. Sort of. On our way to NY. Keeping options open, probably do touristy stuff for our first date in the big city.
TORI: Ooooh. Nice. So, I don't wanna ruin your date or anything…
ANYA: Tori. Do not fuck this up for me.
TORI: It's aether stuff! It'll take maybe like, ten minutes, tops! Just

meet me at Maria Hernandez Park, in Brooklyn. The one that had that book festival last year.

ANYA: Fine.

TORI: Ttfn

"Tori?" Samaira asked as she leaned to the side to catch Anya's eye. Anya put her phone away and nodded as she swiveled around in the co-pilot's chair.

"Yeah. She wanted to see if you'd be willing to spend ten minutes with her to talk about the aether. Something she wanted to get your opinion on," Anya said. Samaira brightened a little, her eyes actually glowing a faint blue for a split second.

"Ooooh. My only student wants to pick her teacher's brain. I guess I can spare a few minutes," she chuckled. "But not too much time. I've got a hot date, after all."

"Okay, you're allowed one temperature related pun per-day. Tori has made more than any one person should. Her and—" Anya was about to say the Flame Dominion and all of its heat and fire-related metaphors, but stopped herself. "—well, other people."

Samaira laughed again and held her hands up. "Fine, fine. I promise, no more heat or fire-related jokes. For now."

The rest of the flight was spent fiddling with the Shadow Ray's radio, trying to find some decent music, and chatting about the various DERD agents that might also be dating each other. It wasn't long before Manhattan lay below them, and Arya flew in for a discrete landing.

Brooklyn had mellowed somewhat from the frigid grip that had clutched it in January. However, it wasn't that much of an improvement. It had progressed from frozen to soggy, the sky from a gray slate that threatened snow, to a slightly paler gray slate that threatened rain. The people who were outside were in a hurry to get back inside, and sloshed their way through puddles of half-melted snow.

They met Tori, and she walked a few feet ahead of Anya and Samaira, allowing them a modicum of privacy and the opportunity to hold hands. Samaira gave Anya a few sideways glances as their fingers intertwined.

They'd barely gone a couple of blocks when her grip on Anya's hand began to loosen and her gaze wandered.

"What's up?" Anya asked after Samaira took her hand away and began to turn in a slow circle. Tori stopped ahead of them and raised her eyebrows.

"Wow. We're not even at the park yet," she said.

"What is it? What's going on?" Anya asked.

"Nothing bad. It's okay," Samaira replied. She reached out for Anya's hand, gave it a reassuring squeeze, and then stepped away. She looked up into the air, her eyes following something invisible.

"I'm relieved, but still in the dark. Obviously something to do with the aether?"

"There's… more of it," Samaira said and squinted. She looked at Tori, who nodded.

"Bingo. I can't feel it yet unless I'm reaching for it, but when I get to the park, I don't even have to try. It's like out here, it's quiet, but there's a whole concert in the park," Tori said.

"Show me," Samaira said, and all three of them hurried on. The Maria Hernandez Park wasn't nearly as big as Prospect Park, but it was still large enough to hold the occasional local event. It consisted of a playground for kids, a tennis court, basketball courts, plenty of trees just starting to show some new growth on their naked branches, and benches along winding pathways. A large, circular area of gray and brown bricks lay at the center of the park, with four straight paths radiating out from it to the corners.

Samaira's eyes got wider and her mouth fell open a little more as they reached the center of the park.

"Whoa," she said.

"Yeah. I don't even have my focus right now. I think it's gotten bigger or something since I've been in Alaska," Tori said and closed her eyes and began to hum to some unheard melody. Anya looked around but neither saw, heard, or felt anything.

"Okay, can you give me the basics, please?" she asked. Samaira blinked, then shook her head. It wasn't in a negative, but more as if she were trying to clear something out of her hair.

"Sorry, yes. Remember when I first spoke with Tori about learning the aether?" Samaira asked, and Anya nodded. They'd done it in a cafe, and Anya had used the Archive's store (along with Samaira's guidance) to buy a small guidebook and focus for Tori to use and attempt to manipulate the aether with. "Well, back then I told her that the best places to find concentrations of the aether in New York were in Central Park..."

"...and a bodega in Queens," Tori finished. "And for a while, she was right. Those were the only places of 'dense,' aether, and that's being generous. Everywhere else it was like smoke. In those places it was like really sad cotton candy. More substantial, yes, but not by much."

"And now I'm guessing that's changed?" Anya quirked an eyebrow and looked around again. All she saw was the gray sky and the park around her, felt nothing but the slight chill in the air, heard nothing but the wind through the trees and the constant rumble of big city traffic.

"Oh yeah," Samaira said. "It's stable too. Before there were just a few tiny little streams, but this is like a river. I can feel it flowing away and through other parts of the city too. I bet the places I found in Central Park and Queens are bigger now too, if this is anything to go by."

"And you'd win that bet. I went there a week ago, and they're a little bigger than this," Tori said.

"So... what? The aether moves around, right? You pull it out of thin air when you're fighting," Anya said.

"Not thin air. I pull it from other places. I've encountered a few spots that have aether wells as big and bigger than this, but they're rare. It's mostly seemed random at this point, but now I'm wondering," Samaira said and looked at Tori. "Where have you been doing most of your practicing?"

"Central Park at first. Easier to hide what I'm doing there than in a cramped bodega with security cameras. I'd just go behind a tree in the park. A few people noticed me, but they probably just thought I was messing with LEDs or something. After I got the basics, I did all my practicing in my apartment," Tori replied.

"Central Park is... that way," Samaira turned and pointed, then looked at Anya, who nodded. Then, she pointed in the opposite direction and added, "And Tori's place is back that way. Which puts this place somewhere in the middle."

"Wait," Tori said and held up her hands, "are you saying I did this?"

Samaira pursed her lips and adjusted her glasses. "Not consciously. The aether does its own thing unless acted upon. Normally it just flows around, but since there's so few aetheric users on Earth—two at the moment that I'm aware of—it means it doesn't take much to influence it."

"But you're kinda, y'know, just a wee bit stronger than me," Tori said, deadpan, and Samaira chuckled. "So shouldn't the aether be swarming all over you all the time?"

Samaira tapped her chin and then shook her head. "Not necessarily. I travel around a lot: for patrols, for meeting people in DC, Canada, and Alaska, to visit my family in Chicago. Going out with Anya a few times," Samaira smiled at her as she said this. "I could be spreading it thin. I also tend to use a lot of aether, and store more of it in my foci. But you stick to the city for the most part, and so it just builds up and hangs around."

"Huh," Tori grunted. "Neat."

"This isn't gonna cause some magical aether storm or anything, right?" Anya asked.

"No. Like I said, the aether just sort of hangs around until somebody starts making use of it. I'd be curious though…"

"About?"

"Well, the aether isn't just an Earth thing. It's a cosmic energy that runs through everything to some extent. The whole reason I have it is because it was in the Archive, which means some alien or aliens have it. So if Tori is pulling more aether to Brooklyn and New York by practicing here, and just by doing small exercises…"

Anya's eyes widened.

"What kind of stuff are you pulling in from space by going all over Earth?" she finished and Samaira nodded.

"When I started using the aether in January, it was tough. Even with it being my primary skill, it took a lot of effort to get enough juice to make my arrows. But now, it's child's play. I thought that was just because of my skills going up, and I'm sure that's part of it, but not the only part. Based on what we're seeing here. I may be bringing more aether towards Earth."

"Cool. Glad I'm not going crazy then," Tori said. "Wasn't sure if my aether-sense or whatever was off."

"My pleasure. It's fascinating," Samaira replied and looked around her more, her smile widening. Anya was actually glad she couldn't see or sense the aether in that moment, so she wouldn't be distracted from the sight of Samaira grinning and turning in slow, graceful circles around the center of the park.

"I'm gonna make myself scarce so you two can... y'know. Be romantical, and stuff," Tori leaned toward Anya and whispered.

"Thanks, Tori. We'll swing by later," she replied. Tori gave her a thumbs up, then strode away as stealthily as she could while Anya faced Samaira. "I'm happy to stay in the park and watch you watch the aether, or we could go somewhere else?"

"Eh?" Samaira asked, blinking her eyes owlishly behind her glasses and then fidgeting with embarrassment. "Oh! Sorry. I got a little carried away. When did Tori leave?"

"Just now. So! We have the whole city to ourselves. Can I interest you in the Museum of Modern Art? Maybe a show on Broadway? The weather's kinda crappy, but Central Park can still be nice..."

Samaira wrapped her lithe arms around one of Anya's muscular ones, and leaned into her with a pleased sigh. The tips of Anya's ears got a bit warm at the obvious display of affection, and in public. Samaira looked up, then smirked.

"The tops of your ears are on fire," she said.

"Uh, right," Anya said and made a conscious effort to put the fire out. It didn't burn, but it did make her a bit self-conscious. "So? Any preferences?"

"Somewhere... quiet. With food. I haven't eaten since breakfast."

"Now you're talking."

They left the park and the swell of aether behind them, arm-in-arm.

12

Anya gave Samaira a few options, and she eventually decided on an upscale dim sum place in the center of Chinatown. It was a little crowded, but the heavy wood decor, the curtains around the booths, and thick carpets kept the atmosphere quiet and intimate.

They sat by a circular window, in a booth near the back of the restaurant's second floor. A thick red curtain partially surrounded their high-backed booth, closing them off further. Though they were well away from the kitchen, the smells of pork, sesame oil, chili, garlic, ginger, and more were inescapable. Anya was drooling by the time they finally ordered.

They chit-chatted over their dumplings, sharing and swapping across the table. They discussed some of the other agents at the outpost, the Canadian hosts, what they had been doing right before the Archives arrived, and generally what life had been like before everything had gone crazy.

"…and then I'd always come home during spring break to stay with my family and Mom would say my head got bigger but the rest of me got shorter. I'll probably still be in Alaska by the time spring rolls around, but, as long as you're there I think I'll be fine," Samaira said, and smiled across the table at Anya.

Anya tried smiling back, but she couldn't stop a single lightning bolt of a thought from entering her head and souring the moment. It happened any time somebody mentioned their family, especially their mom.

That one maternal word always made a dark shape emerge out of Anya's mind, unbidden and unwelcome.

Anya's mother.

She loomed into Anya's mind like a storm front of thunderous disapproval and judgment.

Samaira's smile faded as she looked at Anya.

"Are you... oh. Oh, god. Sorry. I didn't—" she started to say.

"It's fine. It's stupid of me."

"No! I mean, I don't know what the deal is but I know you have problems with your mom, I guess."

Anya snorted. "That is... putting it mildly."

"We can talk about something else! You mentioned Broadway, back in the park?" Samaira said in a tone that was bordering closer to panic than conversational. Anya reached across the table, palm up. After a moment, Samaira slid her hand into it.

"Sam. It's fine. I'm not mad. I just... still clearly have some stuff to work through."

"Do you want to talk about it?" Samaira asked, and winced even as she asked.

"That's not exactly great date conversation."

"Anya," Samaira said, her tone leveling out, her gaze steady with Anya's. "I like you."

"Oh. Good? Bit of a relief to hear on our third date."

"I mean, I like you, and I'd like to keep doing this. But it doesn't all have to be cute dates and happy stuff. The world's kinda gone to hell. I'm here for the dates, and the hand-holding and... more, I guess. But if you need me to be, I can be here for the serious stuff too. It might sound weird, but I'd like to be here for it. Even if it's bad. Maybe especially if it's bad."

She squeezed Anya's hand. Anya's shoulders relaxed. She'd barely been aware of them tensing in the first place, but realized they had been the second Samaira had said the "M" word.

"If you wanna hear it, I guess…" Anya trailed away and Samaira nodded.

"If you want to tell me."

Anya sighed and nodded. "I still haven't told her, or my brothers, that I'm a host."

"I gathered."

"The short version is, my mom is a control freak, and my brothers are her little toy soldiers. She wanted me to be her dress-up doll. She… Christ. She's got a pre-conceived notion for everyone and everything, and I didn't fit into it. Boys were boys, girls were girls, and they could only like very specific things and behave in very specific ways. I couldn't even wear pants until I was in high school and I had to change after I left the house and before I got back home."

Samaira's eyes widened at that.

Anya faltered at the next bit. She wasn't the only one who had been a disappointment. Nathan, her little brother and the baby of the bunch, had been found wanting by their mother as well. Anya had left when she couldn't take it anymore. But when the pressure became too much for Nathan…

He had taken a more permanent way out.

Anya tightened her lips and shut her eyes.

"Anya?" Samaira asked. There was a beat of silence before Anya was able to respond in something resembling a normal voice.

"As bad as my mom was to me, she was worse to Nathan. My little brother. I saved myself from her bullshit but… not him. He… passed away."

Samaira looked like she wanted to ask for more, but stayed quiet. Anya had only ever spoken about Nathan with Tori, and while part of her wanted to open up to Samaira, the rest of her didn't want to spend their evening together circling a tragedy years past.

"My mom's just… an asshole. I haven't told her a lot of things, so I don't know why I'd start with this, that's all," she said and gestured at herself. She shook her head, and forced a smile. "Sorry for bringing the mood down."

Samaira gave her a look, somewhere between sadness and suspicion, but she didn't push, only squeezed her hand again. They eventually eased back into more mild conversation, like how Samaira wanted to finish her Master's degree in Sociology, maybe put it to some use in the wake of the alien invasion. Anya was more than happy for the change in topic, and just to listen for a while.

"I just think it's going to be fascinating once things calm down a bit. Right now it's all pretty much survival-mode stuff: an enemy has showed up with unknown capabilities, so people are hunkering down. But once the threat is over, we'll be able to focus on all sorts of stuff: who the Engineers are, all this info in the Archive that talks about other alien races," Samaira said and continued on, her eyes bright behind her glasses.

Anya had to admire her optimism, all but saying she knew their victory over the gnosiphages was only a matter of time. Given how the aliens had slunk into hiding, she would have agreed with her a few days ago. But after the encounter at Outpost #2, she wasn't so sure.

Just because the aliens had become quiet didn't mean they had become afraid.

"What's going on out there?" Samaira asked and leaned toward the circular window that looked out onto the street below. Anya turned to see a large crowd across the street, a couple of large vans, and several people with cameras.

News cameras.

"Ah, shit," Anya said. "It's the news. Somebody probably recognized me."

Ever since she had appeared beside President Hanover following the attack on the White House, it happened occasionally. Since she'd been up in Alaska, it hadn't happened much, but the few times she had flown down to DC or New York, somebody tended to spot her and call out, wave, or ask for a photo.

Anya didn't mind that sort of thing, though she did find it a little odd. She wasn't used to having strangers smile and ask for a selfie. It was nice, but weird.

What wasn't nice was the order from MacDougal to never make any sort of statements that could violate their confidentiality agreements or paint the DERD, Hanover's administration, or the government at large, in a bad light. Anya didn't have any plans to shit talk anybody, but the orders made her worry she might put her foot in her mouth. Her interview with Jennifer Chang had been strictly choreographed and monitored.

"To be fair, you do kinda stand out," Samaira said. Anya snorted and rolled her eyes.

"Won't even let us eat in peace," she said.

"I'm kinda full, anyway. How about we sneak out the back and head somewhere else?"

"Works for me," Anya said and left some money plus a large tip on the table. Anya found the manager and explained the situation, and they were given permission to sneak out the back, through the kitchen. The two women exited onto a wide alleyway lined with dumpsters and empty crates. Some movement at the end of the alley caught Anya's attention. One of the reporters had seen them and lights shone down the length of the alley.

"C'mon," Anya said and put her arm around Samaira's waist. Samaira let out a surprised squeal that turned into a shriek of laughter as Anya launched the both of them up into the sky.

"Oh, wow. Head rush," Samaira said and looked a bit dizzy.

"Sorry. Just thought it'd be best to not hang around."

"Yeah, good call. Whoa."

Samaira and Anya both went quiet as they looked out across the sprawl of New York glittering below them. It was already dark, and the countless lights of the city flashed and twinkled, a man-made terrestrial starscape that outshone the natural one above.

"I hope I never get used to flying," Samaira said and held onto Anya. "The first night I used my skills and rode Chandrali over Chicago was just amazing. I don't want to forget what that feels like."

"Me neither," Anya replied.

Samaira looked up at her, then leaned in and kissed her on the lips. It was hesitant at first, more of a brush of the lips than a full-fledged kiss, but then both women leaned into it.

Anya wasn't sure how long they kissed, but long enough for her to become aware of her need for air and pull away, albeit reluctantly.

She looked down at Samaira for a moment, breathing a little faster than she had moments before.

"Sorry, was it… I mean, I just had a lot of those pork and garlic dumplings," Samaira said and covered her mouth. Anya laughed and shook her head.

"No, it was perfect. I mean, I had a lot more of them than you did, so if anybody should be apologizing, it should be me. What now? Did you wanna go do something else, or call it a night?"

"I could do with a coffee. And then how about you take me somewhere with a nice view?"

"I can do that."

———

SAMAIRA HAD INITIALLY REQUESTED coffee from the coffee chain Anya used to work at. Anya refused and told Samaira that the coffee there was basically microwaved sewage water. Samaira had made a face and they'd gone to one of the many smaller, more upscale cafes, gotten their order to go, and then Anya flew them both up to the top of Central Park Tower.

It was a gleaming finger of glass and steel that jutted above the skyline. The dark expanse of Central Park stretched out below Anya and Samaira as they sat perched on the edge of the roof, drinks in hand.

"How many people you figure have seen the city from here?" Samaira asked.

"However many construction guys and maintenance workers gotta come out here. Maybe whoever lives in the penthouse," Anya said and sipped her coffee. One of the downsides of having the Sun's Heart was that hot things—drinks, soup, showers and baths—never really felt hot anymore. She had to essentially boil her coffee to lava-like temperatures to feel much from it. "Can you see the aether from up here?"

Samaira blinked at Anya and grinned, somewhat abashed.

"Yes. Is that why you brought us here?" she asked.

"That and I just figured it'd be a nice view. I kinda gathered you were itching to come and inspect it after your chat with Tori."

"Yeah. A little."

"Sam. Please. You were practically jumping out of your skin when Tori mentioned it."

"I wasn't that bad."

Anya smirked and arched an eyebrow at Samaira.

"Okay, maybe I was a little excited."

Anya raised her other eyebrow and Samaira swatted her on the arm.

"Stop teasing me!"

Anya chuckled.

"How's it look?" she asked.

"It's… a lot," Samaira replied. "More than I guessed. I sensed an awful lot of energy, but I figured I was just feeling it from farther away, other locations. But it looks like it's pretty much all there."

Samaira pointed toward the Upper West Side of Manhattan and the side of the park. Anya couldn't see, or sense, anything but a bunch of leafless trees, streetlights, cars and pedestrians and buildings. It looked like the city always had.

"I'll take your word for it," she said.

"It's fascinating, but it makes me worry," Samaira said.

"Worry?"

"In nature, there's always a danger when introducing a foreign element. It's why importing animals and vegetables is so carefully regulated. If you smuggle in something foreign that the ecosystem can't handle, it could destroy the whole thing."

"Right. Like those frogs in Australia, I think?"

"Cane toads, and yes, exactly. The Australian ecosystem wasn't prepared for them and their population exploded. Societies can be affected too, like when a highly advanced culture makes contact with a developing one."

"Like aliens and Earthlings."

Samaira nodded. "It can be harmful, even disastrous for the developing civilization. But I'm wondering…"

Samaira trailed off until Anya prompted her by asking, "Wondering what?"

"Well, usually when a more advanced society makes contact with a developing one, it's bad news for the developing one, like the Spanish and the Inca Empire. But what if it's more like the Cane Toads with us? All this stuff, the aether, the Dominions, magic and psychic powers, none of it was here before. But apparently it's been out there," Samaira pointed up at the cloudy night sky and the countless stars beyond, "for thousands and thousands of years. There's notes in the Archive about the aether that says it was first used something like 80,000 years ago. Humans were still cavemen back then, using bone tools and not much else."

"And now we have all this powerful stuff just handed to us," Anya said. Samaira nodded.

"The academic in me is fascinated by the implications and what's already happening. But the rest of me... it's worrying."

"But the Cane Toads, they thrived, right?"

"They did, still are, but they're recognized as causing harm to their habitat. It isn't natural. The ecosystem hasn't had time to adjust. So yes, short-term, the toads are experiencing an explosion in population. But long-term, they may wind up just killing themselves off, and the environment with them."

"Cheery," Anya said. "I liked it more when all I had to think about was setting a creepy alien puppet on fire."

Samaira laughed at that, then leaned over and rested her head on Anya's arm. Anya leaned back a bit, enjoying the feel of Samaira's weight against her.

"I wish you could see the aether like I do. Central Park looks beautiful with it flowing around... but I'm also worried about what it means. The big picture," Samaira said. "It could be a miracle: people learning to use the aether, or getting the Dominions, solving problems, saving the planet from the invasion. Or... it could all turn really, really ugly."

"Flamethrower or campfire," Anya muttered before she could catch herself.

"What's that?" Samaira asked.

"Uh, something somebody mentioned," Anya said, fumbling for something, "Riley, I think."

Samaira looked at her, face shifting from open curiosity to suspicion.

"If you don't want to tell me, I won't make you," she said. "But don't lie to me please."

Anya considered—briefly—doubling down and insisting she wasn't, but the combination of Samaira's steady, unblinking gaze and her own aversion to being dishonest with her made the lie die before it ever reached her lips.

"I'm sorry. It wasn't Riley," Anya admitted.

"May I ask who?"

"It's… complicated."

"If you don't want to, don't. But I'm relatively smart. I can keep up."

Anya bit her lip. Would Samaira think it was weird? Scary? Maybe too much of a risk, and worth reporting to MacDougal?

Maybe too much of a risk to bother being around her?

Do you really want to be with somebody you can't trust, and who doesn't trust you? a familiar voice asked inside her head. For a moment, Anya wasn't sure if it was the Flame Dominion, or herself, and then smirked when she thought that distinction didn't really apply.

"So, you know how I took the Flame Dominion?" Anya asked.

"I've noticed the fire powers, yes," Samaira said dryly. Anya chuckled at that, but then took a deep breath as she explained everything. How she'd first heard the Flame Dominion, how it contacted her in her sleep, how it had changed shape after she joined the DERD, all of it.

"An interdimensional personification of the cosmic element of fire —that is also sort of your subconscious—told you to ask me out?" Samaira asked.

Anya blinked at her.

"That's what you're focusing on?" she asked.

"For now, yes."

"It encouraged me to do what I was already thinking of doing."

"Wow. I'm not sure whether to be flattered or embarrassed for you."

"Hey!"

"I'm teasing. A little."

Anya leaned forward, elbows on her knees, and looked from the city below her to Samaira beside her.

"Well?" she asked.

"Well, what?"

"I dunno. You don't have any reaction to this?"

"Oh, I'm having a few of them," Samaira's eyebrows went up and she dangled her feet over the edge of the roof in a display of nervous energy.

"That bad?" Anya winced.

"Not like how you're thinking. It actually goes back to what I was saying about the Cane Toads. The aether concentrating around a novice like Tori, and what is apparently a cheap counterfeit Sun's Heart becoming capable of making contact with the Flame Dominion, despite it and the Archive saying that shouldn't be possible."

"Well, maybe not impossible, but very unlikely," Anya said.

"I'm getting the impression that a lot of the things happening here with the Archive are beyond the scope of what the Engineers intended," Samaira tapped a finger against the side of her coffee cup.

"Like the fact that some of them apparently didn't even know what planet they had sent it to?"

"That, but not just that. What does that say about them? Probably that the decision to send the Archive to Earth was made at the last possible moment, that the grunts didn't even get a memo about where it had gone. They must have sent it here as an absolute last resort."

"But why?" Anya wondered.

"Do you remember the last thing that Engineer said to us before its signal got scrambled? Back after the fight outside the White House?"

"Yeah, I asked it if it could unlock the redacted skills, like FTL-travel and the redacted Dominion. It said no, and then the line died."

Samaira shook her head and replied, "It didn't just say no. It said some security protocols were set up by its boss due to the threat level of humanity exceeding normal Archive classifications for distribution."

"Ah, right."

"You talking to the Flame Dominion, me and Tori affecting all this aether without even really trying to, and who knows what else with other people. At this point, it's naive to think we'd be the only people pushing against the norms of what the Archive has set out.

"It's probably what the Engineers meant: something about us is beyond what they're comfortable with, why they waited until the last second to send us an Archive even though we were already next on the gnosiphage's menu. If they were willing to risk sending the Archive to a race they had pre-existing threat levels for, that implies a couple of pretty big things."

"Pretend I'm maybe not as smart as you. What, exactly, does it imply?"

"Well first, that they studied us to some extent prior to all of this. The Archive had skills and information redacted before the Engineers first made contact, so they had to set that up before the Archives got here. I don't know how long they had studied us before the invasion, but there's stuff in the Archives that makes me think the Engineers have been observing humanity for a long, long time.

"Skills like Atlantean wrestling, mammoth hunting, stuff like that. Things that nobody in recent history would know of. And yes, I checked on both of those skills: the Archive lists Atlantis as an actual place that developed a style of wrestling similar to Grecian pankration. Mammoth hunting, well, they went extinct a while ago."

"All right, so they've been watching us for a long-ass time. What's the second implication of them having a threat level for us?"

"That something serious is going on up there," Samaira jerked her chin upwards. "How bad are things that they would risk violating whatever security procedures they have by giving us the Archive?"

Once more, Anya felt like she was out of her depth, and more than a little intimidated by Samaira's extrapolation of the limited information in front of her. Anya hadn't even seen it, and she was directly affected by it. She'd just accepted it and wondered how to hit the bad guys harder next time.

"I get obsessive about this stuff. I feel like my brain's been all over the place since this started, running from one idea to the next, just coming up with more questions," Samaira said and put her hand over Anya's.

"Well at least one of us is asking them," she replied.

"That's its own problem. I get stuck in a loop, asking and wondering and not doing anything. Like before you had everybody meet in Greenland, I was just going with the flow. Still was, I guess, but you gave me and Gary some direction."

Anya smiled at her and chuckled. "It's funny. The bird—Flame Dominion—mentioned that about you."

"Mentioned what about me?" Samaira asked and tilted her head to the side.

"They said you're like water, and if you took the Water Dominion, you'd probably talk with it like I was with mine," Anya said and shrugged her shoulders, then turned to look back at the city. She jumped a little when she felt Samaira give her a soft peck on the cheek.

"Thank you for telling me about your Dominion," she said.

"Thanks for listening. And not running away screaming that I'm possessed."

"I don't know you as well as Tori, but I feel like I know you enough. And I trust you to know yourself. You don't feel possessed?"

"No. And like I told Tori, the Dominion's never asked me anything besides what I want. If I thought it was actually dangerous, I'd never agree to stay at the outpost with all those people until I could get a respecification token."

"But you don't want to tell MacDougal? Or anybody else?"

"No. I think it would just make them paranoid. Maybe Gary. If Pan ever starts talking to his Earth Dominion, I'll tell him."

"Do you think he will?"

"No idea," Anya sighed. She was about to ask Samaira if there was anything else she felt like doing, or if maybe—just maybe—she'd like to stay somewhere with Anya for the night. The words came up to the back of Anya's throat and then Samaira spoke up.

"I should get going," she said.

"Yeah. It's getting pretty late," Anya replied. "Did you want me to take you somewhere? Back to the outpost?"

"God, no. We got a couple days off, I intend to use them. And while I'd love to spend them just with you..." Samaira trailed off for a moment before meeting Anya's gaze, "I should also spend what little free time I have visiting my family. So, I'm off to Chicago. You gonna stick around here or go back?"

"Fuck yeah I'm gonna stick around here," Anya said. She managed to keep the disappointment out of her voice, mostly because the idea of just her and Tori hanging out in New York for a day or two sounded pretty damn good to her. She would have preferred to spend it with Samaira, but she didn't want to get in the way of her seeing her family. Just because Anya would've rather licked a razor blade than see her mother didn't mean everybody else felt the same about theirs. "Did you want a lift to Chicago? Probably take thirty minutes in the Ray."

"I have my own way of getting there," Samaira said. She withdrew her long, white bow from thin air. She flicked it, and the bow extended into a much straighter staff-like shape. Samaira set it on its side and it floated horizontally at waist-height in the air. She perched on the side of it, legs crossed daintily, like a young witch on her broom.

"Fancy," Anya said.

"Not quite as fast as the Ray, and not great over long distances, but here to Chicago? No problem. Besides, I'd like some time to mull over some ideas," Samaira said as Anya stood beside her. Even floating on her transformed bow, Samaira wasn't quite level with Anya's face, and had to levitate herself upward several inches.

"Thanks for everything. I had fun."

"Me too," Samaira said, and Anya gave her a quick kiss. Samaira returned it, then slowly, reluctantly, pulled away.

"Mind picking me up in Chicago when you leave for the outpost?" she asked and floated away from the roof.

"You got it," Anya replied. "See you then."

Samaira gave her a wave, and then she shot away, trailing a thin line of blue sparks behind her that faded as they fell.

Anya stayed on the roof, staring after her for several moments.

Do we have a girlfriend now? the Flame Dominion asked.

"Might be a little early to call that one, but it's looking that way," Anya said.

Good for us.

"Yeah, good for us," Anya grinned, then went to go find Tori and tell her everything.

13

I t was a very disappointing fact of life that having a high regeneration skill meant that Anya, no matter how hard she tried, could not get drunk. She had never been addicted to booze, but sometimes, at least a couple times a month before the Archive came to Earth, she and Tori liked to get properly smashed in the noraebang, and drunkenly sing all their favorite songs.

Anya found Tori at her place after Samaira had left. Tori congratulated Anya after she learned how the date went, then insisted they go celebrate together for the rest of the evening, and Anya could crash at her place. They spent the rest of the night trying to get drunk. Tori was wildly successful at this, needing only a pair of martinis and a hard lemonade to get silly, while Anya chugged an entire bottle of vodka and felt nothing.

"I got an idea," Tori said as she leaned against Anya's shoulder, slurring the sentence into a single word so it sounded more like "*Igot-tunideer.*"

"Jesus Christ. Two martinis? Cheap-ass drunk," Anya shook her head.

"Hey. Hey. And a hard lemonade."

Anya rolled her eyes and Tori giggled.

"Let's go to some tough-ass bar, and challenge some guy there to a drinking contest. You drink, not me. I would… definitely lose," she said and belched.

"You want me to use my alien superpowers to beat some random dude in a drinking contest?"

"Yuh."

"Sounds fun," Anya said and slung Tori over her shoulder like a bag of laundry as they left the noraebang. She waved good-bye to Mr. Choi as they left and she paid the bill, tipping more generously now that she had an actual, livable wage.

"Okay, but you gotta stop flying. I'm gonna get sick if you fly," Tori groaned.

Anya was walking along the sidewalk at a normal pace. She laughed and rolled her eyes.

The still-crisp air of early spring cleared Tori's head out after a few blocks, and she was able to walk on her own, and they reached a sufficiently seedy, rough looking bar at the edge of Brooklyn. It had a lot of dim red lighting and loud music pumping out of speakers that shook the brick exterior of the building.

"Uh, maybe this is a bad idea?" Tori said as she looked up at the bar.

"Oh no, you're not backing out of this. This was your idea," Anya said. "You're gonna be my hype-man. Hype-lady. Whatever."

Anya dragged Tori behind her as they entered the bar. It wasn't crowded but there were more than enough people to get a general idea of the clientele: young and middle-aged men and a few women, most of whom had the general appearance of somebody who might be on the verge of kicking somebody else's ass. Probably whoever made eye contact with them for more than a split second.

Anya and Tori got a number of looks as they approached the bar. Anya had never actually gotten into a drinking contest before, so she wasn't sure what the procedure was. Thankfully, Tori was still a little too drunk to care, and loudly proclaimed Anya as the best drinker in the city and its boroughs, and would drink anybody else under the table.

It didn't take long after that.

A crowd of challengers formed quickly enough, the largest of which, a hulking man almost as tall as Anya herself, was first. He made it through a heroic fifteen shots of whiskey one after the other before he finally succumbed.

Anya swigged what was left of the bottle, and was met with applause when she was done.

"Should we get this guy an ambulance or something?" Anya asked and pointed at her opponent, passed out on the floor.

"Nah, he's had worse," somebody replied. Another man approached the bar next to her, raised a glass, and started the challenge anew. Anya toasted him, and ordered another bottle for herself.

———

AS THE NIGHT WENT ON, Anya acquired an entourage of roving cheerleaders, a mob of cheerful drunks that grew as they moved from one bar to the next. At their fourth bar, Anya finally started to feel something like a buzz. She had just polished off her second bottle of rum (following three bottles of vodka, two bottles of whiskey, and four bottles of tequila), when the bartender handed her a decorative glass jug full of some green liquid.

"Absinthe," the man said as Anya eyed the label. Her eyebrows raised a bit as she saw the alcohol content. Seventy-four percent. She took the cork off the top of the jug and gave it a sniff. It smelled like black licorice and herbs.

"That smells like a leprechaun's ass," Tori slurred. She'd had a couple more cocktails and several glasses of wine and was barely coherent.

Anya nodded, braced herself, and began chugging.

"Christ, lady. You some kinda mutant?" the bartender asked when she was done and slammed the empty jug on the counter to wild applause, whistles, and hoots behind her.

"Woo!" Anya shook her head and blinked. She had a bit of a head-rush, and the familiar, playful tingling, wiggly sensation that came with the early stages of getting drunk. A sort of vague, peaceful happiness settled over her.

"Check this out," she said and turned her face to the side. She held her finger up in front of her mouth, and summoned a tiny flame at the tip. She belched, and the alcohol fumes coming out of her mouth were enough to create a gout of fire that flared up above her and over the crowd.

There was a moment of stunned silence, then more applause.

"Show off," Tori said.

Anya giggled, then shook her head again. The buzz was already fading. Her stomach felt a bit sick for a moment, but then that too, passed.

"Uh oh," Anya said later as they left the bar with their impromptu party brigade. The gray light of dawn was sliding up over the city. The approaching daylight wasn't what gave Anya pause, however, but a number of news vans and crews parked across the street. As soon as Anya and the crowd emerged, a dozen cameras swiveled toward them.

"We're on TV!" somebody shouted.

"Guess the party's over," Anya said. Tori was leaning against her, half-asleep, and Anya picked her friend up and darted back inside the bar, then out the fire exit near the back. She took to the sky with Tori in tow, and landed several rooftops away.

"Urp," Tori burped and covered her mouth.

"You gonna puke?" Anya asked.

"No," Tori said, then shoved herself away from Anya's side and ducked behind an air-conditioning unit and was loudly sick.

"Just like when I first came to the city," Anya mused and laughed.

"It was the flying that did it," Tori said. "You gotta warn me before you take off like that."

"Sorry. Saw the news crews and didn't wanna stick around."

"You mentioned they showed up during your date. They always like that?"

"This is the first time I really noticed. It's also the first time I've just hung around in the open since this all went public. I guess it was inevitable. Gonna be a pain in the ass to go anywhere if this is what it's gonna be like, though."

"At least you can get away quick. Speaking of, I think I'm ready to go home."

"Don't you have work today?"

"Nope! DERD benefits give me paid sick days. I get ten a year, and they carry over. Government worker for life." Tori said, then clutched her stomach and made a face.

"All right. C'mon. I'll fly us back to your place, and I promise to take it slow."

"You sure you're safe to fly? Thought I saw you getting tipsy for a second there."

"I'm good," Anya said as she had Tori put her arm around her neck and put her arm around her friend's waist. She was very much aware of how fragile Tori felt. When she'd picked Samaira up, she had been light, true, but there had been something about her that made her seem sturdier. She guessed it was either the aether, or some other skill or stat increase.

But Tori was just a normal person.

It felt like Anya was cradling a baby bird, and any wrong move might crush her friend's spine. A wave of terror rushed over Anya at the mere thought of it.

"Whoa!" Tori said, her arm tightening around Anya's neck as Anya's grip on her loosened. "You sure about that?"

"Y-yeah," Anya said and took a deep breath.

The feeling had come back to her in a rush, the same sensation she'd had on the beach fighting Jiro and Grant.

It would be so easy to kill somebody.

Anya swallowed and pushed the thought away. She had no desire to hurt Tori, of course, but just the thought that she might, by accident, was causing her throat to close up and her palms to sweat.

"Anya?" Tori asked, her tone filled with obvious concern. She put a hand on Anya's arm. "What's going on?"

"Nothing," she said. "Just been a long night. I could definitely use some rest too."

Tori didn't push and held on as Anya flew them both to Brooklyn and her apartment. It was the same as the last time Anya had been there: clean and tastefully decorated. Tori had actually fallen asleep mid-flight, and Anya tucked her into her bed, then flopped down onto the couch in the living room.

Her mind spun with the events of the last several days, and what was to come. She had to have a psych evaluation, more meetings about the psychic parasites and teaming up with Renn, whatever the news was probably going to say about her drunken night out…

Anya shut her eyes and thought of the city stretching out below her, Samaira at her side, the two of them flying through the crisp night air.

She smiled to herself as her mind calmed, and she finally slept.

————

"WHY DID you make me drink so much?" Tori demanded later that evening, wincing from her hangover and hugging Anya as she stood next to the Shadow Ray on the roof of the apartment building. Anya laughed and patted her on the back.

"It's not my fault you can't hold your liquor," Anya said.

"Next time you're in town we're gonna have to throttle back on the partying. I can definitely feel myself getting older every time we do this."

"Next time I'm in town, I suspect Samaira will want to tag along and chew your ear off about whatever aether stuff you've learned."

"Deal. Fly safe. Don't let the feds work you too hard!" Tori called out as Anya boarded the Shadow Ray, and waved at her through the cockpit as she lifted into the sky.

It was less than a half-hour to Chicago at almost full-speed, thanks to Gary's upgrade. Anya noticed again that while incredibly fast, the upgrade definitely chewed through the Shadow Ray's battery.

Samaira had messaged Anya through the menu earlier, and said she'd meet her in Jackson Park when she was ready to pick her up. Anya landed the Ray in a wooded area near a Japanese pagoda, and spotted Samaira waiting on a precisely manicured lawn.

"Hey! Thanks for getting me. How was New York?" Samaira asked as she strapped herself into the seat while Anya took off once more.

"Probably made the news for starting an impromptu bar crawl and drinking about twenty gallons of booze," Anya said. Samaira stared at her and Anya grinned.

"You're... joking?"

"Nope. Blame Tori. How was Chicago and the family?"

"Chicago was great, as always. Family was... nice."

Anya felt the weight of the silence that followed and she turned the pilot's seat around.

"Sam. You're allowed to talk about your family around me. I'm not gonna have traumatic flashbacks or anything if you mention them."

Samaira seemed relieved to hear it and went on at some length as she described her day with her parents and siblings. Anya smiled as they flew; it was nice to hear about a normal family that had a baseline of compassion and respect for each other.

Samaira started to get sleepy after several minutes of talking, apologizing as she yawned.

"Sorry. Little brothers and sisters kept me up late last night showing them aether tricks and telling stories. How long is it to the outpost?" she asked.

"About two hours at our current speed. We could go faster but I don't want to drain the battery," Anya replied.

"Makes sense. You mind if I catch a nap? The drone of the engine is making me drowsy."

"Go ahead. I'll wake you a few minutes before we land."

Samaira yawned again and was asleep in moments, her breathing deep and steady. She really must have worn herself out tending to her family.

Must be nice, Anya thought.

It could be nice for you, too, the bird whispered to her. *No rules that say you have to stick with the family you're born into*

Blood is thicker than water, Anya thought back.

You know that quote gets misinterpreted a lot, right? The blood of the covenant is thicker than the water of the womb. It means the opposite of what most people think it does: the bonds you make by choice are stronger than those you're born into.

Anya thought about it for a moment, and then pulled away from the idea. Having a family you couldn't stand wasn't fun, but having a family you loved had its own dangers.

I got enough on my mind already, thanks, Anya thought. The bird didn't respond, but she felt something from it: a silent disapproval, or worse, disappointment. For the rest of the journey, there was only the drone of the engines and the muffled roar of the wind outside.

Anya woke Samaira shortly before they landed, the latter yawning a mumbled thanks and stretching as the Ray descended on the hangar of Outpost #1.

Back in New York, Anya could have almost forgotten they were on the tail end of winter. No such luck up north. Sometimes she felt like it would never be spring again. The invasion had a way of making things seem longer than they were.

No sooner had Anya and Samaira emerged from the Shadow Ray upon landing, than a squat, rotund figure came waddling at her from across the hangar, stubby arms spread wide in preparation to hug.

"Anya! Samaira!" Pan all but squealed as he hurried forward, his shuffling steps awkward. He was still bundled against the cold in his puffy coat, pants, and lopsided ushanka.

"Hey, little guy," Anya knelt and swept Pan up in a hug, and the pangolin laughed with delight as she raised him up and spun him around. She set him down and he hugged Samaira's leg. Chandrali appeared from somewhere and arched her back against her other leg, purring loud enough to be heard over the wind.

"We got a present for you," Samaira said, and reached inside her coat.

"A present?" Pan asked. Samaira withdrew a rectangular box and presented it to Pan. "It's a box? Thank you! I like boxes. I think."

"It's what's inside the box," Samaira said and pointed at the words. Anya glanced at it and smiled.

It was an ant farm.

"An ant farm?" Anya asked.

"Ants?" Pan's tiny black eyes twinkled at the word.

"Yeah, you can set it up in your room and watch them. You could eat them, but I figure you have enough of those to eat anyway," Samaira said.

"Watching them is fun too. I cculd watch them while I eat other ones," Pan wondered as he took the box. "Thank you Samaira! Thank you Anya!"

"Oh, I didn't—" Anya started to say but Samaira winked at her. "You're welcome, Pan."

"Riley! Lookit!" Pan turned to show Riley as the agent ambled forward.

"I can't believe I didn't think to get a gift for him. I was just..." Anya started to say and Samaira shook her head.

"Both of us were relaxing and taking some time for us. The only reason I got it is because I took my baby sister to the toy store like she wanted, and she pointed it out. She saw Pan on the news a while ago and is now, apparently, obsessed with pangolins. I've also been forced to swear a blood oath that she gets to meet him at some point," Samaira replied. "You can get him the next present."

"Will do."

"Hope you had a good break," Riley said to Samaira, then glanced at Anya and added, "We know you did."

"Uh oh," she said.

"Nah. MacDougal might give you the stink-eye for whatever drunken mob you were leading around New York, but you didn't actually do anything yourself," Riley waved a hand. "If the government started chastising its workers for going on a bender every time they had a break, they'd never get anything done. Bureaucracy makes everybody need a drink. You didn't break anything, so you're good."

Anya let out a little sigh of relief.

"Meeting tomorrow at nine sharp, right after your psych eval," Riley said, and pointed at Anya. "MacDougal wants to go over some things. No emergencies, thank God, but we'll need to reassess security and response procedures in the wake of what happened at Outpost Two. And maybe see if we need to conduct search-and-rescue for the missing personnel, or just... write them off."

Silence fell over the group.

"Well, you folks have a good night. See you bright and early tomorrow," Riley said, perhaps too cheerily, and strode away to the administration building.

"Back at it tomorrow, I guess. Time and tide wait for no woman," Samaira said.

"It was nice to pretend things were normal for a couple days," Anya said.

"It'll get better."

"You think?"

"I hope."

Anya smiled, but inside, she felt a familiar and unpleasant knot forming just above her guts. Hope was well and good, but it couldn't do shit on its own. She thought of the missing people of Outpost #2, and she knew it wouldn't matter how hard she or anybody hoped: they were gone. That place had been a graveyard.

Anya said goodnight to Samaira and Pan and retired to her dorm. It had been a wonderful couple of days, but there was no running from the war. Anya closed her eyes, and slept to ready herself for whatever came next.

14

The psych eval took less time than Anya thought. It was little else but an interview with the DERD's shrink, who said that she was fine, apart from some stress.

The meeting afterward was just as Riley said: no emergencies, but just going over recent developments. There were continued reports of disappearances around the globe, from Australia to Chile to Japan and more.

All of them matched the reports of what happened at Outpost #2: groups of people just gone, little to no signs of struggle.

"I'll confirm that the disappearances were gnosiphage attack sites in my report. It'll be distributed to any affected nations via the state department. Not much on it, but it may bring some closure," MacDougal said from her position at the head of the table. Riley sat beside her, while Anya and Samaira sat a bit further away. Arvo and Jiro had also joined them in-person, while a holographic screen at the opposite end of the table showed Gary, Esmeralda, and Renn.

Pan, not being much for meetings, was outside playing in the dirt and looking for ants to put in his farm.

"So, we're classifying all personnel at Outpost Two except for Yamada and Gomez as KIA?" Riley asked.

MacDougal let out a low breath and nodded.

"Yes. I don't think spending resources looking for people who are almost certainly dead is going to help anything. I'll start the paperwork on notifying the families," she said, then looked across the table at Gary. "Please tell me you have some good news, Hendricks."

"For the most part, yes, but there's a few snags," Gary said. MacDougal scowled, but gestured for him to continue. "The psychic tracker we made works. The parasite is no longer a threat. I've contained it in a small box that'll keep it alive and allow us to use it, if we have a psychic."

"And you have two right there, if I'm not mistaken," MacDougal said. "What's the problem?"

"Well, the first problem we ran into was that it would take a while to find anything with this critter. It's a receiver, not a sender. At first it was just looking for a signal to receive, but its range was shit. So we would be flying around for a while, chasing our own ass, and even then, we'd only find the one alien it was trying to receive from."

"Great," MacDougal said. "Are we sure this alien that made this thing is still even out there? Or that it still has psychic powers? These freaks can change their abilities when they choose, right?"

"The direction is too vague to tell, but yes, whatever made this thing is still out there and still broadcasting," Esmeralda said.

"The continuation of disappearances following the assault on Outpost Two would also suggest this alien remains at-large," Riley added, and MacDougal nodded. "Just gotta find the bastard."

"It's just like before, when we were flying over the States hunting signals down," Anya muttered. "Didn't find a single one."

"Actually, that's what gave us our next idea, kiddo. When you, me, Sam, and Pan were flying in circles looking for people, and then you had the idea to make them come to us," Gary said. Anya glanced at him, then at everybody else around the table as they turned to look at her.

"Originally, the parasite could receive signals only. But with Doc's help rewiring the bastard and some guidance from Esmi and Renn, we turned it into a sender. And with some confirmation from our Archive

AIs and a lot of pain-in-the-ass fiddling, we managed to make a duplicate Archive signal."

MacDougal narrowed her eyes at the screen and asked, "You've duplicated the Archive?"

Gary was quick to shake his head, the gesture emphatic.

"No, not even close. Just the signal. There's no actual Archive besides the ones we already have, but I've made the parasite broadcast a sort of psychic brainwave that looks a helluva lot like an Archive signal. That is, when it's switched on. It's currently in stasis. But when we switch it on, it emits a signal similar to the ones that were broadcast across the planet prior to the Engineers hiding them."

"Fishing for aliens with your psychic bait, huh?" Riley asked.

"That's the idea."

"And it really works? It's really a fake host signal?" Samaira asked, and Renn nodded.

"As Mssr. Hendricks said, we have had our AIs confirm that they are picking the signal up via the Archive. We cannot be certain the aliens will be able to do the same, but yes, it has the basic appearance of a host signal."

"So the Archive is some kinda psychic thing?" Anya muttered.

"We don't know what the actual Archive uses to transmit information and signal itself, but we're at least able to fake it with Renn and Esmi," Arvo said.

"And are you sure the aliens will bite?" MacDougal asked, and Gary shrugged.

"No way to know for sure until we try."

"All right. Is that the problem? You're not sure if it'll work as bait?"

"Not quite. The problem is that we'll need a psychic literally touching the damn thing to make it work. They won't be in any actual danger from whatever's left of the parasite, but if the bait works, they'll be at ground zero for an attack."

"I've already said that I'm willing to act as the bait," Renn said. "And no offense to Esmi, but between us, I am the more powerful psychic and should be able to boost the signal to its maximum."

"None taken. It's all you," Esmeralda said with obvious relief.

"We'll have back-up waiting nearby," MacDougal said. "If Renn is going, I'm sure other hosts in Europe will be happy to join. I'll make some calls and get the Canadian government's cooperation as well. We'll set up a sizable strike force and hit them hard."

"When are we doing this?" Anya asked.

"Is the device ready?" MacDougal focused on Gary, who nodded. "Then only as long as it takes to notify President Hanover and other relevant parties. Renn, does President Bisset know about your progress?"

"I've informed him. He is of a mind similar to yours."

"Hopefully this won't take longer than a day or two, tops. Now the question is just where to set it up," MacDougal tapped her chin and trailed off.

"Middle of the Pacific, or as near to it as we can get on whatever deserted island we can find out there," Gary said. MacDougal and Samaira nodded, almost in unison, as if this made total sense.

"Why there?" Anya asked.

"The disappearances," Riley said. "California, British Columbia, Japan, Chile, Australia, Philippines, New Zealand, and Outpost Two in Guam. They're all around the Pacific. There's a few more we've noted: Sri Lanka, Thailand, etc., but they're outliers."

"Some countries have been unaware of the disappearances, or lax in making news of them public," MacDougal added. "Took us longer than it should have to put it together because of that. All right, Hendricks. We'll find a suitable island to stick your bait. But I have a question: if this thing works and draws out the aliens, but it gets destroyed in the fight, what then? Do we only have one shot at this?"

"Nah. With Doc's help, we generated some samples of the parasite. We can make another one, but it'll take a while. Better to not let anything happen to this one," he said.

"At least there's a back-up plan. All right, I'm going to get the ball rolling. Everybody is to stay here at the outpost and be ready to go at a moment's notice. Any questions?"

Esmeralda raised a timid hand from the screen and MacDougal nodded at her.

"Gomez. What is it?"

"Uh, who's going to ambush the aliens if they show up?" she asked.

MacDougal smirked and said, "All of you."

———

MACDOUGAL ORDERED Anya and the other hosts to strategize and inform her of their plan of attack if the aliens showed. She wanted everybody to know their role ahead of time, and avoid as many mishaps as possible.

Anya, Samaira, Pan, Jiro, and Arvo gathered in Anya's living room after the meeting. They sat assembled around the coffee table, Anya on the sofa between Samaira and Pan, while Jiro and Arvo had taken the chairs. Chandrali was there too, taking up a lookout position on the windowsill and promptly falling asleep.

"I am happy to stand in the front line," Jiro said through his automated translator. He was still in his armor, top-to-toes, while everybody else wore regular clothes.

"Good to know. What about Esmi? You've fought with her before, right?" Anya asked.

"Ms. Gomez and I have practiced together. She is not an ideal offensive fighter. But she has utility outside of direct combat."

"I can fill in anywhere as needed," Samaira said. "But I'll probably be best at staying near the back and taking shots at whatever is most vulnerable."

"Pan?" Anya asked. The pangolin looked up at her and twiddled his claws. "We might need you to help, okay?"

"O-okay," Pan replied, unable to keep his tiny voice from quavering.

"You're a lot stronger than you were at the White House. You leveled up a lot after that. So it should be easier this time."

"I guess. I just don't know how to fight. Whenever I think about it, my stomach gets tight and I just wanna curl up in a ball."

"You may not have to fight," Samaira said. "If one of us gets hurt, just make sure your golems protect us, and get us away to Dr. Immonen."

"I don't like fighting much either, Pan," the doctor said and smiled at him, "so we will keep each other company, and help our friends."

"That sounds nice. I can do that," Pan said.

"If you're in trouble, dig down and hide," Anya added. "Maybe dig a hole around the bad guys. Otherwise, stay safe and let your golems deal with the danger, okay?"

Pan nodded and gave a determined little huff, his nostrils flaring. Anya rubbed his head and he grinned.

"And I'll do my best to keep you all in good health," Arvo said.

"Which means I guess I'm going to be leading the charge with Jiro," Anya finished. She didn't mind it. In fact, her Sun's Heart flared at the prospect of being the primary source of damage in a fight. It was what she was good at.

It was what she enjoyed.

As long as it was monster aliens and not people.

"Gary's probably going to send a lot of robots," Samaira added.

"Renn will be there too," Jiro said. "From what Ms. Gomez has told me over chat, he is built more for offense than she is."

"We'll probably get at least a couple more hosts from the EU or somewhere," Samaira said as she tapped her fingernail against her knee. "But I'm not sure about anything beyond that. This is an experiment, after all. I can't see everybody throwing all their eggs into this basket until it's a sure thing."

"MacDougal mentioned she would rather not involve any hosts from the New Allied Territories," Arvo said. "The Finnish government's position is similar. They're rather hesitant to work alongside a rogue state, at the moment."

"Do we want to try and ask anyway?" Anya asked. She still had all of their contact info in the Archive. She hadn't spoken with them at all since after the fight in DC weeks ago, despite making a few efforts. Pan had kept in close contact with Ursula the polar bear, mostly talking about how weird humans were.

"It'll be the five of us, Esmi, Renn, Gary's robots, and at least one or two other hosts. I think aside from the scuffle we had in Greenland, that's the biggest gathering of hosts in one place outside of the NAT," Samaira said.

"But if this bait signal works, it'll be the first clear sign the aliens have had of us since the Engineers blocked them. They could all decide to swarm us," Anya said.

"I don't think they will. The last time they tried a big coordinated attack, we routed them," Arvo said. "They were also fairly subdued in the attack on Outpost Two, just a handful of hosts and a few parasites. They're playing it safe, probably since we already killed one of their overseers. Well, you did. Which brings me to a concern: what if it's just mind-controlled hosts again?"

"Ms. Gomez can focus on disrupting the psychic connection between the parasites and whatever is controlling them, now that we know how they work," Jiro said. "She should be able to scramble the signal so they're not as much of a danger to us or themselves, until Dr. Immonen can remove the parasites."

Anya breathed a sigh of relief.

"Good. If he can do that, that's a huge load off of us," she said. "Jiro, if Esmi disrupts a controlled host, can you make sure Arvo's protected while he removes the parasite?"

Jiro nodded.

The rest of the session was spent going over their equipment, and asking Gary what sort of robots he would be sending. Gary promised two dozen Guardians, with another dozen in reserve if need be, as well as a small fleet of shield and medical drones that could provide support. He'd also be setting up a containment perimeter to keep whatever alien or aliens they were fighting from getting away. After a few hours, MacDougal sent them aerial photos and coordinates of a small scrap of land in the middle of the Pacific.

It wasn't so much an island as it was a ring of sand: a shallow lagoon of turquoise water within it, and the expanse of the midnight ocean outside.

"Tekokota Atoll," Samaira read from the attached memo as all of them looked at the projection on the wall. "French Polynesia. Looks like Hanover got permission from the local government."

"It's pretty," Anya said, and it was. Despite being almost nothing but sand and a few scraggly clumps of grass surrounded by the ocean, it did look like a lovely, serene place to spend an afternoon. Anya thought of the conversation she had had with Samaira when they had been in Florida weeks ago, about retiring to some sunny beach somewhere.

"Gonna be pretty much destroyed if this works," Gary said from a floating comms window nearby.

"Where will we be? I assumed we'd hide nearby but there's nowhere to hide," Anya said.

"How many people can fit in that fancy stealth car of yours, kid?"

"Me, plus six people. Maybe eight or nine if some of them don't mind squatting on the floor."

"Mm. That'll work in a pinch. You'll fly up above Renn as high as you can get, activate whatever stealth abilities that thing has, and wait. Not sure how well the aliens can sense the scrambled signals, but it's clear they have at least some ability to, or they likely wouldn't have found Outpost Two like they did. If they sense too many hosts, they may not bite."

"But if we're flying above Renn and the bait, they may not be able to differentiate between our signal and the fake one," Samaira finished.

"Bingo."

"What if we have more hosts than can fit in the Ray?" Anya asked.

"I'll jury rig something up just in case. Won't be pretty, but it should work. You leave that to me. Probably best for all of us to get some rest now. Well, you should. I got building to do."

"See you soon, Gary," Anya said, and closed the window. They threw out a few more ideas, but it was obvious all they were doing at that point was guessing. They could strategize all night and attempt to anticipate every contingency, but eventually, they'd just have to wait until whatever happened, happened.

Anya, Samaira, and Jiro were in the dining hall when MacDougal approached them hours later, looking exhausted, but pleased with herself.

"We're good to go. You'll all leave here and meet at Tekokota Atoll tomorrow at noon. Along with the American hosts and Dr. Immonen, you'll be joined by Renn and that British host, Mona," she said.

"The one with the skeletons. Ick," Samaira said and made a face.

"That creepy kid from Canada with the demons or whatever-they-are will be there too. I've reached out to other governments, but most of them gave me the same response: we're not willing to risk our hosts on an experiment and leave ourselves open to alien attack, but if this works, you have our future support. The NAT didn't even respond."

Anya nodded.

Ten of them.

It was more hosts than Anya had ever been with at one time, outside of Greenland. With that number of people with that much power, they could level a city, blow up a mountain.

And yet, Anya couldn't help but wonder if it would be enough.

15

nya arrived at Tekokota Atoll ahead of schedule. She wanted to get a feel for the place, and both she and the other hosts didn't see much point in waiting around. Anya took Jiro, Samaira, Pan, Chandrali, and Arvo along with her in the Shadow Ray. Renn and Esmeralda arrived along with a squadron of Gary's Guardians and assorted support drones.

"Safe flight?" Anya asked as Esmeralda emerged from a sealed compartment on the side of one of the Guardians, looking rather sick.

"Ugh, sort of?" she asked and then put her hands on her knees and took several deep breaths. "I just get airsick, and these things weren't designed with passengers in mind."

"Sorry about that. At least it was a short ride," Gary said from one of the Guardian's speakers. Renn emerged from another one, immediately removing his reflective gold helmet and also taking several deep breaths of fresh air.

"I am thankful for the lift, but perhaps next time, we could find another way," he said, and covered his mouth as he burped.

"Oh, stop. It wasn't that bad," Gary said.

"It was like riding inside a cannonball," Esmeralda said.

"Or being trapped inside a laundry machine," Renn added.

"Kids these days."

Anya smirked and looked up at the nearest Guardian, then at the swarm of dozens of lesser drones. Each of the drones had a rectangular, boxy shape, and a pair of small anti-gravity discs extending from their sides. They had a variety of different attachments on their front "face" and sides depending on their function: prongs to deliver electric shocks, small barrels to fire weaponry, projection arrays that would deploy forcefields, and more.

The drones flew around the inner ring of the atoll, then submerged themselves in the shallow turquoise waters. They were all but invisible within seconds, even a few that had landed right near Anya could have been mistaken for rocks.

The majority of the squadron of Guardians took up positions along the atoll's outer ring, sinking beneath the much darker waters and out of sight. Only one remained on the beach, projecting a holographic screen with Gary's face on it from its head.

"All my bots will stay hidden until the aliens show up and close on Renn. They'll be entirely focused on protecting him until the rest of you drop down and can back him up, and then they'll do whatever's needed. I can directly control about half of them at a time. If any of you are in trouble, don't be afraid to use one of the Guardians as a shield. I can build more later," he said.

"Thanks Gary," Anya said, then turned to Renn and asked, "You got the thingy?"

"The 'thingy,'?" he asked.

"The bait," Samaira clarified.

"Ah, of course. Gary?" Renn approached the Guardian, the same one he had ridden inside of, and patted it on the leg. Another compartment opened and a matte black rectangle the size and shape of a shoebox emerged. It was featureless but for a barely visible button on top.

"That's it?" Anya asked. "The parasite fits in that little box?"

"Yeah. After we stripped it down to its basic nervous system and the parts of its brain we needed to project the psychic signal, there wasn't much left," Gary said.

"I know the aliens are literal monsters, but this all seems kinda ethically dubious," Samaira said and winced as she looked at the box.

"I don't like it much either," Arvo added, "but when I was inspecting the creature, I found no sign of sapience. Just a basic instinct to attack us. It has no pain receptors, no consciousness outside of the singular function the gnosiphage programmed it with. If it even had the basic awareness of a mouse, I'd be against this. But it's necessary, and it's only alive in the most rudimentary sense. Closer to a Venus flytrap or a reactive potato than any animal we think of."

"Still gross," Anya said. She tried not to think of how the parasites had looked tearing their way out of the backs and skulls of their victims. "How's it work?"

"I press the button and open a small portion of the box on the back where I will be able to make physical contact. That will make syncing up to its psychic signal easier, and then I will add my own ability to the signal and project it as far as I am able. Then… we see," Renn said.

"They will come," Jiro said, scanning the sea and the horizon. His mechanical translator didn't have much emotion in it, but the underlying certainty in Jiro's actual voice was unmistakable.

"I'm as ready as I can get," Gary said. "But we're still two people short. They coming?"

Renn opened the map window of his Archive and pointed at a pair of dots speeding toward them. He looked up and Anya followed his gaze. At first she didn't see anything but a small wisp of cloud, but then that faded and a huge, black, gothic carriage emerged from it.

The carriage was pulled by a team of four skeletal horses, whipped into a rattling frenzy by a cloaked, faceless coachman wearing spiked metal gauntlets and boots. Spectral blue flames that emitted no heat trailed behind the carriage's wheels, as well as from the eye sockets and from between the ribs and jaws of the horses. Despite its antiquated appearance, the macabre vehicle flew across the sky with supernatural speed, and had pulled to a stop a few yards away from the group within seconds of Anya spotting it.

"Ah, the tropics!" said the woman who emerged. The last time Anya had seen Mona, she'd been in an elegant dinner gown, but now she was dressed for battle. A suit of plate armor and a dark black and purple cape covered her from the neck down, the edges of both deco-rated with swirling filigree.

"Reminds me of visiting Singapore," she continued and smiled cheerily at everybody, hands on her hips. She sauntered over to Renn and poked the tip of his nose with her finger. "You always take me to the nicest places."

"Mon chou, merci," Renn sighed, exasperated. He could not entirely stop a smile from tugging at the corners of his mouth as Mona gave him a kiss on the cheek.

"This is an island? It's barely a beach," another voice said from the carriage, and a familiar horned figure in a red cape and dark leather armor emerged. Harrison looked even more devilish than he had when Anya had last seen him at the DERD gala. His skin had reddened more, and his black horns had grown larger. Not for the first time, Anya wondered if his physical appearance was due to changes made through the Archive's cosmetic options for hosts, or a natural result of his skills.

"Just means less stuff is gonna get destroyed during the fight," Anya said. Harrison sniffed at her and said nothing.

Gary cleared his throat and everybody looked up at the Guardian.

"Good. We're all here. Renn has the bait, and we've confirmed it works, so we'll get started soon. In addition to all my Guardians and drones that'll be backing you up, I've set up some heavy duty force-field projectors and motion trackers about a mile out to sea in every direction. If this works, and the aliens close in, we'll have some warn-ing. I'll activate the forcefields and trap anything inside once we've got at least a few within the ring of generators. If it seems like too many are coming, the forcefields will keep the extras out for a little while.

"But remember: we're not here to kill all the aliens. We want to see if our bait works, and then kill at least one to get its data stream. If things are looking bad, we retreat. Everybody on board with that?"

Gary asked and everyone nodded or made some form of assent. "Right. Take up your positions and let's do this. When everybody's in place, Renn'll activate the bait."

"I won't be far," Mona said and cupped the side of Renn's face.

"Is that carriage of yours gonna stick out?" Gary asked.

"No. It can hide just as well as that sleek little car."

Gary grunted and then the Guardian stomped to the outer edge of the atoll and sank beneath the water.

Everybody went back to their respective vehicles, though Anya lagged behind as she looked at Renn. He put his helmet back on, and turned the mirrored faceplate toward her.

"You'd better get into position," he said.

"Yeah. Just… thanks for sticking your neck out. We got your back," Anya said.

"I know."

"Anya?" Samaira asked as she stood just outside the Shadow Ray.

"Coming!" she hurried to the cockpit and took off, and then began to wait.

THERE WAS nothing for the first hour.

Or the second.

Pan fell asleep during the third.

"I didn't expect an immediate response but how long do you think we should wait?" Samaira asked.

"Probably until Renn gets too tired to broadcast anymore," Anya replied.

"During the tests at Gary's factory, Renn said it didn't take much effort to broadcast. He compared it to going for a leisurely stroll in a park," Arvo said.

"I can second that. I did some tests with the beacon as well," Esmeralda said. "It's not difficult, just kinda boring."

Pan snored from his position beside Samaira and Chandrali, the latter of which had curled up on Samaira's lap and was purring contentedly. Jiro remained silent, as usual, his thick arms folded across his chest. He had to hunch to fit in the Shadow Ray, even while seated.

"The Ray's probably got a few more hours of juice with all the stealth features activated," Anya said as she glanced across the control panels. They weren't taxing the engines at all apart from just hovering in place, but the vehicle couldn't stay invisible forever.

Renn had notified all of them sporadically that there was no change as the hours dragged by. Esmeralda had kept her psychic feelers retracted, worried that her sweeping the area might cause interference with the beacon, or somehow alert any approaching gnosiphages.

"Maybe this was too obvious," Samaira said. "It practically screams that it's a trap. A big, bright host signal, all on its own, in the middle of nowhere? I wouldn't take that bait."

"You're also not an alien," Arvo said. "When I connected to the overseer in Washington, it felt very single-minded, in more ways than one. It was a single consciousness, but it was also bent on consuming. If these creatures do literally eat knowledge in some way, and the hosts are their preferred food source, they must be starving. I think if I hadn't eaten for weeks, I wouldn't care if a nice big meal laid out for me was bait or not."

Anya stayed focused on the display screens in front of her while the others continued to talk in hushed tones. The Ray had multiple cameras along its outer surface, including several on its underside. She clicked on one and enlarged the screen to have a wide view of the atoll below.

Renn sat on the largest strip of sand, his hand on the black box beside him. He looked as if he were just enjoying a day at the beach, his hand atop the black box and staring out to sea. He'd been that way for hours now, and had even laid back a couple times.

Anya shook her head and then checked the other cameras to see if she could catch sight of Mona's carriage. A cloud of cold mist had swirled around it as it took off from the beach hours ago, and then it had vanished. The Ray's scanning systems couldn't pick it up, and there was nothing to be seen outside but the occasional bit of cloud.

She flicked back through the displays to Renn again, and paused.

He was standing up.

His head was also cocked to one side, as if he had heard something.

Anya's ear beeped.

"Message from Gary!" Felix said inside her ear.

"Something triggered some motion sensors," Gary said when Anya raised her comms window. He was glancing at several different displays on his end, his eyes narrowed and focused. There was a lot of shuffling behind Anya as everybody moved in to peer around the pilot's seat.

"Wha-whass happenin'?" Pan mumbled as he sat up.

"Alien or a whale or what?" Anya asked.

"Too big to be a whale."

"Too big...? Oh geez," Esmeralda said and began to take several deep, rhythmic breaths.

Renn appeared in a window beside Gary and said, "They're here."

That was when the ocean exploded.

16

The ocean swelled upward in a rolling hill of water before it burst into a white froth of foam and salt spray. The thing that reared up out of the depths was a segmented tower of overlapping armored chitin that rose high above the waves and trailed down to unknown lengths beneath them.

It was an enormous centipede, or an alien equivalent. Countless legs squirmed along its sides, and a pair of massive jaws with serrated interiors emerged from its front end, along with a set of large antennae. Its body was bigger around than a shipping container, and an unearthly, frigid blue light seeped out from between the plates of its armored hide.

The front end of the towering gnosiphage was mostly dominated by a circular mouth, ringed with churning lines of triangular fangs. A tiny face, eerily human, was set above the mouth and the four pairs of glowing eyes all focused on Renn and the tiny black box. Anya recognized the tell-tale black armored body and blue light: the snake from DC had the same features, before she had burnt it to cinders.

The centipede below was an overseer.

"Go!" Anya shouted and punched the button that opened the hatch at the back of the Shadow Ray. She grabbed Pan and Arvo, just as they had planned, while Samaira jumped out carrying Chandrali. Jiro followed, a shrieking Esmeralda under his arm.

Chandrali transformed into her armored tiger form as she fell, blue and white fire swirling around her powerful paws as she ran through the air, Samaira atop her, bow drawn.

"I'm scaaaaaaarrrrred!" Pan wailed as they fell.

"It'll be okay! Just dig!" Anya shouted back, feeling a pang of guilt even as her adrenaline rushed through her, her Sun's Heart glowed, and the wind whistled past her ears. She landed with a resounding boom, sand exploding around her, and released Pan and Arvo at the same time. Pan leaped into the ground and disappeared, while Arvo darted to one side, becoming a blur and then nothing at all.

The ground shook beside Anya as Jiro landed and set Esmeralda aside, and gave her a perfunctory pat on the shoulder as her scream petered out. Samaira circled overhead, an arrow nocked in her bow, while Mona and Harrison descended in the carriage. Renn had also summoned eight duplicates of himself, and each took up a defensive position round him.

Shimmering waves of light emerged from the ocean some distance away from the atoll, and rose up to meet above its center high in the sky. The water along the edges bubbled and then burst upward as the Guardians emerged, trailing sheets of water off their hulking mechanical frames.

The small, human-esque face of the centipede overseer studied the numerous hosts before it, its many eyes narrowing with suspicion and malice.

"Thieves," the centipede said in a rasping voice Anya had last heard from the snake overseer outside the White House. It let out a piercing shriek, and several sections of its back and sides opened with wet, cracking sounds. Plates of armor rose up like doors, and a small horde of gnosiphages emerged.

They were all shapes and sizes, just like the curious mimics Anya had fought before. One was a red telephone booth that walked on cloven feet, its interior filled with what appeared to be loose skin. Another was a dining table and chairs, all moving as one, and the underside of the table was lined with enormous fangs and a lashing tongue.

A floating chandelier made of crystalline fingers.

A large video camera that walked on storkish legs and had a single, segmented insect eye where the lens should have been.

A flock of books, flapping covers made of skin like wings.

A hovering mirror that reflected a distorted image of the atoll.

And more.

More every second.

There were at least thirty of the things that rushed out of the centipede and formed a defensive perimeter around it. It was a menagerie of nightmare mimics, each one familiar enough to be over-looked in passing, but impossible to ignore if stared at closely for more than an instant. Anya thought of the first alien, the puppet, and how eerily terrifying it had been to see something familiar and mundane twisted just enough to be wrong.

She'd gotten used to the idea since then, and she could only grin at the prospect of burning each of the unnatural freaks down to their bones. She wasn't some confused, under-leveled host anymore. And she wasn't alone.

She paused, as three more figures emerged from the centipede's body, most notable for their humanity among the inhuman figures. There was an elderly Asian woman with gray hair, a bald, middle-aged man with tan skin and thick arms, and a younger black man with a body as thin and fragile looking as a reed.

Anya recognized the peculiar movements of the three humans as the same as Jiro's from when he had been controlled. The old woman's eyes glowed blue, and the middle-aged man grew to several times his normal height. The reed-like young man made a white spear appear from a swirl of mist, and leveled it at Renn. There was a second of calm, where each side studied the other.

"Scatter!" Anya shouted, and Esmeralda and Jiro darted in opposite directions: the latter toward the towering centipede, the former as far away from it as possible.

The old woman pointed a finger at Anya, and there was a crackling noise a second before a web of jagged electrical bolts shot out towards her. Anya cursed and dodged to one side, just as most of the bolts struck the sand where she had been. A few tendrils of lightning still managed to grab her, and delivered a powerful shock that turned her elegant dodge into a tumbling fall. Her muscles spasmed, but only for a moment. Her regalia took the worst of the damage, smoking and crackling with residual energy as she got to her feet.

It still hurt like a son of a bitch, though.

No absorbing that, then, she thought.

Gary's Guardians rushed forward along with his drones, and all of them converged on the monstrous attackers. Mona and Harrison emerged from the carriage as it touched down and then flew away. Jiro reached the giant centipede after literally tearing his way through an alien shaped like a jacuzzi full of blood. He grabbed one of the giant creature's legs, the limb longer than he was tall, and tore it away from the alien's body with a sickening wet snap.

The centipede roared at Jiro, and several of the neighboring legs struck him hard enough to send him soaring away over the atoll and into the water on the other side. He'd just splashed down when Anya saw that the gooey stump was regrowing another leg.

Anya tried to warn the others of the centipede's healing ability when she was forced to dodge a bolt of glowing green energy one of the aliens flung at her, followed by another bolt of lightning. The first missed, but the second seemed to seek her out, regardless of how quick she was. Anya cursed as the electrical current forced her jaw shut and made her twitch for a moment before fading.

The muscle spasms wore off just as a shadow loomed over Anya. A hand.

The controlled, middle-aged host had increased his size even more, turning himself into something of a giant. His hand slammed down on Anya, attempting to crush her beneath it. She braced both of her hands against the palm that almost covered her, and then gave it a hard shove to one side as she flew out from underneath it.

"The centipede can regenerate!" Anya shouted as she threw herself at the giant host's side, battering him in the ribs with her entire body and sending him rolling.

"We'll have to put a stop to that then, won't we?" Mona asked as she flew past Anya. She flicked her wrist and a gleaming silver and onyx scythe appeared in her hand, its blade trailing a cloud of frost. Her huge black and purple cape unfurled, and a legion of undead figures emerged: skeletons in heavy plate armor wielding claymores and tower shields, hooded figures with grasping hands made of smoke and shadow, pale-skinned humanoids with stretched out bodies and mouths like lampreys, giant wolves and bats partially covered in rotting flesh, and other undead Anya only caught glimpses of.

Red flame surrounded Harrison as he followed Mona, and the ground opened up to allow his own horrible horde out: impish demons, hulking draconic figures, serpentine creatures made of dark crystal, goat-legged fiends with halberds and tridents, and more. He wielded a long spear made of polished brass, and hurled it at the centipede while his troop of demons swarmed over the nearest lumbering monstrosity the overseer had unleashed.

It was chaos.

The air swarmed with Gary's drones, and all of his Guardians were preoccupied with the smaller aliens the centipede had brought with it. The Guardians themselves were outnumbered two-to-one, and there were still more of the small aliens left over to battle the hordes Harrison and Mona had summoned. Samaira had filled the sky with a hail of glowing blue arrows, each of them splintering into countless tiny shards and zipping through the air to their targets.

Jiro had emerged from the ocean, clinging to the side of the centipede like a tenacious tick on an oversized hound and trying to rip its huge armor plates off with his bare hands.

The centipede was not idle, and Anya gaped in shock as its tail end rose up out of the water. The creature had stretched itself along one entire side of the atoll, nearly a kilometer in length. Its tail whipped up out of the Pacific, trailing a thick sheet of foaming water behind it, and coiled around Jiro.

"Shit!" Anya said as a mantis-armed jukebox lunged at her, demanding her attention. Its limbs were coated in bronze-like metal, and vibrated slightly. Music blasted from its sides, in some awful, hideous language that made Anya's ears ache. It wasn't loud enough to conceal a crackling noise behind her, however.

Anya dodged to the side and shoved the juke box between her and the incoming electrical bolt she knew was coming. The lightning intended for her was instead drawn to the jukebox gnosiphage's metallic arms, zapping between them and skittering across the alien's body. The jukebox slumped forward, arms twitching, body smoking.

Anya wasn't taking any chances.

She condensed a large mass of heat into the palm of her hand until it looked like a glowing white marble floated in front of her palm, then struck the alien in the back as hard as she could and released the tiny fireball. The sudden release of such volatile energy burst outward, melting through the creature's armored body and blasting it in half.

She turned to face the old woman before she could fire off more lightning, but she had gone somewhere else after her first shot missed.

"Felix? Is it dead?" Anya asked and looked at the ruined jukebox.

"Locked out of any Archive functions since the overseer showed up, remember?" Felix asked. Anya cursed. She was pretty sure the lesser gnosiphage she'd just blasted apart was very much dead, but she would have preferred confirmation.

She glanced quickly around the battlefield for the nearest person that needed help. Anya couldn't find lightning lady, and the giant was currently too close to the centipede, struggling to pry Jiro off it. Anya didn't want to do anything with Arvo that close to the overseer. It had been preoccupied with Jiro and the Guardians for the most part so far, and if it was anything like the snake overseer had been, likely still had a few tricks to show off.

She settled on the reed-like host. Despite his thin and fragile appearance, he was somewhat formidable. His white spear was long, flexible, and quick, and he turned into some kind of mist or smoke when he dodged an attack. He solidified just long enough to strike with his spear, destroying a drone or one of Mona's or Harrison's summoned creatures, and then he darted back again.

"Doc!" Anya shouted. Her first thought was to use her comm window to talk to him, but that was out with the overseer right in front of them. "Doc I'm going for spear-guy! Help me if you can!"

Anya didn't wait for a response, trusting that Arvo would stick to their plan and keep his focus on any mind-controlled hosts. She didn't know if Pan would even be able to hear her if she shouted, but hoped the little guy would make himself useful if he had to. His golems were out, running interference and generally getting in the way of the lesser gnosiphages and defending anybody who fell or needed help.

Anya soared overhead, passing by Esmeralda as she focused on the centipede while Renn and a dozen of his clones defended the both of them. Anya was pleased to see the mind-controlled hosts having trouble: tripping over themselves, or grasping at their heads occasionally, twitching at inopportune times and missing an attack.

They were still a threat, however. The old lady managed to short-circuit a Guardian and a small squad of drones. The giant had gained some sort of crystalline, glassy growths along his knuckles and finally managed to pin Jiro beneath one hand while pummeling him with the other.

Anya spotted the spear-user at the edge of the melee, far from the tail end of the centipede. The tail was wrapped around a Guardian, slowly crushing it as the robot drilled into its armored hide with a series of lasers. The spear-user was trying to close on Samaira as she rode by on Chandrali.

"Hey!" Anya shouted at him as she closed in, and swung at his head with a wide, flaming haymaker. His body dispersed into a cloud of mist, her fist arcing through it and hitting nothing but air.

That was fine.

Kan had been quick, but predictable in his attacks at Outpost #2. He had done the same trick over and over: vanish into bloody sand, and pop up behind Anya. The parasites controlling the hosts were nasty, but they—or their controller—didn't have a lot of imagination.

Anya had watched the spear-user do the same thing to Mona's undead, Harrison's demons, and others with varying degrees of success. Dodge an attack by turning into mist, disperse, then reform behind or to the side and lunge with the spear.

Anya's heat sense told her she had guessed right, as a heat source coalesced behind her. She dodged just enough to avoid serious injury, then grunted when the weapon connected with her side. It was sharp enough—whatever it was—to pierce her regalia and stab into her muscled side.

Anya grabbed it, very careful not to grab the host himself in case he decided to vanish again and leave his spear behind. She cried out with pain, somewhat for show but mostly because it really fucking hurt, and hoped Arvo would be quick.

She caught a shimmer moving through the air out of the corner of her eye, and grinned.

"Got him!" Arvo said, his hand and arm appearing from the air and touching the side of the spear-user's neck. Anya yanked the spear out of her with a hiss and a curse, then took up a defensive stance next to Arvo as the other host collapsed into a heap. Five golems formed into a ring around her, along with a wall of condensed sandstone. Two of the golems stepped away to tackle one of the lesser gnosiphages nearby, while the other three closed ranks around Arvo and the spear-user.

"Great work, Pan!" Anya shouted, hoping the pangolin could hear her from wherever in the ground he was. She leaped to assist the other golems, delivering a series of rapid strikes at the gnosiphage—a random knot of metallic pipes that spewed noxious gas—and then shooting a shotgun blast of fire into the alien. It blew open, spraying pale white guts and black ichor over the golems. The sandy humanoid constructs ignored the mess, and pummeled the alien's remains with brutish fists.

"He's clear!" Arvo said as he fully appeared kneeling next to the spear-user, and holding a limp parasite in his hand.

"Pull!" Anya said. Arvo threw the parasite away, and Anya fried it to ash the second it was clear. "Go hide! Gary!"

"On it," the doctor gave her a pained smile and vanished again. One of Gary's Guardians swooped down, grabbed the unconscious spear-user, and soared away, all in one smooth motion.

The centipede emitted an ear-piercing shriek from its giant mouth, and the air literally vibrated from the force of the sonic emission. Anya's sense of equilibrium faltered as the shriek rattled inside her skull.

Something hard and heavy struck her in the side and she was knocked down like a gnat and sent spinning across the sands. She slid to a stop in the center of the atoll, water splashing around her as she overcame the aftereffects of the sonic attack.

Another of the gnosiphages, this one a washing machine with clus-ters of whipping tentacles emerging from its front, had targeted her. It shot a jet of foul green fluid past her from a tube near its back, and Anya recognized it as a similar acid to what the snake overseer had used against her. It would slow her regeneration, drain her energy, and sting like a mother fucker.

Anya ducked around another blast of acid, but the gnosiphage anticipated the trajectory of her movement, and spread its tentacles in a wide net to catch her. The slippery appendages were ropes of pure muscle, each one thicker than Anya's powerful arms, and their suckers latched onto her. Worse, they had the same acid it had just spat at her, and Anya screamed as the corrosive fluid began to eat at her exposed flesh and chew at her armored regalia.

"I gotcha!" Esmeralda said, and a pink psychic construct of a guil-lotine materialized around the alien's writhing limbs and snapped down with efficient finality. The alien reeled back as its tentacles were severed, and then a huge pink cartoon hammer appeared above the alien and slammed it flat with a sickening crunch. The hammer continued to beat it into the sand for good measure, and more of Pan's golems appeared on the sides to continue beating the shit out of the alien until it was nothing more than a smear of broken white plating and pale guts.

"Ow, ow, ow!" Anya hissed as she peeled the still acidic tentacles off her arm and waist. A bolt of cool blue energy struck her in the chest, and the pain faded as her regeneration sped up. Her regalia even partially repaired itself. Anya grinned as Samaira soared past on Chandrali, firing more healing arrows at anybody who was injured.

"Behind you!" Samaira shouted and fired another lance of cerulean light over Anya's shoulder. It pierced the front of a gnosiphage shaped like a moped, but with a huge eye instead of a headlight, and a pair of razor-sharp antlers in place of handlebars. The lance expanded into a bubble that surrounded the moped, and then began to constrict, crushing it and holding it in place.

Anya kicked the bubble high into the air like an over-sized soccer ball, and Samaira shot a volley of arrows at it, further impaling the alien within, and then causing the bubble to explode in a shower of sparks and inhuman gore.

Anya blew Samaira a kiss and then took cover behind a golem as another bolt of lightning shot towards her. The golem took the hit, but exploded on impact.

"Right. You next," Anya said. "Doc! Coming up!"

She didn't need subtlety for the lightning lady. She was relatively fast, but lightning seemed to be her only real trick. Probably a low-level host that had gotten unlucky. Anya face-tanked the next couple of bolts thrown at her, her teeth clamping together as the current forced her jaw shut.

Pan seemed to know what Anya was planning, as a large pair of earthen hands rose up on either side of the old woman, clamping around her and holding her in place before she could zip away. Her lightning attacks did nothing to the hands, and Anya felt a sense of triumph as the air behind the woman shimmered and Arvo's hand materialized inches away from her neck.

The parasite ripped its way out of the old woman's skull a fraction of a second before Arvo could touch her. Anya shouted in horror and fury as the parasite reared out of the woman's spine, trailing blood and bone and skin behind it. Its wriggling limbs flailing as it turned towards Arvo. The doctor's eyes widened in realization and terror as he tried to fling himself away.

Anya flash-fried the thing, taking Arvo's eyebrows and some of his hairline with it, but keeping him intact. The parasite, what was left of it, crumbled to the ground along with the body of the old woman.

"Th-thank you. I thought I had it, b-but I-I..." Arvo stammered.

"Not your fault, Doc. We got one more," Anya said, and turned to the giant host. Renn and Esmeralda had disrupted whatever psychic connection the centipede overseer had, and the giant flailed in the water beside it. The centipede let out another furious roar, and the parasite burst out of the giant's neck, killing him and causing him to shrink back to normal size as it did. Esmeralda screamed and clutched at her head as Renn crushed the parasite with ease.

"You fucker!" Anya screamed at the centipede.

"It is losing and it knows it," Arvo said, his voice heavy. "It's taking from us what it can."

"It's fucking done is what it is!"

She locked eyes with the centipede, flames literally flaring out her nostrils and ears as she shot herself off the beach, straight at the towering monster.

It widened its pincer-like jaws, and a dot of crackling green energy appeared between its pincers. Anya was too blinded by anger to even consider what the new, toxic looking substance might be, and she didn't care. She was going to fly right in the thing's face and put her fist through its eye sockets.

The orb of crackling energy expanded to several times its original size, and Anya's certainty suddenly faltered. It shot towards her in a wide web of crackling lines, too fast and too big for her to dodge.

A skeletal hand larger than Anya's torso held onto her leg and swung her like a baseball bat at a gnosiphage disguised as a wardrobe.

Her forward momentum was redirected and her head and back struck the alien hard enough to crack its faux wooden exterior and reveal insides made of metallic bones and something like a beehive full of swarming alien hornets. Anya temporarily lost control of the heat she had been building, and it exploded on impact with the gnosiphage, turning the wardrobe and its hive to cinders.

The skeletal hand released Anya onto the beach just as a huge crack split the air, and the toxic bolts of energy passed above.

Right where Anya had been.

The poison energy, or whatever it was, seemed to warp whatever was next to it, including the very air. Dozens of Gary's drones and five of his Guardians were destroyed in a blink. They weren't so much torn apart as just converted into slag. The drones became hissing puddles, while random bits of the Guardians fell to the ground, the remains warped and melted into unrecognizable shapes.

"The fuck?" Anya demanded and glared at Mona and the hulking armored skeleton looming over her in a defensive posture. She had replenished her undead horde somewhat, but looked like she'd paid for it. There were dark circles under her eyes, her dark skin waxen and sweaty.

"Needed to borrow you for a tick, darling. You're very welcome for saving your ass in the process," Mona said. "Carry on!"

She gave Anya a playful wave, then swung her scythe at an encroaching mob of lesser gnosiphages. A spray of icicles veined with some sort of violet quartz sprung up in a wall before her, impaling the aliens and forcing them back. Anya grumbled, but then turned to face the centipede again. To her surprise, she saw several of Renn's clones soaring around its head, distracting it.

"Anya," Renn said, suddenly beside Anya, and made her jump.

"Shit! Dude!" she said.

"Many of us are wounded, and the doctor is tiring. We can still win, but not without cost. We need to act quickly or we risk losing some of our own."

"You got an idea? I thought you and Esmi could mess up that thing's brain or something?"

"We are. It is… formidable. It also has several brains, all of which I am attacking. It's slowing it down, but it's not enough."

"No shit! These fuckers aren't helping either!" Anya said and weighted herself to the ground as a coffee table-shaped gnosiphage charged at her on equine legs. It had the speed of a race car, and Anya grunted in pain as it slammed into her, even as her regalia and kinetic dispersal took the brunt of the impact. The gravity well she'd created in a four foot circle around her also managed to slow the table down somewhat, but not enough to take all the force out of its charge.

"That hurt, you asshole!" Anya snarled and brought both her flaming fists down on the table in an overhead smash that bent it in the middle. It looked as if it was made of wood (including the hoofed, muscular legs holding it up), but dented more like metal.

Anya heated one of her hands to absurd temperatures, so much that it glowed, and plunged it into the table's surface, melting through it and seizing hold of something inside that was soft and organic. She detonated her glowing fist inside the alien, causing its metallic exterior to bubble outward and shriek in protest. It thumped over to its side, smoking and unmoving.

"Yes, well, at least they all seem fairly weak," Renn continued. Several of his clones were scattered around the battlefield, providing support to others or ganging up on the aliens "But we won't win just by focusing on them."

"Tell me something I don't know. I tried taking the centipede out just now but your girlfriend yanked me out of the sky," Anya said and ducked under a bony spine that an alien had thrown at her. One of Renn's clones lifted it into the air and proceeded to slam it into the side of the centipede, distracting it from pursuing Jiro as he continued to tear its legs off and use them as spears.

"She saved your life," the Renn standing next to her said. "But you had the right idea. I'm going to need you to do that again when I tell you, along with Jiro, since I think you have the greatest capability of hurting it as quickly as possible."

"You got a plan?" Anya asked, and noticed one of Renn's clones speaking to Jiro across the atoll as he casually mutilated an alien.

"Yes. I can hold the centipede and prevent any movement or attack, as well as cut off its psychic connection, but only for a few seconds. Maybe. After that, I'll be useless."

"What're you gonna do?" Anya asked.

"No time to explain now," Renn said and as if on cue, the shadow of the centipede fell over them. Its human face leered down, and its giant pincers spreads wide as another orb of green energy formed between them.

"Thieves," it rasped again.

Anya and Renn both darted away in opposite directions as a crackling web of green bolts blasted toward them. A wall of sandstone erupted up from the ground between Anya and the bolt as its crackling fingers raked toward her. The bolt hit the sandstone and blasted it to pieces just as Anya flew out of the way.

"Are you okay?" Pan asked, peering up through a tiny hole he had made in the ground at Anya's feet.

"I'm good, buddy. Thanks for the save! Stay under there!" she said. Pan gave her a quick nod and the ground sealed up over him.

"Are you ready?" Renn asked at her side—or maybe it was one of his clones—as he flew beside her.

"What do I need to do?" Anya asked.

"Just hit it as hard as you can with as much as you can."

"Some plan."

"Yes, well. I know Americans like to keep things simple and direct."

"Just do whatever you're gonna do and tell me when I need to hit that fucker."

"Any moment now. Jiro's ready," Renn said. Anya looked up at the centipede as it swept its upper body across the far end of the atoll. It destroyed several of Mona's undead and Gary's robots in a single pass.

Harrison's demons kept the majority of the lesser aliens busy, but they were on the defensive now. Esmeralda had crafted a trio of glowing pink knights to defend herself from the aliens targeting her, while Samaira and Chandrali stood beside her, attacking any who tried to get near.

All of them looked tired. Their faces were strained, their postures drooped. Dead aliens lay scattered across the atoll, but there were still more. The centipede also seemed to be shaking off whatever psychic interference Renn and Esmeralda were causing it.

It was starting to go badly for them.

Then, as if to make things even worse, all of Renn's clones retreated from the positions across the battlefield and converged on him, disappearing into his body and becoming a single figure.

"What are you doing?" Anya demanded. The loss of Renn's clones had freed up several of the lesser gnosiphages to attack the others.

"Shh. Be ready," Renn said, and then he changed.

It wasn't a dramatic shift, but a subtle change along the edges of Renn's figure. He seemed to blur, like he was vibrating at a high speed. Renn moved his hand, and it left some kind of hazy after image behind it, a slow-motion echo of his movement.

There was something else, too. When Anya had been at Outpost #2, she had felt how empty it was, how hollow. She now felt the opposite. The atoll, already crowded with undead, aliens, demons, and hosts, now felt like it had an entire stadium's worth of people crowded into it. There was an invisible presence of consciousness stretching around Anya, countless invisible eyes aware of her.

She looked around, wondering what the trick was, and saw that Samaira and the other hosts had noticed as well. Esmeralda had gasped and fallen over, twitching as if she were having a seizure. Jiro was the only other one who didn't seem confused, and rushed straight at the centipede's front. He leaped onto its head, towering above the battlefield, and began yanking on one of its pincers from behind, tearing it off and distracting it from Renn and Anya for a precious second.

"Now," Renn said, and his voice had a strange echo to it. It wasn't loud, but it was layered, multiple voices speaking the same word.

"Esmeralda—" Anya started to say.

"*Now!*" Renn said, louder.

The centipede had frozen in place. It trembled, its legs twitched, and its eyes rolled in its head. The horde of lesser aliens all fell to the ground, twitching and writhing. Their shapes had also begun to distort, their eerie mimicry devolving into random shapes of flesh and metal and bone.

Anya didn't understand what was happening, or how, but decided she didn't need to. She blasted off from the beach beside Renn, and shot straight toward the centipede.

Its body was too heavily armored to do enough damage to in just a few seconds, even if it couldn't regenerate. Anya thought of the puppet alien from Prospect Park. It had armored itself too, and could also heal from attacks. She'd had to blast all its armor off before she burned it. That wasn't an option with the centipede, though. It was simply too huge.

So instead of attacking the armor from the outside, why not do it from the inside?

The centipede's huge mouth had been frozen while it was wide open. It might as well have thrown out a welcome mat.

Yes! Do it! Right in its kisser! the bird cheered as it saw the arc of Anya's flight. She grinned ferociously, her body becoming a miniature comet that left a flaming tail behind her.

Anya summoned the heat from her Sun's Heart, and condensed it around her body with gravity. It created a dense inferno around her that struggled against her control, straining to burn outwards and only becoming more volatile the longer she held it. She layered another inferno on top of that one, and again, the process taking only a few breaths, until she was armored in shuddering, chaotic waves of glowing fire.

She vanished into the centipede's mouth, soared down its throat, and then she released the raging tempest of fire around her.

It was like being inside a star going nova. The centipede's exterior was heavily armored, but that armor now worked against it. It contained the fire Anya unleashed inside itself, making the raw force of the explosion bounce around within it, looking for an escape. It shot up and down and all around, to the point that Anya lost control of it.

Might have overdone it, little ember, but hey, what a way to go, right? the bird asked. Anya had a confused moment to wonder what that meant, and then she too was being thrown around by her own attack. There was only fire and force, and Anya pinballing against the sides of the centipede's interior.

She lost any and all sense of direction, and then of time. Had she been in this cascading explosion for a couple seconds? A couple hours? Her lungs ached with a need for air, but the fire consumed it all.

While the fire didn't harm her, the repeated impacts did. Her kinetic dispersal skill was utterly eclipsed by the countless impacts, and her regalia wasn't much defense against them after the first few.

Anya's arm broke, then her shoulder, then her hip. Something tore at her side, and the skin along her neck split. She would have bled, but her blood evaporated in the heat as soon as it was exposed. Despite the flames, Anya's vision started to darken as her lungs burned.

Something finally gave way within the centipede, and Anya was blown out into the clear blue sky. She arced through the air—gasping for breath as she did—and trailing flames, smoke, and bits of charred guts behind her. She struck something hard and flat, and then it enveloped her in a rush of cold and bubbles.

She'd landed in the ocean. The water surged around her, and all the blood and smoke and muck that clung to her washed away in a murky, swirling cloud.

Anya sank within the cool blue of the ocean, looking down at herself and the lattice of webbed light across her body as the sunlight pierced the water's surface. Her brain pressed against the walls of her skull, swollen and throbbing, and her broken bones sent rail spikes of pain through her body. However, as Anya drifted below the cerulean deep, it was easy to let go for a moment, and sink.

Somewhere in Anya's mind, she was shouting at herself that she was probably concussed, internally bleeding, maybe even in shock, and still needed to breathe. Plus, there was still a fight going on up there. Her friends were in danger, aliens were still on the rampage, and there was no guarantee her attack on the centipede had killed it.

Anya fought against the pain, against the weight of the water around her, and flew up and out of the waves. She faltered in mid-air, still partially concussed from the impacts within the centipede. She managed to aim herself at the atoll and came to a tumbling, graceless landing in the shallow center.

"I-I'm okay!" Anya said, though her vision was blurry and it felt like the ground kept tilting from one side to the other.

"There she is!" Samaira shouted from somewhere overhead. Somebody put their hand on Anya's shoulder, and all the pain and fuzzy-headedness vanished in an instant. Her bones cracked loudly as they went back to their proper arrangement, and Anya winced at the pain before that too vanished.

"Easy, I got you. All better," Arvo said beside her. He wasn't hazy, but just as visible as anybody else. Anya blinked at him, then around the battlefield.

The atoll was a mess of alien guts, machine scrap, skeleton bones, dead demons, and craters.

And one extremely dead giant centipede.

"Hot damn," Anya said and grinned. "Gotcha, you bastard."

17

"'ve got good news and bad news!" Felix said. The AI floated over her shoulder and looked between her and the corpse of the giant centipede. Anya stood a few yards away from the giant gnosiphage's still-smoking head, staring at the ruin of its mouth, and the human face above it. The face had been split down the middle, smoke floating up out of its mouth, nostrils, and eye sockets. Thicker clouds of smoke also billowed out of the larger mouth below, as well as numerous cracks and breaks across the alien's lengthy body.

"What's the bad news?" Anya asked.

"You can't level up anymore."

"What?" Anya demanded her eyes going wide.

"That's also the good news. You hit the level cap! Congratulations!" Felix cheered and their cozy orange glow expanded as they grinned.

"I'm level 50?"

"Yup! See for yourself," Felix said and Anya brought up her menu.

Felix was right. She had gone up nine levels and reached level 50. That meant a new class, or a respecification token if she wanted entirely new skills. It also meant a lot of extra RAC due to bonuses.

"Hell yeah!"

"Whoa. Level 50?" Samaira asked as she approached Anya's side with Chandrali and saw her menu. She brought up her own and her eyes widened as she saw that she too had hit level 50. "Oh wow!"

"Nine levels for me, eleven for you. Pan! What's your level right now?" Anya shouted across the atoll. Pan sat with some of his golems and Esmeralda, who was lying down on a platform of sandstone the pangolin had summoned for her. Arvo was with them, resting his hands on Esmeralda's temples.

"Uh, I dunno," Pan said and shrugged, then brought up his menu and cocked his head to the side. Arvo glanced at it and his eyebrows raised. "Is that a lot?"

"He's level 43," Arvo said, and then checked his own stats. "A gain of 16 levels. So yes, quite a lot."

A quick survey of the other hosts revealed that all of them, except for Pan, had hit level 50.

"What about Gary?" Samaira asked.

"What do you mean?" Anya replied.

"I mean, you have to be within a certain range to get the experience from the win, right? He's in Antarctica. He wouldn't have gotten anything from that."

The rumble of a car engine drew everyone's attention to the far side of the atoll. An old, beat-up truck drove out of the water, as if it were just going over a puddle and not emerging from the depths of the Pacific. Gary opened the door and stepped out, popping his back with a grunt and waving.

"When the hell did you get here?" Anya jogged over to the old man, grinning as she did.

"I've been here, kiddo. I was hiding near the entrapment field when it all went down and started constricting it as the fight went on. If things started to go south, I was gonna come help out more directly. Maybe set off another bomb like I did last time we fought one of these bastards."

Gary kicked the limp pincer of the dead centipede.

"Unlike you, I didn't forget about the range on getting experience. And I'm also level 50. Handshakes and congratulations all around for everybody."

"Thank goodness," Samaira sighed.

"A shame we could not convince more people to join us," Renn said as he wandered over with Mona and Harrison. Jiro remained near Esmeralda while she recovered far across the atoll, her head in her hands and looking like she might puke. Meanwhile, Arvo, Pan, and his golems kept an eye on the scattered alien remains. "Likewise, a shame that the beacon was destroyed in the fight. My apologies."

"It did its job. I can make another one with the doc," Gary shrugged.

"Felix, is there any kind of experience reduction for more people helping to kill an alien?" Anya asked. "Like if we all ganged up on one weak alien, would we get the same experience if just one of us killed it solo, or would it be split evenly among everybody?"

"I don't have access to that information. The finer details of how the Archive distributes experience is admin access only. I only know that higher level aliens give more experience, and that the higher your level, the more experience you need to advance. Though I guess that's kinda a moot point now."

Anya started to ask another question when her ear beeped.

"Someone calling?" she muttered. Before the AI could answer, she figured it out. Everyone's AI materialized in front of them, their postures stiff, and their various flower or plant-shaped heads turned to a mess of static.

"It's them," Samaira said.

Anya had spoken with the aliens known only as the Engineers twice before: once shortly before the gnosiphages arrived on Earth, and again after she had killed the snake overseer.

"Greetings Earth forms. This one is Initiate Engineer Red-507. Please confirm expiration of local gnosiphage administrative overseer," a now-familiar voice emitted from Felix, along with every other AI.

"Yeah, it's dead," Anya said.

"Confirmed. Thank you. This one anticipates many questions, but be aware communication window is uncertain. Estimated time to gnosiphages reestablishing communications block: two minutes or less."

"How many overseers are left on Earth?" Samaira asked.

"One remains. Uncertain of precise location. Primarily northern hemisphere."

"How many aliens are left?" Anya asked.

"Uncertain. Signals overlap significantly. However, with the expiration of the overseer, your AIs should have more information once they decode the data stream it emitted upon its defeat."

"How do we level up beyond the cap now?" Renn said as he stepped forward. "Is it possible?"

"Maximum possible level cap is 100. Current cap restriction is limited to Earth-based hosts: Current cap is level 50. Previous skill and statistic caps were 75, but have been increased to 100. Further level-ups are not possible without approval of Engineer Council. However, while you may not acquire experience, Reward Allocation Currency will still be rewarded beyond the level cap."

"At least there's that," Anya grumbled.

"And those respecification tokens? What about those?" Arvo asked.

"This one is uncertain. The tokens are usually available at level 50, however, after several Archive irregularities have been detected with Earth hosts, the Engineer Council has opted to prohibit their purchase from the RAC store."

"What the hell does that mean?" Anya demanded.

"Earth hosts have violated multiple parameters of Archive usage. Such violations have been committed by local designations Anya Nowicki, Renn, Samaira Upadhyay, Mona de Rozario, Jiro Yamada, and Gary Hendricks. This is only among those assembled here at this moment. Many other hosts have committed similar infractions."

"What are you talking about? We've used the Archives as our AIs guided us to, nothing else," Gary said.

"In this case, an irregularity is classified as any host exceeding the projected numerical value of a skill. Data has been gathered from numerous sources, and run through practical and simulated experiments to determine the most accurate numerical standard for levels of ability. Many humans have exceeded these models, and is the reason why the statistic and skill level caps have been raised. Those humans that have not already exceeded models are on-target to do so in the future. Local designation Arvo Immonen is closest to becoming the next irregularity."

"Oh. Hooray?" the doctor said.

"If everybody's doing it, it's not really *that* irregular," Anya muttered. "And this sounds like your fault. Not ours."

"This one does not have access to all relevant data. This one can only relay information and decisions of the Engineer Council."

"So no respec tokens. Great. And no raising the level cap to 100? Last time you said you were considering it."

"Negative. Level 50 cap remains. Threat assessment of humanity and possibility of success against gnosiphage invasion has caused some distress amongst Engineer Council as well as—" Red-507's modulated voice was suddenly cut off, and another replaced it.

"Initiate has exceeded necessary communication guidelines," the new voice said. It was somewhat deeper, more commanding. "Level cap remains. Respecification tokens will not be made available. All Archive irregularities have been noted and confirmed. Earth hosts are advised to terminate remaining gnosiphage presence to enhance survival probability. End communication."

All of the AIs blinked out of sight, and Anya and the others were left to stare at each other.

"First time that's happened," Anya said.

"I think we made 'em mad," Gary said.

Anya tapped her chest to bring her menu back up and check in with Felix, but nothing happened.

"Felix?" she asked.

No response.

"Felix?"

Tap, tap, on her chest.

No menu.

Even when there was an overseer present, she could at least talk to Felix. Now the little AI was silent. Anya's heart began to beat faster. If she couldn't access her Archive, that meant no more leveling up. No second class, no RAC store. It also meant no communication with other hosts, no map to find them in an emergency, no—

"Anya?" Felix asked and instead of blinking into view like they usually did, they faded into existence before her. "What happened? I'm missing the last few minutes."

"Felix!" she sighed and almost tried to hug the little AI. Everyone else's holographic assistants began reappearing next to them. Anya explained what happened, and Felix rubbed their chin, the petals on their head closing up as they thought.

"That's... weird. Archive protocol states the AI must have access to all communications that involve the host. The Engineer, the second one, must have manually deleted the record of the conversation. Don't know why, though. Oh well! At least you can level up now!" Felix said.

"Yeah, thank God for that. Before we do that though, I guess we should call MacDougal and let her know we won," Anya said and looked back at the scattered alien corpses across the sands of the atoll. She scowled when she saw the two bodies of the dead hosts.

It wasn't a complete victory.

She flew up to the Shadow Ray, which had remained hovering in place high above them during the entire fight, and then directed the autopilot to land while she called MacDougal.

"Nowicki? Good news?" The director asked, and Anya was a little surprised to hear concern in her voice.

"Yup. The beacon worked, and we bagged a lot of aliens. There were three more mind-controlled hosts. Saved one, lost two. But the overseer's dead. We also had a chat with the Engineers again, but that was kinda inconclusive."

"Hmm," MacDougal replied and let out a sigh. Anya had a twinge of sympathy for the director. As scary and chaotic as the fight had been, it would've been worse if she'd just had to wait it out somewhere, wondering how everybody else was doing while she did nothing.

"I'm speaking with the Admiral in charge of the Pacific Fleet," MacDougal continued. "He's been keeping his ships a good distance away, but they'll be moving in soon to aid with clean-up. There'll be a few vessels from Japan and Canada as well. We'll need you to stay there and make sure the aliens are good and dead before they arrive."

"They're definitely dead. Got the experience for them and everything. But we'll hang out. Anything else?"

"Yeah: good job. I'll see if I can get bonuses approved for you and the others."

"Won't argue with that," Anya said and hung up, then left the Shadow Ray to inform Samaira and the others that they would be sticking around for a bit longer.

―――――

THE VARIOUS NAVIES and their crews secured the area, setting up a perimeter of warships and patrolling helicopters miles wide around the atoll. Smaller craft approached the minuscule scrap of sand, and unloaded crews of sailors, scientists, and Marines.

Anya floated high above the atoll, scanning the waters in every direction. They had killed the overseer, but that didn't mean the other one wouldn't be nearby, looking for revenge. And while the number of lesser gnosiphages had been significant, Anya had no delusions that they had defeated most of the remaining invasion force. They'd killed maybe several dozen of the aliens in total.

Last she had checked, there were still well over a thousand.

"You know, I was thinking maybe you would just blast the overseer in the face or shoot a fireball into its mouth. Not go in yourself. It was entertaining, to say the least," a French-accented voice said beside Anya. She'd sensed Renn's heat signature approaching from below, so she wasn't surprised to see him up here. Like her, he floated in mid-air, though his posture seemed less alert. He slouched, hands in the pocket of his long white coat.

"What did you do to it?" Anya asked. "And yourself? You went all… fuzzy," Anya said, searching for the right word. "And I felt weird too."

"A little trick I figured out," he said, and then brought up his primary screen. "This doesn't reflect the level-ups we just acquired. I'm still level 40, for practical purposes."

RENN: LEVEL 50 PSIONIC COMMANDER
Statistics

- Awareness-20 (+10 from gear)
- Dexterity-4
- Fortitude-14 (+8 from gear)
- Intelligence-41 (+17 from gear)
- Strength-4
- Willpower-31 (+14 from gear)

Skills

- Psionics- 40 (+22 from gear) (+5 from Artifact)
- Density Control (Self)- 15 (+5 from gear)
- Self-Duplication- 30 (+5 from gear)
- Hive Mind- 15 (+22 from gear)
- Telekinetic Mastery- 30 (+22 from gear)

Anya studied the list. Three of Renn's skills matched what she already knew: he was psychic and moved things with his mind, and he could multiply himself. The other skills she wasn't so sure about.

"What's up with these two?" she asked and pointed at "Density Control (Self)," and "Hive Mind."

"Hive mind allows the user to link up to any other person of the same species with the same skill, and receive bonuses to skills based on how many people have it. This pairs quite well with body duplication, as I can just make more of myself, which will also have hive mind," Renn said and Anya nodded, impressed.

"However," Renn continued, "there's a limit to how many duplicates I can make of myself dependent on distance. I can make a few duplicates, and they can function within a very large area with autonomy, or I can make a lot of duplicates, but they have to stay close."

Anya furrowed her brow as she looked at the "Density Control (Self)," skill and started to form an idea.

"You can control your density, and make yourself less solid," Anya said, to which Renn nodded. "And your clones can do the same. And hive mind would make it so you'd all be better at making yourself less solid..."

"...and then I can stack myself over copies of myself, all of us standing in a relatively small space, exponentially increasing all of my skills," Renn said. Anya blinked at him and felt a chill run up her spine.

"How many of you did you have stacked on top of yourself during the fight?"

"About 2,500," Renn said. "I like to call it my *Grande Armée,* even though it never really looks like anything but a blurrier version of myself. I don't have an exact number since some of my duplicates will blink in and out depending on my focus. It's powerful, but I can only hold it for so long. And afterward the, ah, the hangover? There is a strong headache afterwards. Very unenjoyable. If not for Dr. Immonen, I'd probably need bed rest for a day or two. Even with his touch, I still have a bit of a headache."

"Jesus," Anya said.

Renn was a min-maxer.

While Anya played a number of games, she'd never gotten into min-maxing, or maximizing a certain type of character build to specialize in a single task to absurd levels. While she never liked being a jack-of-all-trades sort of character, the idea of slotting herself into focusing on one incredibly powerful skillset never appealed to her either. It felt like trapping herself, even just as a game character, and limiting her options to one or none, no margin for error or improvisation.

"I admit, it is not perfect, but it's served me well so far. Only the third time I've had to do that," Renn said. "Mona had to use her skeletons to carry me away afterward. This time was not so bad, but that's because I didn't do it for as long. You shooting yourself into the creature's mouth shocked me out of it."

"Was it that surprising?"

"A little, though based on what I've seen of you so far, maybe not."

Anya grunted.

"You know what you're gonna do with your points yet?" she asked.

Renn tilted the chin of his helmet down and tapped it in thought.

"No. Maybe something to help me recover from using the *Grande*

Armée, or something like that. Although, I suspect that is what caused the 'irregularity,' the Engineer spoke of."

"No shit."

"Any idea what caused your own irregularity?"

Anya wasn't entirely certain, but she suspected. When she'd first spoken with the Flame Dominion and asked Felix about it, the AI had told her that there wasn't any such information about her experience anywhere in the Archive.

That wasn't some big super move though, that was just... talking. Nothing that special.

Don't tell him, the bird whispered to her.

"Probably just beating the shit out of stuff, or like what I did today: flying into that thing's mouth and blowing it up," Anya said. Renn looked at her, cocked his head to the side as if he heard something, then shrugged.

"Well, I wanted to thank you for your help today. I hope we can continue to rely on each other," he said, waved, and floated back down to the sand below.

Anya maintained her vigil above the atoll, and did not relax until the clean-up by the navy was finished several hours later. While she was glad they hadn't been ambushed, she wasn't as relaxed as she thought she would be. One more overseer was down, but every encounter with the aliens—gnosiphage and Engineer alike—only ever served to bring up more questions.

"Anya?" Samaira asked as she stood beside the Shadow Ray with Pan, Jiro, and Esmeralda. "You ready to head back to the outpost?"

"Yeah. Gary? Arvo? You gonna join us?"

"Nah. Got some samples from the overseer that didn't completely burn up. Gonna take that and some other stuff back to the labs and run some tests," he said. "I'll swing by at some point, though."

"I'm going with Gary to check on the surviving host we rescued. Make sure their recovery is progressing. I will come back in the next day or so," the doctor said.

"You better," Anya replied, and then joined the others in the Ray, and flew back home.

18

Anya had crashed into bed as soon as she'd returned to Outpost #1, and slept through her alarm the following morning. Arvo, Samaira, and Pan eventually came to check on her when she didn't arrive at breakfast to see if anything was wrong with her.

"Exhaustion. That's it," Arvo said when he held Anya's hand for a moment and finished his scan.

"But my regeneration…" Anya said.

"Has been overtaxed, along with your Sun's Heart. You can absorb heat from that magic crystal you got, but it's not a perfect way to renew your energy stores. It's like taking caffeine pills: sooner or later you're going to crash, and your body will demand sleep. Same for food. Even my own healing abilities can only take you so far. That explosion yesterday left you severely concussed, and with most of your bones broken, plus a significant amount of internal bleeding.

"I've refreshed you, but nothing is a total replacement for natural rest and regular meals. Your regenerative ability means you don't need nearly as much sleep unless you pull on your Sun's Heart. Then, you'll need a lot. Comparatively. If you didn't have regeneration, you'd likely need days, if not a week or more, of sustained rest to fully recover from using that Artifact in your chest. It's impressive, but demanding."

"Tell me about it," Anya said and thought of the bird. She also thought how far she'd come since first using her powers. After her first fight with the puppet alien in Brooklyn, she'd been unconscious for days. Sleeping in a bit past her alarm was pretty tame by comparison.

"Speaking of recovery," Anya said, "how's that host we rescued from the atoll?"

"He's fine, I assume," Arvo said.

"You assume?"

"He was mostly recovered by the time I finished healing him at Gary's factory. We scanned him for any signs of alien influence, but there were none. He was rather insistent on not remaining with us, and since we didn't want to hold him against his will, we let him leave of his own accord. Garry offered him a ride on one of his drones, but he said he could take care of himself. I tracked his signal to New Zealand, and then it vanished. My AI confirmed the host had removed himself from my contacts list. No idea where he is now," the doctor shrugged. "I would have liked to make sure he was fine after another day or two, but he made it clear he wished to go on his own."

"At least he's all right," Anya sighed. "Just wish we could've helped the others."

"We did what we could. Take it from somebody who has spent many years trying: you can't save everybody, but that doesn't mean you shouldn't celebrate those that you do. And by 'celebrate,' I mean rest."

"MacDougal gave us all the day off," Samaira said. "Which is fine with me because I'm still tired after yesterday. And Chandrali's still asleep."

"We can bring you food!" Pan volunteered.

"I'll get a wheelbarrow," Arvo said and chuckled as he left with Pan.

"Har har," Anya said and then looked up at Samaira as she stood over her bed. Her face tightened as she looked down at Anya. "Something wrong?"

"You scared me. Yesterday. When you flew into that thing's mouth and then it started shaking itself apart and belching fire. I thought…" Samaira's voice trailed off and she shook her head.

"Oh. Sam, I'm sorry. It just seemed like the thing to do, I guess."

Samaira let out a laugh.

"The thing to do," she repeated. "Try to remember you're not alone out there. You don't always have to throw yourself at whatever's in front of you."

"I'll try."

"Rest for now. Maybe decide what you want to do with your level-ups. MacDougal's requested we inform her prior to making any changes, but not that she has to approve them. Just a head's up, I guess."

Anya grunted. It was one step away from having to get permission to use her own Archive. She didn't argue or complain though. If MacDougal or Hanover forced the issue, she'd put up a fight, but until then, she had other things to focus on. Samaira left, and then came back later with the others and a large helping of food for her, then left her to rest and decide what to do with her points.

The Archive had an almost endless number of skills to choose from: everything from combat-oriented dance moves to quilting to summoning inter dimensional lifeforms. Anya hadn't had any points to spend on new skills in weeks, and now, looking at the main screen of her Archive and Felix floating beside it, she found herself stumped.

She'd gained nine levels from the fight with the overseer and the lesser gnosiphages. If all she had were those nine points, she'd just have increased skills she already had. It wasn't enough to change a whole lot, but hitting level 50 would grant her bonus points for clearing another ten levels.

And, according to Felix, once she had her second class, it would combine with her first to give her an advanced class and grant her even more bonuses and points.

"How many points, total?" Anya asked.

"Nine points from raw level-ups, plus ten bonus points for hitting level 50. Then another fifty skill points with your second class. However, forty of those points will be automatically assigned to relevant class skills, so only ten free-use skill points."

"Okay, so far that's twenty-nine free skill points. What about the advanced class?"

"Sixty skill points automatically assigned, plus an additional fifteen free-use points. And none of this is factoring in stat points, only skills. It's sure a lot!"

"Yeah, no shit. God damn. Forty-four points to put where I want?"

"Correct! In addition to the 100 skill points that will be automatically assigned."

Anya whistled.

144 skill points. Just like that.

Anya looked at her current list of skills and their corresponding numbers and added them up. Her total skill points were currently at 158, just a little over what she would get after leveling up and selecting her classes.

It really was a shitload of points.

However...

They were also, potentially, the last points Anya would ever get. And now that she had no way of changing her stats and skills because of the Engineers, she'd be stuck if she ever needed anything else.

Felix had told her when she first got the Archive that a skill with five points was about average human ability. Somebody with the equivalent of ten points in a skill was considered a genius, and fifteen was the stuff of myths and legends.

"Fifteen points should be enough," Anya said.

"Enough for what?"

"To set aside for emergencies. I may not get any more, and if I need something in a life-or-death moment, I don't want to be out of options. I'll still have twenty-nine points to spend as I please, on top of everything else. But fifteen points set aside will give me enough to make one skill great, or a couple skills very good."

"I gotcha! So, you've been scrolling through my suggestion for classes and skills for a while now. Anything stand out?"

"I think so, but I want some clarification first. These two sound cool," Anya said and pointed at a pair of skills Felix had selected for her review: Energy Focus and Flesh of the Starforge. "But I'm not certain what they'd do functionally."

"I thought you'd like those! Energy Focus will allow you to better control your various forms of attack and defense. So you'll be able to channel more heat from the Sun's Heart, stronger gravity shifts with Singularity's Grasp, and better healing from regeneration. You can also focus your strength to hit harder, fortitude to catch your breath, and so on. However, you will have to consciously focus on the increase, so you may not be able to do everything at once unless you really concentrate."

"Will that use up more of my energy if I use it?"

"Not by much. Energy Focus is about increased efficiency more than raw power. Overall, it would likely decrease energy drain."

"And Flesh of the Starforge?"

"An activated skill that will convert your normal skin to a mystical organic alloy. Not forever! You can turn it off and on. The initial energy cost of activating the skill is moderate, but keeping it up costs almost nothing. Plus, it's technically part of you, so it'll work with your regeneration skill. The heat conductive properties of it are really strong as well!

"I've also noticed that energy management seems to be an issue for you, so I've selected skills that require little to no energy input at all, and will help existing management needs. Flesh of the Starforge isn't a perfect defense, but it will reduce the number and severity of injuries you do receive."

"What would I do without you, Felix?," Anya asked and smiled at them.

"Probably be dead!"

"Can't argue with that. Also, definitely taking those two skills. The Starforge skin thing, can it be flicked on real quick in an emergency?"

"Yes. Once you exceed skill level 5, it can be activated almost instantly. There is a slight delay at higher skill levels, but it's negligible. A second or less.

"I don't want to spread myself too thin, but I figured I'd take one more skill: one of the Dominions."

According to Felix, it was impossible to take the opposite of any existing Dominion. She already had Fire and Gravity, so that canceled out Water and Space, and left her with the Air, Earth, Light, or Shadow Dominions to choose from.

Anya considered the two remaining elemental Dominions, but decided against them. Earth seemed like it favored a slower, defensive approach to battle, and air lent itself to avoiding fights rather than taking them on. Anya wanted to remain the focus of any enemy she came across, draw attention away from her more vulnerable allies, but still bring the punishment when she had to.

That left the Light and Shadow Dominions, which is what Anya selected from her floating menu.

"It's not literally just light and shadow, like making things brighter or darker," Felix explained. "These two are sometimes referred to as the 'philosophical,' Dominions. While they can affect the physical properties of light and its absence, a better description might be to describe them as encouraging or discouraging the inherent nature of a thing."

"You lost me," Anya said.

"Light is support and reinforcement, shadow is weakness and entropy."

"Ooooh. Buffs and debuffs," Anya said.

"Like in a game, right! Sort of!"

"Can you give me an example?"

"Hmm. I only have skill data up to level 5 for any particular skill, but that should be enough to give you the basics. Let's say you wanted to set an alien on fire."

"I'm with you so far."

"The Light Dominion would let you enhance the fire to be more stable: burn longer despite a lack of fuel, or be harder to extinguish, letting you conserve energy. The Shadow Dominion would let you make the fire do more damage right away, or cause it to have a greater effect on destroying an alien's defenses.

"With regard to your other skills, both could help your regeneration. Light Dominion would help you heal faster, and maybe even adapt to certain types of damage. So if you keep getting hit with acid, Light Dominion enhancing your regeneration would make those sorts of attacks hurt less. The Shadow Dominion applied to the same skill would allow you to pull energy away from a target to heal yourself more quickly, weakening and hurting them in the process, like the Life Drain skill.

"With your new skills , I'm not so sure, since you haven't taken them yet and I don't have a detailed record of you using them. However, I can make a guess. Light Dominion could enhance the effectiveness of Energy Focus even further, allowing for more efficient power use and stronger overall effects. A shadow-enhanced Energy Focus might enhance any negative affects of your attacks without costing you much extra power. As for Flesh of the Starforge, it could adapt much like your regeneration and adapt to attacks of a similar type, as well as become even better at defense. Shadow Dominion applied to the skill might become reactive, striking out at enemies within range, or becoming harmful to touch."

"All of that sounds pretty badass to me," Anya said. "Shit. I can't take both? You're sure?"

Felix shook their head.

"The Crown of the Firmament and Umbra's Whisper Artifacts are mutually exclusive. Having both bound to a single entity would cause a catastrophic reaction. The Archive strictly prohibits the possibility of such things happening and will refuse any attempt to acquire both artifacts or both skills."

"Fucking weak," Anya sighed and stared at her menu screen, then once again recalled her conversation with the bird. Campfire, flamethrower.

She knew the bird was right: violence was necessary sometimes, but Anya did not want to build her future around it. Samaira had dreams of making an aether academy, Gary had designs for a cleaner, brighter world, and even people like Renn and Vastukar clearly had their own long-term goals.

The flamethrower option was short term.

"Campfire," Anya said and added the Light Dominion skill to her temporary list for confirmation later. "Okay Felix, I think those are the only skills I'd like to add. Is there a class that matches those?"

"There sure is! The best match for your second class based on your new and pre-existing skills would be the Ascendant Skirmisher class.

You'll need to take all three new skills and raise them to level 5 to meet the requirements, but that's it! Oh! You'll need to get the Crown of the Firmament Artifact from the RAC store too."

"Lemme see," Anya said and Felix brought up a separate window with the class's details.

Ascendant Skirmisher

Statistic Bonuses
+15 Fortitude
+7 Strength
+3 Dexterity

Skill Bonuses
+10 Skill Points (Host Choice)
+15 Energy/Endurance Skill (Combat Focus)
+10 Defensive Skill
+15 Support Skill

Store Bonuses
+1 Free Enhancement Item
+1 Free Armor Upgrade (Up to Excellent Quality)

"Yeah, I think that'll work. And this will combine with my Phoenix Monk class to make a whole new advanced class?" she asked.

"Correct! Phoenix Monk and Ascendant Skirmisher will combine to create the Cosmic Warden class," Felix replied, and displayed yet another window with that information before Anya could ask him to.

Cosmic Warden

Statistic Bonuses
+15 Fortitude
+10 Strength
+10 Dexterity

Skill Bonuses

+15 Skill Points (Host Choice)

+15 Elemental-Based Skill

+15 Support Skill

+10 Melee Combat Skill

+10 Healing Skill

+5 Defensive Skill

+5 Combat Strategy Skill

Store Bonuses

+2 Free Item Upgrades (Up to Excellent Quality) (Host Choice)

+2 Free Artifact or Weapon Upgrades (Up to Masterwork Quality)

+1 Free Armor or Clothing Upgrade (Up to Masterwork Quality)

+1 Free Respecification Token [BONUS RESCINDED PER ENGI-NEER COUNCIL DECISION #305-B]

Advanced Class Abilities

Edict of the Cosmos- Receive a +5 bonus to all skills and +2 to all stats when fighting in space. If exposed directly to the vacuum of space, maintain base life signs for a minimum of five minutes (increases dependent on healing and defensive skills). Grants the skill: Zero-G Combat at skill level 10.

Stalwart Sentinel- All defensive, support, and healing skills are 33% more efficient. Armor is 20% more effective. Grants the skill: Sure Footing at skill level 10.

Warden's Jurisdiction- Any hostile combatant within 50 yards suffers the effects of the Enfeebling Touch skill at skill level 10. Any allied combatant within 50 yards gains the effect of the Rallying Presence skill at skill level 10. These skills are not permanently granted to the host.

Anya whistled. It was an absurd leap forward in power. She could only guess at what the Archive was capable of beyond the level 50 cap the Engineers had imposed. A level 100 Archive user would be unreal, practically a living god. The thought was both awe-inspiring and terrifying.

The advanced class abilities in particular caught her eye.

"These advanced class abilities, everybody gets those?" she asked.

"Not those exact ones, but a version of them, yes," Felix replied. "Advanced class abilities may grant permanent or temporary skills, specialized and unique items, increases to existing skills, and more."

"What do these skills do?"

"Zero-G Combat Training is exactly what it sounds like: you'll have some ability to fight in environments that have no gravity. Sure Footing makes you harder to knock down, and grants knowledge of defensive fighting stances. Enfeebling touch will weaken and slow enemies to a degree, while Rallying Presence will strengthen allies and help them recover from exhaustion. Both of these skills have a minor energy cost, but it's pretty negligible."

"I'll have to see what Sam and the others got. But I think that'll do for now. I'll run this all by MacDougal whenever she's free," she said and Felix smiled at her.

"Good! I'm sure she'll approve. And you're okay with this? You haven't locked anything in yet. You could pick another secondary and advanced class."

Anya studied her menu and all the jumps in power she would receive. There were, quite literally, no end to the possibilities when it came to the Archive. She could dither about on her choices for weeks, years, and still have other options.

She would let Samaira see her picks before she showed MacDougal, maybe get her input, and that would be enough.

"Nah, I'm good."

She yawned, still tired despite having done nothing but lay in bed all day.

"Oh yeah," she added, "how much RAC do I have? After the fight with the overseer and all the level-ups?"

"2,983,531 RAC," Felix said and displayed a window showing the number. Anya let out a choking gasp and her eyes goggled in her head.

"What the fuck? That much?"

"You got a million just from hitting level 50 as a bonus."

"Hot damn! Can I buy a fucking spaceship yet?"

"You can! However I would advise against it. The Crown of the

Firmament you'll need for the Light Dominion and the subsequent upgrades for it—along with Singularity's Grasp and the Sun's Heart—will be prohibitively expensive, even with the store bonuses. This is also assuming you don't want to upgrade or purchase any other items like armor, more runes, accessories, or anything else."

Anya grumbled, but knew Felix was right. Besides, what was she going to do with a spaceship? All the gnosiphages were on Earth, after all. Plus, she'd either have to buy a basic autopilot mod for it like she did for the Shadow Ray, or use skill points to learn how to fly it herself.

It would be awesome, but impractical.

"Someday, maybe…" Anya sighed, then yawned again. "How's decoding that data from the overseer going, by the way?"

"Still decoding. It'll be at least another day. There's a whole month's worth of transmissions between the various gnosiphages to go through, so it's taking a while. I promise to let you know as soon as I'm done, though!"

"Thanks Felix. You're the best. I think I'm just gonna shut my eyes for a bit. Lemme know if Sam or anybody comes around or calls."

"Will do!" Felix said. Anya was halfway asleep by the time they replied, already dreaming of all the things she could buy.

19

Anya showed her planned level-ups to MacDougal the next day, who approved them without fuss or fanfare. Samaira was likewise supportive of Anya's choices, and also eager to show off her own changes and upgrades. She brought up her menu when she and Anya sat down for lunch after their individual meetings with MacDougal.

"Whoa, Sam," Anya said and looked over her proposed changes.

SAMAIRA UPADHYAY: LEVEL 50 AETHERIC RANGER
Second Class (Not Confirmed): Elemental Artificer
Advanced Class (Not Confirmed): Strider Magus

Additional skills (Not Confirmed)
Water Dominion
Rune Construction
Item Enchantment
Aetheric Materialization

Advanced Class Abilities (Not Confirmed)
Discerning Craftswoman- All raw materials from the store have

their cost decreased by 50%, and receive one free quality upgrade (up to Legendary quality).

Wisdom of the Artificer- Any crafted or enchanted items or runes that are made with elemental or aetheric abilities receive a 33% bonus to their innate attributes, and refund 25% of any physical materials used in their construction.

Aetheric Longsight- Allows sight through the aether to minimum of 25 miles, with further distances dependent on total combined aetheric skill level and aetheric availability, and Awareness statistic. Limited ability to affect the aether at this distance.

"What is all this?" Anya asked, her eyebrows inching up her head. "I figured you'd pick more archery stuff, or animal stuff for Chandrali."

"I thought about that, but with the points I'm going to be putting into my existing skills, I'm pretty comfortable with leaving my combat skills as they are. I'm okay in a fight, but I want to have some utility off the battlefield too, y'know?"

"Y-yeah," Anya said, yet again feeling a bit slow. While she had settled on the Light Dominion that also had utility outside of just crushing things, it was still going to be put to work during fights, for the most part. Anya started reconsidering her choices for non-combat skills.

"Hey," Samaira said, and placed her hand on Anya's bicep. Anya was—as usual— wearing a short-sleeved shirt, and Samaira's bare hand on her upper arm was cool, soothing. "I was only able to think about taking this stuff because I knew you'd be thinking about making sure I could survive when we get into another fight. I also took this so I can help you. I can put more enchantments on your armor, maybe even make you some stuff from scratch. Same goes for Pan, Dr. Immonen, everybody. And I'm comfortable investing in skills like this and not combat because I know you've got that covered."

"Okay," Anya said and smiled down at her. Samaira got up on her tip-toes and pecked Anya on the cheek. "But what's up with the Water Dominion?"

"Well, I thought about what you told me about your little friend,"

Samaira said, and glanced around the mess hall to make sure nobody was eavesdropping. "The one who talks to you. And I also asked Boo about how Water Dominion might work—or interfere with—the aether. Apparently it pairs pretty well with it, and will give me some extra options in a fight, or out of one. Plus, the artificer class I wanted required some sort of elemental skill, and the aether didn't count. There was a purely aetheric artificer class, but I wanted to branch out a little, not stick to just one thing, but not go into something entirely unrelated. The skill itself has excellent utility, so if I don't get to chat with my own little friend, I've still got a good skill."

"Seems smart."

"I try."

"This aetheric materialization skill, how's that different from what you got already?"

"Permanence. The aether I've been using has just been me modifying the raw currents. They've all been temporary permutations of the aether: arrows that get shot and do their thing, then disappear. With materialization, combined with the other stuff, I could actually make something permanent that I wouldn't have to keep my focus on forever. So with the other skills, I could make clothes out of pure aether and imbue them with whatever properties I want, then add runes or enchantments on top of that."

"Whoa."

Samaira nodded, clearly pleased with herself.

"Curious to see what Pan, Esmeralda, and everybody else got."

The other hosts were all getting the same rubber-stamp approval for their skills from their governments that Anya and Samaira had already gotten. Jiro was in Japan for the day, Arvo had gone back to Finland, Harrison to Canada, Renn to France, and Mona to the UK.

The exception for all this was Gary, who'd said he was going to sit on all of his points and advanced classes for a little while. MacDougal had tried to ask him anyway, and he'd taken the opportunity to officially renounce his US citizenship.

President Hanover hadn't liked that.

"So, when are you gonna finalize it?" Samaira asked.

"Today. No sense in putting it off," Anya sighed. It had been a long time since she leveled-up, but not long enough that she forgot the pain. The changes the Archive brought on each level-up rewired the host, physically and mentally. The more level-ups, the more rewiring was needed. It was a relatively fast process, but far from painless.

Anya had passed out from the agony when she had taken her first class. Taking her second, an advanced class, and assigning her other points would be unpleasant, for sure.

Felix advised performing the level-up process in a series of small boosts. The secondary class would have to be first, then the advanced class, then assigning the free points, in order to avoid the worst of the pain and risking damage. The Archive referred to such an outcome as a "Catastrophic Data Overload."

"Definitely not looking forward to the actual level-up process. But I'm pretty excited for afterward," Samaira said.

"Would you like me to sit with you when you do it?"

"Yeah. Yeah, that would help."

Anya took Samaira's hand and squeezed it.

"No time like the present," Anya said and stood up. Samaira gulped, but nodded and followed her out of the mess hall. They informed MacDougal, who insisted on having a pair of doctors from the outpost's medical ward on stand-by just in-case.

Felix and Boo were both summoned to monitor their respective host's vital signs. Riley was there too, though more as emotional support than anything else. They did it in Anya's living room, seated beside each other on the couch, feeling a bit awkward as a pair of doctors watched them. Their attention was academic, eager to see the show.

Riley sat on the edge of the armchair nearby, smiling warmly at the two women.

Samaira would go first, then Anya. She brought up her blue menu screen, took a breath, and then hit the confirmation button.

Anya winced as Samaira's face went slack with shock, then twisted into agony when she confirmed her second class. There was nothing Anya could do but wait it out, holding Samaira's hand until she passed out.

When Anya confirmed her own second class, the pain was as excruciating as she remembered. Her mind was cleared of any rational thought and transformed into a receptor for pain. It was pain enough to wash everything else away: all worry of the aliens, the other hosts, her family, all of it.

Except one thought.

It did not hurt quite as much as seeing Samaira go through the same process moments before.

That had been worse.

And then, like before, it was over.

She blinked and found herself on the couch with Samaira, both of them staring at each other.

"Was it good for you?" Anya asked and smirked.

Samaira grimaced, but finally let out a chuckle, then hissed.

"Don't make me laugh. My head still feels... weird," she said.

"Vital signs are normal," Felix said and brought up Anya's status screen. The doctors nodded and made some notes, while Riley leaned forward.

"How do you feel?" he asked.

"Like I got my head smashed under a rock, but it's going away quickly. Felix, how long do we have to wait to do the advanced class?" Anya said.

"Your status menu says you're fine, so any time you're ready. This is the big one, though. It's not going to feel great," the AI replied.

"No shit. Let's just get this over with. I'll go first this time."

"You're sure?" Samaira asked and Anya nodded. Before she could come up with another reason to delay, she pressed the confirm button on her menu for her advanced class.

There was nothing but horrid anticipation for a breathless moment, and then Anya had the sensation that something was rushing at her from somewhere, from all around her. It was as if the fabric of reality had turned against her and crushed itself toward her in a death grip.

It was a single encapsulated moment of agony, and then blessed, sweet nothingness.

Anya came to on the couch, but she was lying down, not sitting up. She wanted to turn her head to look around, but found that she had forgotten how. For a moment, she had nothing in her head but a formless, wordless sensation of confusion and mounting terror. She couldn't recall her name, where she was, or what was going on, only that she still hurt, and she was worried about someone.

Someone with hair like starlight and eyes like the ocean.

Then, all of it came back to her and her head rocked back into the couch cushions and her mouth opened in a silent gasp.

All of it came back, and so much more.

A flood of information—about Starforged skin, about the Light Dominion, about how Xhama Thul reacted with them, about how they reacted with her combat cognition, regeneration, Gravity Dominion, and more—slammed into her with the force of a comet.

Her back arched off the couch and her fingers clawed at the air as her mind swelled, pressed against the cage of her skull, and threatened to crack through.

Anya didn't know how long it lasted, but when it was over, she was covered in sweat and panting. Her muscles twitched and spasmed, and her head spun. She vomited onto the floor, mostly bile, and took several deep breaths.

"Holy shit," she said. "That fucking sucked."

But it was over. The worst was done. Her thoughts began to settle and her body started to relax.

"Anya?" Riley asked, his voice coming from the kitchen. He appeared leaning over the back of the couch, his eyes widening. "Damn! You all right? You look like shit."

"Just what every girl wants to hear," she said and managed to smile. "Feels like the worst hangover of my life, but it's going away. Where's Sam?"

"She's in your room. After seeing you go all weird after you confirmed your upgrades, she wanted to lie down, so she went to your bed. Decided not to risk moving you too much, so we just laid you out on the couch."

"Is she okay? How long was I out?"

"She seems fine, doctors are with her. Her AI's got her status screen up and it just shows that she's asleep. Same as you were for the last five minutes."

"Five minutes? Damn. Longest one by far. Felix? Is that normal?"

The AI floated above her and nodded.

"Given the data I have for your other level-ups, yes. It seems in-line. Are you feeling any better than you were a few seconds ago?" they asked.

Anya took stock of herself, patted herself down, then sat up with a grunt. She didn't want to fight any aliens at the moment, but she felt almost back to normal.

"Yeah. Every few seconds I get better. There's a lot in here now," Anya said and tapped her head. "Not to imply it was empty before."

"I mean, I wasn't gonna make a joke about that or anything," Riley smirked and shrugged. Anya shook her head and chuckled, then paused. Something felt different there.

She reached up and felt her temples, the back of her skull, and ran her fingers through her short red hair.

"Something the matter?" Riley asked.

"Not bad, just… different," Anya said. Her head felt odd, as if something were on it, but not, encircling it, but not touching it. There was nothing there that she could feel with her hands, but she felt something with her awareness, like that feeling of being watched, but not creepy.

It was comforting, a feeling not of being watched, but being watched over.

The living room was suddenly flooded with bright, golden light, and Riley cried out in alarm and threw his hand in front of his face. Anya yelped, and caught a look at herself in the reflection of a mirror near the door.

A circle of warm, honey-hued light encircled her head, the front of it rising up in a decorative peak, like a tiara.

Or a crown.

"Is that the Light Dominion thingy?" Anya asked.

"The Crown of the Firmament, yes," Felix said.

"You have a halo now?" Riley asked.

"Crown," Anya corrected.

"Looks like a halo to me. Is it always on like that? That's gonna suck when you gotta sleep."

"Um," Anya concentrated, and the crown disappeared in a scattering of firefly-sparkles that dimmed and vanished. The comforting feeling of being watched over was still there, but in the background. "There we go. Would've been hard to sleep with that on all the time."

"No shit. Good news is, if we ever have a power outage we can just stick you out in the airfield to direct planes in."

"Smart-ass."

Anya waited another minute before she made her last upgrade: the free points she had from her levels, and classes. It was another headache, another brief black-out, but nothing compared to before. When it was finally all done, she examined her menu.

ANYA NOWICKI: LEVEL 50 COSMIC WARDEN
First Class: Phoenix Monk
Second Class: Ascendant Skirmisher
Statistics

- Awareness-10
- Dexterity-37
- Fortitude-73
- Intelligence-18
- Strength-43
- Willpower-10

Skills

- Flame Dominion-58 (+5 from Artifact)
- Kinetic Dispersal-26
- Combat Cognition-23
- Regeneration-47
- Xhama Thul-26
- Gravity Dominion-31 (+5 from Artifact)
- Energy Focus- 21
- Flesh of the Starforge-20
- Light Dominion-35
- Zero-G Combat-10

- Sure Footing-10

And none of that included her gear bonuses, which she wasn't wearing, and which she hadn't upgraded yet.

"Jesus Christ," Anya shook her head.

Movement from the back of the apartment caught her eye, and Samaira and the pair of doctors emerged from her bedroom. Samaira leaned against the door frame and gave a weary smile.

"That was awful," she said, and then Anya was at her side.

"Are you okay?"she asked.

"Getting better, but still feel like I got run over by a tank."

"It took me a minute or two, but it'll pass."

"Mm. Getting there."

The doctors remained long enough to do a rudimentary physical exam for both women: they shone a light in their eyes and ears, tested their reflexes, and listened to their hearts. One of the doctors paused as he listened to Anya's hearts beat in tandem with each other.

"The two heartbeats thing is normal for me," she said.

"Riiiiiight," the doctor replied. After that, they were declared healthy and both of the doctors left. Riley lingered and made Anya and Samaira some tea while they sat on the couch. By the time the tea was ready, Samaira was back to normal.

"Geez, that sucked," she said and took the tea and began to blow on it. "Thanks, Riley."

"What now? You go out in the yard and practice more? Cause I know some of the other agents love watching that stuff. We can set up some chairs or something," he said.

"I'm down," Anya said.

"Sounds good to me. I can't wait to see what all this stuff looks and feels like. I know it in my head, but actually doing it is something else," Samaira said.

Riley left to go alert some other agents about the incoming show while Anya and Samaira strode out to the athletics field. It was sunny outside, but frost still clutched stubbornly to the grass, refusing to give way to the inevitable warmth that approached.

"What's the Water Dominion Artifact called?" Anya asked.

"Ichor of the Ocean," Samaira said.

"You heard any voices yet?"

Samaira cocked her head to the side and shook it.

"No. Did you hear your little friend right away?"

"I didn't know what they were back then, but yeah, as soon as I got the Sun's Heart I heard the voice."

Samaira bit her lip and looked down in thought, then said, "There was a lot of pain when I took the artifact, but I think I heard music? Something? I wasn't quite sure."

"Huh," Anya grunted. It would make sense if different Artifacts for the Dominions communicated differently. She hadn't heard anything from Gravity Dominion or Light Dominion yet... unless that feeling of being watched over was Light Dominion trying to communicate? She reasoned it was probably for the best. She didn't need a head full of interdimensional personalities blabbing at her constantly. The bird was plenty.

Still, she felt a little disappointment that she couldn't connect with the other artifacts enough to hear them.

At least, not yet, the bird whispered to her.

"You know something I don't?" Anya muttered.

I'd say that's an understatement. But about the other Dominions? No. You might hear them, you might not. I think Samaira is starting to hear hers, though. Look.

Samaira was standing opposite Anya in the middle of the field, her head tilted to the side again, as if listening for some faraway sound.

"Sam?" Anya asked.

"Y-yeah?" she stuttered, blinking and then refocusing on Anya. "Sorry. Yeah. I think I am hearing something. It's really pretty. Gone now. Anyway, you ready to try this out for real?"

"Oh yeah. Show me what you got!"

"What, you want me to hit you? With water, or something?"

"Well, yeah. All your other skills were crafting stuff. Besides, I wanna see how two opposite Dominions react with each other."

"Ooookay," Samaira said, and glanced across the field. Riley had returned with a small crowd of other agents and outpost personnel. They had brought chairs. And popcorn.

"Give 'em a good show," Anya said and winked. Samaira closed her eyes, took a breath, and then pointed a finger at Anya. A loud hissing noise filled the air, and Anya found herself within the middle of a dense fog bank within the span of a heartbeat.

"Uh," she said as she looked around. It wasn't fog, but steam. All of the frost on the grass all over the field had evaporated in an instant, and effectively blinded Anya's sight, and heat sense.

"You might wanna turn that star skin skill on, or however it works," Samaira called, her voice muffled by the steam.

"It's just water," Anya muttered and then let out a yelp as a base-ball-sized chunk of solid ice came whirling at her out of the steam and struck her in the butt. "Ow! Hey!"

"I told you!"

Anya wasn't really hurt. The ice chunk had been moving fast enough to dent a car, but her? Not even a bruise. It had startled her more than anything. But then another came at her and she dodged it, and then another, and another.

Anya focused inside of her for a moment, searching for whatever her Flesh of the Starforge skill had taught her. It was like a mental switch, or maybe some kind of new muscle she had to flex. She activated it, and her body instantly felt more solid. The comparison was stark.

Before she was just skin and bones and muscle. Now she felt as if she could stop a train with her face. Her skin took on a faint silvery sheen, but it still looked like skin. Another ice chunk flew at her and shattered on impact. Anya barely even registered the hit. Even better, her kinetic dispersal skill was somehow interacting with her new skin, nullifying the impact to nothing.

"Did it break?" Samaira called from somewhere beyond the steam.

"Yeah. Throw something bigger! Harder!"

"Uh, are you sure?"

"Fuck yeah!"

All of the steam contracted inward at an instant, revealing a frost-free field, and Samaira standing a few dozen yards away. She had contracted the steam into a hunk of ice bigger than Anya's torso, and shaped it into a blunt missile shape. Before Anya could protest, Samaira launched it at her faster than blinking.

Anya didn't even have time to put her arms up in front of her. It struck her straight in the chest… and shattered into a thousand shards of glittering ice. Anya was knocked back a step, but she only felt like somebody had given her a gentle shove.

"Oh my god! Are you hurt? I didn't mean to launch it that fast!" Samaira said and ran forward. Anya looked down at herself. She wasn't wearing her regalia, just her normal clothes. No bonuses to her defense or anything, just the Starforge skill.

Samaira slowed to a jog and then stopped when she was a few yards away from Anya. Her eyes widened as she took in her somewhat reflective, shining skin.

"That's really pretty," Samaira said, then poked Anya in the arm. She then knocked on her bicep like it were a door. There was a flat, rapping sound. "And hard. Dang. No wonder the ice broke."

"You ladies doing all right out there?" Riley called from the edge of the field. More outpost personnel had come to watch.

"Yeah, we're good!" Anya called back, then asked Samaira, "You made ice and steam from the frost. Do you have to use existing water in the environment, or can you just summon it?"

"I can just summon it. I think it's a lot like yours: having it around me makes it easier, but if I have to, I can just pull it from my ichor."

"That's like blood or something right? Is that safe?"

"It's like the Sun's Heart: too much can drain me, probably make me pass out, maybe even kill me. But in moderation? It's fine."

Samaira snapped her fingers and an ice sculpture appeared at the far, far end of the field. It was in the shape of the snake overseer, made to scale, and accurate down to the last detail. The assembled crowd of DERD agents on the sidelines all clapped and Samaira laughed and took a bow.

"Show off," Anya said and smirked at her. "But I'm impressed you managed to make something like that that quickly all the way across the field. I have trouble with anything beyond a distance of a few yards. Drains my energy pretty fast."

"Using the aether gives me a boost, plus my new aetheric materialization skill. But the statue's just target practice," Samaira said, and then pointed her finger at the statue and squinted one eye. A clear droplet appeared at the tip of her finger, grew to the size of a grape, and then burst outward in a perfectly straight jet of pressurized water. The beam of water blasted across the field, and cut through the ice sculpture like a laser, none of its force diminished by the distance of the field or the hardness of the solid block of ice.

More applause from the crowd of agents.

"That's pretty basic, but you get the idea." Samaira said. "I'm sure I'll come up with better uses for the Dominion than just 'throw ice,' or 'water beam.'"

"The steam thing was good," Anya replied. "Blinded me and gave you cover."

"What about your Light Dominion? And that other energy thing?"

"The way Felix described it, Light Dominion is buffs. So let's see," Anya muttered and glanced down at the now dry, frost-free grass of the field. She focused her attention on a single point nearby and a flickering orange flame appeared.

"Sam, can you put some water on that?" Anya asked.

"Sure," Samaira replied. She waved her hand and a spray of water extinguished the flame.

"Very underwhelming," Riley said. "Zero stars."

"That was the normal stuff. Now," she said, and then searched for that comforting presence around her. The field was immediately bathed in warm, radiant light, and Samaira, Riley, and the agents flinched for a moment. "The enhanced version."

Anya drew on the Crown and Heart together. The primal thumping heat of the heart, and the radiant comfort of the Crown spun together, and with a gesture, Anya summoned another fire on the grass. This one was significantly larger, despite her using the same amount of energy as last time, and it was gold. And kind of glittery.

"Oooooh," Samaira said.

"All right. It's pretty, I guess," Riley shrugged.

"Try putting it out again, Sam," Anya said. Samaira did as she was asked, spraying a gentle stream of water from the palm of her hand onto the flame.

It stayed.

Samaira turned the gentle spray into a more sustained stream, like something from a hose. The fire remained, turning the water to steam and continuing to burn. Finally, when Samaira had dumped about a small pool's worth of water on it, the fire went out. Samaira lowered her arm and shook her hand and wrist as if she had a cramp.

"Geez. Were you sustaining that at all?" she asked Anya, who shook her head.

"Nope. Set it and forget it."

"Throw a fireball or something!" one of the DERD agents shouted.

"Turn Riley into an ice statue!" another added.

"Turn Riley into a flaming ice statue, then throw him!" another said.

"When did you all turn into assholes?" Riley demanded, and he and the agents began heckling each other. Anya laughed and watched them until her ear beeped and she froze.

"Anya," Felix said in her ear, "I've finished decoding the alien data stream. You're definitely going to want to see this."

She exchanged a look with Samaira, and saw by the serious look on her face that she'd gotten the update as well.

"Riley," Samaira said and tapped him on the shoulder. "We need to see MacDougal. Right away."

20

The data stream showed over a month of activity. It lasted from when the snake overseer had died in front of the ruins of the White House, to the end of the fight with the centipede overseer at the atoll.

Anya didn't know what she had been expecting, but this wasn't it.

As soon as Felix had told them that the data stream had finished decoding, Riley had contacted MacDougal. She had just finished reviewing Pan's and Esmeralda's skillsets, approved both, and notified President Hanover.

All of them—Anya, Samaira, Pan (who was napping next to Anya), Esmeralda, Riley, and MacDougal—sat in MacDougal's large office staring at Anya's map screen. Felix had expanded it to fill up one entire wall of the office, allowing them to see the various moving dots that signaled the aliens' locations across the globe over the course of the last month.

It wasn't that hard to keep track of them, because the aliens had shrank in number from hundreds, to just several dozen.

The day of the White House assault had been planned. The aliens had coordinated their movements to strike out simultaneously at pockets of hosts across the world, including the NAT in India and the hosts in the EU, as well as other groups across Asia, Africa, and South America. They hadn't had a full picture of the scope of the attack until several days after, but it had been decisively won in the favor of humanity, resulting in mass alien casualties. The first major victory for planet Earth.

The data on the map showed the aliens in full retreat after the assault, and then weeks of them hiding in remote locations: mountains, deserts, but mostly the oceans. A few would go out and scout for days at a time, sometimes happening upon stray hosts by chance, but that was all.

Then, two weeks ago, the change happened. Almost all of the aliens converged at a single point in the Pacific, and stayed there for several days. After that, several dozen signals emerged. One signal remained on its own, while the others stayed close together.

The mass of signals were the centipede overseer and the lesser gnosiphages it had brought with it to the atoll. Felix confirmed the match, but even if they hadn't, it approached the site of Outpost #2 the night Esmeralda had described, and remained during the next day when Anya's and Arvo's signals appeared.

Before and after the attack on Outpost #2, the centipede and the group of other gnosiphages with it made stops at various points along the coastlines of anything that touched the Pacific: America, Mexico, Chile, Australia, Japan, and several others. It also made brief excursions into the Indian Ocean, but didn't stay for long.

Whenever the centipede and the other gnosiphages stopped, they repeated a pattern. First, they would all stop at a coastline, and the lesser gnosiphages would spread out and make excursions inland while the centipede stayed in the water. Next, the lesser aliens would trek about fifty miles in every direction away from the ocean, if the terrain allowed, forming a criss-crossing web and obvious search pattern. After that, they returned to the ocean and the centipede and returned as a group to the singular gnosiphage in the ocean, far away from them. Then the centipede would leave alone at high speed, and visit several locations while the lesser aliens remained behind. The centipede would scout coastlines on its own, searching— usually for half-a-day or so—but never go inland. Finally, the centipede would go back to collect the lesser gnosiphages, and return to one of the locations it had previously scouted, and the pattern would repeat.

"Well, at least now we know the Engineers' signal blocker works for sure," Anya said as she looked at the map data looping back and playing again from the beginning. "And we know the fake signal bait Gary and the others made works. Holy shit, look at it."

The day they activated the beacon, a single dot appeared in the middle of the Pacific, impossible to miss. The other host signals had previously looked like circles of various size and brightness, based on how close an alien was to finding the host in question. The closer they were, the smaller and brighter the circle got until it was a single pinprick of light. But since the Engineers scrambled the host signals, they had all become massive and pale, overlapping each other across the globe, and hundreds, sometimes thousands of miles in diameter.

The beacon was too precise and bright to ignore, even though to Anya, it practically screamed "This is definitely a trap." Maybe the gnosiphages didn't have a concept of traps, or if they didn't before, they did now.

"We know this one was the centipede," MacDougal said and pointed at the dot on the map with the other alien signals. "And we're sure none of the other aliens with it at the atoll was an overseer?"

"Positive!" Felix said. "Having now received datastreams from two of the gnosiphage overseers, I can confirm they're somewhat unique among the aliens. Of the aliens we killed at the atoll, only one was an overseer."

"So that's the last one, then," Samaira said and looked at the single, solitary dot that drifted slowly around the waters of the Pacific. It was really only slow in comparison to the centipede and the other aliens, though. It was still fast enough to cross most of the ocean in a single day, while the rest of the gnosiphages managed it in a few hours.

"The centipede and that one," Samaira said and pointed at the last alien, "are the ones with the highest kill counts too. I think the hosts from the New Allied Territories said it was as big as a house and looked like a crab."

"I'm designating the centipede as Alien Omega, and that last one as

Alien Alpha," MacDougal said and made a note in her report. "No points for originality, but it'll do."

"I don't get it," Riley said. "Where the hell did the rest of the aliens go? There were hundreds of the damn things and then just, poof. Gone."

"We know we don't get stronger and level-up from fighting each other, but maybe they do," Samaira said.

"But I thought Dr. Immonen said they already share information with each other. They're one brain spread out over hundreds of bodies, right?" Riley asked

"But they can't all do everything," MacDougal said. "Those bodies are still limited. Even the overseers can only do so much. Upadhyay, you and Hendricks fought one of them in Chicago, then it got away and you fought it again a few days later. It's abilities changed between the two fights, correct?"

"They did," Samaira confirmed.

"So the lesser aliens at least can't just keep stacking skills. They have a limited number of options. If something like what Upadhyay said is true, and the aliens all sacrificed themselves to the Big Alpha here, that'd be one powerful monster."

"It's just an idea."

"One that fits. There's no way the signals could be hiding somehow?"

"Nope!" Felix said. "From what I can see of the datastream, the gnosiphages don't have the ability to remove their signals from each other, unlike the hosts. Since they're all one single consciousness, that makes sense."

"Excuse me?" Esmeralda said and raised her hand. MacDougal sighed and looked at her.

"Gomez, this is not a classroom. You can speak your mind."

"Right. S-sorry. I just… I don't understand why Alien Omega and the others were going around to all these places and taking normal people? I get why it killed the people at Outpost Two: me and the other hosts were there, and we're the target, and people were in the way. But these other places that have been on the news, there weren't any hosts there. Why bother just killing random people with no hosts around?"

"Cover its tracks?" Anya shrugged. "They've been trying to keep a low profile. If people saw the alien scouting party, they'd kill them to stay hidden. That's probably why they didn't leave bodies behind, either."

"Oh, right. Makes sense, I guess."

"I got a question too," Riley said. "When we were at Outpost Two, it was just the controlled hosts: Jiro, Kan, and Grant. The centipede and its escort of the other aliens never showed up. Why?"

"At the time you and Anya arrived at Outpost Two, the centipede's gnosiphage escort were with Alien Alpha, here," Felix said, and rewound the map display to the time of the attack. They pointed at Alien Alpha's location, hundreds and hundreds of miles away from Outpost #2. "Alien Omega remained about a mile or two away from shore during the fight at the outpost. As for why it didn't engage, or why the other aliens remained with Alien Alpha, I can't say."

"It looks like they're guarding it, for whatever reason. Whenever all the little ones come back to Alpha, it stops moving. Then they all stay near it while Omega goes and scouts around," Anya said.

"How many people were killed by Omega?" Samaira asked.

"You. Felix," MacDougal said and pointed at the floating, rose-headed hologram. "Can you tell me which cities Omega and the scouting party hit?"

"I can! Here's a list!" Felix said and a window popped up beside them with over fifty locations on it, in chronological order, and with GPS coordinates.

"Geez," Anya winced as she saw the number of places Omega and its scouting party had terrorized.

"Riley: make a note of these places and send it to the Bureau and state department."

"On it, Director."

"That seems like an awful lot," Esmeralda said as she studied the list.

"It does, but it's spread across over a month of time and what looks like thirty different countries. Most of those are still developing, so it may have been days before anybody missing was noticed, if ever,"

MacDougal said. "Even under normal circumstances, the number of people that just up and disappear is more than you might think."

"At least the bastard's dead," Riley grunted as he finished tapping out a message on his phone.

"Which leaves Big Al," Anya said as she looked at the single glowing dot in the Pacific. At the moment of Alien Omega's death, the last recent data they had, Alien Alpha was far south, off the coast of Chile. Its movement patterns were random, as far as Anya could tell. Sometimes it wouldn't move for hours, or days at a time, and at others it zig-zagged all over the ocean, even going up into the Arctic Circle on a few occasions. It never got too close to land, however, only ever drawing as close as ten or fifteen miles before scooting back out to sea.

"We can try using a beacon again to lure it," MacDougal said, but her tone was wary. "I doubt they'll go for it. If they really do share one brain, they'll know that any signals they pick up from now on will carry a risk of ambush."

"Worth a shot," Riley shrugged, then looked through some papers in a folder nearby. "The last beacon got trashed in the fight, looks like it'll be a few days before there's another."

"That's fine. We need to make sure our allies are on the same page as we are, and that we can distribute the data stream to any countries that didn't send hosts to the fight with Omega," MacDougal said and sighed. "I think that's enough for now. Stay on-base, but stay alert. Just because there's only one alien left doesn't mean we're out of the woods. Dismissed."

————

THE REST of the day was spent checking in with the other hosts around the world. Gary had reviewed the datastream from Omega on his own, and come to many of the same conclusions as the others, including that Alien Alpha, or Big Al, would likely not fall for their beacon trick again.

"No harm in trying it," Gary said, "But I don't hold out much hope for it working again. Which means it's back to the damn drawing board. On the plus side, word's got around now that our plan worked, so suddenly a lot more people are looking to cooperate. Especially now that there's only one alien left."

"Do they know it's probably a big-ass alien that ate all its little siblings?" Anya asked and Gary chuckled.

"I doubt they've gotten to that part yet. They probably just heard we killed all the aliens except for one and now they think it'll be a cakewalk. If we can find the bastard, maybe. But if it's big enough, I'm tempted to just nuke the thing."

Anya paused.

"Have you made nukes, Gary?" she asked. It was late and she was in her room, but she kept her voice low. Since Gary had helped build Outpost #2, she wasn't too concerned with bugs or listening devices. That didn't mean somebody wouldn't overhear her from outside, though.

"Technically, no."

"Technically?"

"If you're asking me if I've made nuclear weapons, no, absolutely not. Nothing of the sort."

"But?"

"But I have a few very large bombs, yeah."

"How large?"

"They're scalable. The smallest they can be set for is a little smaller than the ones we dropped on Hiroshima and Nagasaki. The largest boom would swallow Chicago and most of its suburbs. Take a good chunk out of the Lake Michigan coastline, too. Those are the terrestrial bombs I got. I got a few bigger ones that are for off-planet only. Too dangerous to use on Earth. Won't even activate in an environment with atmosphere as a failsafe."

"Jesus, Gary," Anya said.

"They're last resort. I had a little one on stand-by during the fight with the centipede. If things were going poorly, I'd have my Guardians snatch you and any survivors up, get clear, and then fire one bomb. The minimum safe distance would've required us to get out of the datastream range. So the aliens would be dead, but we'd lose out on the data. Probably the experience, too."

"I'm glad it didn't come to that. MacDougal and Hanover are

already twitchy enough about you without knowing you have super-bombs."

"Screw 'em. Well, Hanover, at least. MacDougal's still treating you right?"

"Yeah, she's good. Got a bit of a stick up her ass, but she's decent."

"If that changes, let me know. In the meantime, I'll be trying to figure out how to make an alien tracker that isn't total garbage. Have a good night, kid."

"Night Gary. Don't work too hard."

Gary waved and then his screen went dark, and Anya was alone.

The sight of that single dot on the map wormed its way through her brain as she tried to sleep. It was somehow worse than the idea of hundreds of killer aliens scattered across the world. Anya shut her eyelids, but the dot in the Pacific glowed behind them anyway.

21

Everything official that happened over the next few days was over Anya's head. MacDougal had her various political and directorial duties to tend to, most of which included contacting other national defense organizations and distributing the alien datastream, and meetings with President Hanover. Gary was constructing their next beacon and thinking about how to build an improved alien tracker.

This gave Anya, Samaira, and the other hosts time to go over each other's upgrades and practice. Since the loss of Outpost #2 and its partial destruction during the fight, Jiro and Esmeralda had been permanently relocated to Outpost #1. Jiro took to the practice sessions with silent assent, but Esmeralda always acted like she'd rather have her teeth pulled out than practice fighting.

By the third day of no orders to do anything but wait, Anya was starting to go stir-crazy. She'd spent plenty of time at Outpost #1 before, weeks, but things had been different then. The aliens had—as far as anybody had been aware at the time—just been hiding. But now they knew they weren't, and the one alien left on the planet was up to something big.

The fact that only one alien, no matter how dangerous they were, was left made it worse. They were so close to victory, so close to wiping the gnosiphages out, and now they just had to sit on their hands and stare at the walls of the outpost.

Anya was actually relieved to hear MacDougal wanted a meeting with her later that morning, because maybe the director had something for her to do.

MacDougal looked up from her desk when Anya arrived, and Anya winced as she looked at her. The director normally looked like she had been born in professional attire: everything neatly creased, matching, and in its place. But her graying hair now had a few tight curls springing out of place, her nail polish was chipped, and her blouse was wrinkled. She also had heavy bags under her eyes that, for the first time since Anya had known her, appeared to be made out of flesh-and-blood rather than carved from solid wood.

"Nowicki," she said. "Riley tells me you've been pacing around the outpost when you're not sparring with Upadhyay or Yamada."

"Uh, yeah. Just kinda spinning my wheels," she said.

"Have any of the hosts from the NAT contacted you recently?"

"Noooo," Anya said, drawing the word out and arching an eyebrow. "I mean, not since the battle at the White House. I tried to touch base with them a few times, but you have my reports on that. They either ignore my calls, or tell me to 'Connect through official channels.'"

"Well, they contacted President Hanover earlier today. They've extended a formal invitation to you and Pan to come visit them in New Bengaluru."

There was a long pause as Anya's thoughts swirled around her head in confusion.

"What? Why me? And Pan?"

"The only details they gave us were that it had something to do with you being in physical proximity to two of the three overseer gnosiphages, and that it was necessary to finding Alien Alpha. As for Pan, no damn clue. The President has requested that you accept the invitation and meet with them immediately."

"Requested, huh?"

"He initially ordered it. He's within his rights to order you to go.

Commander-in-chief, all that. I told him I'd let you know about the invitation first."

"Just me? Sam, Arvo, Esmi, nobody else can come? Just me and Pan?"

"That Chinese host, the one with the big rifle and invisibility cloak—"

"Zixin."

"Him. He was the one that made contact with the Oval Office. He said any host is welcome in the New Allied Territories, but not if they're employed by any other world government. You and Pan are the exceptions, and only on a temporary basis."

Anya frowned.

"It's unexpected, I agree," MacDougal continued. "Some of the intel reports I've gotten make it clear they're keen on maintaining their privacy. The CIA's lost more than a few satellites that have wandered over NAT airspace."

"And they didn't mention wanting the decoded datastream or anything like that?"

"We gave it to them along with every other government with hosts in it that we know of. Hanover initially wanted to keep our recording to our immediate allies only, but I told him that wouldn't look good for him if the word got out he'd kept vital intel away from other countries."

Anya thought back over her fights with the snake and the centipede. Sam, Gary, Pan, and Arvo had been present at both fights. Arvo had made more significant contact with the snake than she had, but he'd kept his distance from the centipede. Sam hadn't physically touched either, nor had Gary. But then, neither had Pan.

Anya had gotten up-close with both of them but she'd just fought the things. She hadn't scanned the snake, like Arvo had, or interfered with the centipede psychically like Renn or Esmeralda.

"They also said they would consider your acceptance of their invitation as a favor, and be willing to offer you something in exchange. And Pan. Within reason," MacDougal added and Anya raised her eyebrows again. "Frankly, even if they hadn't made that offer, I'd tell you to go."

"Just to spy on them?"

"Hanover would love that. I'll expect a full report on everything you see and hear while you're there, but no, that's not the primary reason. I got the numbers from all the locations the centipede visited and the tally of missing people. 15,678, spread across thirty-eight countries."

"Jesus Christ," Anya breathed. "How did it take so many and nobody noticed?"

"The Pacific Rim and the east side of the Indian Ocean covers a lot of coastline. A lot. And those thirty-eight countries don't always keep a regular back-and-forth going. So we might hear about seventeen people vanishing in California, a couple dozen outside Vancouver, Maybe ten near Tokyo and another thirty outside Beijing. But places like El Guapinol, Honduras? Or Gagidu in Papa New Guinea?"

MacDougal shook her head.

"Our intel network isn't omnipresent, despite what some spy movies might make you think. Even if we do hear about things like that, we might not connect the dots until we have all the data in front of us.

"And I'm sorry to say, it gets worse. I got a report from the Department of National Defense in Canada about an hour ago. You ever hear of a little town called Port Hardy?"

Anya shook her head and MacDougal continued.

"It's in British Columbia, about 4,000 people lived there."

"'Lived'?"

"Yes. Past tense. The town's a ruin, now. Sometime after midnight last night and four in the morning today, something bad happened. Residents from Port McNeil, about three miles down the road, called emergency services after they reported hearing multiple explosions and seeing fire in the distance. Minor earthquakes, too. By the time first responders arrived, the place was unrecognizable. No signs of bodies, but plenty of violence. Some human remains. And non-human.

"Whatever this thing is, it's not done hiding, but it is done being subtle. Whatever the centipede was doing with its raids around the Pacific, Alpha is picking up the slack. We can't let this thing keep wandering around out there."

"Yeah, no shit. All right. I'll meet with the NAT. Seems like a no-brainer."

"Good, because if you'd refused, I'd order you anyway. But you're aware this means no back-up. The political situation with the Indian government in-exile, the States, the UN, and the NAT and its neighbors is complicated, to put it mildly. If they try to pull anything on you, you'll be on your own. At least, officially. That means we can't send in any government-affiliated hosts to pull your ass out."

Anya sighed, but nodded. "Right."

"Hendricks is unaffiliated though," MacDougal added and gave Anya a knowing look. "For plausible deniability, I can't advise you to ask him to keep an eye out for you, but what you do on your own time isn't my business."

"Gotcha," Anya said and winked.

"You leave as soon as you can. I'll let you tell Pan. If he doesn't want to go, he doesn't have to, but they seemed to want him almost as much as you. God knows why. Dismissed."

Anya turned on her heel and left without another word. Her mind was already buzzing with questions, anxiety, excitement, and what felt like a hundred other emotions. She went to Sam's dorm, and they sat together on the couch while Anya relayed everything MacDougal had just told her.

"It sucks, but I get it," Samaira said when Anya had finished. "I don't think it's any kind of trap, but even if it is, it's too good to pass up. If they can help us find and stop Alpha, then it's worth it."

"Yeah. I doubt it's a trap. Seems like a lot of trouble just for me and Pan. And what would they even do, anyway? Kill us? Jail us? They could try that without all this pretending-to-need-my-help stuff," Anya said. Samaira winced when she mentioned the NAT killing her.

"Just be careful. You've told Gary?"

"Not yet. Wanted to tell you first."

"If he can help keep an eye out for you, all the better. I'll see if there's anything we can do that wouldn't cause a war to break out."

"Maybe you guys could just come hang out near the border?"

Samaira chuckled, but shook her head. "I doubt it. The way some of MacDougal's reports with other countries read, it's like they just consider us all walking nuclear bombs. Imagine if some hostile nation started putting nukes in America's backyard. It'd be like the Cuban Missile Crisis, but with super-powered people. Probably not something anybody wants to risk. But if you're in danger... yeah. I'll be there, quick as I can."

"Thanks, Sam. I guess I should pack an overnight bag or something. Give Gary a call," Anya sighed. While she was glad to have something to do, and even more than a bit excited at the prospect of seeing the New Allied Territories for herself, she wished she wasn't leaving Samaira behind.

"I'll go get Pan and tell him what's going on while you do that. Meet you at the hangar and the Shadow Ray?"

"See you there," Anya said, then went to her room to pack and talk with Gary while she did. Her conversation with him was a shorter, terser version of the one with Samaira: Gary didn't like the thought of her going in alone, but agreed it was a tempting offer, and that he would keep an eye out for her. He said he had to prep some things, but to call him again when she was in the air.

Anya met Samaira and Pan by the hangar a few minutes later. Pan also had a little shoulder bag with him, the edge of his ant farm poking out of the top.

"We're really gonna go on a trip? And see Ursula and other hosts?" Pan asked, rocking back and forth on his wide tail with delight.

"That's the plan," Anya said. "C'mon, get strapped in and we'll head out."

"Okay!" Pan waddled into the Ray and began to get himself situated, leaving Anya and Samaira a moment to themselves.

"Come back safe," Samaira said and gave Anya a gentle kiss. She returned it, a bit more forcefully, and was pleased to feel Samaira lean into her.

"See you soon," she said, and then gave her a wave as she entered the Shadow Ray and took off. The cold Alaskan horizon stretched ahead, and the New Allied Territories waited beyond.

22

She spoke with Gary again once Pan fell asleep. She loved the little guy, but he wasn't the best at being discrete. She didn't want him to give away that Gary was helping them in any way once they were inside the NAT.

"I'll be keeping a low profile once you're with those NAT guys," he said. "You won't see me unless something goes wrong, but I'll be keeping a real close eye on you."

"Thanks. Hopefully all this is just paranoia," Anya said.

"If it is, they're just as paranoid about everybody outside their borders as the feds are about the folks inside. That whole country is locked up tighter than a nun's..." Gary stopped himself and cleared his throat. "Well, it's secure."

Anya laughed and added, "MacDougal mentioned the CIA had lost satellites once they passed over NAT airspace. You tried spying on them at all?"

"Not really. I've sent some scouts along the coast, and I've had my asteroid mining bots snap a few pictures if they happened to be in a good position. From what I can tell, Vastukar hasn't been spying on me at all either. Figured I'd return the professional courtesy."

"Really? You're certain?"

"Pretty much, yup. I've got the airspace, land, and underground monitored 24/7 for a couple hundred miles around my factory. Nothing to speak of. A few drones off the coast, but that's it."

"Figured he would've been more up in your business."

"From what I've seen, all of their attention is focused inward. Not a lot of coming and going. I wouldn't be surprised if they were spying on the States and other big powers like China or the EU, but nothing overt so far. If what Vastukar's said about rebuilding India is true, that makes sense. Resources wouldn't be a problem for him if he's got tech anything like mine. And if they have more hosts, it means they can draw on the RAC store more. No need to worry about trade or anything else."

"MacDougal said she's going to want a report on everything I see."

"Doesn't surprise me. I'll be taking pictures and things like that while I watch your back, but you're the focus, not whatever tech Vastukar has set-up."

"Appreciate it."

"How long a flight is it until you're there?"

"Another couple hours. Not a bad trip considering it's about halfway across the planet."

"All right. My advice is to try and rest like Pan. Never know when you might get the chance to get some shut-eye again."

"Is that something you learned in the Marines?"

"Yeah. Served me well, too. If things go well, you won't hear from me again until you're out of the NAT. Good luck, kid, and keep your head on a swivel."

"I will, thanks Gary," Anya said, and closed the communication window. She leaned back in the pilot's seat and brought up her menu, figuring she would apply all her free upgrade tokens and her wealth of RAC before she arrived in New Bengaluru.

It took the better part of an hour until Anya pressed the "CONFIRM," button on her purchases, and her RAC dropped from nearly three million, all the way down to 274,181. Anya winced, but then any buyer's remorse was erased as soon as she touched the quickchange stone on her wristband, and her upgraded regalia, mantle, and chest-guard swapped with her regular clothes.

"Holy fucking headrush," Anya swooned and leaned back in the chair. If she'd been standing, she would have fallen over. It took her a moment to adjust, but when she did, she felt like she could crack open the Earth itself.

EQUIPPED ITEMS & Artifacts

- Shard of the Everstar (x2)
- Alchemical Tincture of Restoration (x2)
- Sun's Heart (Masterwork): Grants access to higher level of Flame Dominion skill. (+33% efficiency when using this artifact)(+14 to related skill for this quality)
- Singularity's Grasp (Refined): Grants access to higher level of Gravity Dominion skill. (+20% efficiency when using this artifact) (+8 to related skill for this quality)
- Crown of the Firmament (Refined): Grants access to higher level of Light Dominion skill. (+20% efficiency when using this artifact) (+8 to related skill for this quality)
- Regalia of St. Llothec, the Ever-Burning (Epic): Provides protection from any and all heat-based hazards, as well as kinetic damage. Also boosts the wearer's innate heat-producing abilities and endurance. (This Epic quality item has a current cap of five lesser-quality runes and three equal-quality runes) (+12 to Flame Dominion skill, +6 to Kinetic Dispersal skill, +5 to Fortitude statistic)
- Rune of the Shield (Excellent): Provides dual enhancements to quality and defense of imbued item. (+100% to item durability parameters and +100% defensive bonus) (+4 to Kinetic Dispersal skill)
- Rune of the Shield's Embrace (Epic): Provides additional defensive covering beyond the standard coverage of imbued item. (+110% of item's base defensive capabilities to any uncovered body parts, additional +33% defensive capabilities to covered areas)

- Rune of the Maiden (Excellent): Provides dual enhancements to healing and stamina of the wearer of imbued item. (+8 to Regeneration skill and +4 to Fortitude statistic)
- Rune of the Warrior (Excellent): Provides dual enhancements to strength and agility of the wearer of the imbued item. (+4 to Strength and Dexterity statistics)
- Rune of the Stallion (Excellent): Provides dual enhancements to speed and stamina of the wearer of the imbued item. (+5 to Fortitude and Dexterity statistics)
- Rune of the Mender (Epic): Repairs damage done to imbued item, provided the item remains above 8% of total durability. Item requires at least twenty minutes to repair per 15% of damage done.
- Rune of the Comet (Epic): Provides dual enhancements to the gravitational and heat abilities of the wearer. (+8 to Gravity and Flame Dominions)
- Rune of Force (Excellent): Provides dual enhancements to the gravitational and kinetic abilities of the wearer. (+6 to Gravity Dominion and Kinetic Dispersal)
- Mantle of the Gale (Excellent): Imbues the wearer with additional speed as well as a light deflective wind-shield. (this Excellent quality item has a current cap of five lesser-quality runes and three equal-quality runes) (+3 to Dexterity statistic)
- Rune of the Vortex (Refined): Provides dual enhancements to any wind-based abilities of the item and speed of the wearer. (+8 to wind-based air skills inherent to item, +4 to Dexterity statistic)
- Rune of the Greater Salamander (Excellent): Imbued item is granted resistance from fire and wearer's fire-based abilities are enhanced. At this quality level, a portion of fire damage may heal the wearer. (+100% to heat and fire resistance for item, +4 to Flame Dominion, +1 to Regeneration)
- Rune of the Brute (Refined): Provides dual enhancements to the power and hand-to-hand fighting ability of the wearer of

the imbued item. (+3 to Strength statistic and +6 to Xhama Thul skill)

- Rune of the Sentinel (Excellent): Provides dual enhancements to durability and a defensive ability of the wearer. (+4 to Fortitude statistic and +8 to Flesh of the Starforge)
- Rune of the Star (Excellent): Provides boosts to any support and energy enhancement abilities of the wearer. (+8 to Light Dominion and Energy Focus)
- Rune of Radiance (Refined): Provides enhancement to any support abilities of the wearer. (+8 to Light Dominion)
- Rune of the Golem (Refined): Provides dual enhancements to power and a defensive ability of the wearer. (+3 to Strength and +6 to Flesh of the Starforge)
- Rune of Channeling (Refined): Provides enhancement to any energy enhancement ability of the wearer. (+8 to Energy Focus)
- Sacred Orichalcum Chestguard (Charmed)(Masterwork): Grants bonuses to protection and healing abilities of the wearer. Provides excellent defense for the covered area. (+5 to Fortitude statistic and +10 to Regeneration skill) (Bonus +3 to Fortitude statistic and +6 to Regeneration skill due to similar bonuses on worn items)

"Lookin' good," she said, and laced her hands behind her head as she settled into her seat.

"With these upgrades, your Fortitude stat level is at 95, and your Flame Dominion skill level is at 96!" Felix said. "That's impressive!"

"It feels impressive. Wait, the stat and skill caps are at 100, right? Am I gonna stop being able to level them soon?"

Felix shook their head.

"That cap is for how many skill or stat points you can enter into a skill. If you had no gear, no bonuses, no anything, the highest you could raise a skill or stat is to level 100. But with additional enhancements—like gear—you can raise it higher than that. I don't have any data on how high it goes though, just that the Archive allows, and has planned for, increases beyond the level cap."

"Some ways to go to the power ceiling, I guess. Damn, this feels kinda crazy," Anya said and put her hand over her Sun's Heart.

It feels weird to me too, the bird said. *Still artificial, but the workmanship is admirable.*

Anya closed her menu screen and let herself get used to the enhancements. It took longer than usual, but after a while, she barely noticed the changes anymore. She hoped she wouldn't need any of her upgrades in New Bengaluru, but if she did, she'd be ready.

———

SOMETHING from the Shadow Ray's console let out an angry-sounding beep. Not quite an alarm, but not a good sound, either. Anya sat upright in the pilot's seat, blinking rapidly and looking across the many display panels in front of her.

One of them had turned red, and showed a diagram of the Shadow Ray in profile. The magnetic lifts in the diagram were flashing, and a blinking message that read, "NOT RESPONDING."

"Oh shit," Anya said and unstrapped herself from her seat. If the magnetic lifts had stopped working, they'd start to fall soon. She'd grab Pan and fly them both out. Maybe she could try and float the Ray down to the water or land or wherever they were and have Gary pick them up, or something.

That was when she noticed something outside the cockpit window. She'd been so focused on the glaring red display panel that she hadn't seen it.

There was a ship outside.

It looked like something out of a sci-fi movie: it was chrome, and had a smooth, organic shape, without any breaks in its structure to indicate where it had been assembled. It sort of resembled a tear drop turned on its side, but the rounder end was spread out further, and the pointed end faced forward. Three narrow lines of glowing green light stretched from the craft's nose to the tail: along the top and on both sides. The only break in the perfect chrome surface of the craft—aside from the glowing lines—was a black, reflective window.

The vessel itself was several times larger than Anya's Shadow Ray, nearly the size of a house. The sunlight gleamed off its surface even as it cast a shadow on the smaller craft before it.

Anya's attention was drawn away from the shiny airship outside to the Ray's display panels once again as all of them lit up with red warning signs.

"POWER FAILURE."

"CLOAKING INACTIVE."

"BATTERY EMPTY."

A dozen other equally severe warnings began to flash and blare around her.

"Anya? What's going on?" Pan asked as he woke up behind her.

"It's okay, buddy. Just hang on," Anya replied, and then everything in the Shadow Ray went dark. The displays all blinked off and the internal lighting failed. However, despite having no power, the Ray floated in place, nose-to-nose with the chrome vessel outside.

Anya's ear beeped.

"Call from Zixin," Felix said.

"Bring it up," Anya replied, and was greeted with a screen showing a middle-aged Chinese man. "Is this you? Did you fuck up my ride?"

"Hello, pleasure to meet you," Zixin said, his voice thick with sarcasm. "We did not 'fuck-up' your ride, we've merely stalled it. We're going to bring it aboard the ship you see in front of you. Your vehicle won't be damaged or altered. We just don't want you flying where you please or setting off the perimeter security. Is that all right?"

Anya grumbled and nodded.

"Yeah, fine. Just give me a warning or something next time. I thought we were gonna crash."

"We're not used to visitors."

"No shit," Anya said, and then Zixin hung up on her.

"Everything's all right?" Pan asked.

"Yeah, Pan, we're fine. Just people being rude. We—ah!" Anya let out a startled yelp as the Shadow Ray lurched forward. The chrome ship outside loomed closer as an unseen force drew the two ships together. The underside of the chrome vessel opened to reveal a docking bay within. The metallic surface of the craft parted in a widening ring of rippling chrome, just large enough for the Shadow Ray to pass through and settle on the deck of the other ship's docking bay.

When the Ray had stopped moving, Anya and Pan exited out the back and looked around. The docking bay was a roughly triangular room with smooth, matte silver walls, floor, and ceiling. Like the outside, it was impossible to see any creases or lines where the room had been assembled or welded together.

A soft, white glow emitted from recessed lights along the ceiling, pointing toward the tip of the triangular room, and a stairway leading up.

"Hello?" Anya called, but received no answer. She extended her hand to Pan, who grasped it gently between his claws, and the two of them climbed the stairs together. As soon as they had passed through the doorway, the metal rippled and closed behind them into another featureless wall.

"Dammit," Anya grumbled. "My bag's still in the Ray."

She decided she could get it later, and she could melt the wall if she absolutely had to. She and Pan continued up the stairs, and then down another hall to a door.

The door opened into a cockpit, but one much larger than the Shadow Ray's. Two black leather chairs with high backs sat facing glossy black counters and the angled window of the cockpit Anya had seen from outside. Nobody was in the chairs, and there was no sign that anybody else had been in the cockpit at all.

Indicator lights, messages, and screens of data flashed across the glossy black counter. That was similar to the Shadow Ray, at least: it was just one big screen stretched in front of the pilot and co-pilot's chairs. Unlike the Ray, there weren't any obvious means of flying the vessel: no throttle, no control discs, nothing. Clouds swept by the window, becoming thicker and grayer as they sped forward.

"Autopilot, I guess," Anya muttered as she and Pan continued to poke around the cockpit.

"Yes and no," a voice said and Anya jumped. The voice was deep, terse, and touched with an Indian accent. Anya had only heard it from internet broadcasts and killer robots before.

Vastukar.

"At the moment, it's more like remote control. I'm flying the ship personally, to make sure nothing goes wrong. However, all of my vehicles are capable of total autonomy."

"Yeah, neat. Thanks for looking out for us. I guess," Anya said.

"Please, take a seat," Vastukar said, and both of the chairs rotated to face Anya and Pan. The pangolin didn't hesitate, scrabbling up into the chair at once, while Anya eased into hers as if it might bite her.

"So, why me and Pan?" Anya asked after a few moments of silence.

"I think it would be better to wait until you are here to answer that. Pan, however, is simple. Ursula requested he come," Vastukar said.

"Ursula wants to see me?" Pan asked. "That's nice!"

"That's it?" Anya said.

"Ursula has a low opinion of humanity. I am trying to convince her otherwise, and I've made some progress. However, she sees everybody outside of the NAT as a problem. It's a bit of a long story, but the short version is that Ursula became very upset when she learned what poor stewards humanity has been for the planet, and our history of war. She wants an opportunity to convince Pan to leave the outside world behind, and show him around. She insisted. I told her that so long as everybody who comes to the NAT does so of their own free will, then it was fine."

"I'm staying with Anya," Pan said.

"She said you'd say that. She's invited you before, yes?"

"Uh-huh."

"And you said the same thing, I believe."

"Yup! I like Anya. Even if she does live where it's cold all the time."

"Not my choice, but thanks, Pan. I like you too," Anya said and rubbed his head.

"Ursula thinks that if you can see the NAT for yourself, you might change your mind. Or maybe, Ms. Nowicki will change hers," Vastukar said.

"Not what I'm here for. I'm gonna do whatever needs to be done to find Big Al, and that's it."

"Big Al?" Vastukar asked.

"Alien Alpha. What we're calling the last alien."

"Ah, yes. Don't worry, we'll get to that. And I won't pressure you into anything you don't want to do. Besides, I think New Bengaluru speaks for itself."

"How so?"

"Well," Vastukar said, paused, and Anya could almost hear him smiling on the other end of the comm. "Look out and see."

The gray curtain of clouds fell away as the ship descended further, and the city of New Bengaluru stretched below.

The city consisted of one enormous circular wall made of deep red stone that encompassed miles and miles of the land around it, almost as far as Anya could see. It was hard to tell exactly how tall it was from the air, but at a rough guess, it had to be at least five or six stories tall and wider than the average house. Elegant towers with domed roofs dotted the wall every half-mile or so, and trees decorated the tops of its ledges while the sides crawled with ivy and flowers.

A smaller circular wall lay within the first, and a third within the second. The whole of the island of Manhattan would have fit snugly within the smallest of the walls, and Anya's breath caught in her throat as the sheer scale of the metropolis below hit her.

Buildings of all shapes and sizes clustered together in tidy pockets, connected by pale gray roads and silver threads Anya recognized as elevated railways. Gleaming bolts of chrome darted along them: trains several cars long that looked like more advanced versions of the bullet trains from Japan. They zipped around the city and followed the silver threads of the rails beyond its walls and past the horizon.

The pockets of buildings were mostly the same reddish stone as the outer wall, but there was more variation to them: warm oranges, pale yellows, ruddy crimson, and pink so pale it was almost white. Sharp obelisks stabbed upwards, hills of domed rooftops rolled along streets, and orderly rectangles of apartment blocks stood tall around a vast lake so blue that it was like a terrestrial sky.

Dotted across the city were towers made of the same silvery-chrome as the ship Anya rode in, or the trains below. These stood at the center of every one of the clusters of buildings, and were the tallest structures by far. Each one stretched up dozens of stories, and the tallest, at the center of the city, had to be the tallest structure on Earth.

It was a shining shard of silver that dwarfed everything around it, and clouds gathered near its top. Ships like the one Anya rode in buzzed around it, docking at ports all along its length, and soaring away to other parts of the city or past its walls.

New Bengaluru wasn't just a single massive urban sprawl, however. The amount of lush plant life couldn't be measured. It wasn't quite a forest, but it wasn't fully just a city, either. Vibrant emerald life bloomed on top of and around the buildings, almost appearing to be designed around them, or integrated with their structure. In an echo of the building design, a great tree sprouted from the center of the city, directly in front of the gigantic tower acting as its hub.

The tree itself would have dwarfed several skyscrapers in New York, and stretched its branches over several city blocks in every direction. Its branches had grown down to support its immense size, forming natural pillars that arched over the bustling streets and railways below and created tunnels of lush vines and leaves.

"Holy fucking shit," Anya said.

"Is it cold out there?" Pan asked.

"The current temperature is 27 degrees Celsius, 82 Fahrenheit. It's a bit humid, but within the city, it's mild. So warm, but not too hot. The walls are for climate adjustment and restoration. New Bengaluru gets its energy from wind, solar, and geo-thermal power, but decades of pollution still require the filtering systems within the walls to do some clean-up. They project some defensive fields as well," Vastukar said.

"No snow!" Pan cheered.

"How tall is that building?" Anya asked and stared at the central tower they were flying toward.

"The Kendriya Adalita Gopura, or Central Administrative Tower, is roughly a mile tall. It's mostly just called Kendra, or Central. The Burj Khalifa is about half that, for reference. The atmospheric stabilizers in the wall keep wind velocity down to help with stability, but the tower itself it also somewhat flexible and can adapt to changes in the weather as needed. The tree at its base is also integral to its support, and runs up and down the length of the building."

"Jesus," Anya breathed. She had to lean forward and crane her neck to see the tower as they neared. They were close enough now that she could no longer see the top, obscured as it was by clouds. "How did you do this?"

Anya thought of Gary's factory, and how huge it had seemed. It paled in comparison to New Bengaluru, and it had taken Gary a month and almost all of his RAC to build, plus a small army of construction robots working around the clock.

"I didn't. We, the people of the NAT, did. I oversaw construction and was a primary contributor, but it would be disingenuous at best to claim sole responsibility for it," Vastukar said. He made a short intake of breath, as if debating whether to continue, then added, "Over seventy hosts assisted with the cleaning of the rubble of old Bengaluru, and what you see now."

"Seventy?" Anya asked.

"Seventy-six, to be exact. More have joined since the start. And before you ask, no. Most of them are not combat-oriented. Many are just people who wanted to be safe, and only a handful have fought a gnosiphage."

Anya shook her head. Even if that were all true, the Archive didn't target children, so the average age—and therefore a host's starting level—would be at least around twenty or so. That was enough levels to become superhuman in just about anything.

"You know Hanover's going to want to hear that, right?"

"Of course. That's another part of your visit. We've wanted our privacy up until now, but it's time we opened up, at least a little. It's become clear to me that no one person or power is going to be enough to stop the aliens, or whatever comes next."

"What do you mean?"

"Another conversation for later. We'll speak soon, Ms. Nowicki."

The comm shut off as the ship finally slowed to a gentle glide upon approaching the tower. The mirror-like surface reflected the ship back at Anya, and then rippled as it slid open to reveal a vast, open docking area. It was bigger than several of the athletic fields back at Outpost #1, and dozens of ships like the one Anya was in hovered in neat rows. Other vessels—some smaller, others larger—also hovered in place, attended to by ground crews of men and women in bright yellow coveralls and hardhats. Small drones, most no bigger than a person and bearing a similar tear-drop shape to the larger ships, floated alongside the human workers and escorted loads of crates.

Anya's ship floated to a gentle stop and the door at the back of the cockpit slid open behind her. Anya looked from the windshield to the door and back again, then down at Pan.

"Time to shit or get off the pot, I guess," she said.

"I don't have to go," Pan replied, and Anya chuckled.

"I mean it's time to go meet these people. You ready?"

"Yes!" Pan said, and took Anya's hand as they disembarked together, and into the heart of New Bengaluru.

23

A pair of familiar faces met Anya and Pan as they strode off the airship: one human, one bestial. Ursula the polar bear and Zixin the sniper stood side-by-side a few yards away, eyes on the new arrivals.

Ursula stood at just over ten feet tall when she was on her hind legs, as she was now. She was clad from top-to-bottom in crude armor made of rough slabs of black iron, with a dark blue cape flowing behind her. Only her face poked out from a helmet crowned with short spikes. Despite the rough appearance of the armor, it didn't seem to encumber Ursula's movements at all.

She clutched a long weapon in her armored paws: a huge maul with a head and handle of the same black metal as her armor. The hammer was almost as tall as Anya herself, and its blunt head was nearly as broad as her shoulders. It must have weighed hundreds of pounds, but Ursula held it as if it weighed no more than a slender tree branch.

Ursula's nose twitched and her lips curled up as she focused on Anya. Her fangs glistened, the two massive ones in front each longer and thicker than Anya's thumbs. However, when she turned her attention to Pan, her lips lowered and her dark, beady eyes brightened.

Zixin was almost comically non-threatening when compared to the grim mountain of iron and hair and fangs beside him. He was short, even by normal standards, and had the lithe, athletic figure of a swimmer. His black hair was cut short on the sides, but longer on top, and tied back in a neat knot. He wore a silvery hooded cloak over a tight black body suit, which covered everything but his face and his right index finger.

A holster was strapped to Zixin's right thigh, but it held no gun, only something that looked sort of like a large bottle made of a single piece of dull metal. Zixin had his hands hooked into his belt like some cowboy, and followed Anya's every movement as she left the airship. Ursula was more focused on Pan, and she was the one to move first.

"Pan! Good to see you in-person again," she said.

"Ursula!" Pan cheered and waddled forward. He had shed his winter clothes aboard the airship, and was now dressed in a pair of baggy green trousers and a thin black coat with flapping sleeves. Ursula dropped her maul and stood on all fours over Pan so he could embrace her front leg. The maul moved by itself and attached itself to Ursula's back, as if magnetized.

"Ahem," Zixin said and glared at Ursula. She let out a rolling grumbling sound at him, but then gently nudged Pan back with her snout.

"We can talk later. Maybe about getting Brody to come here too," Ursula said.

"I'd like that!"

"And I'd like to get on with it. May we? Vastukar is waiting," Zixin said and gestured to the side of the cavernous docking chamber.

"Lead the way," Anya said, and Zixin marched toward a distant exit set in the far wall. A few human workers glanced their way as their entourage passed, and a few even waved and grinned at them.

The workers were mostly Indian men, but Anya saw quite a few women and people of other ethnicities as well. She also noticed that some of the workers were taking it easy: a small group played cards against another wall, another pair chatted and laughed while they smoked cigarettes, and some were having a meal in the corner. Of the many workers who were busy at their tasks, none seemed tired or out-of-sorts. A few even looked cheerful, and would chat and laugh with their co-workers as they assisted the drones in loading or unloading cargo, checking ship manifests, and more.

Anya couldn't help but compare it to her time before the Archive, when she'd been a barista. Every shift felt like a slog, and she was always physically and emotionally drained by the end of it, dreading the next shift. Any relaxing outside of the mandated break-time was strictly curtailed by her old boss. That old, worn-out chestnut of, "If you got time to lean, you got time to clean," was rolled out so often that Anya still heard it in her dreams some nights.

"Seems like a nice place," Anya said. Zixin led them out of the docking chamber and down a short, utilitarian hallway to an elevator. They all fit inside, but Ursula took up most of the room and made it feel cramped.

"It is," Zixin said, but didn't elaborate.

"Better than what the rest of you've done to the world," Ursula said and Anya looked up at her, frowned, but held her tongue. The elevator hummed and began to move upward, picking up speed as it went. Anya's ears popped as it climbed higher, and she wondered how far up the tower they were.

The elevator ride was silent, Vastukar having opted out of forcing riders to listen to shitty music while stuck inside. That raised Anya's opinion of him by at least a few notches. Clean energy, beautiful architecture, happy workers, and a lack of shitty elevator music? Truly an advanced society.

When the elevator stopped and its doors slid open, Ursula grunted at Anya from behind to indicate that she should get off. Anya ignored her and examined the space beyond the elevator.

She was greeted with a short, minimalist hallway: a floor made of some unknown, glossy black material, and white walls. A pair of bright green ferns set in red clay pots sat against the wall opposite the elevator where they flanked a pair of wooden double doors.

"Vastukar is through there," Zixin said and pointed across the short hallway. "Please don't try anything stupid while you're in there. It won't work."

"Your boss is safe as long as he doesn't start shit," Anya said.

"Pan, would you like to come see the city with me?" Ursula asked. Before Anya could protest, Pan shook his head.

"I wanna spend time with you and talk about animal stuff, but I'll stay with Anya for now. Is that okay?" he asked. "Wait. Anya, are you gonna talk about boring stuff? Like you do with MacDougal?"

"Yeah, probably," she admitted.

"Can I wait out here with Ursula, then?"

Anya considered making Pan come in with her. They could trap her, or Pan, or anything if they separated. But they also could have done that already. She was in the heart of New Bengaluru, surrounded by Vastukar's tech and two strong hosts.

"Just stay right out here, okay?" she asked and smiled at him.

"He'll come to no harm," Ursula said to her and placed one huge paw on his back.

"Right. Thanks," Anya said, then muttered as she turned away, "Felix, alert me if Pan's signal leaves the hallway. Immediately."

"You got it!" Felix whispered back inside her ear.

She strode through the wooden doors while the others stayed in the hallway. The doors opened by their own as she approached, and closed shut with an almost silent click behind her.

The room Anya was in was a much larger version of the hallway outside: a polished black floor and white walls, decorated with a variety of plants in red clay pots of different sizes. A white carpet stretched from the entrance of the room to a large desk made of the same wood as the doors. A pair of simple white cushioned chairs sat before the desk, with a larger chair behind it. The desk itself was barren, but for a tiny green fern in another clay pot, not much larger than Anya's hand.

The far wall was a single sheet of glass, and looked out across the vast expanse of New Bengaluru. It was a breathtaking view, but not quite as high up as Anya had suspected. If she had to guess, they were about two-thirds of the way up the tower.

The expansive view was only interrupted by the figure of a man, cast in silhouette as he stood before the bright window, and Anya's eyes adjusted to the room's light. He turned, and Anya recognized him as the man from video broadcasts posted to the net.

Vastukar was taller than Zixin, but still only of average height. The crisp suit he wore accentuated his broad chest, shoulders, and slim waist. He was middle-aged, or a little older, with a few streaks of gray in his beard and on either side of his head. His hair was long, swept back, and combed into precise lines. He smiled at her, and the whiteness of his teeth was a sharp contrast against the dark tan of his skin.

"Good day," he said. "I can't thank you enough for coming."

"Uh, yeah," Anya said and looked around. The office had a high ceiling and wide walls. It wasn't cavernous, but it felt just slightly too large for the minimal amount of furniture.

"It's nice to meet you in-person, Ms. Nowicki," Vastukar said and extended his hand across the desk. Anya stared at it for a moment, well aware of what a handshake between hosts meant. Any physical contact hosts made put them in each other's contact lists. It also meant each host could know the exact location of the other at any time. Anya had long since decided any potential risks were worth the benefits.

But Vastukar had, up until now, gone to some lengths to keep himself secluded. True, he could always remove Anya from his list of contacts at any time and go back into hiding, but him making the offer at all was a surprise.

Anya took his hand and shook it.

"Just Anya is fine. Is Vastukar your first name or last name?"

"Neither. It's an assumed name, one I adopted when the Archive hit. It's Hindi for 'Architect,' which is what I hope to be. But we have other things to discuss, so please, have a seat," Vastukar gestured at the chairs, and he sat down behind the desk while Anya took the seat across from him.

"I had Zixin track your progress via the Archive map. Alaska to India in under three hours is impressive. Did you need anything before we begin? I've heard your caloric intake requirements are… extensive."

"Maybe later. I'd mostly just like to get to the point."

"Your bluntness is appreciated. The point is, I think I can pinpoint the approximate location of Alien Alpha in real time, with your help. You're aware of how the aliens emit a data stream when they're killed?"

"Yeah?"

"And beyond a certain radius, a host cannot intercept said data stream?"

"Of course."

"Well, while there is a sharp drop-off point beyond which no data can be collected from the gnosiphages, there is a more subtle loss of information with any distance between the host and the dead alien," Vastukar said.

Anya squinted at him and pursed her lips.

"So a little data gets lost, even if you're just standing a few feet away from the alien you've killed?" she asked.

"That is correct."

"And I've been in direct physical contact with both overseers at the moment they died, meaning there's as little degradation in my personal data stream as possible," Anya said as it clicked in her head, and Vastukar nodded.

"Correct again."

"And... what does that mean?"

"Due to my particular skillset, I've developed a method to read the—how do I put this?—the surface level information the Archive has. We cannot alter it, but we can read it and transfer it to a machine. Up until now, the only way for somebody to get data from another host's Archive—such as gnosiphage locations—would be to see their map in-person and record it with a video or something similar.

"The surface-level information of the Archive contains decoded alien data streams, lists of skills and items within the RAC store. It doesn't contain information of the Archive's programming or creation, leveled-up skill information, or anything about manipulating prices within the RAC store. We can't change anything about the Archive, but we will be able to understand it better, share information, and read it more thoroughly."

"And you want to read the gnosiphage overseer data streams I have to help you track the last one."

"Just so. We have an incomplete profile created from other aliens we have encountered, but we lack a full overseer transmission signature. That's where you come in. We will scan you, and upload your data streams into our model, and this will help us find the last alien."

"Scan me?" Anya asked, and frowned.

"Yes, and I don't blame you for being suspicious."

"No shit. The first time you introduced yourself was a few seconds before you tried to kill me with your squad of death bots."

"They were multi-functional," Vastukar said.

"One of them had electrified razor whips."

"As I said, I don't blame you. But, we're short on options. The beacon trick devised by Mr. Hendricks, Dr. Immonen, and Renn is unlikely to work again. I'm sure they—and Director MacDougal—have arrived at the same conclusion."

"They have. It might work though."

"It might. But as I said: unlikely. And their progress on an alien locater has had limited success?"

"Pretty much."

Vastukar spread his hands as if that's all there was to say.

"No offense, but what makes you so special? This could all be bull-shit. Gary's not exactly a slouch, and him, Arvo, and Renn figured a solution out before you did. Now you're saying you've one-upped them?"

"A fair question. Mr. Hendrick's skillset is primarily mechanical, correct?"

"Yeah," Anya said, not seeing much use in hiding it.

"Dr. Immonen's focus is on scanning biological matter only. The beacon they made required both of them working together over a period of days, and they were functionally just copying and modifying an existing creature.

"The reason I figured out how to read the Archive is because it—and the gnosiphages too—isn't just a matter of biology or technology. It's both, but not in the sense that it's half of one and half of another. There is no separating them. It isn't black and white, it's gray."

"I... don't really get it."

Vastukar tapped his right wrist with his left index finger, and a pale green menu appeared between him and Anya.

.   .   .

VASTUKAR: LEVEL 42 OMNI-ENGINEER
Statistics

- Awareness-20 (+7 from gear)
- Dexterity-3 (+10 from integrated systems)
- Fortitude-20 (+10 from integrated systems)
- Intelligence-54 (+10 from gear)
- Strength-4 (+10 from integrated systems)
- Willpower-15 (+5 from gear)

Skills

- Mechanical Engineering-28 (+15 from gear)
- Robotics-20 (+10 from gear)
- Biomechanical Integration-25 (+10 from gear)
- Civil Planning and Construction-10
- Biological Engineering-28 (+15 from gear)
- Matter Melding-11

"I think Mr. Hendricks and I have had similar ideas. You recall my 'death bots,' from Greenland? They looked quite a bit different than the technology you see here."

Anya thought back to the fight in Greenland. The robots she and the other hosts had fought had been much less organic looking than the tech she had seen since entering New Bengaluru. They had been clunkier, with obvious joints and screws and plating. Everything today had been smooth, elegant.

"It was that fight that made me realize a single approach wasn't enough. I knew I didn't want to generalize outside of engineering, but knew I shouldn't just narrow my focus to only one type. You've noticed some interesting combinations among your skills, I'm sure," Vastukar said and Anya nodded as she studied his menu. "It was the same with me. It's not putting living components inside machines, or vice-versa. That can be done, but it isn't the only outcome. It's about using knowledge of each to improve both, and make something entirely new.

"This building you're in now, for example: it's a physical impossibility by standard engineering and construction metrics. But the tree at the base of Central makes it possible. Its roots, branches, and vines wind all through the building, providing support, even carrying electric impulses that act as power for the lights. Likewise, the leaves of the tree have been enhanced with solar-collection technology that exponentially increase the amount of sunlight the tree can take in, allowing it to grow bigger, faster, and stronger than ever."

"The tree's leaves are solar panels?" Anya asked.

"Not just the tree. Every plant in the city is a solar collection array. And they're all connected. And if one is damaged, it regrows and repairs automatically, just like a normal tree. All it needs is sunshine and water.

"The Archive is the same. It's rewired your brain and your entire body to receive and adapt to new information, to store untold amounts of data, exponentially more than any computer modern man could devise. But if somebody like Dr. Immonen scans you, and he only has an understanding of biology, that's all he'll see. The same for Mr. Hendricks. He may understand certain mechanical aspects of the Archive, but not the entire picture."

"Okay, fine. I believe you can get data from the Archive, and maybe even use it to find Big Al. But that doesn't mean I trust that that's all you'll do if you scan me. You could do…" Anya trailed off and shrugged. "God knows what."

"It will require some trust, yes, but I wouldn't ask you to put blind faith in me. As the scan is set up to read the Archive, this means it can also be monitored by the Archive. That means your AI can confirm that we have not done anything against your wishes. Whatever you think that might be."

"Felix? Is what he's saying true?" Anya asked.

"That he can read the surface-level data from the Archive directly? I don't know. I can tell you if the Archive is being read and what data is being accessed, however. Kind of like how right now, I can tell you that you're sending your location data to everybody on your communications list," Felix replied. "If all he wants is a direct transfer of the data stream, I can monitor that."

Anya looked down and bit her lip.

"Can he clone me? Levels and all?" Anya asked. Vastukar raised his eyebrows at her.

"Based on data I have up to level 5 of his skills, he could clone a duplicate of you. However, it would be a physical duplicate only. The data on skills, RAC store items, and so on is not surface-level. It's buried deep, deep within the Archive, and is unique to its host. A cloning machine cannot duplicate the Archive, nor data that's been granted to a host," Felix said. "Cloning skills like Renn's are different, and entirely dependent on the primary host to function."

Anya sighed. A dozen other concerns piled themselves around her, but she batted them aside. What if Vastukar was using this as some way to kill her? Well, if he wanted her dead there were a lot of other ways to try it that didn't involve sitting her down and asking her nicely.

Some way to track her? He'd had that with Zixin, Ursula, and Asmund. They had known her exact location at all times since Greenland.

Maybe he just wanted to detain her, remove her as an obstacle to whatever else he was planning. Again, easier ways to do it than having a chat. Also, while Anya was strong, there were a lot of other hosts out there who were at least as strong as she was. Renn, Samaira, Gary, Jiro, Mona, Harrison, and Esmeralda were all at level 50 like her, and most of them were combat-focused, too.

"You just want to use my data to look for Big Al?" she asked.

"That and nothing more."

"So when you're done with the data, you'll delete it?"

"Of course."

"And you realize I'm not just going to take your word for that, right?"

Vastukar smirked.

"I assume you're in contact with Mr. Hendricks, somehow?" he asked.

"Why would you assume that?"

"Because you're not a fool. From what I can tell, short-sighted, reckless, and a bit to eager to throw yourself into a fight, but not a fool. I told you no back-up from government-affiliated hosts aside from Pan. Mr. Hendricks isn't affiliated. You're also both somewhat close, based on the information I've gathered. If you're not in contact with him, I'd be happy to let you call—"

"I'm here," Gary said from a speaker mounted into the wall.

"Mr. Hendricks. Did you hack into Central's entire security system, or just the audio function?"

"Audio and video. Barely. Probably could've done a few more things but I'm long-distance and your set-up is… weird."

"Yet you managed to breach the basic safeguards I had up. Impressive."

"I'm flattered."

"You've been listening this entire time?"

"Yup. Can't blame the kid for being twitchy around you. You're the guy that blew up a city, after all."

Vastukar frowned at that.

"That was an accident that occurred during a rather violent alien attack, and while I was not directly involved, it only occurred due to oversight on my part. If you would like to discuss the matter at a later date, if this all works out, I will accommodate you. But for now I would like to stay focused, please."

"Fine. You got a proposition for me?" Gary asked.

"I do. You and Dr. Immonen were able to create a beacon that replicated an Archive signal over the course of a few days. You've managed to breach the basic levels of my security. I believe you would be able to monitor the machine I will use to scan Ms. Nowicki, and ensure any data I retrieve is disposed of, if she wishes it, after we have what we need to locate the last alien. As a gesture of good faith, I will give you full security access to Central's database."

"Gary?" Anya asked and looked at the speaker on the wall. "Can you do that?"

"I can take a look. If I can't figure it out, we can talk about what to do next."

Anya grunted.

"All right. Fuck it. Between Felix and Gary keeping an eye out, I'm willing to give it a shot. If this'll help nail Big Al, then it's worth it. But if you try to fuck me over, I'm not gonna let it slide."

Vastukar leaned back in his chair and sighed. Not with impatience or irritation, but relief. A phantom weight lifted from his neck and shoulders, and the man visibly relaxed. Once more he extended his hand to Anya, and they shook.

24

Gary had one of his own robots waiting a few miles beyond the outer wall of New Bengaluru. With Vastukar's permission, Gary flew the robot to the Central Administrative Tower, where it was greeted in the docking bay by Vastukar, Anya, Ursula, and Pan.

Gary's robot had the general size and shape of a thin human, and was covered in slim, interlocking steel plates. It was sturdier than any of Vastukar's drones, but lacked their elegance. The head of the robot was a rough oblong shape, and a hologram of Gary's face projected from its surface.

The robot waved at Anya as it flew into the docking bay, its lower half converting from a single rocket thruster and separating into two skinny legs and a pair of wide feet.

"Heya kid. Hey little guy. How's the visit so far?" Gary asked, his voice slightly distorted by the robot's speakers.

"Great! Ursula and I were talking about where to get dinner. I'm thinking I'll maybe have termites, but Ursula says I can have whatever," Pan said.

"Yeah, you guys might wanna get comfy while I check out Vastukar's set-up. I want to be thorough."

"My laboratory is open to you. It's just this way," Vastukar said and gestured at an elevator on the far side of the docking bay. Anya and Gary exchanged a look, and he nodded at her. Vastukar led Gary away from the group, and Ursula let out a low growl as she started to follow them. Vastukar put his hand up to stop her and shook his head.

"You shouldn't go alone," Ursula said.

"This is about building trust. I appreciate your concern, but having you looming over Mr. Hendricks won't help anything. I'll be fine, Ursula. Show Pan and Ms. Nowicki somewhere nice to eat while I entertain our other guest."

Ursula's mouth worked as if she were about to argue, but she huffed and stayed quiet. Vastukar gave her a gentle smile, and then continued toward the elevator with Gary's robot.

"C'mon," Ursula said to Anya as she led her and Pan to another elevator. "Vastukar says you need a lot of food. I can relate. There's a good buffet up near the top, nice views. There's a food court every twenty floors, and they all got some kinda different food type. Dunno what you like."

Anya studied the bear, tilting her head to the side to look up at her. For Anya's entire life, she'd lived with the idea that if something seemed too good to be true, it always was. Her mother had spent decades trying to carve her four children into perfect little models of what she wanted them to be, but it had all been bullshit.

New Bengaluru—or at least, what Anya had seen of it—was beautiful. A lush utopia of technology and nature. But it looked, and sounded, a bit too perfect. So when Ursula started to rattle off options within the tower, Anya decided to push.

"Anything outside? I've been in the Shadow Ray a few hours, and it'd be nice to stretch my legs," she said. She expected Ursula to come up with some reason for Anya to not go outside, something to keep her away from looking too closely at the city and uncovering its faults.

"Fine," Ursula said. "I'd like Pan to see the place anyways."

Anya kept the mild surprise hidden from her face as Ursula led them down hundreds of floors to the main level. The elevator opened onto an atrium the size of a sports stadium, the ceiling made of a web-like pattern of metal and wood with glass in-between. Branches stretched from floor-to-ceiling, arching with the dome or growing straight down like pillars, and gave the structure its support.

Bright signs pointed in all directions, indicating incoming and outgoing trains, airship docks, and other transportation options. The atrium was a hive of activity, with thousands of people switching trains or riding the dozens of large elevators up and down to parts unknown. It was busier than anything Anya had witnessed during rush hour in Manhattan, but it was so well organized. There were a few people who seemed confused, but they were attended to by spherical assistance drones that hovered over to them within moments of them raising a hand.

"Where are they all going?" Anya asked Ursula as the polar bear guided them along a well-lit walkway toward one of the rail lines.

"Some live here and they're coming home. Others work here and live in one of the other city blocks. However, to keep traffic down, Vastukar's arranged most of the city to have anything a person might need within a few minutes walk or train ride," Ursula said.

"So people can't go beyond where Vastukar has them assigned?" Anya said, a certain amount of smug satisfaction falling over her.

"Huh? No, that's stupid. People go where they want. They just don't have to go very far to get what they need. Any resident can go anywhere in or outside the city at any time. The only places off-limits are some of Vastukar's labs, anybody's private quarters, and maintenance areas that could be dangerous. Like the railways."

Anya grunted as Ursula led them to a train platform. It looked a bit like some of the old subway stations in and around New York Anya had seen pictures of: a lot of decorative tile walls, ornate benches, curving lamp-posts, and not a speck of trash in sight. Or a rat.

Signs indicated that they were waiting for the train servicing sectors 1-to-5 of the inner ring, and that it departed every ten minutes. A countdown timer showed that less than three minutes remained until the train arrived, and there was a graphic showing the train's location in real time as it approached.

Several dozen people waited along the platform, sitting on the benches or leaning against the walls. Nobody looked shabby, though a few did look tired. However it wasn't the exhausted, near-death look

Anya had worn so frequently whenever a shift ended. They were people who appeared to have been busy, and were looking forward to going home; not like they'd barely survived a hostage situation.

They also didn't pay much attention to Anya, Pan, or Ursula. They studied their phones, or books, or chatted with whoever sat next to them. A few looked up, but only with passing curiosity. Nobody seemed concerned or worried at the appearance of a ten-foot tall, heavily armored polar bear wielding an enormous hammer.

This included several children who stared at the trio of hosts with obvious wonder. Ursula managed to smile at a few of the kids, who giggled and smiled back. Anya just shook her head as the train arrived with a quiet magnetic hum and a gentle hiss.

Ursula took them across the city to a sushi restaurant near a park. Pan had his run of the park to root around for ants and termites while Anya and Ursula gorged themselves on fish. Neither one spoke much to the other while they ate. That was fine with Anya. She had a view of the street outside: a quiet little avenue of townhouses and gardens and shops. Bioluminescent flowers hung on vines that stretched over the cobblestone road and emitted a cheery glow as the sun set.

"So, how'd you and Vastukar meet?" Anya asked as she set her chopsticks down and belched.

"Asmund," Ursula said. "I ran into him first, tried to eat him. He acted like it was just a game and nearly killed me, then nursed me back to health. Then we went south and hunted aliens across Europe until we ran into Vastukar and Zixin."

"Was this before or after the city exploded?"

"Before," Ursula said, then looked outside at the park across the street. Pan was rooting around in the ground and using his long tongue to scoop up a colony of ants. "He's happy. He doesn't need much. Me or Brody, either. Food, shelter, somebody to talk to. I'll never understand humans. You're all monsters."

"Said the ten-foot tall murder-bear," Anya retorted.

"I'm a predator, not a monster. I'll kill to survive, but that's it. Humans? You're much worse. You kill, you take, you eat so much you starve others doing it. And it's never enough. More, more, more. Until you're all fat and alone sitting on a dead world. Monsters."

Anya balked at the venom in Ursula's voice. That wasn't just anger, but deep bitterness. She wouldn't have expected an animal host to have been capable of something like that. Pan was so childlike, Brody too, in his way: both just simple-minded and happy.

Ursula's black eyes shone with what Anya almost swore were tears before the bear turned away and devoured the last of her meal. She swallowed it with an audible, rumbling gulp, and then turned to study Pan.

"He's happy," Ursula said again. "And for whatever reason, he's happy with you. So I won't take him. But if you have any care for that little one at all, you'll do what's best for him."

Anya watched Pan, then started when her ear beeped.

"It's Gary," Felix said, and brought up a communication window.

"Heya, kid. All done," Gary said.

"Already? That was quick. The beacon took you days."

"Yeah well, that was building something from scratch. This is just me looking around. All the stuff Vastukar's using is weird, but I figured it out after a bit. It's actually been pretty educational. I may not have his bio-engineering, but just looking at this stuff is handy. Plus, the Operating system he's using is pretty straightforward. I'm able to see the whole thing. I'll keep an eye on whatever data Vastukar scans from you, personally."

Anya relaxed a bit. "Thanks Gary. We'll be back soon."

"Vastukar told me that if you want to stay, you can," Ursula said as she and Anya pushed away from the sushi bar, thanked the chef, and left. Anya paused outside, looking around at the people walking the streets in the darkening twilight. Nobody glanced over their shoulder for muggers, no sirens wailed in the distance.

"If this goes well, I'll think about it," Anya said, and then went to go get Pan.

———

URSULA AND PAN stayed in Central's main atrium to admire the plants and people watch while Anya ascended to one of the laboratories Vastukar directed her to. It seemed silly to worry about Pan, at the moment. Even if she didn't fully trust Vastukar, she knew Ursula wouldn't hurt him.

The laboratory she arrived at looked more like an upscale electronics store than a place for scientific research. Glossy white counters lined the walls, and a pale wooden floor polished to perfection reflected soft lighting from overhead. Hanging strands of ivy curled down from ceiling-mounted planters and swayed in the gentle breeze of the temperature-controlled room.

Counters of the same wood grew out of the floor, and had unfamiliar devices spaced evenly apart down their lengths. The smallest of the devices was the size and shape of a cellphone, while some of the larger ones were as big as microwave ovens or mini-fridges. There were larger pieces of tech on the floor, all set up near the far side of the room.

Anya focused on the largest: a flat, circular platform several feet across, and framed on each side by curving metallic bands that arched up. Glowing green sensors glimmered on the inside of the metal bands, blinking in sequence. Gary (or rather, his robot), and Vastukar stood on either side of the platform. Vastukar was focused on a large, wall-mounted screen before him that showed flickering lines of data, while Gary's robot waved at Anya as she entered.

"Is this the thingy?" Anya asked as she looked at the platform and the metal bands curving up along either side of it.

"The scanner, yes," Vastukar said but did not look away from his screen. He gestured at it with one hand. "Please just step into the center and hold still."

Anya glanced at Gary. His holographic face smiled and he nodded.

"I gotcha, kiddo."

"Oooookay," Anya said and stepped onto the platform. There was a beep, and the metal bands spun clockwise around the platform, then counter-clockwise. Vastukar muttered to himself as he stared at his screen.

"Hey, could you use this thing to find other host signals?" Anya asked as she waited.

"No, unfortunately," Vastukar replied. His attention remained fixated on the screen, but one of his hands pointed from his head, to

Anya's, to Gary's robot. "Our signals are far too disparate. The gnosiphages all share a singular consciousness, with the overseers' only having some slight variation. But even that mild difference is enough to make tracking them difficult. The discrepancy between host signals is much greater. And I've had a significant data pool to draw from. The Archive itself remains the only way I'm aware of accurately finding hosts."

"Darn," Anya sighed. The metal bands around the platform spun once more and beeped. Vastukar let out a sigh, and his shoulders relaxed.

"It worked," he said.

"Wait, are you already done?" Anya asked and Vastukar nodded. "That was it? Felix? Did anything happen?"

"Yup! I got a notification that an outside system scanned surface-level data: the collected and decoded gnosiphage datastreams. That was it," the AI replied.

"So you can tell where Big Al is right now?"

"Right at this exact moment?" Vastukar shook his head. "No. It will take some time, maybe a day, to fully integrate the missing pieces of code we will extract from your data stream into the signal tracker I've designed. But by this time tomorrow night: yes, hopefully."

"What now?" Anya asked, and spread her hands.

"You may step off the platform and then return to your country, or stay here for the night if you're tired."

"I came here to find Big Al, and I'm not leaving until I do. Or, you do."

"Very well. There's some accommodations on floors 200-350. I'll have a drone escort you, and put you in a room with Pan near one of the dining areas. Those are open all day and all night, if you need anything. And you may contact me via the Archive, if you wish. Now if you'll excuse me, I have an alien to find," he said, sparing Anya a brief sideways glance before focusing on his screen again.

Anya stepped off the platform and left the laboratory with Gary's robot clanking behind her. She leaned against the smooth, white wall outside the lab when the door hissed shut behind her and let out a long breath.

"I thought it was gonna be some whole procedure, y'know? Like getting in some machine and getting prodded and zapped or something," she said and Gary smiled at her.

"I'll give Vastukar this much: he's a talented engineer. His mechanical engineering skill may be significantly lower than mine, but he's made up for it by finding shortcuts or work-arounds with his bio-stuff. By the way, in case you were wondering, I checked his scans. He's got nothing on you. Felix was right."

"Of course I was right!" Felix said in Anya's ear, and she chuckled.

"I'm glad it worked out and I don't have to worry about him cloning me or doing any other weird shit with my info," she said.

"So, what now? Just go settle in?" Gary asked.

"Yeah. Call Sam and MacDougal, give them the updates. They're probably dying to know what's going on. Tori, too. I know I would be. What about you?"

"I'll leave the robot with you, keep my eye on it. But right now, I'm going to go work on a few side-projects. Just call if you need anything and I'll hear you. Take care, kid."

"See ya, Gary," Anya replied. Gary's holographic face blinked out, leaving the blank, smooth surface of the robot's head behind. Anya looked past it at a floating, cat-sized silver drone approaching from the far end of the hallway. Her escort, no doubt.

The drone showed her—and Gary's robot—to her room, where Pan was already waiting for her. He was asleep, curled into a heavily-armored donut and making soft little huffing noises as he snored. Gary's robot marched into the corner, folded itself into a briefcase-sized rectangle, and went still.

Anya smiled at both pangolin and robot, then surveyed the room. It was like an upscale hotel room suite: a bedroom with two separate beds, a single bathroom, and a living room with a kitchenette. Like the rest of Central, it was decorated with pale, minimalist decorations, some vibrant but unobtrusive plant life, and featured an amazing view of the sprawling metropolis below.

It really was beautiful.

It wasn't just the trees and the gleaming towers, or the pleasing aesthetic designs. It was that the Archive could be used for something beyond just fighting aliens. Gary had made his own advancements, but those had all been in sprawling industrial factories. There was a city outside the window, a country beyond that, being shaped into something new, and better. Millions of people making a new way of life and already making the old one seem like a bad dream.

If it was real.

If Vastukar wasn't one of the monsters Ursula believed the rest of humanity to be.

Anya's Sun's Heart beat faster in her chest. It radiated warmth within her, and her eyes—golden and glowing—stared back at her in the window's reflection.

25

Anya made her report to MacDougal while Pan slept, and didn't spare any detail: the seventy-something hosts living within New Bengaluru, its level of technology, design, basic layout, all of it. While Vastukar had told her that he knew she would be reporting on her trip, Anya still felt an unpleasant hook of guilt in her gut as she spoke to the director. It felt like tattling.

Vastukar had been, so far as she could tell, nothing but honest and accommodating with her and Pan. The people in the city seemed happy, healthy, and safe. While Anya knew that MacDougal herself wouldn't do anything bad with the information, she would be required to give it to President Hanover, and God only knew how he would react. He'd definitely be jealous that Vastukar had more hosts than America, like it was a card-collecting game or something.

She called Samaira when she had finished speaking with MacDougal, and that conversation was much more enjoyable. Samaira's eyes literally lit up and her hair glowed a soft blue the more Anya described the city.

"I take it you'd like to visit?" Anya asked, a grin tugging at the corners of her mouth.

"Of course! I could probably write a hundred papers on it. Human society—regardless of geographic location or era—has always depended on resource management. People have gone to war over trade routes and access to rivers, oil, gold, fertile soil, all of it. If Vastukar's solved those problems on the scale you're describing… well, calling it a paradigm shift is something of an understatement. Gary's started to do it, but just with his factory. I can't believe Vastukar's implemented functioning infrastructure on a country-wide scale in just a month," Samaira said, shaking her head in awe as she did.

"Yeah," Anya said and glanced down. "I'm waiting for the other shoe to drop."

"Gary checked out his tech, right? All above board?"

"For what he wanted with me? Yeah. For other stuff? I have no idea. This is the guy who blew up a whole city, though, remember? He says he wasn't directly involved, but I dunno. Everything still just seems too damn perfect."

"I have to see it for myself," Samaira said. "Maybe spend a few days interviewing people. You said you went to dinner. How did you pay?"

"I didn't. I assumed Ursula took care of it, or the guy who ran the place recognized her and she got to eat for free."

"What about the trains? Were there any turnstiles? Ticket machines? Anybody using cards?"

Anya thought back and came to the realization that no, there had been none of that. No ticket counters, no sales windows, no card scanners or ticket readers. And the more she thought back over her short jaunt through the city, the more she realized there hadn't been any sign of anybody using any sort of currency.

There had been no cash register in the sushi restaurant, or equivalent. Anya and Ursula had gorged themselves for a long time—long enough to see several customers come and go—and not a single one had paid. They had eaten, thanked the chef, and left.

"Nope," Anya said. "Sam, I don't think anybody uses money here."

"People have been using some form of currency since Mesopotamia 5,000 years ago. This is amazing! Is it barter? Trade? Some kind of social credit?" she began firing off questions like an automated turret until Anya held her hands up in a desperate plea for a cease-fire.

"Look, I'll ask Vastukar if you can both chat sometime, or maybe you can come visit like I did. But for now, I think he's pretty focused on finding Big Al. Remember that? The horrifying killer alien?"

"Right. Yes. Geez," Samaira pinched the bridge of her nose. "How is that going?"

"Hopefully have the freak's location by tomorrow."

"How's Pan?"

"Sleepy. He had a pretty busy evening. Seems to like it here, though."

"Do you like it there?"

Anya opened her mouth to reply, shut it, then spoke.

"I don't know. I think... I think I want to. I want something that seems good to be good, and not have it be some shitty mirage set up by another guy on a power trip. I was out tonight and kept getting surprised at how nice things were. Like, I was expecting something horrible to happen, but nothing did. And the longer things keep looking nice, the more suspicious I am that something awful has to balance it out. Does that make sense?"

"It does. Did you ever read that short story, *The Ones Who Walk Away from Omelas*?" Samaira asked.

"Can't say I did. Was it a college thing? Higher education and me didn't exactly work out."

"Not sure where I read it first, but it stuck with me. It was about a utopia named Omelas, but its perfection and harmony all depended on a single child locked beneath the city suffering every day. The citizens could accept that and continue to live in prosperity, or they could walk away into the wilderness."

"That's kinda fucked up."

Samaira chuckled and continued, "It is. But I think that's what you're expecting to find. It's what I'd be on the lookout for. Not necessarily a literal kid, but somebody, some lower class to shoulder all the burdens or something similar. I'm already telling myself why a post-scarcity society without currency could never work, rationally, but that's also because I've never lived in a world like that. It's just as alien to me as... wherever the Archives came from. Our experience, as humans, has taught us to expect Omelas; but, maybe it's different. Maybe nobody has to suffer for this. Maybe nobody ever did."

Anya bit her lip and looked down.

"You should try to rest. I should too. If Vastukar can find Big Al, we're all going to be very busy," Samaira said.

"Too true. G'night, Sam."

"Sweet dreams. I'm here if you need me."

Anya ended the call and stretched out on the sofa. Sleep was a long time coming, and when it did arrive, it was uneasy.

———

VASTUKAR HAD a drone floating outside her door the next morning. It played an automated message that said he wasn't done, would be a few more hours, and to go eat or see the city while he worked. Pan called Ursula and they, plus Anya, took a leisurely train ride around the city. Gary's robot remained behind in the room, after Anya confirmed her schedule with him.

They stopped in the second, middle ring of the city for breakfast, at a vegetarian place that served different sorts of curries. Anya was wary, but Ursula swore it would satisfy. After an hour of gorging herself on spicy, savory dishes, Anya had to agree.

"Do we pay for this somehow?" she asked when she was done and looked around the restaurant. It wasn't fancy, but it was clean, brightly decorated in yellows and greens and hanging flowers, and busy. Once again, Anya couldn't help but notice how little people seemed to care about the huge polar bear and pangolin in their midst. They got occasional glances, but these were inquisitive rather than alarmed, and brief.

"Yeah. Say thank you to the chef on the way out," Ursula said and licked a polished wooden bowl clean of some kind of roasted cauliflower curry that was a vibrant shade of orange.

"No money?" Anya clarified.

"Nope."

"What's money again?" Pan asked.

"Some human bullshit," Ursula said and belched as she stood. "Thank you!"

She waved a giant paw at a woman and several others at the kitchen in the back of the restaurant. Anya left with a genuine thanks and took Pan's claw in her hand as they crossed the cobblestone street with Ursula. She stood on the street corner and watched the pedestrians come and go. There was a school up the road, and the sounds of children playing in a sports field behind it echoed between the buildings.

"You like it here, Pan?" Anya asked him as Ursula lumbered next to them.

"Uh-huh! It's warm, and I can go places and not bother people, and there's no snow, and I get to see Ursula, and it's not cold!"he said.

"Does the heat bother you?" Anya asked and glanced at Ursula. It wasn't sweltering, but it was warm.

"Not really. I'd prefer the snow, but it's not bad here. If it gets too hot, my armor helps regulate my temperature. I usually hang out at an ice-skating rink or indoor ski-slope in my free time," the bear replied.

"Snow inside? That sounds terrible," Pan said. "It's already outside, why would you want to bring it in?"

"For fun," Ursula said and smiled at him when he made a disgusted noise.

Anya's ear beeped.

"Bring it up," she said, not even waiting for Felix to tell her who it was.

Vastukar appeared before her, bags heavy under his eyes. He must have stayed up the entire night.

"It's done. Or it will be in… fifteen minutes," he said and glanced at something off-screen. "I see you're in the second ring. Ursula, take them to the express line and come back, quick as you can."

"You got it. This way," Ursula nodded down another street and toward a distant, elevated chrome platform.

The express train lived up to its name. It took them ten minutes to get to the station, mostly because of Pan's maximum waddling speed, but then only five minutes to cross over half the city. She messaged Gary to activate his robot and meet her at Vastukar's lab, which it did several minutes after the express train arrived at Central.

"Well?" Anya demanded as she practically burst into the lab. "Did you find it?"

"Yes, but you're not going to like where it is," Vastukar said and pointed at a huge screen that hung from the ceiling. It showed a map of Earth, and a rapidly shrinking circle that grew brighter as Vastukar zeroed in on Alien Alpha's location.

"Oh shit," Anya said. MacDougal's meeting with her before her departure came back in a rush. That village in Canada, destroyed, all the people missing or dead. A swathe of destruction that erased several thousand people in the span of hours, maybe even minutes.

If Vastukar's tracking system was to be believed, Alien Alpha was a few hundred miles away from Hawaii, and closing. It was coming at the archipelago from the north-east: a path that would lead it right to Waikiki, and the city of Honolulu.

Anya stared at the glowing dot, her eyes widening, fists clenching, stomach churning.

"This is live?" she asked, and Vastukar nodded, solemn.

"Ten minutes ago the signal was a little less precise, but now it's almost exact."

"How long? I mean—"

"Until it reaches Honolulu? Assuming that is its destination, ninety minutes, maybe two hours, given its current speed."

"We… we have to do something! And why is it doing this now? This entire invasion, the aliens have been keeping a low profile and hiding and…" Anya trailed off, unable to form any sort of coherent sentence from the cascade of words that caused her mind to seize up.

"No, they made a few major attacks out in the open: one on the White House, one in Europe, and one on New Bengaluru. At the time, that was where the largest concentration of hosts were. But nobody's in Honolulu and the most hosts, by far, are still all here," Vastukar said and rubbed his chin.

"Where you chased off the last attack, and have had time to shore up your defenses," Gary added.

"True. They're probably smart enough to know a frontal assault here wouldn't go well for them."

"It's bait," Anya said. "Just like what we did to it."

"Elaborate," Vastukar said.

"When we used the psychic beacon to lure the other overseer out, we used bait. Big Al might not have bait like what we had, but maybe it's figured another way to draw us out: attack a major city and get us to come to it."

"Why now, though?" Gary asked. "Damn things been sneaking around the Pacific for weeks. Why bother causing a ruckus right at this moment when Vastu—ah."

"Mm," Vastukar said and began to rub his temples. "Damn."

"What? What's going on?" Anya asked.

"It is possible that my signal trace alerted Alpha, somehow. Like how a submarine can tell when it has been pinged by enemy sonar. I don't know if that's accurate, or even possible. To be honest, I was mostly focused on getting the signal tracer to work. Which it seems to be."

"Yeah great, you found it and it decided to rush the nearest major metropolis," Anya said.

"We'll just bomb the bastard," Gary said. "I can have missiles in the air in two minutes. They'll take about fifteen minutes to reach Alpha. I'll need exact coordinates though."

"Now that I've got the tracking data uploaded, I can just send it to you," Vastukar said. He tapped a few buttons on a console nearby. "I can send it whenever you're ready. Though, Mr. Hendricks, I have to ask: how many bombs have you made, and what scale are they?"

Gary paused for a moment, his holographic face flickering as he considered, and then replied, "For terrestrial targets? Smaller than early nukes, and they use anti-matter so they're non-nuclear, too. No fallout or radiation or anything."

"Small comfort," Vastukar said. "And I'm to assume you have larger weapons for non-terrestrial targets?"

"Yup. But we got other fish to fry right now. I'm ready for the location data whenever you are."

Vastukar pressed another button, and Gary grunted when he received it.

"What if Alpha has some kind of counter-measure? Or your bombs set off a tsunami or something?" Anya asked.

"We'll come up with Plan B. In the meantime, you should let that director of yours know the situation. I've already sent some drones out to confirm Alpha's location, visually," Gary said. "I'm gonna be busy setting all this up, so forgive me if I'm a little delayed in my responses."

With that, Gary's face vanished from the robot, and the machine stood rigid in Vastukar's lab. Vastukar himself sighed and stared at the screen showing Alpha's location, then at Anya.

"I'm sorry. I should have known it might detect me, somehow," he said.

"We don't know that it did. What matters now is stopping it and saving as many people as we can," Anya said. "I'm going to call MacDougal and tell her what's going on."

"I haven't made any bombs," Vastukar said, and looked at Gary's robot with obvious annoyance, "but I'll see about arranging what I can in case Mr. Hendricks's assault doesn't work."

"What about whatever was used to destroy old Bengaluru?"

"I told you, that wasn't me. That isn't something that can be used like how you want anyway. The overwhelming majority of New Bengaluru's weaponry is built into and around the city as defenses. If Alpha were coming here, it would be another story, but aside from some advanced drones and robots like the ones you fought in Greenland, I haven't planned for offense."

Anya started to question him further, but didn't bother. Arguing or grilling Vastukar for info wasn't what was important at the moment, and they had hours at most, more likely minutes, until the most powerful alien descended upon hundreds of thousands of people.

26

"You're certain? This thing is going to hit Waikiki in two hours or less?" MacDougal asked when Anya called her from a sitting room near Vastukar's lab. The video app showed MacDougal at her desk, glancing between her phone and Anya, and her computer as she hammered something out on the keyboard. Pan had followed Anya into the sitting room and was fidgeting and pacing across the wooden floor.

"Gary should have visual confirmation in a few minutes, but so far, yeah, that's what it sounds like," Anya said.

"All right. I have to notify the President, Admiral Bentley at Pearl Harbor, the Governor of Hawaii, and whoever the Mayor of Honolulu is. I'll need to mobilize DERD forces here and in California. With those troop transports Hendricks gave us, we should make it there in about an hour or so. While I do that, you start contacting every host in that contacts list of yours and do whatever it takes to get them to Honolulu as quickly as they can."

"You got it."

"Good. Text me when Hendricks has confirmation," MacDougal said, and ended the video call.

"This is bad, right?" Pan asked as he shuffled to Anya, and rested both of his tiny hands on her knee. Anya stroked his head, and then took his hands in hers.

"It's not good. But we're gonna try to make it better if we can," she said. "Right now, we gotta get our friends. Felix, can I mass message everyone?"

"Of course!" they said and opened a blank communication window in front of Anya. She stared at it for a minute and then typed out what she hoped would be good enough.

Friends,

Good news: We've located the last alien and we're going to try and blow it the fuck up!
Bad news: it's on its way to Honolulu and if the plan to blow it up doesn't work, a lot of people are in danger. It's gonna hit the city in less than two hours (assuming the "blow-it-the-fuck-up" plan doesn't work).
The NAT and America already know and are sending aid to Honolulu as a back-up. If you get this message, no matter where you are, please come. People need help, and if that doesn't get your ass in gear, then maybe the opportunity to hit level 50 will. Whatever your reason, get to Honolulu, and let's kill this fucker.

"I'm so bad at writing e-mails," Anya said and then sent the message out. She didn't have time to edit her tone or wonder if it sounded "professional," enough. It was a fucking alien attack. Anything more coherent than babbling screams was good enough.

"I got the message too," Pan said, and looked at his menu. "Reading is harder than talking, so I dunno if it's good, but the words look nice."

"Thank you, Pan."

The door to the sitting room slid open, and Ursula poked her head in.

"Hey. Vastukar says Gary's gonna have visual confirmation in a few seconds, and the bomb should hit after that," she said, and led Anya and Pan back to the laboratory. Gary's robot stood beside the primary screen, a small cable connecting the two.

The screen showed an aerial view of the ocean, nothing but blue and the shadow of a large cloud drifting overhead. Vastukar and Gary both stared at the screen, faces tense. For a second, Anya thought the tension was of anticipation, waiting for Alpha to come into view and confirm its location.

Then she saw it.

A cloud drifted past the edge of the screen, casting its shadow onto the water below. The shadow Anya had first assumed was also from a cloud moved again.

In the opposite direction.

Her skin crawled and went cold.

"Hooo-leee fuck," she said.

"Pretty much," Gary agreed.

The enormous shadow was lurking beneath the waves, not laying atop them. Given the altitude of the camera and how the shadow almost filled the screen, it had to be enormous.

"That's Big Al? That huge-ass shadow thing?"

"It would appear so," Vastukar said. "At least my tracking system works."

"That's... really scary," Pan said, and hid behind Anya's leg. "How big is it?"

"Really big," Ursula said.

"Can't say exactly," Gary said. "But at a guess, and based on the scans my drone's sending me, 'Really big,' is an understatement. Maybe as big around as some of the bigger sports stadiums out there, at least twenty stories tall. Probably more."

"Twenty—" Anya sputtered. "That's not an alien, that's a fucking kaiju!"

"A what?"

"Giant monster!"

"Oh. Yeah."

"How long until your bomb arrives?" Vastukar asked.

"Thirty seconds."

"Then for now we wait, and hope this will be over soon."

Anya gulped and folded her arms across her chest. Thirty seconds had never seemed so long. She knelt down beside Pan and wrapped an arm around him. He hugged her as they both looked up at the screen. Ursula caught her eye, and the bear looked between her and Pan. Her gaze softened for an instant, then she too focused on the screen.

"Impact in three, two—" Gary said. A rocket trailing a line of fire and smoke streaked into frame and shot toward the ocean. Anya held her breath and—

A line of strange energy—dark purple, and emitting some kind of otherworldly light—lanced out of the water below, briefly illuminating the surface of something huge and armored beneath. It was only there for a moment, but it was enough to strike the rocket with pinpoint accuracy and blow it out of the sky. The rocket detonated into a huge sphere of white light that blinded everything within view of the camera drone and Anya had to look away from the screen.

"Shit," Anya said and her stomach sank.

"That was the standard. I've got a couple more bombs with tricks right behind it," Gary said. On cue, another missile shot into frame, and was once again blasted out of the sky by a ray of dark light. However, this time there was no explosion. The missile fractured and scattered into dozens of tiny fragments, all of which streaked down toward the ocean.

A trio of purplish beams shot up from the depths and swept across the sky. Each one left a glowing trail of explosive spheres behind it as they destroyed the fragmented missile.

"Shit," Gary muttered. "Was hoping that would do it. All right, last one in three, two…"

No missile appeared on screen and Anya squinted at the screen.

"Where?" she asked.

"Under water. There we go," he said as a huge burst of bubbles and foam exploded beneath the surface, then shot up in a column of water that cast a shadow across the ocean below. The shadow appeared unbothered by the explosion, and continued on.

"Fuck! Nothing?" Anya said. "Wasn't that bomb some nuclear-sized explosive? It didn't even slow it down."

"Ten, thirteen, and eight kilotons, respectively. Also, not entirely sure how much the third one hit. I'm looking at the data the torpedo sent and it connected with the target. Can't get a read on structural damage or anything though. At least we learned it doesn't have those counter-measures on its underside," Gary said.

"Could you launch a lot of those missiles at once? Overwhelm the creature?" Vastukar asked.

"Anti-matter ain't easy to come by. I've got seven more of the little ones, and five of the non-terrestrial big ones. They take a long time to make, so that's all I've got for now."

"Can't we just buy a shitload of bombs from the RAC store?" Anya asked.

"Technically? Yeah. With the money we made fighting the centipede, we could afford quite a few. But they're not cheap. The only bombs I'd be comfortable using are each hundreds of thousands of RAC. There's cheaper, but they're either too small, or they leave some nasty side-effects behind, like radiation, and some other alien stuff I don't even know about and don't want to play with. This is also assuming one of us has the skills necessary to operate an alien-made bomb. I could figure it out, but it'd take me a while."

"Shit. All right. I'm going," Anya said and turned on her heel.

"Kid! Wait!" Gary said and his robot hurried after her.

"We don't have time, Gary. It'll take me at least an hour to get to Hawaii from here. You and Vastukar can plan and do whatever you need to from here, but I'm not just going to sit on my ass."

"She's right. I'm going too," Ursula said. She shook herself and her plated black armor appeared over her body with a series of echoing clanks and bangs. "We'll take one of Vastukar's airships. It'll be faster. Zixin and Asmund are coming too."

"Are those the only hosts you have that are battle-ready?" Gary asked.

"The strongest, yes," Vastukar replied.

"I-if I come, do I have to fight?" Pan asked, his voice trembling. Anya shook her head.

"You don't have to come, buddy," she said. "Stay here where it's safe."

Pan seemed to consider it for a moment, then shook his head.

"No way! If you're going, and so's Ursula and everybody, I can't stay here. I dunno if I'll fight, but I can at least do something!"

"Pan…" Anya started to say, to tell him this alien wasn't like the others, that it was too dangerous.

"Let him," Ursula said. "You're not his owner."

Anya glared at her for a moment, and then knelt in front of Pan.

"If you want to come, I won't stop you, but—"

"Okay! I'm going!" he said.

"All right. But you gotta be careful. Promise?"

"Promise!"

"That goes double for you, kid," Gary said. "Go on. I've already sent a few squadrons of Guardians and a small fleet of drones toward Honolulu. It'll take them a while to get there, but hopefully it won't be too late."

"I'll be sending some repurposed drones and combat droids along as well," Vastukar called from the lab. "Ursula, you and the others take the *Aruna*. It's the fastest."

"Gotcha," Ursula said and began stomping away.

"Good luck, kid. You too, little guy," Gary said and his robot waved before turning back to Vastukar's lab.

"All right, buddy: time to go save the world again," Anya said and picked Pan up, set him on her shoulders, and hurried after Ursula.

———

The *Aruna* was an arrowhead-shaped craft three times the length of Anya's Shadow Ray, and only somewhat wider. Like most of the crafts of New Bengaluru, it was solid chrome, but tinged green. It was almost impossibly sleek and sharp, like it could cut the sky open with its passing.

Zixin sat in the pilot's chair in front of an array of touch screens and floating holographic readouts and managed their take-off. His silvery cloak billowed around him when he sat, and clung to him with every movement.

Anya barely felt the craft move, even as it began to accelerate to Mach 1, Mach 2, and beyond just within seconds of leaving the Central Administrative Tower behind.

Pan and Ursula sat near each other on a pair of soft leather chairs set into the wall. One of the chairs had been designed just for the polar bear, judging by its immense size. Anya sat across from them, near the *Aruna's* other passenger: Asmund.

Asmund had been in Greenland with Ursula and Zixin, and like them, Anya had only met and spoken with him for a bit. During the brief window of time where it appeared as if their initial encounter might come down to combat, Asmund had had the wild, ecstatic look of a child on Christmas morning.

He was currently slumped low in a chair, snoring away. He was a compact wedge of muscle and wild hair. The former was on display due to his lack of a shirt, which also showed off a number of swirling black tattoos that shifted as if they were alive. The latter was a wild mane of fiery orange strands that swayed above his head, as if a bonfire were slowly consuming his brain. He had a long beard of the same color, and both were decorated with sporadic, intricately woven braids. A pair of hand-axes rested next to his booted feet, and when Asmund shifted his legs in his sleep, the axes shifted with him.

He had been onboard the *Aruna* when Arya and Pan had arrived, already asleep and stinking of alcohol.

"We sure he's gonna be good-to-go by the time we get there?" Anya asked Zixin. The older man glanced at Anya, frowned, and then turned his head towards Asmund.

"He'll be fine," Zixin said, and then focused on the console in front of him. Anya glanced out the cockpit window to see that the *Aruna* had ascended to the boundaries of Earth's atmosphere, and the sky had become dark. She shook her head in amazement, then tensed when her ear beeped.

"Christ, I'm gonna have some kinda panic attack every time I hear that," she said.

"Sorry," Felix replied from within her ear. "It's nothing bad. I've been holding your messages until you had a minute. I checked them for anything that was urgent, but it's mostly just confirmation of people on their way to Honolulu."

"Thank you, Felix."

The AI was right: the majority of the messages were just people saying they were coming. The only response of note that Anya paid much attention to was Samaira's.

Anya,
I'm squished into Arvo's flying egg thing with him and Esmi. We should be there in about an hour. Hanover's mobilized the entire Pacific fleet, and he's working with Hawaiian officials to evacuate Honolulu.
Stay safe.
When this is over, we'll celebrate. You and me.
~Sam

Anya smiled to herself as she read the note and closed her menu. She didn't want to speculate too much on what "celebrate," might mean, but if it meant time with Samaira that didn't involve worrying about being attacked by gnosiphages, she'd take it.

The rest of the flight was uneventful, and the sky beyond the cockpit turned from an icy indigo to warmer shades of cerulean. It had been late afternoon when they had left New Bengaluru, but in Hawaii, it was still morning. Tropical sunshine shone in through the window and reflected off the countless windows of luxury hotels and resorts that sat beachside far below.

"Asmund," Zixin said and looked behind him. Asmund had begun to snore, and a thin streamer of drool inched its way down his beard. "Ursula?"

Ursula huffed, stood, reared back a paw, and slapped Asmund across the face with it. The blow was enough to slam the man face-first onto the floor of the *Aruna* with a heavy bang. Anya jumped in surprise, wide-eyed at the display of violence. Zixin put a gentle hand on her wrist, then pointed at Asmund's prone form.

"Mmmm? Whuzzat?" the man asked, his voice rough and thick with sleep. "We hit something?"

"Something hit you. We're here," Zixin said and landed the *Aruna* on top of one of the taller hotels.

"Oh!" Asmund said and leaped to his feet, eyes wide, grin wider.

He blinked when he noticed Anya and Pan. "Were you two here before?"

"No, we got on after you were asleep. Are you okay?"

"Why wouldn't I be? Ursula's love tap? She just does that sometimes. It's how polar bears show affection."

"No it isn't," Ursula said over her shoulder.

"Impact energy conversion," Zixin said. "Getting hit makes him stronger."

"Like having a nice, strong cup of coffee in the morning. Ah!" Asmund said and took a deep breath of air. "Or cocaine! Urse! You got another one in ya?"

Zixin grumbled and followed Asmund off the *Aruna,* and all three NAT hosts stood on the edge of the roof. Anya held Pan's hand as she followed them, trying to figure out if their chances of winning were better with somebody like Asmund, or worse.

You're turning into something of a violence enthusiast yourself, little ember, the bird whispered to her. *Even now. I feel it in your hearts: fear, yes, but not for yourself. And excitement.*

"Shhh," Anya whispered.

"Hmm?" Pan asked and looked up at her.

"Nothing, buddy. So, what's the plan?" she asked and stared out at the expanse of Honolulu's coastline. It was almost too perfect: swaying palms, pale sandy beaches, towering mountains covered in thick blankets of trees, expansive seas of turquoise. She supposed that, on a regular day, the beaches would have been packed with sun-bathers, surfers, tourists, and people playing volley-ball. Today, however, it was chaos.

Police, life guards, and what appeared to be the security teams from the various hotels herded people off the beach. Life guards on jet-skis and small boats went up and down the coast looking for surfers and swimmers and whale-watching tours. The dark, angular shapes of naval vessels floated far out to sea, forming a kind of barricade around the island. There were at least two aircraft carriers, and a half-dozen smaller ships on patrol out there.

The city itself wasn't much better. Sirens blared, firetrucks honked their horns, and a pre-recorded message looped on repeat and echoed along the streets.

"Attention: this is an emergency tsunami warning. Please evacuate the area. Police and other emergency services will direct you to where you need to go. Do not approach any beach or coastline for any reason. Thank you for your cooperation. Attention: This is an emergency…"

"I mean, I guess there might be a tsunami," Anya said.

"People living on an island like this expect something like that. It's a 'normal,' problem to have. The aliens have only been public knowledge for a little while. Telling them a huge sea-creature is on its way to flatten their city wouldn't help anything," Zixin said.

"I dunno. I think I'd like to hear about it if I was gonna get squished," Asmund replied.

"Yes, well, you're an asshole."

Asmund laughed.

"How long have we got until Big Al gets here?" Anya asked.

"About an hour, max," Zixin said. He reached down and grabbed the strange metal bottle-thing that hung from his belt, and pressed a button on its side. The bottle made a series of loud clicking noises, and expanded into a huge matte gray rifle that was almost as tall as Anya.

He threw out six metallic discs, each as big as a dinner plate, until they expanded and grew into hovering cylinders a little bigger than traffic cones. Each one sprouted a nasty looking cannon, and took up defensive positions around Zixin. He nodded as he observed them, then reached into his pocket and produced a tiny plastic nodule which he gave to Anya.

"Ear bud. When Alpha shows up, we might lose our Archive communications. This is a more reliable alternative," he said. "Vastukar's also given the frequency to your friend, Gary.

"Got it, thanks," she replied and shoved the tiny plastic bud in her ear. Zixin gave her a thumbs up after they tested it. "And what're you gonna do?"

"I'm going to set up here, for now. If I have to withdraw, it'll be to that hotel over there, then that cluster of buildings, then the mountains beyond the city."

Zixin pointed at each location as he spoke.

"Fuck me, being a sniper must be dull as a cow's balls. Why'd ya pick it again, Zi?" Asmund asked.

"Because I like to shoot things from far away and not get hurt."

"I'm going to go help the Coast Guard and cops evacuate as many people as I can," Anya said, then used her heat sense on the building below them. It was still full of people, but most of their glowing heat signatures were near the bottom of the hotel. The few that remained in the upper floors appeared to be moving down: either in straight lines, indicating elevators; or in slower zig-zagging paths, indicating the stairs.

"What should I do?" Pan asked.

"Stay with Ursula for now, maybe summon some golems while you can," Anya said. Her combat cognition skill told her of a half-dozen other things Pan could be doing with his Earth Dominion skill, but it depended on whether or not Big Al would be coming to this exact stretch of beach or not. No sense in having Pan set up pit traps to trip the huge alien (if that were even possible), if it was just going to walk up another beach up the coast.

"I'll keep an eye out for him," Ursula said. Anya gave Pan a quick hug, and then flew off the top of the hotel and landed next to a squad car at a nearby intersection. Two cops stood beside the car and directed a flood of tourists towards some waiting buses. One was an older man with a pale face streaked with sweat, and the other was a younger Hawaiian woman with her hair in a tight bun. Both jumped and backed away from Anya when she landed.

"The hell!" the man said and fumbled at his side for his radio. Anya put her hands up in a calming gesture.

"It's okay, I'm with the DERD. I'm here to help," she said.

"Paul, it's okay. I recognize her. She's been on the news, the younger officer said.

"You're one of those alien people?" Paul asked, still eyeing Anya as if she might bite him.

"Not an alien, just a person. Can I help with anything?"

"We've pretty much got this part of the beachfront settled," the younger woman said. "I thought we were evacuating for an incoming tsunami. But if the DERD's here... is it an alien?"

Anya didn't want to lie to the woman, but she didn't want to cause a panic either. Her hesitation was enough of an answer, however, and the woman's tan skin paled.

"Shit," she said.

"It's gonna be all right. Every host from the DERD and other countries are on their way. We've still got time to evacuate the area," she said.

"There's a boat out there, looks like one of them glass-bottomed deals, moving a bit slow," the man said and pointed far out to sea. There was a dot in the distance, chugging its way toward the beach. "All the big ships from the Navy, Coast Guard, and beach patrol are otherwise occupied, so if you could fly out there, I guess? Check on 'em or something?"

"I gotcha," Anya said and didn't waste another second. She shoved off from the ground with a whoosh, and then flung herself across the sky towards the distant boat.

It was hard to judge the distance of things when the ocean was involved. Anya thought she'd make it out to the little vessel in under a minute at top speed, but it took her nearly five to finally reach the tour boat. She had a better view of the smaller navy ships and Coast Guard patrol boats as she flew over the water, but they were even further out.

Calling the tourist vessel a boat was a bit generous, especially when compared to the huge naval craft in the distance. It was a floating platform with a pair of outboard motors on the back and a set of benches bolted to the deck. A white awning stretched over the top, providing some shade from the morning sun.

"Billy's Tropical Tours," had been spray painted on the waist-high railing around the boat, and somebody had crudely stenciled "Glass-Bottomed Girl," on the white hull. The center of the deck was made of thick, clear glass that offered a view of the crystalline waters below as well as a number of colorful fish swimming past.

A group of about fifteen people filled the boat, the surprised circles of their faces popping out from under the awning one-by-one. The passengers ranged in age from children in elementary school, to a couple that had to be in their eighties at the very least. Phones appeared in hands and began to snap pictures and video as Anya hovered beside the boat.

"Uh, hello," she said, feeling quite awkward as several faces and camera lenses focused on her. "Sorry to bother you folks. Are you aware of the tsunami warning?"

"Are you flying?" one of the tourists asked.

"What? Yes, I—look, there's a tsunami coming, and—"

"How?" one of the kids asked.

"That's not important. We need to get you all to shore, So I'm just going to lift up the boat—"

"I've seen you on TV!" another tourist said. "You're that lady that blew up the White House or something!"

Anya scowled. "I didn't blow it up! Aliens did!"

"Not what I heard," the tourist said and folded his arms across his chest as if that settled the matter.

"Look, you're all in danger, and we need to get you to shore, fast. I'm going to pick up the boat and fly you over—"

The man steering the boat, an older man with salt-and-pepper stubble along his tan jowls, turned up the radio beside the boat's wheel. The emergency broadcast Anya had heard repeated on land echoed from a crackling speaker.

"Uh-oh," the man said.

"Yeah, no shit, 'Uh-oh.' Just hang on to something while I figure out how to lift this thing without breaking it," Anya said and flew in a quick circle around the boat. She figured she could just reduce the gravity around the whole thing, float it up, and then stay beneath it to make sure as she flew it to land. She wouldn't be able to fly too fast, or else—

Somebody on the boat screamed.

Then another, and then everybody was screaming and the kids were wailing.

"What? What?" Anya demanded and darted over, just as the sound of cracking glass filled the air.

Something was under the boat. Something about six feet long, and with vaguely humanoid limbs covered in black carapace armor. It had pale, luminescent eyes and more fangs than was even remotely necessary. It let out a bubbling shriek, and then slammed up through the glass bottom of the boat as it lunged at the passengers.

Anya moved before her brain even registered she was moving. The creature—a nightmare shape of glistening spines, armor-plating, claws, and lashing tendrils—emerged from the water in a spray of foam and shattered glass. She activated her Flesh of the Starforge without another thought and slammed into the horrifying creature. She wrapped her arms around it and began to crush it in a vice of gravity and fire as she plummeted down, down, down into the water.

The monster struggled and writhed, slashed at her and bit at her face, but to no avail. Anya's regalia, kinetic dispersal, and armored skin rendered its base physical attacks next to useless. She super-heated herself, causing the water around her to flash-fry and explode in a burst of hissing bubbles. She locked her hands into the thing's armored hide and then tore it asunder.

The crushed, melted, torn fragments of the creature sank away from her, to where the blue waters turned black. Anya stared after it, relieved it was gone and that it had been easy enough, but puzzled as to how it had sneaked up on her.

That couldn't have been Big Al. Felix would have detected its signal if it had been that close, and it was far, far too small. The pale light from the beast's eyes faded to darkness as it sank out of Anya's sight. She began to swim upward when a distant glimmer caught her attention.

Far away, down in the depths, another pale light; a pair close together.

Eyes.

Another one of those things was swimming up towards her.

Then another pair.

And another.

Then a hundred more.

A thousand.

Thousands and thousands more.

They stretched back as far as Anya could see, a river of eye-lights beneath the waves, surging toward her.

And beyond them, a final horror. The lights of the creatures' eyes resembled a scattering of undersea stars, but behind them all was a growing, pale blue radiance. Its source was uncertain, but it threw a towering, black shape into silhouette.

It was the size of a small mountain, or—as Gary had suggested—a stadium. To Anya it looked like a blunted, rough-hewn pyramid. Her mind went blank with terror as legs taller than buildings moved with ponderous inevitability towards her, towards the city behind her.

Alien Alpha had arrived.

27

Anya almost took off then and there.

It didn't matter if she was level 50. Not next to something like *that*. Not next to a fucking walking mountain. Her instincts screamed at her to get out of the water now and fly as far away as she could.

She looked up and saw the underside of the glass-bottomed boat. The glass had broken, and water splashed up through the opening. It would sink if she did nothing. That seemed too optimistic, actually. The boat would be overrun with aliens and its passengers slaughtered well before they had the luxury of drowning.

Anya floated upward and spread her arms wide as she lessened the gravity around the boat to almost nothing. The boat floated above her as she rose out of the water, the screams of the passengers reaching her ears.

"Just hold onto something!" Anya said. She ignored the screams as she shot forward, focusing on keeping the boat balanced above her and making sure nobody fell off. She was only going half her usual flight speed, but it was enough to stay ahead of that swarm of eerie lights below the waves and keep all the passengers aboard.

"Felix, are the Archive comms still working?"

"They are."

"Great. Bring up the hosts on the island for me."

"Got it!" Felix replied and then a comms window split into a four-way grid that showed Pan, Ursula, Asmund, and Zixin appeared at the edge of her vision.

"What is it?" Zixin asked.

"It's here! Well, almost," Anya replied. "Big Al and at least a few thousand little monsters it brought with it."

"Uh-oh," Pan said.

"Now we're talking," Asmund said.

"A few thousand at a guess. Probably a lot more. I'm about five-to-ten minutes away from shore. Big Al and those things aren't far behind."

"Let me see…" Zixin muttered and his face turned away from the camera and to the scope of his enormous rifle. He adjusted something on the side of it, cursed, then adjusted something else. The man went rigid and he leaned back from the scope, both eyes wide.

"Zi?" Asmund asked.

"There's about 50,000 smaller targets, and more coming into range every second. Alpha is at their rear. ETA, thirty-three minutes for the big one, maybe twelve for the the first wave of the smaller ones."

"Fifty-*thousand*?" Ursula asked.

"And more," Zixin added.

"Is that a lot?" Pan asked.

"How high can you count?" Ursula asked.

"What's higher than ten?"

"Eleven."

"Okay, I know that one. What's next?"

"Twelve."

"Excuse me?" Zixin interrupted the two animals. "Focus on basic arithmetic later, and the horde of hostile life converging on our position now, please."

"It's a lot, Pan. More than ever before," Anya said. "But I fought one just now and it was weak. Stronger than your average human, but nothing like the regular gnosiphages. It didn't send off a signal or anything, either. Felix would have warned me, right Felix?"

"Right!" the AI confirmed.

"Hmm," Zixin said, then looked down his scope again. His face jostled slightly in frame, and then Anya felt something zip past her, mere feet away from the boat.

"What was—did you just shoot at me?" she demanded.

"Of course not. If I shot at you, I would have hit you. I shot one of the small ones, center mass, about fifty meters behind you and thirty meters down. It appears to be dead. They're not terribly strong, but with so many of them, they don't need to be."

"Pan, I need you to summon as many golems as you can and set up a wall along the beach. Can you do that?" Anya asked.

"Oh! Y-yes!" he said.

"I'll stay with you," Ursula added.

"If those things are weak enough, maybe the cops, Marines, and the Coast Guard can help clean them out too," Anya said. "Felix, is the RAC store still working?"

"For now, yes! Alien Alpha is still far enough away that it's not interfering with the signal."

"Great. I need you to find me some affordable depth charges from the RAC store or something we can drop as I fly us to shore."

"Got it! Give me five seconds!"

"Vastukar's drones should be arriving within twenty minutes. We only need to hold on for a little while until back-up arrives. Eight minutes or so. Can you—*Diu!*" Whatever Zixin was about to ask was cut off with some form of curse. Before Anya could even begin to wonder what had upset Zixin, a bright light flared behind her.

She looked over her shoulder and almost dropped the boat above her in shock.

A ray of purple energy—almost like a black light—had emerged from the ocean and stretched up into the air high enough to brush the clouds. It had pierced through one of the aircraft carriers, and then swept down to one side, cleaving the entire titanic vessel in half. The ship split, and explosions rocked the bisected hull and sent fireballs blasting into the air along with plumes of smoke.

Another beam shot up from the depths, blasting one of the smaller destroyers to bits, and then a third beam zipped along between another aircraft carrier and destroyer. The second destroyer was vaporized at once, while the carrier was cut at an angle along its length. It fell apart and exploded, much like the carrier before it.

"Holy shit," Anya said. The passengers above her screamed, the sound one of pure terror. She couldn't blame them. The other ships out to sea began to back away from the attacks, and Anya held her breath, waiting for another strike, but none came.

"I guess those ships were just in the way," Zixin said.

"I should go back for them. There have to be survivors, or—" Anya started to say before Zixin cut her off.

"You have survivors. The Navy and Coast Guard can handle themselves. There's too many for you to save individually, and you can't take Alpha on alone. You'd get killed, or do nothing. How far away are you from shore?" Zixin asked, and another shot whizzed past Anya and into the ocean behind her.

"God dammit!" Anya snapped, but knew Zixin was right. "I'm almost there."

"I got something!" Felix said. "Programmable proximity mines. It can be programmed to detect a single specific type of target, or ignore others. Has a pretty good damage potential, and each one is 500 RAC."

"Do I have to scan those monsters?" Anya asked.

"Nope! I can just set it to target anything that isn't a human or native Earth animal. Kind of like how I set-up the Shadow Ray's map and autopilot functions before you ordered it."

"Perfect! Order a hundred, one at a time, every second or so, and just let them drop behind me."

"You got it!"

There was a whoosh and a flash as a black metal ball appeared in the air beside Anya, then dropped into the water. Then another, and another, and another.

She gave herself another burst of speed, and flew in a mild weaving pattern to spread the charges out. There were more shrieks from above, but nobody fell off. Good enough.

Anya landed on the beach a couple of minutes later and 50,000 RAC lighter, and set the boat down on the sand. She waved at some nearby life guards who came rushing forward as soon as they saw

Anya approaching. The passengers all had a wide-eyed, wind-blasted look to them, and none of them moved as the boat came to a halt.

"Get out of here!" Anya snapped at them. "Are you fucking stupid? Go, go, go!"

She clapped her hands at them loudly, clearly scaring them, but at least spurring them to action. They ran towards the life guards, the older passengers getting some help as they hurried away.

"Yeah, you're welcome," Anya muttered. She glanced up at the roof of the hotel the *Aruna* had landed on. The rhythmic crack of gunfire echoed from the hotel as Zi continued to shoot at the incoming creatures. His rifle had to be powerful, but it wasn't terribly fast.

There was a loud boom far out to sea, and a pillar of water shot up from the distant waves. Then another boom and another pillar, then several more. The little ones had started activating the proximity mines.

"Anya! I'm doing it!" A tiny voice called to her from up the beach and she looked away from the water. Pan stood amid a crowd of golems, next to a wall that was taller than Ursula and half as thick. He'd used the sand, compacting it into dense chunks of stone as well as making a sizable moat on the outside of the wall. His golems were even more impressive.

Before, the golems had looked only vaguely humanoid, more like shuffling masses of mud and rock, broad-shouldered and stout. These golems were all made of obsidian, porous gray lava rock, thick slabs of granite, and several had a metallic or crystalline sheen to them. Some even appeared to be made of solid crystal or steel. All of them were taller than Anya and had clearly defined arms and legs, a few even had multiple arms.

"That's great Pan! Wow, you got all this up really quick," Anya said.

"Uh-huh! The Earth feels really nice here. Strong. I dunno why, but it's nice!" Pan said.

Anya glanced from Pan, to some cops and men and women in battle fatigues that stood a cautious distance away, waving the boat passengers toward them. She waved at them and when they didn't immediately come over, she flew towards them. A couple aimed rifles at her, but she had her hands up and floated down a few yards away, and they lowered their weapons.

"Who's in charge?" she asked, and a Marine who looked like he wasn't old enough to buy booze raised his hand. The others around him didn't look much older.

"Uh, I guess I am, ma'am," he said. "Lieutenant Brown."

"I'm Ardent, with the DERD," she said. She didn't use her code-name much at all, outside of press events and internal memos with the government. It felt weird introducing herself like that, but she'd be lying if she said she didn't enjoy it a little.

"I know who you are, ma'am."

"Good. I don't wanna alarm you, but there's a lot of very nasty alien bastards that are gonna be here in a few minutes. So anybody with a gun and some training needs to get down here ASAP: Marines, cops, hotel security, who-the-fuck-ever."

"I-I uh, I'll get on the horn, get some people down. Is that gunfire up there some alien?" Brown asked and jerked his chin at the roof Zixin continued to shoot from.

"No, that's one of us, taking out as many of them as he can before they get here. Now go on, contact your boss or whoever."

Brown cast a glance back up at the hotel, then hurried back toward a Humvee with a gunner's seat and a machine gun sticking out of the roof. He fumbled with a radio and relayed everything Anya had just told him to a harried-sounding man on the other end. The nearby police officers did the same thing, and used the radios in their squad cars.

"Felix, how much RAC do I have left?" Anya asked.

"You have 224,181 RAC remaining."

"Get me some kind of automated turret or something we can throw down on the beach here. If it's programmable like those proximity mines, even better."

"Got it! Annnnnd... here we go! Automated programmable anti-personnel turret. The creature you killed didn't seem too tough, so this should do. 5,000 RAC per turret, and I'll make sure they have the same programming as the mines."

"Let's see," Anya muttered and did some quick math in her head.

"Get me thirty. That should leave me with enough RAC for emergency medical supplies or anything else. I'm gonna fly up and down the beach and then you drop 'em."

"Will do!"

Anya soared over the beach, going beyond the bounds of Pan's wall, all while keeping an eye on the explosions of her proximity mines as they got closer and closer to land. Felix dropped each of the turrets as she flew: little else but six-foot tall, oblong shapes of dull metal on treads, with a multi-barrel cannon sticking out the front. She wanted to get some really big guns, but Gary and Vastukar had that covered.

Pan continued to erect walls along the beach while Anya flew overhead, and Ursula followed behind him. The polar bear's armor rippled as she passed each sandstone chunk Pan had created, and an apple-sized ball of the black metal detached itself and burrowed into the makeshift barricade. Ursula did this for every section of wall that Anya could see, and had probably been doing it since Pan started. To what end, Anya didn't know, but did notice that her armor didn't appear to diminish in size at all.

Movement caught her eye, and Asmund's squat form jumped off the hotel they had landed on and hit the ground below with a heavy thud. He walked it off as if he'd just stepped off the curb instead of twenty stories, and jogged towards Anya. The officers and Marines nearby gawked at the man as he approached, but thankfully none were stupid enough to reach for their guns.

"Zi says the first of the little ones'll be here any second. What's this?" Asmund asked and gestured at the visibly nervous Marines and cops. "We gonna throw them to the little ones as a distraction?"

"No. They've called in back-up. The one I fought felt weak enough that something like that or that," Anya pointed at the machine gun on top of the Humvee, then one of the turrets she had dropped, "might actually be effective. I imagine the military has also got bigger stuff on the way. Helicopters and shit. Do they have tanks here?"

The question was directed at Lieutenant Brown, who managed a shrug.

"I don't think so. Not like how you're probably thinking, anyway. We've got some APCs, but that's about it. If it's got a gun on it though, it's on its way," Brown said. Sirens flashed in the distance as he spoke, and a small convoy of squad cars and a handful of other Humvees sped toward them.

"It'll have to do. Fall back if you have to, and we'll hold them on the beach as best we can," Anya said and then faced the wall Pan had made. It was surprisingly thorough, given the immense length of the beach. It didn't cover the entire sandy stretch, but it came close. The pangolin didn't even look remotely tired after his efforts either, and his team of golems lumbered behind him as he hurried over to Anya's side.

"Ursula and me saw something move out in the water," Pan said and latched onto her leg. Anya caressed his head and back, then gave him a pat.

"You get safe underground and stay there, okay? We'll handle the rest. If things go bad, help these people get away safely," Anya said and nodded back at the men and women behind her. They were checking their guns, body armor, anything to make sure they were ready. Anya had to give them credit: she was nervous as hell, and she had an array of superpowers at her command. She couldn't imagine what it must be like to be standing in front of an oncoming alien horde with nothing but a sidearm.

"I will," Pan replied.

"Incoming!" Zi's shout echoed from the roof of the hotel, and Anya, Asmund, and Ursula all turned to face the wall. The golems took up flanking positions and spread out along the beach, and the men and women at Anya's back cocked their guns. The turrets beeped, their cannons aiming towards the wall.

The beach was eerily quiet for a moment, just the sound of the wind and the waves. The regular thumping explosions of Anya's proximity mines had stopped. She couldn't see over the wall, but she heard the aliens when they arrived. The serene whisper of water against sand became a frenzied frothing, a thrashing of waves and the screeching rasp of claws against stone.

Insectile limbs, whipping tentacles, and grasping talons appeared along the upper edge of the wall, along with an unholy chorus of gibbering howls, shrieks, and hisses.

"Oh shit, oh shit," one of the officers behind her began to mumble.

The aliens came over in a rush. They slithered and crawled over the wall, each one a different form of nightmare. They had scything mantis arms, slithering eel tails, arachnid legs, circular lamprey mouths full of needle-teeth, and harpoon-like proboscises that speared out from insectile faces. Some had the crystalline wings of dragonflies and others the membranous flapping limbs of bats. It was a menagerie of horrors, every angle of the horde designed to kill or maim in some gruesome way.

The only traits all of the onrushing swarm shared were their glowing eyes, their gray-black skin that was frequently segmented like plates of armor, and their average height. While the gnosiphages had ranged in size from only a few feet tall to bigger than Ursula, these creatures all seemed to be about six or seven feet in length. None of them had made any attempt at mimicry, either: no refrigerators, killer puppets, or toilets, just glistening terrors that lunged at Anya and the others, all fangs and claws and hungry luminescent gazes.

For once, Anya was not the first into the fray: Asmund was.

He leaped forward into the thickest patch of them, arms spread wide, an ax in each hand, bare chest thrust forward. They mobbed him at once, burying him beneath their numbers. There was a moment where Anya thought the man had just killed himself, but then a burst of red light shone from beneath the pile of monsters and blasted them outward. Asmund stood in a small crater, his axes, tattoos, and eyes all glowing red. The aliens that had attacked him had been reduced to so much scattered viscera and quivering chunks. Asmund struck his own chest and let out a baying roar, far louder than any normal person could make, and the unearthly horde flinched back from him.

He threw his axes and the spinning blades cut a path through the oncoming surge of enemies. Asmund charged up the newly created lane, deep into the densest part of the mob, and repeated the process. Another swarm, another moment of being attacked, and then another explosion.

Anya took the moment to rush in herself, heart blazing, and her golden Crown of the Firmament glowing. Her Light and Gravity Dominions combined to make a much more powerful vortex around her that was, she was delighted to see, multi-functional. Enemies were pulled in when she was within a few yards of them, dragged across the sand screeching towards her golden, Light-enhanced flames and her burning fists. Meanwhile, any attacks were shoved aside with a force that was as final as it was casual.

One alien swung an armored, mace-like tail at her, and her enhanced field shoved it back so hard that it snapped the creature's appendage in half. It was then yanked forward onto its face and drawn in to meet Anya's burning foot, crushing it flat.

Anything that actually made it through Anya's new defenses was left to deal with her Flesh of the Starforge, now also Light-imbued. She barely felt any of the attacks that landed, and the ones that did actually cause her some pain were healed and forgotten within moments. Anya laughed as she decided to imitate a version of Asmund's attack, and expanded her gravity field to draw in a couple dozen of the swarming aliens. She drew on her Sun's Heart and crafted a trembling bomb of flames in front of her, and then detonated it with her at its center.

The aliens were blasted apart en masse, and her golden flames leaped from their remains to other nearby aliens. They tried to retreat to the ocean to put the fires out, but her enhanced fire burned even beneath the waves. Her turrets chattered through the mayhem, ripping the lesser aliens to bits.

Ursula was no slouch in battle, either. She charged in along with Anya, roaring to match Asmund. Her black armor became almost like a living thing whenever an enemy was near: it lashed out at them, impaled them on spikes or cut them in half all on its own. Apple-sized pieces of the armor detached themselves and rolled away from Ursula. When they stopped, they burrowed into the sand, and then exploded in a hail of black iron shards that shredded anything unlucky enough to be close. It was almost always the aliens that took the brunt of these makeshift mines, but occasionally one would detonate near Asmund. He didn't seem to mind, quite the opposite: his tattoos glowed brighter and he roared his approval at being struck with the lethal hail.

Whenever the bear slammed one of her rear legs down, the earth shook and anything within several yards of her was thrown off-balance. Like Anya, she also had some sort of field around her, but one of ice instead of fire and gravity. Nothing could stand within a radius of several yards of her without starting to freeze over. Anything that survived her armor's active, violent defenses was either forced to retreat, or frozen in place.

She swung her huge maul with the ease of a practiced baseball player, and her targets shattered under its swings or were sent rocketing away through the air, usually in several gory pieces. A wave of concussive force radiated out from the hammer's impact point, sending crowds of the aliens flying backward with each mighty swing.

Zixin upped the tempo of his shots, as well as their variety. Some of his bullets scattered into fragments and pierced multiple targets at once, others exploded on impact. A few times, Zixin fired some kind of tracer bullet that zipped around the beach, almost with a mind of its own. The tracer rounds left glowing lines behind them as they ricocheted between the aliens, killing five or six with a single shot, then swiveling around in mid-flight and reversing course to take out another half-dozen before stopping.

The four hosts were more than managing to keep the horde at bay; they were actually pushing them back. Pan's golems protected the stream of cops and Marines that arrived in squad cars and Humvees. The men and women in the vehicles stayed back, holding their fire in part because they had no targets to shoot at, and also because most of them were too distracted by the theater of destruction before them to even think of aiming their weapons.

Anya had just started to think they could handle this, they could hang on until back-up arrived no problem, when her ear beeped.

"Be ready," Zixin said over the open comm. "That was the tip of the spear. The rest are emerging… now."

There was a tremendous roar from the other side of the wall, one that echoed up and down the beach. Sections of Pan's barricade shattered and fell, allowing a tide of creatures to pour through. Worse, they were no longer focusing their attack on the small, half-mile section of beach they had been, but had spread their numbers in either direction. The turrets Anya had placed farther up the beach sprang to life and began mowing aliens down, but it was clear they wouldn't last long.

"Shit," Anya said. The initial surge of alien creatures had been a lot, hundreds, maybe. This was something else. This was all of them. They came as a great wave, an ocean unto themselves, and flooded the beach as they rushed past the shore and towards the line of hotels and buildings.

"Open fire!" somebody yelled from behind Anya, and the Marines and cops let loose with every weapon they had. Machine gun turrets chattered, sidearms popped, rifles rattled, and even a few rocket-propelled grenades whooshed past Anya and exploded in the midst of the onrushing tidal wave of murderous life.

To Anya's surprise, the conventional weapons did a fair amount of damage. Not enough to stop the charging horde, but enough to make sections of it falter and regroup. Anya and the other hosts spread out further, forced to cover larger areas of the beach. Anya spread her gravity field as far as she could and stayed in front of the Marines and cops. Anything that came within a dozen yards of her died a quick, fiery death. She crushed and blasted and dive-kicked alien after alien, often getting several at once, but for every one she killed, ten more were right behind it.

There was no way Anya and the other hosts and the handful of cops and Marines could hold the beach. Some of the aliens took flight, and were already making headway into the city and crawling over buildings. Anya's turrets faltered and crumbled under the assault.

"Get out of here!" Anya shouted back at Lieutenant Brown just as she rocket-kicked some octopus-wasp hybrid thing into a spray of flaming giblets. "Shoot anything you can but get away from the beach! Evacuate anybody who's left!"

Brown didn't even bother responding to her. He tapped the helmet of the Marine nearest him and made a circular hand-gesture and shouted at the other men and women to begin falling back. The message was repeated over radios, and they all began a fighting retreat.

Anya focused on giving them enough space to get free, but she couldn't be everywhere at once. She managed to keep Brown and the other vehicles near him safe as they sped away, but she winced as she heard other Humvees explode further up the beach. She grit her teeth in fury as the screams of men and women were cut off by the continuous flood of aliens swarming over them.

"Anya? What do we do?" There's too many!" Pan said in her ear.

"They're starting to climb the hotel I'm on. Moving back to second position," Zixin said.

Ursula roared wordlessly over the din as she became bogged down in the waves of monsters. Many were frozen as they wrapped their bodies around her, slowing her down and allowing other aliens with projectiles to take shots at her.

"I'm starting to get winded," Asmund said. His breath came in ragged pants over the comms, and there was a manic edge to it.

Anya didn't have time to think. She wrestled four aliens to the ground and turned them into a charred paste, then flung herself at the next group. Her upgrades were allowing her to stay unharmed and to put out incredible amounts of damage. Wherever she went, aliens died by the handful, several every second. But all that output was draining her, and no matter how many monsters she killed, more slipped past.

Anya was about to demand that everybody just keep fighting, to not stop, to hold on until their friends arrived, when the flood of aliens paused. It was eerie, seeing so many thousands of creatures all freeze in place, even for a moment. Then, as one, they all turned to look behind them at the ocean, and issued an undulating, rattling cry.

Something was coming.

A dark, triangular rock several yards tall stuck out of the ocean like a huge, stony dorsal fin. It was still far off in the distance, but it had a wake behind it and was closing fast.

The point grew, stretching into the air and broadening along the base as more of it became exposed. Anya dropped the pair of alien corpses she had throttled to death and stepped back, mouth agape, as Alien Alpha emerged from the ocean in all of its terrible and monolithic majesty.

28

t's a god damn mountain, Anya thought.

It was a fair comparison, but if it had been an actual mountain, Anya would not have been impressed. It was smallish, by mountain standards. Really more of a hill with goals.

But mountains (or even hills with goals) tended to just sit there and do absolutely nothing.

Seeing something that size move, to see it moving toward Anya, to watch it block out the sun and tower over her, the hotels, the beach, was another matter. Nothing that size should ever move. And it was only after several full seconds of mute, horror-struck staring at the sheer size of Big Al did Anya actually start to take in its shape.

It appeared to be a broad pyramid made of overlapping plates of rocky armor. Dark, milky crystalline growths sprouted along the top and sides of the pyramidal main body. The underside of the behemoth was a paler shade of gray, and made of the same interconnected plates as the top. Frigid blue light shone out from between the plates, bathing the ground beneath in a chilly glow.

Ocean water ran off it in cascades and curtains, sluicing down the angular sides of its body. It was dotted with barnacles and other marine life that had clung to it, and pieces of kelp and seaweed dangled from cracks and crevices between the rocky plates.

Legs sprouted from its sides, three on each. They were long and thick with armor, segmented and jointed to bend beneath the huge weight of the thing. The legs ended in blunt tips, and every time one of them slammed into the ground, Anya's teeth rattled in her skull. The limbs were crab-like, except they moved the beast forward instead of to the side.

Another pair of limbs, also crab-like, extended from the front of Alpha, almost near its belly. Pincer claws, each longer than a city block, swept overhead. One of them casually slammed into a hotel and bashed it in half with a single blow. The building crumbled as though it had been made of stale crackers and toothpicks, and Anya flinched back.

Clusters of eyes glowed blue along Alpha's front, sides, and top. They twitched and swiveled, hundreds of them focusing everywhere at once. The largest of them, a pair of glistening orbs each as large as tanks, were front and center. They focused on something distant, and then several of the crystal formations on Alpha's craggy back began to glow with dark purple light that became more intense by the second.

"Oh shi—" Anya started to say, but was drowned out by a deafening shriek as the now-familiar lances of dark light shot out from the crystals. They shot out from Alpha and swept across Honolulu's skyline in a criss-cross pattern, then vanished.

Any structure over six stories tall was cut short. A series of explosions boomed across the city as building after building blew apart and crumbled down upon themselves. The destructive paths of Alpha's lasers had decimated miles of the city in a single instant.

Anya only had a moment to reflect on the chaos before the onslaught of lesser aliens forced her attention back to the beach. Another wave of the creatures had hitched a ride on Alpha's sides and legs, and dropped from its mountainous body and rushed inland.

The aliens had already broken past numerous barricades up and down the beach and were making their way deeper into the city. Anya stared up, and up, and up at Alpha. Its shadow fell over her and the whole of Honolulu, and the horde of shrieking thousands surged forward under its pall.

Something glinted in the sky above Alpha, a wink of sunlight on silver.

An egg.

Samaira, Arvo, and Esmeralda had arrived, and not alone. Dozens upon dozens of bulky shapes flew with them, revealing themselves to be Gary's Guardians, and each of them carried a huge shipping container. More vessels flew in behind the Guardians: the deployment ships Gary had made for the DERD. Each one landed up the road from the beach, and unloaded crowds of DERD troops in advanced armor, heavy machine guns, and rocket launchers.

More silvery glints in the sky came from the opposite direction. Anya recognized the teardrop-shaped vessels in the distance as Vastukar's drones, an entire fleet of them, all shooting forward in formation.

Alpha noticed them too, and a different group of crystals glowed on its back, brighter and brighter.

"No!" Anya shouted and blasted herself free of a mob of aliens that swarmed over her as she rushed towards Alpha. She spun in mid-air, dodging a devastating but clumsy sweep of Alpha's gargantuan claw, and landed on its back at the nearest glowing crystal. The luminescent, glassy growth was taller and thicker than one of Pan's golems.

Anya's Crown of the Firmament glowed as flame and gravity coalesced into a spiraling orb of light and force at the tip of her Star-forged fist. She swung it at the crystal outcropping, popping off an explosion behind her elbow to further propel her blow forward. She connected, detonating the enhanced fireball and punching through the glittering, golden explosion of fire and force that resulted upon the booming impact.

The crystal cracked and shattered. The deadly light within dispersed in a flickering web of weaker rays—at least a hundred of the small, deadly beams—but most of them missed her, had a reduced range, and faded after a short distance.

The few that did hit, hurt. A lot. Her metallic skin kept the beams from fully impaling her on their deadly violet light, deflected some, but not all. Her regalia was no match for them either, even in their weakened state. Two of the narrow purplish lances struck her just over her heart, but bounced off her sacred orichalcum chestpiece.

Anya landed on her back, bleeding from the numerous holes that dotted her body. Her wounds glowed a soft gold, her blood flowed back into the injuries, and then closed.

"That was fast," she grunted as she leaped to her feet. Without her Starforged skin, she would have been shot through in at least a few more places. While it might not have killed her, it certainly would have left her a mess, and there were at least five other crystals powering up to blast her friends and backup out of the sky.

A mad scream shook the air as Asmund ran up Alpha's side like some kind of rabid monkey. His eyes were glowing red along with his tattoos, and he flung himself bodily at the nearest glowing crystal, and brought his axes down. The crystal broke as if it were about as substantial as a cheap wine glass.

The weakened, directionless dark light shot from the ruined crystal just as it had under Anya's attack, but Asmund didn't have the benefit of Starforged skin. He took a face-full of the lethal glowing lights, several of them impaling him through the chest and gut, and one slicing an entire arm off.

"Holy shit! Asmund!" Anya said. The man barely registered her presence. He picked up his fallen ax, gripped it in his teeth, and charged at the next crystal, leaving his arm behind. After a moment, his arm stood up on its hand and fingers, and crawled after him.

"Gross," Anya said, but followed Asmund's example and rushed to the next crystal. Ursula was up here now as well. She smashed a crystal and the weirdly dark light bounced off her armor. Two of the glowing outcrops cracked from distant gunfire, then exploded as Zixin took them out from a distance.

There were still dozens, maybe hundreds of the outcroppings left on Alpha's back, but they had smashed all of the glowing ones for now. Anya's skin, enhanced by the Light Dominion, had become quite adept at deflecting the beams, and both she and Asmund were fully healed by the time they stopped to examine the damage.

"Anya!" a voice called from overhead, and Samaira flew down with Chandrali, Esmeralda hanging on tightly to her waist from behind.

"Sam!" Anya waved. Arvo's silver egg sped past, and a flickering shape emerged from it mid-air. The doctor landed some distance away, still in his shadowform, and then hurried to meet them just as Samaira landed.

"This thing..." Samaira said and looked below her, mouth agape. She managed to shake her head and little else.

"Doc, can you paralyze it, like you did with the other aliens?" Anya asked. Arvo's shape consolidated back to normal as he knelt and placed his hand on Alpha's rocky armor.

"No. Whatever this is," Arvo said and rapped his knuckles against the blackish-gray surface beneath them, "it's inorganic. I can't reach Alpha's body through it. I can do some scans though. Whatever this outer layer is, it's thick. At least several meters, and incredibly dense."

"What about its eyes?" Samaira asked and nodded toward a cluster of glowing blue eyes not far away. Arvo shook his head.

"Those aren't eyes. They can see, but they're like the ends of telescopes. The actual eyes are probably deep beneath the armor, farther than I can scan. Those crystals you smashed, they won't work either. They're also regrowing, but slow. I can see parts of Alpha's insides, but it's so big I can't get a complete picture. Multiple hearts, clusters of brain cells, redundant organs all over."

"So no going for a singular weak spot, I take it?"

"I'm afraid not."

"Fuck."

Anya glanced overhead as Gary's Guardians slammed down into the city below and began to push back against the hordes of swarming aliens. The DERD dropships flew further into the city and continued deploying field agents in protective gear. Vastukar's drones soared overhead and dropped clusters of bombs along the beach.

It was helping slow the assault, but not push it back. Asmund— now with his arm reattached—had gone off to one side of Alpha's back and had been slicing it with his axes since the others arrived, but he had barely made a dent in it. Ursula had been doing the same, but stopped to listen to the others. She hadn't had much luck in doing anything but cracking the hard armor plating either.

If any of Gary's bombs had connected with Alpha's back, they might be able to get a feel for what level of damage was needed, but...

"Arvo, I need you to come with me. We're gonna fly under this big bastard and I can show you where Gary's bomb hit its belly. Hopefully," Anya said.

"Uh, okay," Arvo said.

"I'll run interference," Samaira said and hopped back onto Chandrali. Esmeralda immediately hopped off, shaking her head.

"I'm getting away from this thing. I'll go help people evacuate and see about pushing the little ones back toward the beach," she said.

In the distance, Asmund screamed and continued to attack Alpha's back.

"I'll handle him and we'll go give Pan some back up," Ursula said. She ran at Asmund, grabbed him by the throat with her mouth, and then leaped off Alpha's back and into the fray below.

"Ready, Doc?" Anya asked as she tucked Arvo under one arm as if he were nothing but an over-sized duffel bag.

"I suppose. You just want me to scan it?"

"And look for anywhere you can touch. Maybe it's got an exposed asshole, or something."

"Disgusting, but possible. Ready when you are."

Samaira readied her bow and urged Chandrali forward with a nudge of her heels. The armor-clad tiger bounded forward, blue fire leaping around her paws as she ran across the air. Anya flew after them and clutched the doctor tightly to her side.

The patches of eyes along Alpha's back and sides tracked them as they flew. Anya saw that some sections of Alpha's body were more porous than others, and were dotted with holes almost as big as Anya's fist.

"Holes?" Anya asked Arvo and nodded at one as they soared past, approaching the titan's lower side.

"Not big enough for me to fit in, and depending on how shallow they are, may not be much use. Although, if—oh. Oh dear," Arvo said and stiffened in Anya's grasp. She looked to the side and thought she might be hallucinating. The more porous sections of Alpha's armored shell looked to be squirming. Then Anya realized it wasn't the rocky armor, but the things emerging from it.

Squishy, winged deformities writhed their way out of the holes in the armor, looking like a cross between an overfed slug and a mosquito. Their bulbous bodies shone with slick fluid, and their numerous, hair-thin legs twitched along with their wings. Their heads were little more than knives flanked by segmented eyes. The smallest of the loathsome critters was about the length of Anya's foot, while the largest was bigger than a medium-sized dog. Their soft, squishy bodies compressed themselves as they pushed out of the holes along Alpha's side, then expanded once free.

A small swarm of them locked onto Anya, Arvo, Samaira, and Chandrali, their knife-like faces glinting as they zipped forward.

"Absolutely not," Samaira said and fired an arrow into the swarm's midst. It burst in a spray of aether and water that coated the entire swarm. Bolts of electricity followed the initial blast of water, connecting every single repulsive creature in a web of twitching lightning. Most of the monstrosities were reduced to ash, but the few that managed to survive found themselves frozen as the water crystallized around them, encased their wings in ice, and dropped them like stones to the sea below.

The group flew down past the edge of Alpha's side and finally reached its underbelly. They had flown far to Alpha's right to avoid the claws, but now had to contend with the legs. Each was as big around as several houses, and trudged forward with implacable force. Samaira tried creating thick blocks of ice around them in the water, but Alpha tore free of them as though they weren't even there. The only saving grace Anya could see was that Alpha was slower on land than it was at sea. Its sheer size and density worked against it, forcing it to amble rather than sprint.

"Get me as close as you can!" Arvo shouted over the force of the wind rushing past them as Anya flew between two of Alpha's legs. She focused on her flying rather than looking for any weak spots. Samaira flew literal circles around them with Chandrali, her bow never ceasing its aetheric barrage.

Now that they were closer to the ocean, Samaira was able to make better use of her Water Dominion. The ocean below rose up in swirling pillars that lashed out at anything that came close. Some of them spat icicles thicker than palm trees at the swarming aliens below, or any more of those knife-faced mosquito-slugs. If anything got past Samaira's arrows and water blasts, Anya blasted it out of the sky as soon as it came within range.

Arvo, for his part, managed to stay focused. His eyes had a distant, glazed look to them and he was muttering to himself. After several moments, his vision cleared and he patted Anya on the arm.

"Would you like the good news or bad news?" he asked.

"Dammit. Bad news."

"Alpha is armored from top to bottom. No mouth or opening of any kind more than several centimeters wide, and those appear to only go a short way in before they close off. I think this one learned from you flying into the centipede's mouth."

"Asshole."

"No, it doesn't have one of those, either."

"I mean—forget it. What's the good news?"

"I can detect some weakness on the back right side," Arvo said and pointed at a place far behind the rear legs. "There are some hairline fractures in the armor, and what may be some missing plates. However, it's still covered quite heavily."

"Got it. Thanks, Doc. Let's get out of here for now," Anya said and then waved at Samaira and pointed back towards the beach. Samaira nodded and they all soared out from under Alpha's shadow and to where Ursula, Asmund, and Pan had cleared a significant area and were holding firm against the horde of mindless aliens.

"Well?" Ursula demanded as soon as they touched down. Anya pointed at where Arvo had indicated.

"That spot's the weakest, but it's still tough," she said.

"I can't get a shot from anywhere but ground level, then," Zixin said over the radio. "And I doubt even that would work. I've been shooting this tsou hai with my best armor-piercers and they only manage to get about a few meters into the outer shell. It looks like it gets denser the further in it goes."

"It's regenerating too," Anya added.

"I can target most of the crystals from my current position, but I'll need at least one other person to cover Alpha's far side, preferably two people," Zixin said. "If we can do that, at least we can cripple one of its weapons."

"Me and Asmund," Ursula said.

"I've got the beach covered," a familiar voice said, and a squad of twenty of Gary's Guardians, accompanied by a sizable swarm of the smaller support drones, landed nearby. All of them spread out at once, opening fire on the waves of crawling horrors that continued to emerge from the sea. One of the drones stayed behind and projected a hologram of Gary's face.

"I'll use my boys to stretch along the beach and keep as many of those freaks from making it into the city as we can," he continued.

"But what about Alpha?" Samaira asked.

"I can slow him down," Vastukar's voice said from the speaker of a nearby drone ship, similar to the one that had brought Anya into New Bengaluru. There were dozens of them, and unlike Anya's ship, these had a variety of weapons on their sides. They flew overhead in squads of four or five, surrounding Alpha and opening fire. Several of them attempted to tie its legs together with glowing wires, while others acted as decoys as they flew in and out of range.

"And the other hosts? This bastard's still screwing with our maps. Can't tell where people are," Anya said as she double checked the Archive to make sure. It was definitely still not working.

"Everybody else is gonna be at least another half-hour, I'm afraid," Vastukar replied.

"Shit. But, even if everybody's here..." Anya said and trailed off as she stared up at Alpha. "How the fuck are we gonna take him out without blowing up the city, too?"

"I'm working on it," Gary said. "I'm modifying a couple of my bombs to focus on armor piercing. They'll be ready in ten minutes or less, then two minutes in the air. Vastukar says he's working on retrofitting some mining lasers he's got attached to satellites to help with the armor-piercing angle. If we can think of some way to flip that big bastard over, we've got a shot. In the meantime, you should just try to get people as far away from the beach as possible."

"Its back? Are you serious?"

"And preferably at least a half-mile back out to sea, but yeah. Haven't figured that part out yet."

An idea popped into Anya's head. Pan's earlier statement, about the earth feeling stronger here, had been bouncing around in the back of her brain since he'd said it. She had been focusing on Alpha's approach and then attack afterwards, but now it came back to the forefront of her mind.

Why would Pan think the earth was stronger here?

It seemed pretty obvious now.

The idea was crazy, and dangerous, and would probably get her in a lot of trouble with Hanover, MacDougal, maybe everybody. Assuming she even survived.

Ah, but doesn't it also sound like an absolute blast? Pun intended, the bird said, and Anya heard the excitement in its voice.

Could we even do it? she asked.

Oh yeah. We'd need the little one's help, though. But yes, it's possible.

"I think I have an idea of how to flip Alpha over," Anya said.

Everyone turned to look at her, expectant and curious.

"Go on, kid, what is it?" Gary asked. Anya took a deep breath and then pointed behind her. Her finger aimed past the beach, the ruined buildings, the distant suburbs, and to the lush mountains far in the distance.

"I'm gonna hit it with a volcano."

29

Anya stood atop the volcano nearest the city. It stood at the edge of Honolulu, a few miles inland, and looked like any of the other tree-shrouded mountains. However, deep beneath the earth, Anya felt it.

The heat.

The fire.

A potential for an explosion so immense it made her shudder.

It was asleep now, a gentle warmth that wouldn't awaken for ages to come.

Unless she poked it.

Which she absolutely intended to do.

"This feels.... weird," Pan said beside her.

She and the pangolin had soared up from the beach, leaving the others to begin their preparations. Anya could see for miles in every direction from atop the mountain, including Honolulu far below, and the carnage Alpha had wrought. Tendrils of black smoke rose from across the city, and Alpha itself was a dark mass on the coastline that continued its advance. It had emerged from the ocean and was stomping its way across the beach, towards the edge of Honolulu. It smashed any buildings within range to dust, a promise of carnage to come for the rest of the city.

"The volcano?" Anya asked and Pan nodded.

"I like it, it's a strong feeling. But also kinda scary. It's a lot of stuff that could happen, but isn't. But maybe it can help us, so it's okay."

"Do you think you can do what I asked you?"

Pan closed his eyes for a moment, and the ground rippled beneath him. There was a distant *Thud!* as something far below the surface moved.

"Yeah, I can do it! You just want me to make a kind of tunnel?"

"Funnel. There's gonna be a lot of moving earth and stuff. I don't need you to stop any of it, I just need you to direct it that way," Anya replied and pointed at Alpha. "Keep it from going all over the city and hurting people until we get to the beach, then help me push it up, right in that big asshole's face."

Pan nodded.

"Okay. But you'll be helping me, right?" he asked.

"You know it. I'm going to use my Dominions to help you keep it on course and from blowing up too soon. All you gotta do is help me funnel, and let go at the end. Got it?"

"I got it!"

"All right, little buddy. I'm gonna check with Gary real quick," Anya said and touched the radio in her ear..

"Hey kid. How's Operation: Batshit going?" Gary asked.

"It's not batshit!"

"Kid."

"Okay, but I didn't hear anybody else throw out ideas. We don't have time to take this to a committee!"

"I'm on your side, but it's a crazy-ass plan. We've done our bit, though. Vastukar says he's rigged his meteor mining laser or whatever, and I've got my rocket on its way. It'll hold above the water until Alpha's at a good enough distance. Sam, the other hosts, the cops, and the military have managed to clear the path from the volcano to the beach that we decided on. It's nothing but aliens in there for now."

"And the shields?"

"My Guardians and Vastukar's drones are set up along the

perimeter of the eruption's path. We'll throw up some forcefields to help funnel the worst of the debris and lava and whatever else. Did you get far enough away for your RAC store to work?"

"Felix?" Anya asked.

"I managed to reconnect a few minutes ago, and have been looking for what you asked about on the flight over. You can afford two seismic alteration devices. 35,000 RAC each. That'll bring you down to 4,181 RAC remaining," Felix said.

"But they'll work?"

"They will help redirect and channel any and all seismic activity within a given area to a desired location, yes. There are more powerful versions, but these are the best you can afford. These also have advanced enough automation that you just need to turn them on."

"Get them," Anya said. Two white, metallic devices that looked like industrial refrigerators but were covered with blinking lights, and had some kind of spiked drill in their base, appeared beside Anya. One of Gary's Guardians flew towards them, and landed just long enough to pick up the seismic alteration devices.

"I'll make sure these get put down somewhere optimal. Keep as much of the aftershocks and such away from the city and push them towards Alpha. But kid, it's a volcano. It's gonna make a mess."

"I know. But Alpha will make a bigger one if we just leave it. At least this way, it's just some buildings that get trashed, and not the people in them."

"Good luck, kid. See ya when you're done."

Gary clicked off as the Guardian flew away with its cargo, and Anya turned to face Pan. The pangolin wriggled his nose and regarded her with his shiny black eyes.

"No time like the present, huh, Pan? Lead the way to the spot you feel has the most... I dunno, Earth power?"

"I think I know. Follow me!" Pan said, and spread his claws wide. The dirt and stone parted before him, and fell away to reveal a tunnel that opened like a throat into the ground below. Anya flew them both down, clutching Pan closely to her.

While she could sense the build-up of heat and potential explosive force, it was still some distance away. Affecting such a large amount of heat from so far would strain her Sun's Heart too quickly, and leave her drained well before she reached the shore and Alpha itself.

Pan maneuvered them ever deeper into the gullet of the mountain. Past rock that was older than mankind, older than the dinosaurs. Anya glanced up and saw a pinprick of blue sky far above them. She had a moment of claustrophobia, as absurd as that was. She could fly or blast her way out, no problem. But being this deep in the ground, with the air and sky so far away, it made something primal in her want to scream that this was a bad idea.

This is a fucking great idea, the bird said. *I love it.*

If it works, Anya thought.

If it doesn't, you'll probably explode.

What?!

Your regenerative abilities are impressive, but being at ground zero for a literal volcano blast? The kinetic force is going to vaporize you if you make a mistake. But hey, better to go out with a bang than a whimper, right?

No!

We both know you don't believe that, the bird said, then chuckled and became quiet.

"Jerk," Anya muttered.

"Hmm?" Pan asked her.

"Nothing, buddy. I think we're as close as we can get. Does all this heat not bother you?" Anya asked as they stood at the bottom of the gaping pit.

"No. My upgrades and scales and stuff protect me. The Earth Dominion too. It's really nice! Gives me all kinds of stuff to keep me safe."

"Good to know. I'm gonna set off my big bang, and then we just gotta go… Uhhh," Anya looked around the narrow walls of the pit they stood in, having lost all sense of direction.

"The ocean and Alpha are that way," Pan said and pointed. "I can feel it shaking the ground. It's scary."

"Thanks, buddy. It'll be over soon. I just need you to pop me an escape tunnel to fly out of here, but still kinda close to the ground, at an angle."

"I can do that!" Pan said and waved his claws again. Another tunnel opened up before Anya, this one tilted up slightly. It was all encased in shadow before another tiny dot of light opened up far, far away.

"This'll take you up and out," Pan said. "I'm gonna stay in the ground and do the funneling thing like you told me."

"Thank you, Pan," Anya said and knelt in front of the pangolin. She hugged him close and stroked his back. "Be safe, okay?"

"You too. It's here, when you're ready," Pan said, and dove into the black rock as if it were water without another word. He made another smaller tunnel that led down in a different direction for several dozen yards. The smaller tunnel had glowing red light welling up from it, primal and ancient.

Anya clapped her hands together in front of her and popped her knuckles. She checked her Shards of the Everstar to make sure they were as full as they could be. She drew in as much of the ambient heat as she could to top off her Sun's Heart, and took several long, deep breaths.

"Okay. Okay, okay, okay. Just gonna... hit a kaiju with a volcano. I'm good. I'm good to go. Good and read—"

You're stalling, the bird said.

"Yup. Okay, fuck it. *Onetwothreego!*" Anya said and reached out to the glowing mass of heat below her. It was huge, tremendous, but it was also patient. The sarcophagus of layered stone and dirt piled onto the would-be explosion over the eras kept it contained, made it stew in its own potential energy. It probably would have waited thousands of years for its moment to burst forth if Anya didn't decide to just...

Tickle it.

That's really what she was doing, acting as the feather under the volcano's nose.

She created a bowling-ball-sized orb of condensed fire, smashing it down as tightly as she could between her hands and enhancing it with the Light Dominion until it gleamed golden.

She chucked it down into the small tunnel Pan had made, and detonated it.

Something thumped far below Anya, and the red surface magma bubbled.

And then, the earth *moved*.

Words like "Super Volcano," and "Cataclysmic Event," popped into Anya's head. The force that awoke beneath Anya was more than just an explosion. It felt like a living thing, like she had just awoken a sleeping leviathan of rock and lava, fire and thunder, and it was coming up from Hell itself.

"Oh shit," she said.

Ha haaaa! Too late to back out now, little ember! Ride or die! the bird crowed, delirious with excitement. It laughed, and Anya couldn't stop herself from laughing too. This was insanity, but damn if it didn't feel amazing.

Anya focused all of her energy and will into grasping that terrifying energy below her. She couldn't control that much. Not even close. But she might be able to guide it, just a little.

Flame Dominion connected her to the roiling explosion and pulled it onward, while gravity held it to a single course, and the Light Dominion enhanced all of it, and her energy focus skill ensured everything was operating at maximum efficiency. With Pan helping to funnel all of it from far below, Anya lassoed the volcano's fury and rode it up and out of the earth's guts like a shrieking, laughing demon.

Calling what rose up from the earth and broke through its surface a mere explosion would be to do it a great injustice. The force of nature that Anya rode was an event, a memory from a distant age that had only been witnessed by mankind on a handful of occasions.

The ground tore open before the volcano's might like a tissue in front of a grenade. There was no resistance to be had from the strata of rock and dirt. The force Anya rode commanded that the earth open and allow it passage, and something of that magnitude could only be obeyed.

Or, as Anya thought as she blasted along at the eruption's apex, it was a really fucking big kaboom.

Her vision was clouded by flying debris, clouds of smoke and sulfur, and sprays of lava that splatted onto her face. She wiped it away as if it were nothing more serious than warmed up pudding, and tried to maintain her focus on keeping the eruption focused and forward.

It was a wild animal beneath her, trying to throw her off and run free. It fought against her gravitational shackles, more each time she used the Flame Dominion to tug it back on track. Anya didn't know how fast she was going, but it felt like double her normal flying speed. Her energy, already taxed from the fighting, was draining fast. She focused on her Shards of the Everstar and drained them as she flew on.

She was surrounded by buildings within moments of shooting out of the ground, and the structures simply dissolved before the eruption's overwhelming might. Huge blue panels of light popped up on either side of Anya, a few blocks away on either side. Gary and Vastukar's forcefields flickered and rippled against the eruption, but they held.

The eruption itself did not push back at the forcefields too much: it had its way forward, and its target. Anya locked eyes with Alpha as she approached the beach at rocket-speed.

She didn't actually know if Alpha could see her, but she sure hoped it could. Her hair had become a glowing mass of flames, the Crown of the Firmament ablaze with radiance that matched the flare of her eyes. Anya stuck out from the front of the eruption's towering cloud of fire and fury like the figurehead jutting from some hellish ship's prow.

Pan must have sensed they had finally come to the beach, because that was when the funnel stopped, and the full power of the eruption was finally, at last, given free rein. Anya gave it one final yank of gravitational force, her hands shaking from the strain, and a tremendous blast of fire and light. It all struck Alpha from below and surged upward in a furious roar that shattered every window for miles, and sent waves crashing across the ocean.

Anya couldn't see it from her position, but to her it felt like the Earth itself had just delivered an uppercut to Alpha, right in its gut.

That was when Anya realized this *might* have been a bad idea.

The explosion hit Alpha in its underside... which meant she found herself plastered to heavily-armored kaiju tummy by an ongoing volcanic eruption.

Uh-oh, Anya thought.

The eruption lifted Alpha off its crab-like legs and flung it up and back through the air as if the towering alien behemoth were just another piece of debris. There was a secondary explosion and then a sudden, horrible pressure at Anya's back. Her bones creaked, then broke, then shattered, and then one of her arms was just gone. There wasn't pain, only a sudden numb sensation below the shoulder. Her Starforged skin could only take so much.

Her eardrums burst from the sheer din of it all, and even if she could have opened her eyes there would have been nothing but smoke and dirt to see.

She had to get out, had to make sure Alpha was on its back, and get away before Gary's bomb hit, along with Vastukar's laser. Anya forced herself to focus on flying, to making a buffer of space between herself and Alpha's underbelly.

There was a floating, weightless moment where Anya thought maybe she had lost control of Gravity Dominion. The eruption had reached its apex, and thrown Anya and Alpha together through the clear Hawaiian sky. The pressure on her back abated, and Anya was free to move.

Her regalia was in tatters, her right arm missing. But, she was alive. The eruption had dispersed enough to Alpha's sides and around to allow her light-enhanced regeneration and Flesh of the Starforge to keep her from being blasted entirely to pieces.

She sighed with relief as she began to fly away, exhausted and beginning to really hurt now that the shock was wearing off. They were far enough away from the beach, at least half a mile, that Gary's bomb could go off without issue.

Except, there was another issue. Alpha was in free fall, but not on its back. It was tilted somewhat backward, but just before the tipping point that would make it fall over entirely. If it hit the water like that, the impact could knock it back forward, and all that work, all that destruction, would be for nothing.

Anya's Shards of the Everstar were tapped. The crystals were dark and cool against her skin. She had one barely functioning arm, and two broken legs. She probably had just enough energy to fly back to shore before the bomb hit.

Or to tip Alpha that last little bit.

It wasn't even a choice.

Anya flew up to between Alpha's huge frontal eyes and grinned down at it, just as they both reached the apex of their flight. She regenerated one of her legs just enough to plant it between the huge, glowing blue eye balls. The black pits at their centers swiveled forward and focused on Anya as she leaned down.

"THIEF," Alpha said from somewhere deep within it's body, its voice rumbling and resonant; an earthquake that had learned to talk. "NOT OVER YET."

"Give it another second, big guy," she said, and then blew a kiss at Alpha as she put every last ounce of energy she had into a fiery kick. The force was enough to shatter Anya's leg all over again, and she growled at the pain. It was also enough to crack the armor between Alpha's eyes... and push it over that precarious balancing point that sent the titanic alien falling backwards.

It also blasted Anya away and back towards land.

Though not by much.

Anya fell from the sky, energy spent. She made an effort to slow her fall, but gravity no longer obeyed her. Her Sun's Heart was cool, her Crown of the Firmament dark. She stared up at the wide blue sky as something glinted high above, and then a column of white light blasted down from above the clouds and pierced Alpha's fragmented underside.

A rocket streaked across the heavens, curved in the air, and hit Alpha's gut just as the kaiju splashed into the ocean. Anya shut her eyes as the whole world became consumed with a blinding white glare. There was a rush, and then a deafening roar of wind and air as she was thrown back across the waters.

The world became a tumbling mess of wind and sea, and Anya's body cracked, bounced, cracked again. The air was knocked out of her on the first impact, and the second almost made her pass out. She realized she was skipping across the ocean like a rock across a pond, and then she plunged beneath the waters as her momentum slowed.

She sank.

A few bubbles emerged from her mouth, but the impact against the waves had knocked most of the breath out of her already.

It seemed pretty stupid to survive everything up to this point, and then die because she drowned. Though she did find it appropriate that water would be the thing to snuff out her fire. Maybe the bird would think that was funny.

Anya had started to come to terms with her death when something splashed through the water overhead and rushed towards her. Blue firelight flared around fuzzy paws, and white saber fangs glittered as Chandrali opened her mouth and seized Anya by the back of her regalia, and then lurched upwards.

Normally, Anya would have been focused on a giant, armor-clad tiger running underwater straight at her, mouth agape, but all of her attention was on Chandrali's rider.

Samaira's hair billowed around her in the water, a silken nebulae of glittering stars. Her gloved hand extended to grab Anya's, and helped Chandrali carry her from the ocean's sodden grip.

They landed on the beach moments later, and Chandrali dropped Anya to the sand with a gentle thump. Samaira was at her side immediately, cradling her head and looking down at her.

"Anya! Oh my god! Anya, please! Are you okay?" she asked, her voice cracking.

Anya looked up at Samaira, then let her gaze wander past. Smoke rose from countless fires, and collapsing buildings sent rumbling echoes across the sky, punctuating the wail of countless sirens. Plumes of debris-laden dust rose for miles from the wound Anya and Pan had opened in the Earth, and cast a black cloud over the entirety of Honolulu.

"Think they'll let me pay off the damage in installments?" Anya rasped.

Samaira blinked down at Anya and tears fell from her eyes. Her mouth twitched, and then she sputtered and began to laugh even as she cried. Anya snorted as well, even as her own eyes began to sting with tears of relief and joy at seeing Samaira above her. She reached up with her remaining arm and the two women held each other on the ruined beach as they laughed and sobbed together.

FROM SPACE #2

From an intercepted communication between the Engineers via Luorian Intelligence Ministry (LIM) (Translated from Luorian Basic):

Initiate Engineer Red-507: Elder Engineer Green-28, please acknowledge message request.

Elder Engineer Green-28: This one informed you not to message unless there were important—

Initiate Engineer Red-507: The humans have defeated a siege-class gnosiphage, Elder.

Elder Engineer Green-28: …

Initiate Engineer Red-507: Elder?

Elder Engineer Green-28: Is this an error? You have many mistakes on your extended record of service.

Initiate Engineer Red-507: Negative. This one has confirmed the data many times. The communications disruption between Earth and this Enclave has ceased. This one was the first to confirm the data, but this one suspects other initiates will begin confirmation soon.

Elder Engineer-28: Siege-class? Confirm again.

Initiate Engineer Red-507: Confirmed. A siege-class gnosiphage. Scans indicate it had personnel manufacturing capabilities, as well as anti-matter rays, Class A-2 armor, electric discharge, and several other offensive and defensive capabilities. It was defeated within roughly two hours of its first confirmed sighting by the humans.

Elder Engineer Green-28: How many casualties?

Initiate Engineer Red-507: Of hosts? Zero. Other casualties are not conclusive. Somewhere in the low hundreds.

Elder Engineer Green-28: Unexpected. Alarming. How many gnosiphages remain on Earth?

Initiate Engineer Red-507: Zero. Shall this one establish communication with Earth hosts?

Elder Engineer Green-28: Negative. This one is currently meeting with Grand Engineer Black-3 and Mr. Prospector. They will need to be notified of this. Wait on this line.

Initiate Engineer Red-507: Mr. Prospector is here?

Automated voice: You have been placed on hold. Please do not leave your station during this time.

Grand Engineer Black-3: Initiate. Confirm report: siege-class gnosiphage has been defeated by Earth hosts. Zero host casualties.

Initiate Engineer Red-507: Ah! C-confirmed, Grand Engineer! This one is humbled to address you so directly!

Mr. Prospector: Didn't I tell you they'd be better than the Melarusians?

Grand Engineer Black-3: Your assessment was accurate.

Mr. Prospector: Mm-Hmm. You're welcome. Tell me, Initiate, you've been keeping a steady eye on the humans, correct?

Initiate Engineer Red-507: Y-yes! Mr. Prospector! Th-this one is also humbled to address you! Thank you for your guidance thus far.

Mr. Prospector: It's the least I could do. Now, how many of the humans have broken Archive parameters?

Initiate Engineer Red-507: This one is aware of 205 hosts of remaining 371, or 55.256%, have committed Archive parameter breaches in some capacity.

This one will need to review new data, but as of the previous cycle, most of the parameter breaches were minor. However, based on breach data by Sol-3022 and Sol-4507—local classifications, Anya Nowicki and Renn, respectively—initial parameter breach is indicative of continued and successively greater breaches.

This one posits that all Earth hosts will commit some level of Archive parameter breach within another forty-eight cycles or fewer. This one further posits that at least one-quarter to one-third of those breaches will be significant.

Grand Engineer Black-3: I will review your data now. Is it available on central messaging?

Initiate Engineer Red-507: Yes, Grand Engineer.

Elder Engineer Green-28: Could the Archive breaches be a result of system corruption? Redistribution and calibration for humans was done in haste. Error potential could have escalated as a result.

Grand Engineer Black-3: Possible. However: improbable. Archive integrity remains constant according to data. Conclusion from that would be that Engineer data collection methods are flawed, or Earth hosts are displaying the exact same inclination for parameter breaches as the primary host.

Elder Engineer Green-28: Primary Earth host, designation Sol-1, only had access to prototype version of Archive. Breaches were inevitable. Current version of Archive is up-to-date. Approved by Grand Engineer Council and Prime Engineer. Breaches should not be common occurrence.

Grand Engineer Black-3: Agreed. Yet, the data does not lie. Prospector, is this what you wanted when you proposed alternative Archive assignment to Earth?

Mr. Prospector: We've tried it your way for how long now? I've tried my best to work within your confines, and where has it gotten us? Nowhere. The gnosiphages have multiplied, and swarmed, and claimed system after system. We have only delayed their advance, not stopped it, let alone turned it back. Initiate?

Initiate Engineer Red-507: Yes, Mr. Prospector?

Mr. Prospector: Do you have footage of the siege-class gnosiphage's defeat?

Initiate Engineer Red-507: Yes, Mr. Prospector.

Mr. Prospector: Play it.

—ATTACHED FILE: SOL-521109—

Grand Engineer Black-3: And you think this is a positive outcome, Prospector?

Mr. Prospector: I do.

Grand Engineer Black-3: The human used a geological event as an improvised weapon. That is not conducive to peace and stability.

Mr. Prospector: Peace and stability bid you a fond farewell quite some time ago, as I recall. What you have now is a ravenous enemy that you—we—are responsible for. I am trying to help clean up this mess, which is what I have always done. I understand your trepidation, but things are reaching a breaking point.

Speaking of, the LIT has sent another comm spike. That seems to be happening a lot lately. Looks like it's interfering with long range communications with the humans as well.

Initiate Engineer Red-507: Oh. Oops.

Elder Engineer Green-28: Unacceptable response.

Grand Engineer Black-3: Unacceptable response.

Mr. Prospector: For gods' sake, give the initiate a break. You overwork the poor things.

—SIGNAL LOST—

From the recorded minutes of a private meeting in the Prime Minister's office as archived by Luorian Intelligence Ministry (Translated from Luorian Basic):

Prime Minister Axun: Recording to begin. This is an official classified meeting, and has an informational rating of 1-3, and may not be accessed by any individuals except LIM agents with a rank of seeker or higher. So say I.

Defense Minister Feuxellian: Acknowledged and seconded. This meeting is so ordered.

Intelligence Minister Qohara: Have you both seen the latest communication spike?

Prime Minister Axun: We have. The Defense Minister has also confirmed visual on the Enclave's location, thanks to your scouts. I think we should move in at once, unless you have something else to report?

Intelligence Minister Qohara: That depends. Have you heard back from the Cosmic Wardens, Defense Minister?

Defense Minister Feuxellian: Yes. They're going to "wait and see."

Prime Minister Axun: Wait and—are they mad? The humans just took down a siege-class gnosiphage with D-ranked weaponry, and did it with a natural disaster less than two clicks from a major populated area! They don't give a damn about collateral damage or endangering innocents, even when it's their own people. If they get off-world again with something like the Archive, we'll have another disaster on our hands.

Defense Minister Feuxellian: At least we've blocked the Engineers from sending them any more updates or messages, for the time being.

Intelligence Minister Qohara: Ah. I take it you've seen the communication spike, but not the attached scans we intercepted from the Enclave?

Prime Minister Axun: No, I've barely slept. I was up all night looking at Feuxellian's reports from the front in Sector 42. The Tuhd system is likely lost to the Empire, at this point. Unless that's what your scans were about?

Intelligence Minister Qohara: No, Prime Minister, apologies. However, I believe the situation with the humans will sort itself out. Please examine scan number one.

Prime Minister Axun: What is this? It's their tiny little solar system, isn't it?

Intelligence Minister Qohara: Indeed. And there, on a direct course for Earth…

Defense Minister Feuxellian: Is that…?

Intelligence Minister Qohara: It is. C-Class. We've also confirmed that there is a single Herald present. It's the same one that destroyed Melarus-III. We are confident it will have a similar outcome with Earth. There's also a chance they may wipe each other out. The Wardens have already seen the scans. That's why they're going to "Wait and see." No need to send Wardens to a barren rock.

Defense Minister Feuxellian: Poor bastards. A C-Class and a Herald with it? Bad luck.

Prime Minister Axun: On the off-chance the humans survive, have the Wardens indicated they would still be willing to provide assistance?

Intelligence Minister Qohara: They have. I showed them some of the aetheric flow charts. There's been a 157% increase of aether flow towards Earth in the last few cycles. They must have an army of aetheric users to be diverting that much of the flow to their planet. On average, it's slowed down somewhat since the first several cycles of Archive integration, but it's still higher than what we anticipated.

The Wardens weren't too pleased when they saw the charts. They were quite incensed, actually. I think the commander's exact words when I spoke to him were, "Complete quarantine of the system." But, this is dependent on the Herald and its transport not wiping them all out.

Prime Minister Axun: I hate to hope for the extermination of a planet. Space is bleak and lifeless enough as it is. But, in this case— gods help us—let this be the end of it.

PART THREE
HERALD OF THE ABYSS

FROM EARTH #8

From the *Honolulu Star-Advertiser*

GIANT ALIEN DEFEATED BY DERD, INTERNATIONAL FORCES: CASUALTIES LOW, BUT CITY IN RUINS

The citizens of Honolulu and Oahu bore witness to an event that will hopefully never be seen on this planet ever again: a giant alien rampaging along the beach and firing upon the city, along with a horde of other smaller extraterrestrials, and finally being destroyed in a controlled volcanic eruption and a massive explosion.

Witnesses claim that among the hostile aliens were many of what some have identified as "rock men," a polar bear in armor, and a small army of robots. All of these aided in forcefully evacuating civilians from the area of the attack, along with a number of police, military, and agents of the DERD.

While many citizens and tourists have been understandably traumatized, very few of them were harmed, given the scope of the calamity. 158 people have been reported as deceased or missing, which, while tragic, has many saying that it was a miracle more lives weren't lost. While many suffered injuries in the attack, the Finnish host going by the call sign "Mender," has gotten all survivors back on their feet, and in many cases, healthier than they were before the attack.

But many are claiming "psychological damage," in the wake of the incident, and not just from the aliens.

"My family and I were grabbed by these…I think they were giants made out of dirt and metal. They just grabbed my kids and ran away with them. Then some robot tucked my wife and I under its arms and took off in the other direction. We were separated from our children for hours," said a man who wished to remain anonymous.

Others had similar complaints of being separated from family, some of whom were in need of medical attention during the attack. Senator Kalawai'a praised the hosts for their bravery and quick response, but condemned their rash actions that left much of the city of Honolulu and a nearly seven mile stretch of the O'ahu National Wildlife Refuge in ruins, which includes a significant chunk of the Ko'olau Mountain Range.

"Our island is very small, but precious. Again, we are thankful for the help, we would not be here without it, but defeating the enemy at the cost of destroying our homes is not a sustainable strategy."

Members of the Hawaiian Senate echoed Senator Kalawai'a's state-ment, and many are backing her up. Some of Oahu's representatives, as well as those from other islands and the mainland, are calling for the government to curtail the reach of the DERD, and hold its members accountable for severe property damage.

"Buildings can go back up. Forests can grow back. Senator Kalawai'a is right about one thing: this is our home. And we mean to kick any intruders out," Director of the DERD Suzanna MacDougal said in response to questions during a press-conference.

"We will, of course, be covering all damages. One of the hosts is volunteering the use of over 250 construction robots to rebuild the damaged parts of the city, while Agent Mender is continuing to aid any harmed during or after the attack. Agent Pan is also stabilizing the volcano and ensuring that it remains dormant. We're also looking at using some recently discovered, advanced methods to regrow the forest," MacDougal went on to say. "So overall, I'd call this a success.

Yes, it was a frightening experience, but without our hosts, it could have been much, much worse."

———

From *The Washington Post*

SENATE HEARINGS FOR DERD OVERSIGHT PROPOSED

In wake of the destruction of Honolulu, many have called for more rigorous training and damage mitigation from the newly formed government organization and the hosts it commands. Senate hearings to discuss the future of the DERD and the super-powered humans (and pangolin) within it are scheduled to begin next week.

"We need to discuss plans for combating extraterrestrial threats that do not require the destruction of a major city," Senator Diaz from Florida stated.

"It's important, but the priority is people, not property," President Hanover said in response. "When the White House was destroyed nearly two months ago, we rebuilt. We were able to rebuild because we were alive, because the hosts made sure the enemy was dead. We did not choose Honolulu to be the latest battlefield, but we eliminated the enemy that did."

Senator Kalawai'a (HI) and Senator Diaz are both making the push for more oversight, while Senator Norris (NY) and Senator Ricci (IL) are more in favor of supporting the DERD as-is.

"All this alien stuff," Ricci said, "it's not like anything we've ever dealt with before. When the hosts start getting my people killed, I'll put my foot down. But from what I hear, they made evacuating the attack site in Hawaii a top priority and didn't blow up that mountain until it was safe. They've got my support."

Similar discussions are happening in governments across the world, with British Parliament seeking to pass a law that would hold any host guilty of "gross misuse of power" subject to fines, and possibly even imprisonment. When asked how a rogue host might be contained, Hanover only said that "We hope it doesn't come to that."

30

Anya managed to stay conscious long enough to finish her laughing fit with Samaira, and then everything stopped, as if something had just cut Anya's feed to reality. She wasn't aware of anything, including the fact that she wasn't aware, until she opened her eyes to the Flame Dominion.

The bird was there, and it had grown again. At first it had been a tiny sparrow, and then something like a small peacock and an eagle crossed together. Now it still looked the same, but was as big as a very large dog, or very tiny pony. Its glowing tail feathers trailed behind it in a flickering train of fire and lights, and its carnivorous beak clicked at her.

"Welcome back, little ember," it said. "Thought you might be a goner there for a while."

"A while?" Anya asked. "How long has it been? Last I remember I was on the beach with Sam…"

"I'm not entirely sure. I get most of my perception of time as you understand it through you. The Dominion in its natural state has a more fluid definition of time. Less linear. But at a guess? Maybe a little less than two days."

"Fuck. It's dead though, right? Big Al?"

"That'd be my guess, yeah. Although, again, hard to tell with your consciousness stuck in here while your body recuperates. You really put on a show, I'll give you that."

"Is that why you're bigger again?"

"Partly, yeah. But also because of you going to New Bengaluru. I think some of the NAT hosts are warming up to you. And that city of theirs, it's kindled something in you, hasn't it?"

Anya reached down and touched her chest. When she had been eating with Ursula in the sushi restaurant, and glancing outside at the city, it had seemed... nice. Like how things should be. How things could be, with some work. Maybe how things should have been all along.

She still wasn't sure if what she had seen in New Bengaluru was real or not; genuine or illusory. But she did know that she wanted it to be real, and if what Vastukar was making was just some shallow facade, then maybe she could make something genuine.

"Starting to think long-term, now, huh?" the bird asked and cocked its head at her.

"Maybe. Now that the aliens are gone, the future's something I have the luxury to plan for. Hard to do that when a gnosiphage could bite you on the ass any minute."

"True, true."

"But first, I think I'm gonna take a vacation. Hopefully with Sam. My Sun's Heart got drained to hell during that fight."

The bird laughed. It was a sardonic, knowing sound, and Anya didn't care for it.

"What?" she asked.

"I told you before, little ember: that thing in your chest is as much a Sun's Heart as dogshit is a diamond. Listen to you. 'Drained.' Look around, little ember," the bird said and spread its wings wide. A flurry of sparks rose from the bird as it did, the flicking motes of light blinking out like fireflies before the dawn.

"You sit in the Flame Dominion, the realm of fire and heat. The universe is made of this! The Big Bang, every star in the sky, supernovas, solar flares, rolling tides of fire that could consume your entire solar system in a blink. How could such a force ever be drained? Do you want to know the real difference between a true Sun's Heart, and the toy in your chest?" the bird asked.

Anya nodded.

"What you have now is a battery, but a Sun's Heart is a doorway. Your facsimile was made by people trying to put a bridle on a supernova. In a way, I can respect it. It's what you did with the volcano. But while you only tried to temporarily direct a force of nature, whoever made that," the bird jabbed a wing towards Anya's chest, "made the mistake of trying to control it. They wanted to put a supernova in a box, but it doesn't work that way. You know it from experience, now. Riding that eruption was fun, wasn't it?"

"Oh yeah. Scary, but fun as fuck."

"Mm-hmm. Think you could have held onto it forever?"

"Hell no."

"Then what makes you think your little sun toy there will hold onto all of this, hmm?" the bird asked and gestured at the expanse of the Flame Dominion with its wings. The eternity of wavering reds and oranges, the nebulae of burning yellow stars, and constellations of fiery pinpricks of light that stretched away to forever.

Anya wasn't sure whether to be scared or excited.

"Are you saying the fake Sun's Heart I got from the Archive is going to break?" she asked.

"I'm saying that you're reaching beyond the boundaries of the neat little boxes that the Engineers have placed around you. Sooner or later, you're going to break their toy. All of you are. I think that's why I like humans. You all, as a species, seem to have an affinity for it. Some of your oldest stories are about fire. Prometheus, for example. Always liked that one."

"Yeah, I—wait. What do you mean you 'always,' liked humans?"

"Time for you to wake up, I think. See you soon, little ember," the bird said, and then pecked Anya on the nose.

Anya stared up at a blank, white ceiling. She blinked, then looked around to find that she was in her room, back in Outpost #1. She was in bed, dressed in a hospital gown and sweats. She had an IV attached to her arm, which she found extremely odd, and a monitor beeped beside her bed as it tracked her heart rate. It was a bit off, as it was tracking both of her hearts, the beeping faster than normal, but still steady.

The arm in question had an odd look to it: smooth and pink, like she'd had the world's worst sunburn from shoulder to fingertips. That was when she recalled that she had lost that arm in the fight with Alpha, and let out a sigh of relief at having it back. She didn't know if her regeneration had done that, or Arvo had.

Gary sat in a chair beside her bed, snoring lightly, slumped low, chin against his chest. Pan rested on the floor beside him, curled into a ball, also dozing. Somebody had brought another chair into the room and set it near Gary, but it was empty.

The room was dark, but for the small bedside lamp, and the window looked out onto a dark sky and falling snow. Her bedroom door was open a crack and light from the living room and the clatter of dishes from the kitchen filtered through. It was a cozy, domestic scene to wake up to, especially given what she had last seen.

A spike of guilt went through her as she recalled Honolulu. She'd done her best to save people but maybe it hadn't been enough. She'd absolutely ruined a good chunk of the city and the outlying mountain range.

But, Alpha was dead.

The last alien, gone.

It was over.

"Thank God for that," Anya said.

"Muh!" Gary said and started awake. He gave Anya a bleary look as he adjusted his glasses, then almost fell out of the chair in his haste to stand.

"Kid!" he said, and Pan let out a squeak of surprise as he awoke. "Sam! She's awake!"

The sound of breaking glass came from the kitchen and then Sam practically threw herself into the room. Pan's head appeared over the edge of her bed, black eyes bright and glittering, nose snuffling in her direction.

"Uh, hey," Anya said, her voice a croak. She coughed and looked down at herself, wondering what the hell was going on. She was actually weak. If the bird had been right, she should have had plenty of time to regenerate, given all her recent level ups and advanced class.

Her worries went away when Samaira knelt on the bed beside her and wrapped her up in a hug. Gary reached over and gave Anya a soft pat and a squeeze on her shoulder before withdrawing, and Pan touched her knee with his claws.

"We were getting worried, in case you couldn't tell," Gary said.

"Yeah, I picked up on that," Anya said.

"Are you okay? Are you still hurt? How's your arm?" Samaira asked, and her hands emitted a gentle blue glow as she waved them over Anya's new arm and her head.

"I'm fine. I'm just... worn out, I guess. Which is weird, since my regeneration should've kicked in..."

A toilet flushed from the bathroom, followed by the sound of the faucet, and Tori stumbled out.

"Of course you'd wake up while I'm in the john," she said and also came in for a hug. "Your new arm is super gross, by the way. I got to watch Arvo regrow it. I'll never eat meat again, so thanks for that."

"You're full of shit," Anya said and hugged Tori back.

"Yeah. I could never say no to meat."

"Speaking of..."

"Say no more, we've been planning for this," Samaira said and rushed out of the room. There was a muffled conversation from out in the hallway, and then more voices at her door minutes later. Gary, Tori, and Pan helped arrange Anya's pillows so she could sit up in bed, and she grumbled at them fussing over her.

Samaira and a handful of DERD agents entered the room carrying boxes of pizza, Chinese take-out, burgers, sandwiches, trays of salad, and huge bottles of water and sports drinks. Anya's eyes widened at the food and her mouth began to water. Her body took over, demanding the food with a primal need, and she began wolfing it down.

The others joined Anya as she ate, though their portions were much more reasonable. By the time Anya was ready to talk, she had demolished six pizzas, five take-out boxes, eight burgers, four sandwiches, and multiple drinks. She was still ravenous, but she had reached a place where her body was no longer screaming at her for food.

She also felt about a hundred times better. The weakness was becoming a memory, and relief washed over her as it did.

"Better?" Samaira asked with a smirk and Anya nodded.

"What happened after I passed out?"

Everyone exchanged a look, except Pan, who scrambled up onto the bed and latched onto Anya's side as she continued to eat. She wrapped an arm around him as he nuzzled his head against her.

"Bad news?" Anya asked.

"Kind of?" Samaira said, and winced. "Everybody's glad we killed Alpha, but a lot of people are upset about the city getting sort of destroyed. A little."

"It's not destroyed," Gary said. "Thirty percent of it was wrecked, and the other seventy suffered cosmetic damage, at worst. I've already got construction droids fixing everything up free of charge. Hanover's taken credit for that, of course, but whatever."

"But the people?" Anya asked.

"Fewer than 200 casualties," Gary said and Anya's stomach sank, which must have shown on her face because Gary continued. "Kid. Not your fault, not mine, not anybody's but the aliens. All the casualties were a direct result of Alpha's blasts, and those little freaks running around. We managed to clean the rest of them up after you went down. Took the better part of a day, but we got 'em all. Buncha other hosts finally showed up to help with the clean-up: Renn, Mona, Brody and Cooper, some others."

"Turns out that's where all the missing people were going," Tori said. "The DERD's been going over Alpha's remains non-stop for the past couple days. With Arvo and Gary helping, we figured it out. Alpha had turned itself into some kind of giant, mobile monster-creation fortress-factory thing. The centipede was the hunter-gatherer, and Alpha was the queen. Or king. Whatever. Point is, it needed food and decided people worked best. Apparently it was using them for spare parts, nutrition, whatever."

Anya paled.

"Wait, so the things we were fighting were humans?" she asked.

"No, thank god," Samaira said. "Arvo scanned the bodies. What we fought weren't gnosiphages, but they definitely weren't people either. They were just drones. Some of them did incorporate parts of human biology into their structure, but that was it. I think Arvo described them as being like 'Really big wasps,' as far as their intellect went. And they would have kept coming out of Alpha if you hadn't helped stop it."

"And me! I helped!" Pan said and Anya patted him. "I put the volcano back to sleep too. It seemed pretty happy it got to act up for a while, but it was tired afterwards."

"You were the only one close enough to get Alpha's datastream when it died. Has Felix finished decoding it yet?" Samaira asked.

"Oh, shit. Yeah, sorry. I didn't—Felix!" Anya said and the AI popped up in front of her.

"Hello! Super glad you're not dead! And yes, I'm decoding the datastream. It's not done yet, though. As you can imagine, Alpha had a lot of information to sort through. It shouldn't be too much longer, and I'll let you know as soon as I'm done!"

"Thanks, Felix."

"Of course!"

"Hey, how much RAC did I get from killing Alpha?"

"Zero!"

"Excuse me? I should be rolling in it."

"Not quite," Samaira sighed. "None of us got anything. We thought it might be an issue with our proximity to Alpha when it died, but we didn't get anything for fighting the little ones either. And we still should've gotten partial rewards just for fighting the alien. But nothing's changed. No word from the Engineers, either."

"This is bullshit!" Anya said. "I got the datastream, I should get the RAC, too! The Engineers said they wouldn't be capping our RAC!"

"The datastream comes from the aliens, while the RAC comes from the Engineers," Felix said. "Not sure what the Engineers are up to, but at least you got Alpha's information. That's pretty good!"

"Still bullshit," Anya said and then winced as her side twinged.

"Easy there, kid. I'm gonna go call the doc and let him know you're awake and doing better," Gary said and stood. "He's still in Honolulu, helping the DERD scan pieces of Alpha and healing anybody that needs it. Anyway, he'll be thrilled you've made a recovery, probably come right up to check on you."

"I'll go let MacDougal and Riley know, too," Tori said as she followed Gary out of the room. "Pan, why don't you come help me?"

"Huh? Why? I don't like talking to Magoogle. She's scary."

"Just… c'mon, Pan."

"Is this so Anya and Samaira can be alone? Are you gonna do private stuff?"

"Jesus Christ, dude," Tori sighed.

"We're just gonna talk," Samaira said and patted his head.

"Okay. I'll be back later if you need me," Pan said, then waddled out with Tori. When they were alone, Anya took Samaira's hand and squeezed it. Samaira lifted it to her own cheek and leaned into it with a soft sigh.

"You really scared me, you know?" she asked.

"Scared myself, a bit."

"MacDougal said that once you were awake and recovered, we'd need to have a debriefing, go over some stuff. It sounds like political bullshit, restructuring or something, now that the gnosiphages are gone."

"Have they told people yet? That the invasion's over?" Anya asked, and Samaira shook her head.

"No, they're waiting until Felix decodes the last datastream to make extra sure. No surprises. Hanover wants to give us all medals or something, have a big party. I heard Riley mention an actual ticker-tape parade in New York."

"Damn. They still do those?"

Samaira shrugged and chuckled.

"I guess we'll find out. But when things calm down, I'd like to go to a couple places with you."

Anya raised her eyebrows.

"Oooh. A couple places. Is it a surprise?"

"Well, the first one should be somewhere relaxing. Private. The second place, I think, should be New Bengaluru."

"You really wanna see it for yourself, huh?"

"I do, but not just that. I'm fine working for the DERD so long as it's to fight monsters like the gnosiphages. Beyond that? I don't know. If Vastukar is making something better, then I want to help. And if he isn't, then I want to know."

Samaira squeezed Anya's hand, and the two locked gazes. Anya thought of what the bird had said before she woke up.

Thinking long-term.

"Okay. We'll go back. Take Pan with us so he can visit Ursula. Speaking of, what happened to them after the fight?"

"They stuck around to help with the clean-up, then they and all of Vastukar's drones left ASAP. Zixin's messaged Gary a few times to check on the status of the datastream, but besides that, nothing."

They spent a little more time in private together, but after a while it was clear that Anya needed more rest. She slept, then woke in the middle of the night to find Sam on her couch, asleep, with Pan resting in the corner. She had herself a midnight snack, and returned to bed.

Arvo arrived the next day to check on her while she relaxed with the others. She felt almost entirely back to normal, but the doctor insisted she take at least another full day to recover. Samaira said they could spend the time watching movies together, and since that sounded fine to Anya, she agreed.

They were halfway through their third film of the day when Anya's ear beeped and Felix floated over Anya's shoulder.

"I finished decoding Alpha's datastream," they said.

"Great!" Anya said. "What's the status? All aliens gone?"

"Better if I show you."

Anya and Samaira exchanged a worried glance as Felix brought up the map of Earth. The gnosiphage counter in the corner read "ZERO," and Anya breathed a sigh of relief.

But then the map zoomed out to show Earth as a spinning globe with the moon orbiting it. The map continued to zoom out, and out, and out, and out, until Earth was just a tiny point of glowing light with a label.

Anya was barely aware of Samaira's hand gripping hers, both of their palms becoming slick with sweat as they stared in silence at the screen.

Mars appeared next, just another insignificant dot of light with a name. The map zoomed out again, and finally, stopped.

A third dot appeared on the far edge of the map, this one moving towards Mars, and Earth beyond. It was labeled "ASTEROID C-276."

A message in some alien language flashed across the bottom of the screen, scrambling into English moments later.

"Oh no. No, no. God, please," Samaira said beside Anya.

Anya herself had gone numb. The screen and the message at its bottom had become surreal, a thing that shouldn't be. But it remained, despite Samaira's pleading, despite Anya's revulsion of it.

The message glowed at the bottom of the screen like a brand seared into flesh.

INITIAL ASSAULT WAVE STATUS: ELIMINATED.

ZERO ACTIVE.

PRIMARY ASSAULT WAVE STATUS: INCOMING.

21 DAYS / 14 HOURS / 45 MINUTES / 13 SECONDS

752,083 ACTIVE.

31

"The asteroid shifted trajectory, here," MacDougal said and pointed at a screen at the front of the conference room. She stood at the head of a long table, around which Anya, Gary, Samaira, Arvo, Esmeralda, Pan, Riley, President Hanover, and the Joint Chiefs of Staff sat.

MacDougal and everybody from Outpost #1 had flown to the Pentagon from Alaska as soon as Anya had broken the news. There had been a flurry of activity, disbelief, shock, and horror. MacDougal and Gary had been the first to emerge with something resembling clear heads, and the director had arranged the meeting in DC with Hanover within minutes before ordering them all (and politely asking Gary) to get moving.

The picture MacDougal pointed to was from NASA, who'd managed to get some scans, photographs, and charts made up that showed the asteroid, its original path, and its current one.

"About a day after Nowicki, Hendricks, and Vastukar defeated Alien Alpha, the asteroid—which Nowicki's Archive has identified as 'C-276,'—made a hard turn towards Earth. Since asteroids don't just randomly make hard right turns, we can assume that the gnosiphages are guiding it," MacDougal said.

"And it's how big?" Hanover asked.

"About the size of Australia," Riley said. "The notes from NASA have it at, uh," he flipped through a file in front of him, "2,000 miles across. They also say that if something that size hits Earth, it's pretty much The End. Not just for people, but for everything. The planet itself'll get smashed open and get scattered across the solar system."

Silence weighed in the room for several moments before MacDougal spoke again.

"Hendricks. Do you have anything that could stop something that size?" she asked.

"Right now? No. I could *maybe* get something in the days we have left, but it would be dicey. Also, if you're talking about blowing it up, we don't have twenty-one days. We have nineteen, at most," Gary said.

"What're you talking about? The timer Agent Nowicki showed us said we have twenty-one days until that thing gets here," one of the Joint Chiefs replied.

"We'll need a buffer of a couple days to give any major debris time to disperse. If we blow the thing up too close to Earth, we might avoid the obliteration of our planet, but we'd also have a shitload of smaller, also deadly asteroids on a collision course."

"What do you need to blow something that size out of the sky?" Hanover asked. For once, he'd been relatively quiet. It seemed to Anya that his concerns for re-election had finally taken a backseat in the face of immediate annihilation.

"It's not what I need, it's what I don't need. Namely, the 700,000-and-some odd aliens crawling around that rock. If the asteroid was just a big chunk of space minerals, I could handle it. It'd still be a major undertaking, but I could do it with some help. But a missile, or a laser, or whatever, those aliens are gonna have counter-measures."

"What about that Vastukar guy?" Hanover asked. "Does he know yet?"

"I've had Felix send a message to every host in my contacts list, and MacDougal called everybody in the UPRC who needs to know. I got some confirmations, but nothing else yet, really," Anya said.

Hanover drummed his fingers against the table.

"We'll need to tell people," he said. "It's gonna be a shitshow."

"It will, but we should wait a few days, weigh our options. No sense telling people of an incoming disaster when there's nothing they can do to escape it, and we don't have a plan yet," MacDougal said.

"No word from the Engineer fellas yet either, I take it?"

"No, Mr. President," Riley said. "Unless one of you've managed to get through?"

Anya and the other hosts shook their heads.

"I've had Boo try any available option they can. Nothing. I've also had them combing through the RAC store for any way to contact them, or anything that might be capable of destroying the asteroid. No luck," Samaira said.

"In that entire god-dang alien store you got, there's nothing that can blow up that asteroid? No death rays or mega bombs or anything?" Hanover asked.

"Oh, there's plenty of those," Arvo said. "But they're too expensive or too small. I could afford possibly ten of the medium-sized weapons, but after looking at their destructive capacity, they would barely scratch the asteroid."

"Nowicki, shouldn't you have a shitload of that currency from killing the big alien?"

"I should, yeah," Anya said and couldn't keep the irritation out of her voice. "But it looks like we've all been cut-off. No more experience, no more level-ups, no more RAC. I spent the last of mine fighting Alpha."

"Even if we all bought as many bombs as we could, it'd be the same problem as before. That many gnosiphages on that asteroid would just knock-em out of the sky," Gary added. "Same issue we had with Alpha, before Anya knocked it on its ass."

"All right. I'm going to talk to NASA, get all the information they have, and take stock of our nuclear arsenal. MacDougal, keep me appraised of whatever's going on with these folks and their international counterparts. We'll meet again in twenty-four hours, unless something changes," Hanover said as he gestured at Anya and the other hosts. He stood, along with the Joint Chiefs of Staff, and strode out of the conference room.

"I'm going to spend the next several hours contacting our allies in the UPRC and see what our options are. I need the rest of you to figure out how the hell we're going to stop that thing," MacDougal said and glared at the picture of the asteroid on the screen before turning back to the others. "Dismissed."

———

Esmeralda had a full-on panic attack shortly after the meeting, and Arvo had helped calm her, then escorted her to the nearest hospital.

"I might as well stay and do some good as long as I'm there. I'm not much use against an asteroid. Call if you need me, though," he had said before leaving, Esmeralda in tow.

Anya, Samaira, and Gary sat on a pair of benches in the center courtyard of the Pentagon along with Tori, who had joined them after the meeting. Pan was rooting around in the grass and dirt a short distance away, digging for his lunch. Tori had brought them all sandwiches from the building in the middle of the courtyard. Anya had assumed the building at the center of the Pentagon was some sort of super important meeting room, or maybe an elevator to a bunker.

It was a donut and sandwich shop.

Anya sat, elbows on her knees, and stared at the ground. Samaira leaned against the back of the bench beside her and stared at the sky. Gary chewed his sandwich in silence, while Tori tapped her foot.

"When you were talking with Vastukar about bombs to blow up Alpha, you said you had some non-terrestrial ones. You're sure none of those will work?" Samaira asked Gary.

"I'm sure. The big bombs I made could damage the asteroid, maybe nudge it off course if the gnosiphages weren't 'steering,' it somehow. But to take out the thing? Nah. I thought about drilling, maybe dig deep and set something off."

"Like in that movie," Anya said and snapped her fingers.

"Yup. But it'd be the same issue as just shooting the asteroid. The aliens wouldn't give us time to drill. They'd stop anything we sent at them before it had a chance."

"What about the aether? It can do pretty much anything, right?" Tori asked and turned to Samaira.

"It can, but to destroy an asteroid of that size? I could channel a huge amount of the aether, burn myself out doing it, and for basically nothing. I just don't have the capacity to make even a dent. It might be able to help with some smaller things, but... I don't know."

"Pan could probably make tunnels pretty easy, but he's just one little guy," Anya said, recalling how the pangolin had tunneled into the volcano.

"It's just too damn big," Gary muttered. "I've already sent some of my mining drones to scan the thing. They'll intercept it in two days, but unless the thing's made of cotton candy, I don't see how I'm supposed to drill through it enough to blow it up."

Anya sighed and looked up. Samaira sat beside her, gazing into the middle-distance and biting her thumbnail. Tori and Gary sat across from them, both staring down.

Anya had a sudden memory of her, Samaira, Gary, and Pan back when the invasion had first started. They had been on the run, camping out at night and taking turns at standing watch. Gary had set up the tents and Samaira had set up some aetheric runes around their camp to act as alarms, and Anya had started the campfire.

Campfire and flamethrower, a voice echoed at her.

Anya's memory of them all seated around the campfire shifted. The campsite was bigger, with lots of empty chairs around the little flame at the center. Gary and Samaira's words also bounced around in her head, knocking against her skull with insistency.

"I don't see how I'm supposed to drill through it enough to blow it up."

"I just don't have the capacity to make even a dent."

Vastukar spoke up from the back of Anya's memory, from when she had been in his office right after arriving.

"You've noticed some interesting combinations among your skills, I'm sure? It's about using knowledge of each to improve both and make something entirely new."

"Uh!" Anya shouted and shot to her feet. The others around her flinched back from her and stared. There was a soft *Fwump!* noise as a little fire appeared on top of Anya's head, like a lightbulb turning on.

"Kid?" Gary asked.

"Idea! I got a… thing!" Anya said, words failing as every thought she was having piled up on themselves and tried to force their way out of her mouth.

"Is Arvo still around?" Tori asked.

"I'm not having a panic attack! I just… okay. All of our skills, they sort of talk to each other, right? Like, the combinations click together in ways we wouldn't think of. My Dominions and Xhama Thul fighting style turned into this explosion-and-gravity-based pro-wrestling martial arts thing. I can't punch the asteroid, Sam can't stop it with the aether, and Gary can't bomb it. But what if we could do all of that?"

Samaira furrowed her eyebrows.

"You mean we all go up into space, together?" she asked and Anya shook her head.

"No, I mean what if we could combine them all?"

"How?" Gary asked.

"Vastukar's scanner."

Gary's eyes widened, then closed and he shook his head.

"Wouldn't work. The man said it himself, and Felix confirmed it: that scanner of his can't take skill data or RAC store information from the Archive."

"It can't copy skills, true, and it can't duplicate anything from the RAC store that we haven't ordered. But it could scan existing items that we already have. My Sun's Heart, Samaira's aetheric foci, Arvo's bio-generation whatever-it-is, Esmeralda's psychic thingy, anything. You're worried about a drill taking too long to dig into the asteroid? Pan can make huge tunnels in seconds. The rockets or bombs or whatever need protection? My Light Dominion could buff any forcefield you could think of, ditto for my Starforge skin."

Samaira and Tori looked at each other, then Samaira turned to Gary.

"You inspected Vastukar's scanner, didn't you? Is she right?"

Gary rubbed his chin.

"Maybe. We were only letting him scan the data stream, nothing else. And I made sure he deleted it afterwards. But technically, what I saw seemed pretty effective at scanning… just about anything. It was comparable to a lot of things I have set up in my lab, just different. But even if it does work, do we want one guy having all that information?"

"You can make sure he deletes it again," Anya said with a grin.

"And your plan is to what? Make some kinda super bomb with all of our skills?" Gary asked.

"I don't have a fucking clue!" Anya declared. "But that's my point. None of us know how all these things could interact with each other. But what if you could find a way to translate Pan's Earth Dominion into a drill? What if Esmeralda's psychic constructions were infused with Samaira's aetheric manifestations? I have no idea if this will even work, but c'mon, Gary, it's worth a shot, right?"

"All of this is a moot point without even asking Vastukar, but what the hell? I've got my factory set to make as many anti-matter bombs as it can in the meantime. If he's willing to try, I am too."

"Samaira?" Anya asked.

"Of course. I'm willing to try just about anything."

"Tori?"

"Huh? Me? I can't do squat compared to you guys," she said. "I made an aetheric butter knife yesterday and used it to make a PB&J. That's about the extent of my abilities."

"But you've made foci, right?"

"Shitty little ones, sure."

"We'll take 'em. You in?"

"Yeah, fuck it. If my magic butter knife can help save the day, let's do it."

"Pan!" Anya called out. The pangolin popped up out of the ground, startling a couple of staff sergeants as they walked by. "You wanna go see Ursula again?"

"Okay!" Pan replied and hurried over.

"Planning a trip?" a voice said from behind Anya and she nearly jumped. She'd sensed a pair of heat signatures behind her, but there were dozens of them in the courtyard. She'd been too excited to notice MacDougal and Riley approach.

"Uh," Anya said and regarded the two of them. MacDougal wore a mild scowl while Riley managed to look apologetic for not calling out a warning.

"Heading to see Vastukar?" MacDougal asked.

"M-maybe?" Anya said. MacDougal arched a thin iron-gray eyebrow at her. "Fine. Yes. We had an idea and we're going to try it."

"And it never occurred to you to run this up the chain-of-command?"

"Give me a fucking break," Gary said. "The planet's about to get smeared across the solar system and you're gonna pull this bureau-cratic crap?"

"To see if I can help? You're damn right I'm going to insist one of my agents comes to me with her ideas, Hendricks. We had a deal, Nowicki. You work with the DERD, and I work with you. Have I done something to lose your confidence?"

"No! You've, actually been okay, I just… I got excited and time is of the essence…" she stammered.

"It is. So, you're gonna fill me in on everything while you're en route. If it's not totally insane, I'll let Hanover know and we can divert resources as needed, or help you come up with something else. I'm not against you, Nowicki, but you can't be against me either. All our asses are in the same sling. I can't imagine you'd enjoy being left in the dark, either."

"That's fair," Anya said.

"You taking Corsetti?" MacDougal asked and looked at Tori.

"I was thinking about it. Why?"

"As a friend for moral support, or something else?" Something in MacDougal's tone suggested she knew, or at least, suspected some-thing. Anya considered bullshitting her, but didn't think that was wise, given how the conversation had gone so far.

"It'll take a while to explain, but the short answer is, Tori can use the aether, and we think that might help, even if it's just a little."

"She what?" Riley almost spat the words out. "Since when?"

"Since she started wearing that jewelry with the same blue crystals Upadhyay wears. So, a little over a month, at least," MacDougal said and glanced down at the silver bracelet with the blue aether focus on Tori's wrist. "I'm not thrilled with that. You selectively choosing who gets to know what doesn't sit well with me."

MacDougal glanced between Anya, Samaira, and Tori, then sighed.

"If we survive the next twenty-one days, we'll talk. Until then, get going. Tell me the rest on the way."

"Thanks, Director," Anya said.

"Call me when you're in the air. Go," MacDougal said, and then turned and left. Riley looked after her for a moment before waving at Anya.

"I'll catch you later, I guess. Good luck!" he said, then hurried after MacDougal. Anya watched them go, then turned to leave with the others.

"So, India, huh?" Tori asked.

"Hospital first. We're grabbing Arvo and Esmi, but after that, yeah," Anya said. "Hope Vastukar won't be too mad I brought company this time."

32

MacDougal hadn't said much when Anya explained her idea to her, only grunted and told her they'd see how it went, one way or another. She'd messaged Vastukar on the way to tell him she was coming, and with company, and what her plan was.

"First of all, you're assuming I'll let you and your cohort into New Bengaluru at all," Vastukar said over the communication screen.

"Uh, yeah. I guess I am," Anya replied. "But, since I got this idea from you, I figure chances are good."

"From me?"

"You talking about your skills talking to each other, it not just being one thing that got New Bengaluru running, not black and white but gray, that stuff."

"I see."

"So?"

"I seem to recall that you were rather hesitant to let me scan you, last time. And that was just the data stream."

"Yeah, well, things change."

"A giant asteroid does tend to have that effect. Very well. I make no promises, but your friends, and any other host, are welcome to enter

New Bengaluru for the purpose of testing your theory, provided they do not cause problems."

"Thank you, Vastukar," Anya said and smiled as she let out a sigh of relief. She would have felt pretty stupid if he'd said no and she had to pull a U-turn back to DC. Plus being back at square one with the giant asteroid.

"Thank me if it works," he replied, and ended the call.

Anya and the other hosts spent the remainder of the flight spreading the word to every host on their contacts list. Some scoffed, others balked, and others jumped at the chance. By the time they had finished the calls and explaining to the various hosts on their lists, they were almost at New Bengaluru.

"Y'know, I'm gonna be disappointed if this place doesn't live up to the hype," Tori said as the Shadow Ray crossed the Bay of Bengal.

"What hype? I didn't hype it," Anya said.

"'Oh it's so cool, there were trees, and a big silver tower, and nobody used money, and there were no rats on the subway. Coolest place ever!' That was you."

"It was not."

"It's pretty nice," Gary said.

"I liked it!" Pan added.

"Take a look for yourself," Anya said as they flew over the land and shot towards the outer wall of New Bengaluru. There was a sudden rush forward as Tori, Samaira, Esmeralda, and Arvo crowded around the pilot's chair to stare out the cockpit window. Even though Anya had seen it all before, the sprawl of New Bengaluru's natural and urban jungles still managed to awe her into silence along with the others.

"Herranjumala," Arvo whispered.

"Oh wow," Samaira breathed.

"Oh my god," Esmeralda said.

"Huh," Tori grunted.

By the time Anya landed in the Central Administration Tower, everyone was chattering at each other about the different things they had seen during the flyover. They barely noticed Vastukar, Zixin, and

Asmund walking across the landing bay to meet them until Pan stepped forward.

"Hello! Is Ursula here?" he asked.

"She's busy. Apparently one of the other hosts you invited stopped in one of the outer sectors of the city to relieve themselves and have a smoke break," Vastukar said.

"Brody and Cooper," Anya sighed.

"Brody's here too? That's great!" Pan said and checked his map to see that Brody's location marker was indeed within New Bengaluru.

"This way, please," Vastukar said and waved them onward. Zixin and Asmund trailed behind Anya's group while Vastukar led the way to his labs. The place was the same as when Anya had last seen it, although now there were a number of football-sized drones and scientists in the lab, all studying scans of the asteroid.

"What've you learned about the asteroid?" Gary asked and gestured at one of the nearby scans.

"I've only managed to take long range photos and readings of it so far. My drones are about a day away from being within what I'd consider acceptable range to get the most accurate scans but it doesn't look good. The asteroid is made primarily of haxonite, which isn't positive news for us, but it could be worse."

"Iron, nickel, and carbon, basically, for the non-science crowd," Gary clarified.

"On a scale of one-to-ten, with ten being the hardest, this is about a five or six. Again, these are preliminary scans, and may be subject to change."

"It matches what my mining droids have seen. They're gonna run into it at about the same rate as your drones."

"What about the aliens?" Anya asked.

"Difficult to say. Some movement has been detected on the surface, but not much," Vastukar said, then gestured at the scanning platform. "Now, if you please? If this is going to fail, I would like to know sooner rather than later."

"I'll go first," Anya said, and stepped up. "Felix, monitor what's scanned, just like last time."

"You got it!" the AI replied from her ear. Vastukar tapped a few buttons on the terminal next to the scanning pad and nodded. "He got the data stream from Alien Alpha, as well as the information of your RAC purchases, skills and their recorded levels, and your biometric data."

"He got my skills?" Anya asked and her eyebrows shot up.

"Just what they are, not the actual powers themselves," Vastukar said. "Most of this isn't much good. The data stream is handy, but what I'm really after are your biometrics. That thing in your chest... the Sun's Heart Artifact. That's what you use to make fire?"

"Yup."

"Can you summon some now? Just a little?"

Anya held up her finger and lit the tip of it with a gentle, flickering flame.

"Interesting. Like a battery," Vastukar said.

"What you have now is a battery, but a Sun's Heart is a doorway," the bird's voice echoed from her memory.

"It's not entirely organic, but it isn't inorganic either. These pieces, like crystal, but also some kind of possible protein structure..."

The laboratory had grown silent as everybody looked at Vastukar, and he flinched when he finally glanced up from the terminal.

"That's not conducive to a productive environment," he said and frowned.

"Can you do anything with it?" Anya asked.

"I've only been looking at it for a few seconds. I'm not sure. Just the basic structure? Not an issue. But having it function as yours does? Unlikely."

"We wouldn't need it to function as a perfect Sun's Heart, just as a proof-of-concept. If we can get one thing working, even a little, we might be able to get others to as well," Gary said and adjusted his glasses as he looked over Vastukar's shoulder at his screen. "Y'know... I've been working on some replicators. Mostly for recycling trash and crap like that. But some of this stuff... Yeah, I think they could make it. Mind if I plug in here?"

"Be my guest," Vastukar said and stepped aside. Gary pulled a long, thin wire out of the side of his wristwatch and held it next to the terminal. The wire stuck to the side, and the screen flickered for a moment, then began to flash with images of schematics, diagrams, and code.

"Any of this making sense to you?" Gary asked.

"About half of it. But... yes. Yes. We have replicators too, but they're not the same, but with that bit there and this..."

"Uh-huh. This doo-dad. What the hell is that?"

"It's like an enlarged synapse," Arvo said as he stepped forward and squinted at the screen. "Good lord. Is this what you use to make electricity?"

"In some structures, yes," Vastukar replied.

"Can you zoom in on the middle of the heart, there? That's fascinating. I didn't pick that up when I scanned Anya."

Gary, Arvo, and Vastukar spent the next minute getting into more and more inscrutable terminology, until Anya finally cleared her throat.

"Hey, so, can I get down now, please? Anything else you need from me?" she asked.

"Yes, actually. Make fire again, but maintain it for a bit," Vastukar said and Anya did as she was asked. Vastukar, Gary, and Arvo began muttering to each other again for a while until Vastukar waved his hand at Anya to stop.

"Next, please," he said.

"Pan? You just need to stand here, okay?" Anya said, and she and the pangolin switched places.

"Is it gonna hurt?" he asked.

"It's already done," Vastukar replied. "Do we have some dirt or stone you could move?"

"I'll grab something from mineral analytics," a nearby assistant said, then left with a drone following after, and returned in moments. Pan was presented with a chunk of ordinary-looking rock, which he began to play with as if it were clay. He split it in half, merged it back together, made it look like one of his golems, and a crude approximation of Anya.

Vastukar, Gary, and Arvo resumed their clipped conversation as they pointed at the terminal. Samaira and the aether were next, then Esmeralda and her psychic abilities. Arvo also took his turn on the platform, but kept rushing back and forth to study the terminal, then get scanned again.

"I think... yes. We can do something with this," Vastukar said after exchanging another look with Gary and Arvo, and both men nodded.

"Something?" Anya asked.

"It will take some time to look at the implications. But if we can replicate approximations of the Artifacts—Sun's Heart, Mountain's Bones—as well as biological components like the psychic nodule Ms. Gomez has, we could get them to 'talk,' with each other. From what I understand of the aether and what Ms. Upadhyay told me, it will be vital in helping the different components communicate, due to its inherent malleable nature. We'll also need to record more complete data of you all using your skills at higher levels of output, but I need to run more tests first," Vastukar said.

"Anything you need."

"Right now all I need is time, which is in short supply. But... no, I don't want to speculate yet. Please just stay within the city if I need you."

"Got it. Should I stay in the lab with the others?"

"No. Mr. Hendricks, Dr. Immonen, and Ms. Upadhyay should stay, but the rest of you can go. Yes, you two, as well," Vastukar said and looked at Zixin and Asmund as the former started to protest while the latter lazily rotated his index finger inside of one nostril.

"You gonna scan them too?" Anya asked.

"I scanned them days before I first scanned you. They and Ursula were my test subjects. But back then, I was mostly focused on reading the Archive's data stream and trying to find Alpha. I think eventually I would have tried this, but maybe not in this particular way. Regardless, thank you. Now please, I'll require space. If you'll excuse me?"

Anya and the others left the lab and stood out in the hallway. Asmund and Zixin took off on their own, while Tori, Pan, and Esmeralda stayed with Anya in the hallway.

"It sounded... encouraging?" Tori said.

"Yeah, but I'm not gonna get my hopes up just yet," Anya said.

"We've done everything we can, for now I think I need to find a quiet place to sit. Everybody's emotions were going a mile-a-minute in there," Esmeralda said, and rubbed at her temples.

"I could use a drink," Tori said and followed after Esmeralda.

"I wanna go see Brody and Ursula!" Pan declared and tugged on Anya's hand. She smiled at him and went with the others as they left the laboratory behind. All there was to do now was wait.

Anya had to force herself to not stare at the countdown clock on the Archive's map, to not stare at the tiny dot of the asteroid as it drew inexorably closer. She and the others met Brody, Cooper, and Ursula after Brody had been scanned.

"I think this one's gotten smaller since I last saw him. I can barely fucking see you down there, mate," Brody said and laughed as he stared down at Pan. Pan giggled as he sat between the orca and Ursula, comically tiny wedged between the two hulking creatures.

They had all settled in a lounge on one of the upper levels of the Tower: one with a stunning view of the city sparkling in the night below, and plenty of soft sitting areas. They tried making small talk at first, but it inevitably drifted to their individual scannings, and what their back-up plans might be.

Vastukar, Gary, Samaira, and Arvo entered the lounge after a few hours, and all conversation stopped as Anya and the rest caught sight of them. A ringing started in Anya's ears as she focused on them, and both of her hearts began to beat a rapid tempo beneath her breast. Her breath caught in her throat, and aside from her hearts, her entire body froze, muscles taut, eyes unblinking.

Gary's mustache twitched upward in a smile, and he gave her a thumbs up. Samaira grinned and nodded, and Arvo drooped with obvious, exhausted relief.

"My friends," Vastukar said and spread his hands as the subtle trace of a smile tugged at his mouth, "we have a plan."

33

While "bomb," might have described what Vastukar, Gary, Samaira, and Arvo had planned to build, it was an overly simplistic term that only encompassed a fraction of what the device would actually do.

"I'd describe it as something closer to an artificial host, or a recording device, but for actions and abilities rather than sound or images," Vastukar said to everybody when they had assembled in his lab again.

"It's not powerful enough to do everything we can, but it can do multiple simple things, which should be enough to do what we want," Arvo said.

"We'll also be making a few of them, as redundancies," Gary said. "We should have just enough time to make fifty of them between my factories and Vastukar's facilities, along with a lot of more conventional weapons to act as decoys and back-up if we need it."

"We've only had a day to theorize and make some rough plans, but that's been enough," Vastukar continued, "And we've developed a basic blueprint for a multi-phase device that will incorporate all of our skills. We've used some of the details of the Sun's Heart to act as the primary catalyst for the explosion, as well as its secondary power source. Ms. Nowicki will need to provide us with scans of her creating some explosions of varying sizes."

"Not an issue," Anya said.

"Primary power will come from the aether," Samaira continued, "converted to current via runes and foci I'll make. It's also going to be the glue that binds a lot of this together. Tori, I know you're new at this, but you're the only other person with an inkling of understanding of the aether, and I need all the help I can get."

"You got it, Teach," Tori replied.

"If you would be willing, I can also request volunteers from the city, if you would be willing to instruct others," Vastukar said. Anya caught a gleam in Samaira's eye at the prospect of teaching.

"We'll see," was all she said, however. "The more complex runes and constructs I'll have to make myself, but if it's just pulling the aether in... yes, I could probably do that."

"But how're ya gonna blow up the big fuck-off rock?" Brody asked.

"By fracturing it," Gary said. "We'll use a simple version of the Mountain's Bones Artifact from Pan to create a series of dividing hairline fractures throughout the asteroid. Essentially it's just a tunnel maker. It'll create a big tunnel going down, let's say, twenty miles, then split into two smaller tunnels that are each a little shorter, then each of those two will split into two more even smaller tunnels, and so on, until it hits its limit, resets, and does it again."

"Just tunnels?" Cooper asked. "That's it?"

"That's the best we can reasonably do on such short notice. But if we can get enough of them, then those hairline fractures running throughout the asteroid should be enough to let the explosive phase do its thing."

"And the aliens? You said just blowing the asteroid up by itself was doable, but that the gnosiphages wouldn't just stand around and let you," Esmeralda said.

"We actually got the solution to that from you," Arvo said. Esmeralda pointed at herself, eyebrows raised in doubt. "When we fought the centipede, it was you and Renn that disrupted the overseer's psychic signals, and caused the lesser aliens to go haywire. We think we can produce a similar, magnified effect that will help protect the device, and temporarily disperse any opposition."

"This is also where Sam's aether batteries and such will come in handy: I can make some reactive forcefields to protect the device that the aether will be able to charge and enhance, based on some basic functions Sam can provide," Gary added.

"There's a lot of other things as well," Vastukar said, "Mr. Hendricks has filled in several gaps in my own mechanical knowledge, while Dr. Immonen has aided tremendously in any aspect that required insight into organic components, and I was able to weave them together. However… there is one aspect of the design we are not able to replicate: a conscious mind."

Everyone exchanged glances, then looked at Gary as he spoke.

"It's like the beacon Doc and I made. We could fake the psychic signal, but we needed an actual psychic to help. The psychic disruptor that'll keep the aliens away—at least for a while—needs somebody to keep it active. We can chain the effect from one device to another, so if we get one working, the others will too. But the problem is getting one to work at all."

Everyone turned to look at Esmeralda, who let out a squeak and paled.

"There are two psychics on this planet that I know of," Vastukar said. One of them is here, and the other is on his way. Correct, Zixin?" Vastukar asked and turned to the sniper. He checked the map on his Archive, and nodded.

"Well, if one of us has to go, we might as well all go," Anya said. "I'm on-board for that. Not fair to insist somebody go up there alone like that."

"Waitasec. Maybe I've smoked myself stupid, but if we're gonna go to space anyways, why bother with the fancy fucking device? Let's just make some spaceships or something and kick some ass?" Brody asked.

"The device is still necessary," Vastukar replied. "While any one of us could do better than a single function of the device, none of us can do all of them. Plus, we'll need many of the devices to have a chance at making enough fractures in the asteroid.

"Currently, there's only one of us here with the ability to tunnel instantly, only one who can use the aether at an expert level, one that could provide the raw explosive force, two that could act as psychic disruptors, and so on. We simply do not have the human—or animal— resources to do this first-hand. As I told Ms. Nowicki, the dozens of hosts that live in New Bengaluru aren't suited to combat, and are of much lower level than everyone else here," Vastukar said.

"There's also the matter of the energy required," Samaira said. "I can make a ton of aether batteries that can have the energy sucked out of them and be replaced. But if I tried to channel that much aetheric current in one go, I'd burn out, faint, or die. The devices are disposable. We aren't."

"Which is why we need to stay here, on Earth," Gary said. "This is about redundancy. If this doesn't work, or only partially works, we'll need to come up with something else. That means we need hosts here. Even if this plan succeeds and blows up the asteroid and every alien on it, we all know that's not gonna be the real end of it. There's probably more of those bastards out there, plus the Engineers and whatever's caused them to go radio silent. Somebody has to stay behind on Earth, and the more of us, the better."

Silence fell over the room.

"I've got fifteen points saved up," Anya said. "That's enough to get to a pretty high psychic level, right?"

"Anya—" Samaira started to say.

"It might be," Vastukar said. "I want to speak to Renn when he arrives, and we'll see what our options are. I'm positive we can find an alternative to sending one of our own up."

"That's a lie," Esmeralda said. "Sorry, Mr. Vastukar. Can't lie to an empath. Though right now, I kinda wish you could."

"No, perhaps honesty is best. I don't know if it's possible, but I'll look into it all the same. For now, Mr. Hendricks and I will begin building what sections of the device that we can, and Ms. Upadhyay will begin work on the aetheric components. We will need to take multiple scans of all of you performing your skills at varying levels, so please remain near the laboratories for the next few days."

So dismissed, the hosts began to mill around while the lab techs went to their stations. Tori hurried over to Samaira's side and the two walked over to a table covered in blue aetheric crystals. Anya approached Esmeralda and rested her hand on her shoulder.

"Hey. Whatever happens, I got your back. I'm not letting you go up there alone, if that's what it comes down to," she said.

"I don't even know if I can, even if they made me I—I think I'd just die of fright or something stupid," Esmeralda said. She shook under Anya's gentle touch, tremors of fear making her short, stout frame visibly shudder.

"Nobody's making you do anything. We'll find a way. If I gotta spend my points on psychic skills, then that's what I'll do."

Esmeralda crossed her arms over herself, her head hunching low between her shoulders.

"I'm sorry. It's stupid. Bet you wish somebody else had gotten my Archive, huh?"

Anya thought of how irritated she had been with Esmeralda, back when Outpost #2 had been hit. How she had run and hid while the outpost had been cleared out by the centipede and its parasites. She had fought, eventually, but at first, she had fled.

It had seemed stupid at the time. Cowardly. But that had been a losing battle for Esmeralda. Her retreat had, long-term, saved Jiro and helped them counter the centipede.

Not everybody was a fighter.

Arvo wasn't, and neither was Vastukar, or Gary, or most people. As Anya looked around the room and studied the diverse crowd, she was glad it wasn't the case. If Esmeralda had been like Anya, she would've dove in head-first, and been killed.

"No, I don't wish somebody else got your Archive. If they had, we wouldn't have gotten this far. You were there with me at Outpost Two, you were there against the centipede later, and you're here now. None of us would have gotten as far as we have without the others. Do what you can, and let others help with what you can't."

"Thank you," Esmeralda said and sniffled. "I guess I'll go see if they need more scans or anything."

She shuffled away and began speaking with Vastukar and Arvo, just as Tori and Samaira approached.

"We're going to take over one of the smaller labs and get to work on the aetheric batteries. Gonna see how Tori does with some basic rune work as well," Samaira said.

"If nothing else, I can help Sam pull in some more aether," Tori added. "Anyway, you can come hang with us, but we're not gonna be much fun."

"Nowhere I'd rather be," Anya said, and followed the other women out of the lab.

———

OTHER HOSTS TRICKLED into New Bengaluru over the following day. Everybody on Anya's contacts list had arrived, and the laboratory levels of the Central Administration Tower were a bustling hub of activity. Anya was eventually called away from Tori and Samaira, and into one of the labs that had been designated for explosives testing. She allowed Vastukar to scan her while she used her Dominions to make multiple enhanced, condensed spheres of fire.

"Why don't you just throw them?" Vastukar asked as he studied the trembling, golden spheres of heat and light. "It seems like it would be a more efficient method of fighting."

"Because keeping them under control over distances uses more energy. Makes them more likely to miss, too. Up close and personal is more energy-efficient, and a guaranteed hit. Well, almost guaranteed," Anya said.

"It's amazing how hot they burn. That's the Light Dominion?"

"Yeah. I've never actually checked the temperature of these things. I just kinda make 'em."

"And you're not straining now?"

"Nope."

"Good to know," Vastukar tapped something out on a holographic screen that floated in front of him, smiling as he did.

"You seem cheery," Anya said as she watched Vastukar tap away.

"Do I? I guess... I did not expect such cooperation. Seeing people of so many different backgrounds coming together. It's a surprise. I think my previous career left me more jaded than I had suspected."

"Which was?"

"I worked for a charity organization, out of New Delhi. There was no shortage of work to be done here. It became… depressing."

"Seeing people in need?"

"No. No, that I could tolerate. It was sad, yes, but it was also what I expected. It was what I signed on for. Yes, many people were poor, homeless, starving, sick, but I was there, and I could help. The organization could help."

"I'm sensing a 'but,' coming up."

"Mm. Yes. It could help, but too often, it did not. The problem with human generosity and empathy is that it is human. It tires. It falters. It lies to itself in order to preserve its own comfort and status. Even good people, when faced with the endless misery of the world, will grow tired. There is no end to suffering, but there is very much an end to a person's ability to withstand it."

"People quit?"

"No. Worse. They stayed. They looked for shortcuts and loopholes to secure more funding to secure their jobs. They told themselves they were doing good work, but they were really just working for themselves. People I looked up to, people I respected: all the same. The weight of it all threatened to crush them, and they did whatever they had to to take the pressure off. Even if it meant the people they were supposed to be saving were crushed instead."

"Jesus," Anya said. "I'm sorry."

"I was too. But then I realized that is just how it is. That's humanity. It's good to see people cooperating in the other labs, but it's a shame too. The only thing that ever truly seems to make us work together, is when we're trying to kill something else," Vastukar said. The smile had faded from his lips as he spoke, and his tapping on the screen had become sharper, a staccato of rapid jabs.

Silence settled over the lab until a notification beeped from a monitor nearby, and Zixin's face appeared on the screen.

"Yes?" Vastukar said.

"Renn's finished his scans. Says he wants to talk to you. Now," Zixin replied. "He was rather pushy."

"I'm in lab 6. Send him over," Vastukar said. Renn walked in a few moments later, Mona following behind him. Renn's helmet was off, and he had his usual sleepy expression. Mona didn't look quite so relaxed. Her neck muscles were tense, lips drawn and tight.

"Mr. Renn. Welcome. I'll be finished with Ms. Nowicki in anoth—"

"I'll do it," Renn said, and Vastukar paused with his mouth open. Anya blinked and stared at him. "You need a living psychic to maintain the disruptor field around this device of yours?"

"Correct, however we're looking into alterna—"

"That's unnecessary. I will go."

"Renn—" Mona started to say, desperation obvious in the single syllable, but Renn shook his head.

"If a living psychic goes, it will ensure the device is a success?" Renn asked.

"Nothing can guarantee our success, but it will greatly increase the chances of it working to maximum capacity," Vastukar said. "The models Dr. Immonen and I have been discussing would have only limited functionality, and would be prone to failure. A skilled psychic would make such concerns irrelevant, and would also allow us to divert our attention to other matters."

"Then it's settled. I will go."

"Renn, please!" Mona said.

"I have a request, though. If I am to be focused on this device, I will want somebody to watch my back."

Mona sighed with relief and said, "Of course. You don't need to ask, darling. We'll go—"

"Non, mon chou. I don't want you to go for the same reason you don't want me to. It is hypocritical, and I won't blame you if you hate me for it. You. You will come with me."

Renn looked across the room and locked eyes with Anya. Anya found herself under the combined stares of Mona and Vastukar as well, the former seething, the latter mildly surprised.

"Wha—buh," Anya sputtered, and all of her little burning spheres sputtered with her, then vanished. "Why me?"

"Because you can hurt things the most. And I think that is what I will need up there. I need somebody who is strong—and perhaps stupid—enough to use a volcano as a weapon and live. Besides, I heard from Esmeralda that you were already planning on going if nobody else would, and that you have fifteen skill points—unassigned —that may be of use later."

Anya frowned.

She had meant it when she said she would go.

If their only options were to die in a huge asteroid impact, or take a shot at saving the planet but probably die in space, it wasn't even a choice. Of course she would have gone. A slim chance at victory over absolute defeat was a no-brainer.

But being *told* she had to go rankled her.

She knew it was stupid, but it still set her hackles up.

Ever since she had first met Renn, he had seemed... pushy. He had taken over her meeting in Greenland. She hadn't minded too much at the time, because all she wanted was for people to meet and talk, but Renn had silenced everybody and taken charge.

Then there had been the dinner at Outpost #1, where he had not-so-subtly implied that Anya should be listening to him and not MacDougal.

And then there was the fight with the centipede, which he had also taken over, mid-battle. The fight had worked out, and he hadn't said anything at dinner that she definitely disagreed with, and he'd helped organize people in Greenland...

Nothing terrible, and definitely some real good. If not for Renn, the fight against the centipede could have gone a lot worse.

And yet...

He just seemed like kind of an asshole.

Anya wondered if she had some ingrained, subconscious bias against the French, and then decided it didn't matter. It didn't matter if Renn was pushy, or if he was an asshole, or even if he was French.

If he was going to save the world, and he needed her help, then that was it.

"Okay," Anya said. "I'll go."

"Merci," Renn replied and inclined his head toward her. Mona gripped his sleeve and glared at Anya. Despite the blazing look of fury on her face, her core temperature plummeted, causing a layer of ice to form over the floor and lab equipment around her. Shadowy fingers and skeletal limbs began to crawl their way out of the darkness of her cape, all reaching for Anya.

"Mona," Renn said, and put his white-gloved hand on her cheek. She continued to stare at Anya until Renn gave her chin a gentle tug and she was forced to look at him. The undead horde withdrew with a resigned sigh. "Mona."

"You can't! She said she would go alone, so let her! If you… I can't lose you, too. Please," she said, and tears welled up in her eyes before freezing on her cheeks. They made glittering diamond streaks as they froze.

"We'll talk about it. But not here. Vastukar, I will be at your service later, but for now, I think some privacy is best."

"There are private rooms a few floors up. Take whatever time you need. You've freed up a significant portion of my schedule," Vastukar replied.

"Anya. We should also talk. Later," Renn said, then left. Anya scowled after him.

"I have everything I need for now if…" Vastukar trailed off as Anya stepped off the scanning platform.

"Yeah," she said, and left. She had to tell Samaira.

34

"He can take Jiro," Samaira said later that evening. Anya hadn't wanted to tell her while she and Tori worked.

And, if she was being honest, she wasn't in a hurry to tell Samaira about her decision. The thought of blasting off into space and landing on a hurtling asteroid that was also ground zero for hundreds of thousands of ravenous gnosiphages didn't weigh on her nearly as much as what Samaira's expression would be like when she told her.

She had expected her to be angry, or maybe incredulous, hurt, or disbelieving. However, as Anya sat on a bench in the aether laboratory, Tori asleep on a bench nearby, Samaira barely looked up from her work. Her long black hair was tied up in a messy bun that had tilted to one side, leaving the slender line of her neck exposed as she leaned over the table.

When Anya had last left them, Tori and Samaira had assembled a few dozen individual aetheric battery crystals. Now, they had several dozen *boxes* of them.

"Or, Mona wouldn't be a bad choice, if she's for it. She can summon the dead, so maybe she can control dead aliens. Something like that? Kill them and then get them forming a defensive line. Brody wouldn't be a bad pick, either. He can adapt to just about anything, from what Cooper was telling me," she continued, still not looking at Anya. Chandrali, in her cat form, lay on the edge of the table, her tail swishing over the side.

"Sam, he asked for me. And he's right: when it comes to hurting stuff, I'm the one that's kind of specialized in that. Jiro's tough and strong like me, but he can't blow shit up like I can. Brody might adapt, but he can't hit as hard as me or Jiro. He's also not level 50. And if there's some emergency, I got skill points to spare. It's—"

"It's fucking stupid," Samaira said, and her eyes finally snapped toward Anya, who flinched at the edge in her voice. "He can take somebody else."

"Sam—"

"Do you want to go?"

"I—No! I'd rather stay here, with you. But if this means we have a better chance at winning? I have to go. It's not like it's a total suicide mission. If this device works like it should, me and Renn'll come back. It's gonna be dangerous, but—"

"Please don't treat me like I'm stupid, Anya."

"I'm not. But we've been risking our lives this whole time. How is this any different? I've almost died at least…" Anya trailed off as she counted in her head for a moment. "At least four times in the last several weeks. Maybe five. So have you."

"But you had back-up here, except for maybe in the very beginning. And even if you didn't, you could just run away if you had to. You can't just run out there," Samaira gestured at the ceiling. "It's space! It's hostile to all life, and its going to be who-knows-how-many miles away from any help!"

"I'm not saying it's not risky. I'm saying it's less risky than doing nothing. And if this can help people—you, Gary, Pan, everybody—and I can do it, but I don't… I couldn't live with myself."

"When we were on our date in New York," Samaira said, her voice becoming measured, careful, "you said you couldn't save your brother. Throwing yourself at something that'll kill you… you know that won't bring him back, right?"

Anya's jaw tightened on a reply she knew she would have regretted had she said it.

"I just mean—" Samaira started to say.

"No. It's fine. I should go tell Gary, Pan, maybe the others. Let Tori know when she wakes up," Anya said, and didn't wait for Samaira to reply before she left the lab.

———

ANYA DIDN'T EVEN KNOW it was possible for a pangolin to cry, but when she told Pan, he did just that. She tried to reassure him as best she could that she would be coming back. He took it as well as he could, and made her promise to return. She did, but she was glad Esmeralda wasn't there to pick up on her lie. Arvo seemed pretty broken up about it too, but not nearly as much as Pan.

Despite what she'd told Pan and Samaira, this time felt different. Maybe because there was a lead-up, to see what was coming before it was in her face. With her first encounters with the aliens, and the volcano, that had been spur-of-the-moment stuff. She didn't know what the hell she was doing until she was already in the thick of it.

"You'll need a spaceship," was all Gary said at first when she told him. They were leaning against a railing and overlooking the city far below. It was more beautiful in the day, when the greens of the jungle and the reds of the buildings really popped, but the night gave it its own charms.

"Guess we will. I figured that sort of thing would be small potatoes for you and Vastukar," Anya replied.

"Mm-hmm. Few days. Maybe a week, we'll have it ready. We could buy one from the RAC store, but it'd be a waste of the currency, and most of us are broke or damn near it already."

"Thanks, Gary."

"Seems kinda strange to be thanking me for sending you off to an asteroid full of those things."

"You know what I mean. And you're not sending me."

"I'm helping."

"You are."

"You know what I mean."

Anya smirked. "I do."

"Sam took it pretty bad, I guess?"

"Yeah," Anya sighed and hung her head. She was already sorry she'd stormed out of the lab like that.

"You tell our little dirt-digger yet?"

"Yeah, just before I found you. He cried, but he stopped when I told him I'd come back."

"Pangolins cry?"

"Pan can."

"Huh. So. You gonna come back?"

"I'm gonna try."

"Good."

Gary turned away and meandered back towards the entrance to the Tower. Anya looked at his back and asked, "That's it?"

"Kid, you've tried a lot of wild shit since we met. You've come out of it beat-to-hell and missing a limb, but you've been okay. If anybody's got a shot at this, it's you. Besides, I've also learned you can be pretty hard-headed since we've met. Me fussing at you wouldn't do much."

"Probably not."

"I'll do my best to make sure everything works. Least I can do."

"Thank you, Gary."

"Mm-hmm," he said, turned to leave, then stopped.

"Gare?"

"I just wanted to… well, I'll make sure the ship has plenty of food for you, okay?"

"You're the best," Anya replied. Gary paused for a moment longer, as if debating whether to say anything else, waved at her, and left.

She stayed out on the balcony for a while longer, and watched the city sleep.

———

HANOVER, along with pretty much every other world leader, agreed to submit raw materials and any staff needed to provide assistance for the project once it began to proceed. Vastukar allowed a small army of engineers, scientists, and other assorted workers and researchers from various countries into New Bengaluru, provided they wouldn't cause trouble, and the construction of the device advanced.

The next several days were spent prepping Anya and Renn with as much information about the asteroid as they could. During that time, Anya only caught glimpses of Samaira. Neither seemed certain how to speak to the other, and the silence between them grew. Anya cursed herself for not being better at this sort of thing. However, every time she tried to make time to speak to Sam, to catch her alone, she was either working with Tori to construct aetheric components, or Anya herself was called away for some task.

Eventually, when everything had been checked and double-checked, full-scale construction of the devices began in earnest. Vastukar called a meeting of hosts, some government representatives, and the various engineers and scientists. They assembled in a large lecture hall that reminded Anya of one of the few university classes she had attended: a semi-circular room with rows of tiered seating curving around a central presentation floor.

Anya tried to catch Samaira's eye when she entered, but failed to. She sighed, took her seat further down the row as the lights dimmed, and Vastukar gestured at a huge screen at the front of the hall.

The briefing was, thankfully, brief, and outlined the basic functions of the devices. Renn's hive mind skill would allow him to link with every device, effectively empowering them all so long as he was near at least one of them. That would increase his psychic disruption signal, boosting it to a better version of what he'd used against the centipede.

Anya would run interference around Renn and the primary device. There would be another thousand decoy devices scattered amongst the handful of genuine ones, each acting as a tempting target, but exploding in a devastating bomb if attacked.

Vastukar and Gary calculated they would need two hours and at least fifty-percent of the devices to survive to crack the asteroid into small enough fragments, and annihilate the majority of the gnosiphages. From there, conventional weaponry would do the rest.

Gary was already working on defensive satellites: improved

versions of what Vastukar had jury-rigged to fire at Alien Alpha. Those, plus the remaining hosts on Earth, plus a few more planetary defenses should be enough to finish off the asteroid's largest fragments. The rest would either burn up in the atmosphere, or be small enough to cause only minimal damage if they struck land. Hosts would be on alert, and they'd be making use of the same global tracking system they'd used to find Alpha to track down any aliens that made it to Earth, and wipe them out.

"A much less daunting task now that we've confirmed the gnosiphage signals can be tracked," Vastukar said at the end of a briefing.

The screen displayed a number of high-definition photographs and video of the asteroid. Vastukar's and Gary's drones had gotten close enough to take photos of the aliens themselves, and Anya's skin crawled as she looked at them. These weren't built for mimicry, like all the gnosiphages before—save the overseers—had been. There was no attempt at any disguise: every gnosiphage on screen was a killer made of fangs and claws and black armored plates, surreal biology and nightmare forms.

"Y'know, I don't mind going up to that asteroid thingy. Sounds like a good fucking time to me. Whaddya say, Coop? Space? Kill some of them ugly bastards for a while?" Brody asked and whapped Cooper on the arm.

"Ow! Mate! You can't do that when I'm not wearing my armor," Cooper said and rubbed his bicep.

"We considered a larger strike force to assault the asteroid, but we think it's better to stick with a duo, for the time being. Mr. Renn can act as the much-needed psychic to activate the device, and Ms. Nowicki will act as bodyguard. She can also, in event of an emergency, function as a back-up power-source and trigger for the primary explosive," Vastukar said. "There's also the matter of surviving in space. Mr. Renn can form a sort of psychic cocoon around himself that will enable him to survive in a vacuum, and Ms. Nowicki has a similar ability with her Starforged skin and Light Dominion. You also have some sort of bonus from your advanced class, I believe?"

"Yeah," Anya said. "It's not much, but it'll let me survive in a vacuum for a few minutes if all else fails."

"A few minutes?" Brody scoffed. "You just said they'd need a couple hours!"

"We have some methods to assist in their survival. I'm working on a deployable atmospheric bubble based on your environmental adaptability, Mr. Brody.

"Besides, as I've said before, we'll need as many hosts available here. Even if the device is a complete success, we still anticipate at least several thousand gnosiphages to make planetfall at some point prior to or immediately after the asteroid's impact date. We only have about forty high-level, combat-capable hosts that we are aware of. A precious resource we cannot waste. There are a few hundred more hosts out there, but we do not know their status, capability, or anything else.

"Sending two hosts to the asteroid will have to do. They won't be alone. Mr. Hendricks will be bombarding the asteroid's surface with bombs to keep the alien horde distracted and clear what he can of their number. We will both be sending a small fleet of drones as well to assist with defense. It's not perfect, and no plan survives contact with reality for long, but it's what we've agreed has the best chance of success. Now: questions?"

"I've got a question, here," a mellow voice tinged with a South African accent said from the back of the room. A man in his early-thirties stood up from his seat. He dressed like a farmhand—well-worn jeans and a t-shirt—and had a windblown bush of sandy hair on his head, along with a bushy beard, and a light tan across his skin that paled some as his raised arm revealed a tan line near his shoulder. Something like a lemur perched on his shoulder, except it had bright red hair, a fox-like face, and flames licked from its mouth whenever it yawned and licked its lips. Anya's heat sense told her the thing was hot enough to melt steel, but the man—Bernard, she thought his name was—acted as if it was no different than any normal fuzzy critter cuddling his shoulder.

"Yes. Mr. Van der Berg?" Vastukar said.

"How're they getting home?"

There was some silence in the chamber before Gary stepped forward onto the stage.

"I'm building a ship. It's almost done. Renn and Anya will land it on the asteroid along with the primary device. Once it starts its last phase, they'll have a few minutes to get on, and get clear before the big boom goes off. After that, they'll have another few minutes to get up to speed and away from the blast radius."

"A few minutes?" Bernard asked.

"Best we could do," Gary replied and glanced at Anya. She just nodded at him. They'd spoken about this beforehand, with Renn and Vastukar. Speed was key. The decoys, missile bombardment, and their defenses had a finite window of operation. All the models Vastukar and Gary had run gave them a maximum time of three-and-a-half hours on the asteroid before they were fully overrun.

"Aren't there only about 700,000 aliens on that thing? And it's as big as Australia? That's a lotta room. Will the aliens even notice them?" Amahle, the woman next to Bernard, said. Her voice boomed across the room, and had a similar accent to his.

Her hair was an explosion of dark curls that arced in graceful parabolas around her head, and her dark skin had a blue sheen to it, almost like crystal. Like Anya, her eyes glowed a faint yellow, but Anya didn't detect any unusual heat from her. She was dressed like some kind of monk, with loose pants and a flowing, sleeveless top, both of bright turquoise.

"Ms. Kekana. Our scans show the aliens spread out in roughly equidistant squads, each one several miles apart. They move constantly, likely using their mental connection as a singular entity to maintain maximum coverage. Ms. Nowicki and Mr. Renn will have some time to themselves upon landing, but not much. We hope for an hour, but at least a minimum of thirty minutes, if we can get the landing area between squads."

"And if it doesn't work? If they die and the devices all break?" Amahle asked.

"We got a few aces up our sleeves if that happens, but that's extremely unlikely. If the worst-case scenario happens, and all the devices fail completely, it doesn't mean game over. The planetary defenses we're setting up as a last resort will work, but the aftermath ain't gonna be pretty," Gary said.

"However, we're confident this will succeed. The devices will be finished in a few more days, which will coincide with the construction of Mr. Hendricks's spaceship, and give us just enough time to send our brave volunteers up with the devices, and shatter the asteroid. If there are no more pressing questions...oh, uh, I see," Vastukar mumbled as a hundred more hands shot into the air.

"If you're from a government, no, we're not sharing this tech with you, and yes, all of the data will be deleted or locked away after the crisis is over, and only opened in the event of another emergency, on mutual agreement of everybody involved. And if you've been trying to email data or whatever out of the city, we've already caught you and put a stop to it," Gary said and several hands went down, but not all of them. He sighed and added, "Look, just come up here and ask whatever and let us get back to work."

Several people descended toward the presentation area, while others turned to each other and spoke in excited whispers. Many others left the lecture hall, and Anya almost leaped out of her chair towards Samaira, but she had already left.

"Hey," Tori said from beside her. Anya looked down at her friend and tried to smile. Since Tori had been working with Samaira, she hadn't seen much of her either.

"Hey," Anya replied. "So, uh..."

"Yeah, you kinda suck for making me worry about you, but I'll let it slide since you're about to save the planet. C'mon, I'm hungry," Tori nodded toward the exit, and they took the elevator down to street level where they found a Mexican-Indian fusion place a few blocks away from the Tower.

"Tori... I'm sorry. I've wanted to spend more time with you lately, I've just been swamped," Anya said as she stared down at the small mountain of butter chicken and paneer nachos before her, unable to meet her friend's eye.

"Me too. I don't blame you. I get it. Besides, good-byes suck."

"I've been trying to talk to Sam, but every time I see her, or try to send a text, I just… I dunno. I'm not good at this shit. Has she… mentioned me?"

Tori scoffed and then coughed as she partially choked on a bit of chipotle curry.

"Is that a joke? God, she won't shut up about you. All day we're working with the aether and she keeps asking me how to talk to you or what to do, or if you're angry with her, or blah, blah, blah," Tori said once her coughing fit had passed. "You two just need to kiss and make up."

"How?"

"Literally just kiss her and make up. This isn't complicated. You both want to be together and back to normal, so stop doing the teenage angst thing and just go talk. Start with 'Hello,' or maybe 'Hey,' or even, 'I'm sorry.'"

"Yeah," Anya sighed and looked down at her nachos.

"These are mine, now, by the way," Tori said and took the nachos away from Anya.

"Hey!"

"Uh-uhn. You've pissed away enough time. Go talk to your girl-friend. We'll get dinner together some other time," Tori said.

"Some other time? Tori, It's a few days until I take off for space and…" Anya trailed off.

"When you get back."

Tori's voice might have cracked a little as she looked down at her plate, or it might have been some leftover chipotle curry in her throat.

"When I get back. Thank you, Tori," Anya embraced her from the side, and Tori did her best to wrap an arm back around her. They didn't say anything else, but Anya thanked the restaurant owner as she hurried out.

———

ANYA DIDN'T BOTHER with a text. She wanted to speak to Samaira, hear her voice. She used the Archive's map to find her in one of the private rooms in the Tower's upper levels. She stood in front of the door, finger hovering over the call button.

The door slid open with a near-silent *swish* before she could press it, and Samaira stood in front of her.

"Oh! Hey, uh, good timing I was just about to... " Anya said.

"I knew you were out here. I was thinking about texting you, and then Boo said your signal was coming up," Samaira said. She and Anya stared at each other in silence for a moment before Chandrali meowed behind them and Samaira stepped to the side. "Would you like to come in?"

"Sure. Thanks."

Anya swallowed, disliking the formality between them. Their tones each had the careful trepidation of somebody speaking to a stranger, or maybe a stray dog that might snap at any moment. Anya turned, ready to blurt out anything to break the rigid quiet between them as the door slid shut behind her.

Samaira's finger on her lips stopped whatever she was about to say.

"Just let me say this before I lose my nerve," she said and Anya remained silent as Samaira lowered her finger. "I was in love, once, when I started college. It was pretty slow-paced, but I remember the early days when I first started dating her, and how good it felt.

"I'm not in love with you," Samaira continued and Anya's throat constricted to a narrow point. "Yet. Like I said, I remember what it felt like, before I was in love, and the things that led to it. This is better. We're better. And I think part of the reason I've been taking it slow, or maybe even avoiding you, is because that scared me a little. We're in the middle of this crazy thing, and it's so dangerous and I was just... afraid. I *am* afraid. Afraid of feeling like this, afraid for you, and now you're leaving. And the thought of you not coming back is scarier than any of it."

"Sam... " Anya said and rested her palm against Samaira's cheek. She leaned into her hand, and cradled it within her own.

"I want you to come back. Because I don't love you, yet. But I want to. So please, Anya—"

Anya kissed her. She wrapped her arms around Samaira's slender waist and picked her up and held her. She didn't know how long they kissed, but finally she was forced to lean back and take a breath.

Samaira cupped Anya's face in her hands, her own face flushed, stray strands of her sable hair curving in front of her eyes.

"Stay here tonight," she said. "Stay with me."

Anya's hearts burned inside of her chest.

Oh HELL yes, the bird said.

No. NO. This is going to be private and you will absolutely fuck off, Anya snapped back at it mentally.

Fine. I'm still you, anyway, so I'm gonna know, but I won't bug you, the bird replied, and then became silent.

The door to Samaira's room slid open a moment later, and Chandrali was tossed out into the hallway with an indignant yowl. The door swished closed again, and beeped as it locked. Chandrali stared up at the door, then haughtily turned from it and strolled away as if that had been her plan all along.

35

The next few days were a blur. Any free time Anya had was spent with Samaira. Some of it was in public, usually with Pan, Tori, Riley, and others. But when they could, they spent time alone, together. Free time was a precious commodity, and in short supply.

Samaira still had aetheric runes to make, batteries to charge, and connections for the devices to forge. Anya, meanwhile, spent most of her days going between Vastukar and Gary, studying the asteroid and possible insertion points with the former, and practicing basic space-ship and space travel scenarios with the latter.

Gary said he was installing a basic autopilot into his ship, similar to Anya's Shadow Ray, but he wanted both her and Renn to have some comfort with manual piloting. He'd made it as simple as possible, almost like a video game, and had even managed to set up a simulator for them to practice.

There was also the prospect of being in a zero-gravity environment, a concept Anya initially dismissed given her Gravity Dominion.

"Your Flame Dominion absorbs heat and runs off that, right?" Gary asked as he, Anya, and Renn stood in a testing chamber away from the main labs. The chamber consisted of a huge, empty white room for almost all of it, with an observation room with a long window attached to one side. It looked like what might happen if somebody combined an empty school gymnasium with a sterile operating room.

"Right," Anya replied.

"So will your Gravity Dominion need existing gravity?"

"No. It's not an energy producer like my Sun's Heart. It's just kind of there. It'll be easier to use, actually, since I won't be fighting against Earth's gravity."

"And you?" Gary asked and turned to Renn.

"My psionic abilities won't be any more affected out there than they are here. Mind over matter, as they say."

"All right, well, let's give it a shot," Gary said and gestured at the center of the chamber. He went into the observation room, and the door sealed shut behind him with a hiss. Anya watched as he tapped a few buttons, and the familiar pull of the Earth's force faded, then vanished entirely. She tapped her foot on the ground and was sent floating upward. Renn stayed where he was, but his helmeted-head and its reflective golden faceplate followed her movements.

"Fine so far," Anya said. "Feels like when I usually float around, just without the strain of using Singularity's Grasp."

"Move yourself around some," Gary said and Anya obliged. She did as she usually did, pushing herself forward, and then her brain was flooded with information from her Zero-G combat skill.

She initially overshot, then adjusted and steadied herself before she slammed into a wall. The combat skill was useful, but it was also interacting with her Gravity Dominion skill, both of them intermingling into something new.

"Not bad, a little rough," Gary said. "Renn?"

"As I said: no difference," Renn said and floated himself around with ease before landing again.

"Fine. Go practice in the ship simulator again or see if Vastukar needs you for the hive mind link-up. Kid, you good?"

"I'd like to practice a little more," Anya said.

"Good luck, then," Renn waved at Anya as he left through the airlock on the far side of the room.

Anya continued to practice, having to adjust how she normally used Gravity Dominion. Her fire attacks behaved differently, her ability to condense flame and light felt weird, and even her regeneration seemed to have been altered when she was mildly injured during the tests.

"Blood flow," Arvo said when he joined them later. "I can see it in you now. It's gathering mostly in your head and chest. Also your human heart has changed shape very slightly."

"Damn, that's weird," Anya said.

"Get used to it. Imagine if you were having to adjust to all this mid-fight," Gary said and Anya sighed.

"Are we done?" she asked.

"Nope. Now I'm gonna drag all the atmosphere out of the chamber and turn it into a vacuum.

"Are you serious?"

"Yup. That's why Doc's here. If you pass out, he's gonna revive you. I know you said you can do it, and you got that advanced class bonus, but we gotta make sure. We'll be testing those atmospheric bubbles later as well."

Anya groaned, and testing resumed.

———

AND TOO QUICKLY, the final days of prep were gone.

Anya woke up on the morning of the launch as the sun streamed into her and Samaira's now-shared bedroom. The sunflower-yellow rays of light spread over New Bengaluru and made the countless trees glisten and sparkle with the water from the previous night's rains.

It was too beautiful a day to leave.

A shaft of sunlight filtered through the window, holding motes of dust inside it, and coming to rest across Samaira's sleeping figure. Her hair lay scattered around the pillow, sleep-tousled and erratic. Anya sat up in bed beside her, and thought that if she ever got to see her like that again, she'd never take it for granted.

Part of her faltered in that quiet, sun-dappled moment. After days of training, planning, working, meeting, and more, she hadn't stopped at all to reconsider her choice. There was a problem, and she wouldn't run away from it. Not again. Not ever.

But looking at Samaira, her insides trembled. The forward momentum she'd had the last few days wobbled and stalled. Anya reached for her, thinking to wake her up, and ask her if she just wanted to go, to run, to get off the whole fucking planet if they could. Just get in the spaceship Gary had made, cram as many of their friends and Samaira's family into it as they could, and fly the fuck out of there.

Anya's outstretched fingers hesitated above Samaira's bare shoulder. She bit her lip and then closed her hand into a fist, and brought it to her side.

She suspected Samaira would go with her. But even if they all left and had decades after today together, Anya would never leave this room, this moment when she asked Samaira to leave. It would be like how it had been with Nathan all over again.

Instead, she leaned down, and kissed Samaira on the forehead. She blinked her eyes, smiled at Anya, then frowned when she saw the sunlight.

"Oh," Samaira said, her voice heavy with dread.

"Yeah," Anya said, and gave her a sad smile.

"Never thought I'd be so scared of waking up in the morning."

"Me either."

They held each other for several long moments, but none of them long enough. Finally, dreading the inevitable became too much, and Anya pulled away from Samaira.

"I should go," she said. "I think Gary said launch was around noon, and there's probably stuff to do before then, so…"

"Yeah," Samaira said, and they both got ready. Gary had said it would be a few days to fly out at top speed, so Anya dressed in her normal clothes and the storage gauntlet that contained her regalia, as well as a couple changes of clothing. It felt weird packing such mundane things as clothing for a trip to outer space.

That was when Anya realized that she had subconsciously packed for just a couple days.

In other words, a one-way trip.

She hadn't even thought about it, but she had put just enough clothes into a small shoulder bag for the journey out, but not the return.

"You ready to head out to the launching platform?" Samaira asked.

"Yeah," Anya said, and zipped up her bag. She didn't mention it to Samaira as they left.

They were silent in the elevator as it descended. Anya had about a thousand things she wanted to say, but they all piled around each other and lodged in her throat. She took Samaira's hand and held it as the elevator continued to hum downward. Samaira squeezed it, then let go as the elevator slid to a stop and the doors opened onto a short corridor, and the launching platform beyond.

Anya took a deep breath and walked out, Samaira at her side.

The launching platform had been constructed along with Gary's spaceship over the last few days. It was a square slab of white material, something between concrete and metal, with blinking lights at its corners, and leading into its center. For a moment, Anya forgot about her dread, her sadness, and everything else as she beheld the ship Gary had assembled.

"Holy shit," she said.

"Yeah, that's… that's something," Samaira said.

The ship sat upright, resting on its engines. It was roughly triangular in shape, almost like an elongated, three-sided pyramid with rounded edges and a smooth point at its apex. Its sides had a stretched look to them, similar to the Shadow Ray, and formed subtle, elegant wings. The entire thing had been painted bright red, with white stripes, almost like an old muscle car.

"She's a beaut, eh?" Gary said and wandered over. He had a tablet in his hand, and looked up from its glowing surface to Anya.

"You made this in the last few days?" Anya asked. Gary laughed and adjusted his glasses.

"And nights. Paying for it too. Basically running on pure caffeine at the moment."

"It's amazing. Love the color."

"Figured you would."

"Can it shoot lasers? Plasma missiles? Torpedoes?"

"It has some basic defensive counter-measures, but no, no weapons to speak of. The drones and rockets Vastukar and I are sending as your escort will take care of the offense. This thing is meant to go fast, and keep you and Renn alive. That's it. All the energy goes to the magnetic pulse engines and the shields."

"Makes sense I guess," Anya said, and looked around Gary as Vastukar stepped around the side of the ship.

"Just doing final checks. It'll be ready before noon," Vastukar said. "Mr. Hendricks did fine work, given the limited time frame."

"He always does," Samaira said and Gary waved a hand at her as if to bat the compliment away. Others filtered down to the launching platform as the morning wore on and the pre-flight checks continued, Renn and Mona first among them. Renn was dressed as he usually was, in his white coat and armor and helmet, while Mona looked like she had just fallen out of bed. She had bags under her eyes and her cyan hair was still rough and unruly from sleep. She shot a few glares at Anya, which she tried to ignore.

Gary escorted Renn and Anya into the ship and gave them a brief tour. He'd sent them the basic layout before, and familiarized them with a model of the cockpit during training sessions, but it was quite a bit different actually being inside the ship itself. Tilted on its end as it was, Anya had to float herself and Gary around with her Dominion.

"Artificial gravity will kick in once you're out in space. A bit lighter than what you're used to, but enough to feel a little bit like home," Gary explained as they floated back out of the spaceship and landed on the platform. "Your quarters are nothing special, but they're comfortable, and private. And you'll only have to put up with it for six days, max. Three days out, three back."

"It is wonderful Monsieur Hendricks. I'm sure we'll be quite cozy. I can't thank you enough," Renn said.

"You blow up that asteroid, and we'll call it square," Gary replied.

"A deal. Now, excuse me. I'm going to spend the time I have left before take-off with Mona," Renn said, then left with her at his side.

The rest of the pre-launch procedures seemed both to drag, and to fly by. Arvo, Tori, and Pan came down to see her off, of course, and the latter two were both equally inconsolable.

Tori had clearly been drinking at least a little, and made Anya repeatedly swear to come back and take her to the noraebang again. Pan gave her a baggy full of squirming ants and one of his scales, for "A snack and good luck," respectively. Arvo gave her a couple of concentrated calorie mixtures he had made, just for her.

"I can't guarantee the taste, but if you need a lot of caloric intake very quickly, it will help," he said. "Just don't ask what I put in it," he said as he handed her a pair of finger-sized glass vials, each full of a beige paste.

"Well now I definitely—actually, no. I'm good. Thanks, Doc."

"Always my pleasure. See you soon."

She glanced away from Arvo as she noticed Riley and MacDougal making their way across the platform.

"Nowicki," MacDougal waved at her as she stood beside the others.

"Director."

"Would've been here sooner, but things have been busy, as you can imagine. How long until launch?"

"We were just about to board."

"I'll make it quick, then. The President sends his regards, wishes you the best, etcetera, etcetera. He had one of his speech writers make some bland statement he's going to read tonight when he announces the asteroid to the nation, along with every other world leader. You being up there is going to mean the difference down here between total anarchy, and whatever composure the world can still hold onto. Whatever else happens, I'm glad we got this far together. So, thank you."

"Thanks for not being a shitty boss," Arya replied, and the two women shook hands.

"Breakfast at that place in Brooklyn when you get back? What was it?" Riley asked as he also shook Anya's hand.

"Mal's Deluxe Diner."

"I promise the feds won't raid the place, this time."

Anya shook a few more hands from other hosts like Brody and Asmund and others, some of the lab techs she had worked with over the last few days, and representatives from governments all over the world.

"All right. Everybody not on the cleared list, get inside!" Gary shouted, and Vastukar's drones began to escort the now enormous crowd off the launching platform. Gary gave a quick glance to Anya and Samaira, then walked away with everybody else.

"I've said everything I want to, for now," Samaira said as she looked up at Anya. "The rest can wait until you come back."

"Looking forward to it," Anya said, and they kissed, a quick touch of their lips, and then Samaira ran after the others. Anya watched her go, tried not to let it hurt too much, failed, and then flew up and into the ship.

She strapped herself into the cockpit just as Renn flew in behind her and did the same. The two of them went over the final checklist with Gary over the radio, and then it was done.

"I'll activate the launch from here. You two just keep an eye on everything. We'll maintain radio contact as long as we can, but it might get a bit dicey from time-to-time, especially when you get close to the asteroid."

"Got it. Thanks Gary."

"Merci, Monsieur Hendricks."

"Good luck, you two. Godspeed."

There was a loud thud from below them, the rapid CLANK CLANK CLANK of clamps unlatching around the perimeter of the ship, and then a resounding, pulsing hum. Anya looked over at Renn, and let out a shout of surprise as the ship flung itself into the sky. She barely had time to register that they had left the ground before the blue, early-afternoon sky turned to indigo, then to black.

And just like that, Earth was behind them, and before them was only void and starlight.

36

t was more than a little awkward in the spaceship.

After the initial thrill of blasting off, of seeing space, there was nothing else to distract Anya from the fact that it was just her and Renn, alone in a spaceship, thousands of miles from Earth already and getting farther by the second.

There was nothing but the steady hum of the engines to hear and the black void of space to see. There was no point in even pretending to study the control panel. While Gary had made it plenty easy to understand, it was all saying the same thing: systems normal, autopilot engaged.

Nothing to do but wait for them to get out to the asteroid.

And likely not come back.

While she fully intended to try not to die, every second they got further from Earth, the further away her chances of making it back felt. It was one thing to be optimistic back in the sunlight, surrounded by friends. It was another thing entirely to keep a cheery outlook when all there was to look out at was...

Black.

Emptiness.

She paced around the small confines of the ship, going back and forth between her room, the small dining area, the communications room, launching bay, and the cockpit. All of it was utilitarian, but cozy.

Renn never moved.

He never looked away from the infinite nothing outside, never turned his reflective gold faceplate to her whenever she entered the cockpit. The void reflected itself in his helmet, creating an utterly empty visage, a black hole where a face should have been. Anya was reminded of the old Nietzsche quote about staring into the abyss.

After a full day of pacing, lying in her bunk, and having Felix scroll through random items in the RAC store she could no longer afford, even the possibility of dying started to bore Anya. She could only dread her death for so long, and honestly, the hard part was over. Leaving Gary, Pan, Tori, the others, that had been awful. Like its own kind of death.

Especially Samaira.

Especially after their nights together.

I want you to come back. Because I don't love you, yet. But I want to. Her words beat a steady tempo inside Anya's skull; a melody she couldn't shake.

She would go nuts, or start crying, or both, if she stayed in here and did nothing but run over her last few nights on Earth. And she had a couple more days in this tiny ship, with nothing to do but scroll through the Archive, eat, sleep, and be around Renn.

She finally returned to the cockpit and flopped back into the chair beside the Frenchman with a sigh. That finally elicited a response from him, and he turned his head a few degrees to the side to look at her.

"I'm bored," she said.

"I was picking up on your rather subtle signals," Renn replied. Anya snorted.

"I never thought I'd be bored flying to my death. Well, maybe my death."

"I think most of us have faced death so frequently over the past few months that it has lost some of its… *Comment dit-on?*… notability? I'm not sure if this is the right word."

"I get it. Hard to get too freaked out for too long when you've spent weeks on end figuring an alien might chomp your ass at any minute."

"Oui. Chomping ass."

Anya frowned when she turned to face him and saw only her distorted reflection looking back at her.

"If we're gonna talk, you need to take that helmet off. It's weird. Like I'm talking to a droid or something."

Renn didn't respond, but he did reach up and tap the helmet's underside. It hissed, then folded and collapsed backward into a wide collar around his neck. He looked as he almost always did: like he'd just been woken up from a nap. His brown hair was a shaggy mess, and his green eyes were droopy.

"Better?" he asked, his voice much softer now that it wasn't coming through the modulator.

"Yeah. Thanks," Anya said, and then the silence reasserted itself between them. Anya had never been great at small talk. Renn taking off his helmet clearly signaled he was fine with chatting, but now that he had removed it, Anya had no idea what to say.

"Your skills," Renn said after the silence almost started to become a physical presence in the cockpit, "do you think if you ever get the chance to change them, you will?"

Anya blinked and thought about it.

"I don't know," she said. "I might change some of them, but I'm starting to like them. They feel like… me."

Renn nodded.

"I agree. I like my skills. It's almost a sort of personality test. Not quite, but always enlightening."

"Yeah."

"Your fire powers, for example: very interesting. So up-close and violent, but also more diverse than I would have thought. I saw them in Greenland at first, and I thought, 'Ah, how very American. Explosions and punching.' But then I also saw you using it to warm the snowfield, to gather people. Surprising."

"Thanks, I think. If I'm being honest, I'm still kinda on the fence about you and the whole psychic thing. Seems weird to me."

"But not your friend Esmeralda?" Renn asked, a wry smirk stretching one side of his mouth.

"Her's seems more like it's for defense and navigating people. Yours... I dunno. Even after Arvo and Esmi and everybody said mind control is pretty much off the table—except if there's an alien parasite involved—I've still been paranoid about it. Somebody shooting a lightning bolt and swinging a sword faster than the speed of sound, or building a death ray, that doesn't bother me as much as I thought it might. Psychic stuff though... not clear on the rules."

"You may relax. As the doctor and others said, mind control is impossible. Even what the gnosiphages did was not mind control, but crude, physical puppetry. Do you want to know something I learned about us? Humans, I mean."

"Yeah, why the hell not? I got nowhere to be for the next million miles or so."

"You know the gnosiphages share a single consciousness?"

"Yeah."

"And we do not."

"No shit."

"Around each of our minds is like a fortress. Or maybe a prison, would be more accurate. It protects us, naturally, but it also confines us. Even normal humans, without the Archive, they have this. Animals possess a lesser version, but the animal hosts, like Pan, are the same as humans. I think this is why we—Esmeralda and I—cannot read minds. We hear only the vague echoes of thoughts. So, yes, while I could theoretically use my psionic powers to harm you—just as you could use your fire powers to harm me—it is not in the way you think. Not by turning your mind against itself. Only you can do that.

"And if you do not believe me, I will not try to convince you otherwise. Just believe that I want to see Earth again, and keeping you alive and at your full power is in my interest. You're not the only person on this ship who has someone waiting back home for them."

"Yeah, I'll buy that, at least. Speaking of: did you spend any time with family before we left, or just Mona?"

"Just Mona. I spoke with Harrison some, and a few other hosts, but mostly her. You?"

"About the same. Spent most of my time with Sam, but hung out with Tori, Pan, Gary, a few others. I haven't spoken to my family in ages. Wanted to spend my time with people I actually care about."

"I can empathize."

"You don't like your family either, or what?"

"Is it normal to ask personal questions like this in America?"

"Not always. But the way I see it, we're stuck in a tin can in space for a few days and we might die at the end. The typical social niceties don't seem like they'd apply here."

"True enough," Renn said with a slight chuckle. "Well, my only family were my mother and father, and they've been dead for a few months now."

"Oh, shit. I'm so sorry. That was right around the time of the invasion. That must've been awful for you."

"More of a relief. They were not good people."

"Harsh. Can I ask what they did?"

Renn paused for a moment, and stared out at space before he said, "They lacked empathy. Not just for me, but everyone. It's like I said earlier, about our minds being like prisons. But theirs had become worse. They thought only they existed, only they mattered, and they spared no thought or care for anybody else. It's why I had the Archive change my name, along with almost everything else. I wanted none of them, not even their name, to follow me."

Anya recalled that while the Archive did show her full name, along with almost everybody else she had met, Renn's status screen had only displayed his chosen name. Pan's was similar, as was Vastukar's, in that regard.

"Sounds like we have something in common then," Anya said as she thought of her mother. She hadn't given a damn about Anya, or any of her children, only that they do as she said, when she said, and how she said. Anya had run, but Nathan had broken.

She thought that when her mother finally did die, it would likely be no small relief to her, either.

She left the cockpit without a word, and went to the dining room and the food replicator. She had it serve a couple glasses of whiskey, which she took back to the cockpit, and gave one to

Renn. He took it, looking up at her quizzically as he did. Anya sat back down in the pilot's chair beside him, then clinked her glass to his.

"To getting away from shitty family," she said.

"*Santé*," Renn replied, and raised his glass, then took a sip. He raised his eyebrows in surprise at it. "Not bad for recycled algae and plastic, or whatever it's made from."

"Gary does good work."

"Well, if this is any indication of how well the devices are made, we may have a chance after all," Renn said as he looked at the amber liquid in his glass. Anya smiled for the first time since they had left, and hoped he was right.

———

THEIR COMMUNICATIONS WENT DOWN HALFWAY through the second day.

Their Archives still worked fine, but the options for getting in touch with anybody back on Earth had become unstable. The ship's signal had also become unreliable: lots of static and fuzzy images. This was all exacerbated by the sheer distance between them and Earth. Any message sent over the ship's comms took hours to get to Earth and come back.

She and Renn stood in the communications room, and waited for a message from Gary to finish transmitting. The room was a bit cramped, with its center dominated by a wide, circular table that acted as a 3D holographic display. Screens were set into a pair of the walls, along with multiple read-outs displaying radio signal strength. The latter showed that the signal was currently fluctuating between nothing and fifty-percent, and a progress bar showed that whatever Gary was sending was almost complete.

"The ship radio and transmission stuff being slow, I get. But why the Archive? We can still message each other if we want, and the RAC store and stuff works fine, so it's not gnosiphages screwing it up. Why just the comms?" Anya asked and Renn shrugged.

"You're asking the wrong person. If I had to guess? Maybe there is some main signal from the Engineers that gives us access to the

Archive and RAC store, but the local communications only act within a certain range. But, as I said, just a guess."

"I swear if I ever meet the Engineers, I'm putting my foot up their collective ass."

"I may help you."

The display nearby beeped as the transmission from Gary finally finished downloading, and a holographic image of the asteroid appeared rotating above the central table. A text message typed out on another screen nearby.

MOST RECENT SCAN OF ASTEROID. NO SIGNIFICANT CHANGES BUT ONE: STRONG UNKNOWN ENERGY SIGNATURE DETECTED. MOBILE. VERY STRONG. NO DETAILS. CONTACT IN 26 HOURS AS OF SENDING THIS MESSAGE. COMMUNICATIONS UNCERTAIN AFTER 6 HOURS, LIKELY LAST TRANSMISSION UNTIL YOUR RETURN.
GO GET 'EM, KID.

Anya smiled as the text message typed itself across the screen, then glanced at the time stamp that followed. Gary had sent the message seven hours ago, which meant they had nineteen hours until they got to the asteroid.

"Looks the same," Renn said as he studied the asteroid. Clusters of red dots crawled across it in coordinated patterns. Each cluster represented a large group of aliens, and they were usually spread apart, equidistant from each other. It wasn't much different than the previous scans they had seen, save for one difference: several clusters had formed in the center of the asteroid, forming a single huge mass several times the size of the largest regular cluster. At its center was a single glowing white dot, that had a label floating above it.

DANGER

That was all it said. Anya tapped on the label, and the message that expanded over the hologram didn't do much to explain why that white dot was a danger. There were some details about an energy signature, and how it hadn't been detected until now, but that was all.

"Fuck whatever that thing is," Anya sighed.

"Agreed. We'll aim to land opposite wherever it is, stay away from that mob around it as well," Renn said. "We're likely going to lose Archive access upon arrival or shortly after, thanks to the gnosiphages. However, I think it would be good to make any store purchases or skill changes now, to be safe."

"Right. I'm pretty much broke for RAC, but I still got my fifteen skill points. I guess I'll just boost my regeneration and Dominions as best I can. Give us the best shot at staying alive."

"Actually… I have an idea," Renn said and looked at Anya. Something in his voice sounded off, and Anya realized that it was hesitation. Renn hadn't been shy about stepping into the spotlight in Greenland, or getting bossy with her during the fight with the centipede. He hadn't even asked her to come along with him on this mission, just pointed at her and said what he wanted.

"Okay?" Anya replied.

"I have five skill points and just over 130,000 RAC. I believe that is enough for me to acquire a Sun's Heart and the Flame Dominion skill, yes?"

"Uh, yeah. But it'd be weak as hell. We don't need more fire stuff. You're psychic guy, I'm fire gal. You do psychic stuff, I do fire stuff."

"I am proposing that I would no longer be the psychic guy, and you would not be the fire gal. We would each be both, and better versions of them."

"I don't think I understand," Anya replied and narrowed her eyes at him.

"You have enough skill points to acquire what you need for the self-duplication and hive mind skills. If you take these things, each of us will benefit from the other's powers. Our tiny team of two will expand to an army of thousands. Instantly."

Anya blinked. Her mouth opened, but no words came out as her thoughts began to pile up inside of her. Would it work? What were those skills again? If Renn took the Flame Dominion and a Sun's Heart, then cloned himself, would the effects of the Heart stack upon each other and create a kind of endless, rechargeable battery?

"Wait," Anya said as one thought in particular bashed through all the others. "Hive mind. That would link me to you, right?"

"Yes, and open the door to allow us to enhance the other's skills. My weak Sun's Heart and Dominion would become as strong as yours, and your ability to duplicate yourself would become as strong as mine."

"And throw open that same fucking door to my entire brain. You said it yourself just the other day: only I can turn my brain against itself. What the hell? I'm not giving you the keys to my head, man. Are you fucking nuts?"

"Your head would become my head. Hurting you would hurt me. All this would do is unlock the prison you're in. You would have access to my power, just as I would have access to yours."

"Yeah but your skill level for hive mind would always be higher than mine! And how would that even work, beyond just the skills? Would our personalities get all churned up? Our memories? Do you even know?"

"I know it's worth the risk, and whatever would affect you, would affect me. As we are now, I think we have a decent chance of setting off the devices, maybe less-than-decent, given whatever that thing is," Renn said and pointed at the white dot on the hologram. "But that chance does not include our survival. I think even if we destroy the asteroid, we're still unlikely to live through the process. But if we do this, if we truly work together, it's all but guaranteed. My brains, your brawn, and then both will be ours, together."

"Absolutely not," Anya snapped and turned to leave the room.

"What about Pan? Gary? Tori? Samaira? I may not have Esmeralda's expertise for seeing emotions, but even if I had no psychic ability at all, I could tell how much you care for them. Are you willing to give them only half a chance at living?"

Anya stopped in the doorway, her back to Renn and the room.

Dying—even dying heroically—wasn't her first choice. But if it meant saving people back home, then it was a fair trade. Some trash-talking ex-barista from Brooklyn, who'd failed to save her little brother, weighted against the entire population of the world? No contest. She'd rather die as herself than take even a chance at living as... whatever would become of her if she took Renn's offer.

But it wasn't just her.

Anya had felt the dread welling up in her as soon as she had seen the vastness of space. The asteroid loomed in her mind, and that white dot, whatever it was that drew the red lights of the other gnosiphages to it, couldn't be good.

It wasn't just dread of dying, but of dying for nothing.

It was dread of failure.

"I know you're afraid," Renn said. "Not for yourself. For them, back on Earth. I feel it too. But if we do this, we can win. Everyone can be saved. And not just now, but if something like this happens again. Do you think, even if we stop the asteroid and nobody dies, that it will be the last? That the gnosiphages, the Engineers, they will just be finished with us and leave us in peace? Maybe this time we win, but next time? And the next? I don't know if you've been paying attention, but our problems only seem to keep growing with each victory."

Anya rested her hand on the door frame, then leaned against it.

He was right.

It had started with that killer puppet in the park in Brooklyn, and now she was flying out to space to stop a chunk of iron and stone as big as a continent.

And he was right again.

This wasn't all of the gnosiphages. There were more, out there, somewhere. The Engineers too. And if the Archive's notes on the various skills were to be believed, an entire galaxy of aliens with magic powers, advanced tech, and who-knew-what-else.

And he was also right about her being afraid.

Her human heart pounded in her chest, and her stomach churned its bile around. All she could think of was Samaira, lying next to her in bed, hand on her cheek.

Pan, clinging to her leg, and asking her if she wanted some of his ants.

Gary, leaning back in his armchair in his lab, laughing as they talked shit about Hanover.

Arvo, always tending to her and everyone else.

Tori, leaning against her, drunk off a pair of watered down cocktails and singing her lungs out in the noraebang.

"Don't be selfish," Renn said. "This isn't about you, or me. This is about them."

Anya grit her teeth, and her hand hovered over her chest, where her Archive had struck her. A tap, a couple button presses, and a confirmation, and she could make sure everyone was safe. Her hand lowered, and felt the heat coming from her Sun's Heart.

I have a question, little ember, the bird said. *Why ask now?*

Anya's hand froze over her chest.

What?

I've never gotten the impression that this Renn guy is stupid, the bird continued. *He just came up with this idea? Now? He asked for you to join him days ago. You're also one of maybe a handful of hosts on the entire planet that had points in the bank.*

I don't understand, Anya thought.

Just seems pretty fucking weird that he's asking now, just as communications have failed. Also that he didn't ask it when you had access to the only other psychic, and one who could tell if he was lying or not.

"Wait. Yeah," Anya said aloud.

"Yes. It's about th—" Renn started to say.

"Shut the fuck up," she snapped and looked over her shoulder. Something in her eyes must have warned Renn she wasn't kidding, as the sleepy look was all but slapped off his face and he took a step away from her.

I'm not psychic, and neither are you. But he's asking you to put all your eggs in his basket, and he's done it when you're isolated, and he has all the information. At least, when it comes to this hive mind thing, the bird said.

But would it work? Would it guarantee we'd stop the aliens? Anya thought.

It might. But you might do that anyway. Gary worked hard on the devices with Vastukar. Sam and Tori pulled a bunch of all-nighters making the aether components. It might fail. But you might fail if you go Renn's way too. Your choice, little ember. Nothing in life is certain. Listen to your heart. It's gotten you this far.

Anya let out a sigh, then turned to face Renn.

"No," she said.

"Why? You think stubborn refusal to cooperate will protect your friends from the aliens?"

"No, but it might protect them from you. Really fucking amazing timing bringing this up now, huh?"

Renn didn't answer for a moment, then asked, "Who were you talking to, a moment ago?"

"What?"

"My power does not allow me to read thoughts like a book. But I can sense when a mental conversation is happening, and when more than one person is around. Just now, it was faint, but somebody else was here, and you were thinking at them. They're gone now. What was this? What are you hiding?"

"Don't fucking change the subject—"

"*Non.* You imply I'm acting suspiciously, while you are having secret conversations with some phantom. You can't—"

"You just tried to manipulate me into letting you into my head, you fucking creep! You planned it from the start. Waiting until just the right moment, when I'm alone, feeling me out for when I'm the most scared, and then making it sound like I have to do what you say or my friends are gonna die."

"They *will* die! Everyone will die!" Renn snapped and threw his hands into the air. His face flushing with anger, eyes wide and white and focused on her. "Because you choose now to be stubborn and self-ish. You insist on staying in your mind's cage, even when I offer you the key!"

"I don't think you want to let me out of my 'prison.' You just want to be the warden. Hard pass, asshole," Anya said and then turned and left. She half expected Renn to duplicate himself, surround her, and attack, but he stayed in the communications room, muttering to himself in French.

Anya spent the rest of the day in her tiny room. She watched the blackness outside the small, circular window, and asked herself the same question, over and over.

Is this the right thing?

She had a new answer, and a new reason for it, every time.

She put her pillow over her head and cursed into it, then rolled onto her side with a resigned grumble.

She was, at least, still herself.

It would have been pretty cool to have duplicates of herself fighting with her, though. Or some kinda ultimate power move.

"Hey Felix?" Anya asked.

"Yes?" The AI replied as they materialized beside her head.

"Bring up the Archive. I got a few skills I wanna look at. I have an idea."

37

An alarm sounded and Anya jolted awake.

"Whuddufuk!" she mumbled as she looked around her room, searching for the noise. It shut off a moment later, replaced by Gary's voice.

"Hey. Asteroid's two hours out. The first wave of rockets and assault drones should be hitting right about now. I'll update you with the raw statistics. Get ready and good luck, you two. Also, this is a recording. I'm not actually on the radio," the recording said.

"Oh shit," Anya said and scrambled out of bed. She threw her regalia on, and made sure she had everything she needed: her two Shards of the Everstar, healing potions, and Arvo's little vials of calorie sludge.

Anya felt like she was in the middle of one of those didn't-study-for-the-test nightmares, except a million times worse. She'd passed out after she'd spent the last of her skill points, and then must have slept through the night. Or day. Or whatever it was.

She barged out of her room, fiddling with the belt of her regalia as she hurried toward the cockpit. Renn was seated in one of the pilot chairs, helmet up. He did not turn to face her as she sat down.

"We good?" she asked as she studied the displays in front of her.

"You heard the recording?" Renn asked.

"Of course!"

"Then you know that, for now, we're good. I've confirmed with the ship's autopilot to land us as far away from that glowing white anomaly from the hologram as it can. Our landing position, along with the primary device, will determine the location of the secondary devices. I've already conducted my checks to make sure I can link to all the devices and power the psychic distortion field and initial activation. Everything was cleared for operation. How was your nap?"

The disdain in Renn's voice was difficult to miss.

"Fucking peachy. Slept like a log since I didn't have nightmares about my conscious mind being controlled by a snide Frenchman."

"Enfant égoïste."

"Look man, I went to public school, so any language that isn't English is *no bueno* for me."

Renn only shook his head in response.

Anya rolled her eyes and let out a huff.

"So, I'm not gonna lie because I know you'd be able to tell, and also because we don't have time to waste on bullshit. I wasn't a big fan of yours before this, and now, I think you're a manipulative bastard. But We—me, and everybody on Earth—need you for this. I give you my word: I will do everything I can to keep you alive. And if you want a chance at making it back to your big-titty goth girlfriend, you need me alive. So how about we agree to just stay focused on killing aliens, deal?"

Renn did not turn away from the void for several moments, and the cockpit was filled with nothing but the hum of the engines to break the silence. Anya was about to press him when he looked at her and extended his white-gloved hand.

"Deal. You think I am a manipulative bastard. I think you are a stupid child. But so long as you are pointed at the aliens, maybe we have a chance. Though, if we die, I am saying it now: I blame you entirely."

Anya almost laughed at that, and shook his hand.

"Fine by me."

———

THE UPDATES from the first and second waves of rockets and drones came soon enough.

Wave one suffered 80% losses and only managed to eliminate about 3% of the total alien presence on the asteroid. Wave two managed only 30% losses and cleared out 11% of the remaining aliens.

The third wave was the largest, and would act as cover for Anya and Renn landing. The two of them stood in the launching bay, next to a silver orb that was at least three times as tall as Anya. The device was deceptively simple-looking, given everything it could do: just a huge metal ball, with a few subtle etched lines in precise geometric patterns across its otherwise flawless surface, and a few buttons.

Renn had programmed their chosen landing site to be as far away from whatever the glaring white dot was, and its roaming escort of gnosiphages.

"We should have thirty minutes, minimum, to ourselves, according to the computer," Renn said. "After that, the aliens will start to descend on us. Though, given our luck, I suspect we will have even less time than that. But even if we do get an entire half-hour, that still leaves ninety minutes we must protect the device."

There was a warning alarm over the ship's speakers, and Gary's voice emitted once more.

"Third wave of rockets and drones is set to hit in three minutes. You'll launch in two, and arrive during what is hopefully a lot of chaos for the aliens. Get ready," the recording said. Red lights began to flash in the launching bay, and the device hummed to life between Renn and Anya.

Anya put her hand on the side of the device, and a glowing outline appeared around her palm. The light extended from the device and expanded into a transparent blue-hued bubble that surrounded her. Anya couldn't see Renn on the other side of the device, but she saw a similar glow from around its silver curve.

"Host connections made. Psychic distortion field activated. Linking to secondary devices," an automated voice said from the device itself. "Linking successful. Launch will commence in eighty-seven seconds."

"Fuck," Anya let out a breath and bounced on her feet. She'd been over the procedure to know how this would work. The bubbles the device emitted would secure her and Renn during the launch, and allow them to breathe until they landed. At that point, it would deploy the larger atmospheric bubble, and then get to work. She would be perfectly safe during the launch, and the landing.

Except for the aliens, it'd be fine. Like a roller coaster, maybe.

No big deal.

"Sixty seconds," the voice said.

"Jesus Christ, just do it already," Anya muttered.

"Easily the longest sixty seconds of my life. *Merde*," Renn said from the other side of the device.

"Wish I could say it's been fun."

"Based on how you act when you fight, I'd say the fun is about to begin."

"Yeah, but the waiting sucks."

"Indeed."

"Thirty seconds to launch," the automated voice interjected.

"The third wave of drones and rockets will be hitting the asteroid as we land. Hopefully it will give us enough cover," Renn said.

"Just gotta go down and kick ass," Anya replied.

"Ten seconds to launch."

"Oui. And not die."

"As long as I take them with me—"

"Five seconds to launch."

"—I'm happy."

The launching bay door opened with a blare of alarms and flashing red and yellow lights. There was a deafening hiss and a rush of air as everything was sucked out into the black empty eternity beyond the hull of the ship. Anya stared outward, face-to-face with infinity.

A single gray dot floated out there in the great beyond. A speck.

The asteroid.

Points of light burst across its surface and in the space around it. Beams of energy lanced down at it and up from its surface as the third wave of the assault unleashed as much hell as it could before Renn and Anya arrived.

Anya's breath stuck in her throat as she stared at it.

"Launching," the automated voice said, and there was a sudden jerk as the device was blasted out of the launching bay. Anya had a moment to glance behind her, and see the red shape of their ship shrink into non-existence as they shot away from it at several thousand miles a minute.

The protective barrier emitted by the device kept her and Renn secure, attached, and alive as it hurtled forward. The asteroid grew in Anya's field of vision, and then it loomed, going from a speck to what looked like a planet unto itself within the span of a minute.

"Holy God," Anya whispered.

The surface of the asteroid was an uneven, chaotic terrain of peaks and valleys that bore a closer resemblance to a stone sea, frozen in a moment of tumultuous frenzy. Hills of iron and rock surged up like waves stopped at the apex of their surge. Anya had a brief view of explosions scattered across the surface, some of them domes of light and death that stretched for miles. She had a glimpse of tiny black figures scuttling around, but they were almost microscopic at their current distance.

The device slowed as they approached, and then landed. The impression of a roiling ocean was still present, but the jagged curves and swelling slopes of the alien terrain were somewhat more subdued when seen from up close. The device had landed in the center of something like a sloped plateau, and as soon as it touched down, a huge dome of translucent blue light sprang out from it.

The dome was taller than Vastukar's tower, and wider than Manhattan. It seemed huge, but it was a single, tiny pocket of precious air and atmosphere across the unforgiving surface of the asteroid. As soon as the atmospheric bubble deployed, the smaller fields around Anya and Renn vanished, and she removed her hand from the device's side.

"It's active," Renn said, still touching the device as Anya walked around to his side. She bounced once, twice, getting a feel for the gravity. The asteroid had enough mass and density to have some gravity of its own, but not nearly as much as Earth.

Anya glanced down as a hole appeared beneath the device, about as big around as the device itself, then began to expand outward and stretch down into the asteroid's core. It was fast, gaining about a few feet down every second, and picking up speed even as it continued to expand. Renn floated beside it as the ground vanished beneath his feet, and Anya was forced to do the same a moment later.

"I can feel the other devices. They've all landed," Renn said as he looked up and around. "They're active, too. No problems, yet."

"Don't fucking jinx us," Anya said, and let out a quiet sigh of relief. "I'm gonna fly up and be on lookout. You stay down here, conserve whatever energy you can and focus it on the device. Felix, is the Archive still working?"

"It is!" Felix replied. "Did you want to buy something? You don't really have any RAC left."

"No buying, but let me know the second we start getting interference. I don't suppose we can track the aliens on the map?"

"Not precisely, no. Vastukar's tracking thing is back on Earth, and the Archive just has their general location, which is just 'HERE,' basically, and then it shows me the asteroid."

"Great. Okay. Just lemme know when the Archive shits itself, then."

"You got it! Good luck! I hope you don't die!"

"Me too. See you, Renn," Anya said and then shot up as high as the atmospheric bubble would allow. The view from above wasn't that much different from below, except she had a better impression of the chaotic landscape. Flashes of light blossomed and then winked out of existence beyond the horizon in every direction. Blinking lights of drones and Guardians soared by over head, firing salvos of missiles and lances of energy.

All of it was silent.

Anya rotated slowly in place, trying to keep an eye on everything at once.

The horizons.

The explosions.

Renn.

The device.

The hole.

The landscape.

Her muscles remained tense for the first five minutes. She expected a kaiju gnosiphage to rise up out of the ground at any moment.

After ten minutes, she thought she kept seeing movement out of the corner of her eye. It was always just shadows, leaping across the deformed landscape, thrown into sharp relief by the light of distant explosions that continued to rock the asteroid's surface.

At thirty minutes, her fists were tight, quivering balls at her sides, and she barely dared to believe they had made it this far without an alien jumping them. She began to think that they had the wrong asteroid. They'd gone all this way, and just found the wrong hunk of rock. That was it. It was stupid, of course; the drones and the rockets wouldn't have triggered and attacked an empty asteroid, but the quiet was getting to her.

She flew down toward Renn, and paused a moment to gape at the side of the tunnel below the hovering device. She could no longer see the bottom, and the diameter of the tunnel had gotten so large that it could have swallowed most of a city block. The device had released a series of fist-sized orbs, floating at distant intervals, all the way down the length of the tunnel, until they also disappeared. Anya recalled Vastukar saying something about extending the device's signal once it dug deeply enough and the tunnels began to divide.

"How's it going?" Anya asked. She forced herself not to bug Renn, and only come down once every ten minutes or so.

"Not bad. Several of the devices have been destroyed, but not as many as we feared. All the dummies Gary and Vastukar made must be doing a good job," he said. "No aliens?"

"Not yet. It's making me fucking paranoid."

"Every second we remain undisturbed is a blessing."

"Don't jinx us," Anya repeated.

"Go back to your watch. I have this handled."

Anya grunted at him and flew back up. She folded her muscular arms over her chest, and tapped a finger against her bicep as she scanned the horizons once more.

Forty minutes.

Fifty minutes.

Sixty.

Anya began to hope this would all be sealed up and done without them having to do anything. They had one more hour, half-way there, and then they'd activate the return function on the device which would take them back to the ship as well as trigger the final detonation. Then it would be done. Mission accomplished.

Sixty-five minutes.

Seventy.

"How many devices have they destroyed?" Anya asked when she floated down again. She'd started to space her check-ins out to twenty minutes after the half-hour mark.

"More than I'd like. We're down by slightly less than half now. Maybe sixty percent remaining. The two hour limit only applies if we can keep fifty percent of the devices up and running."

"Yeah, I gotcha," Anya said, and flew up again.

Seventy-five minutes.

That was when Anya noticed that the explosions had stopped. The silence was nothing new, but the sporadic flashes of light had been a near-constant reminder of the ongoing third wave.

And now it was gone.

Eighty minutes.

Eighty-five.

Nine—

Movement.

Anya froze in her silent rotations, her glowing, golden eyes focusing in on something far in the distance. Not a shadow.

A flock of winged nightmares soared over the edge of the far horizon and sped toward Anya. Their myriad shapes came into focus as they flew closer: wings of thin crystal, mottled leather, feathers that glittered like shards of obsidian, and more kept the hellish flock aloft. A tide of scuttling horrors surged over the land below them, cresting the lip of the horizon and moving as a single mass of fangs and claws and thirsting tongues.

"Company!" Anya shouted down. Renn only waved his acknowledgment up to her, and then his clones materialized around him. Nearly thirty of them in the blink of an eye, all spreading outward in a defensive ring.

Anya turned to give the skies a last look, and was unsurprised to see another horde, and then a third, rushing toward them from different directions.

They had been lucky. Eighty-five minutes of undisturbed progress. They had to hold on for thirty-five more minutes, and pray the other devices could hold out for as long. If the third wave of the assault was finished, then she and Renn would have to serve as the big distraction.

"Anya, the Archive is no longer functioning," Felix said in her ear.

"Yeah, no shit."

Anya turned herself into a golden beacon of flames, her light shining across the barren, iron wastes of the asteroid. She shot forward as the nearest flying gnosiphages entered the atmospheric bubble, and slammed the first one with an elbow drop that decapitated it and sent a shockwave of glittering flames out from its body. The alien—something that resembled a dodecahedron made of scaled flesh and with the head of a skinless dog—splattered to pieces, and the shockwave sent its golden flames crashing into the next twenty aliens around it. They all writhed as their wings and bodies caught fire, unable to get rid of the enhanced flames, and tumbled to the ground below as they turned to ash.

Anya stretched her arms wide, making the air around her heavy enough to drop anything that flew within a wide radius of her. She, and about fifty aliens all plummeted onto the heads of more aliens below. They struck with a thundering boom, and pillars of light and heat leaped up from around Anya as she cratered the ground below her and turned anything close enough into smears of burning paste.

As soon as the area was clear, a mob of gnosiphages charged in to fill the gap. Acidic barbs, beams of energy, and a hail of projectiles fired at her. Her Starforged skin and Gravity Dominions deflected most of them, sent many back at their attackers, and blunted the impact of anything else that got through. Anya's body blurred as her energy focus increased her speed, allowing her to use Gravity Dominion to dart more effectively around attacks.

Anything stupid enough to try and close to melee range had to fight through the swirling vortex of gravitational claws that pulled them down, and in, towards the nexus at Anya's feet. Its force crushed anything as it pulled it closer, and the radiance of her Flame and Light Dominions ignited anything that wasn't pulped and torn to pieces.

The few stalwart gnosiphages that survived all of that met a gloriously brutal end at Anya's fists and feet. Every punch was a localized bomb, every kick a focused hurricane.

Anya couldn't tell what the gnosiphages levels were at, but all of them displayed a multitude of powers and abilities. The lower level aliens she had fought had maybe two or three tricks up their sleeves, but each one of these—the ones that lived more than a few seconds once they got close to her, anyway—had an array of skills.

A low, droning noise filled the air, and Anya looked up to see something like a whale floating overhead. It was whale-like in its size as well as its general shape: a long tail, fat body, and a multitude of fins extending from its sides. Its underbelly inflated like a bullfrog's neck, expanding into a huge sack of opaque, stretched flesh. Some kind of embryonic life swarmed within, briefly visible as the stretching thinned the flesh and allowed Anya a glimpse inside.

The whale thing began to open its mouth, and Anya didn't bother to see what it was going to spit out. She wondered if the gnosiphages —linked mentally as they were—had forgotten what she'd done to the centipede.

She would remind them.

Anya flew up and into the whale-thing's mouth just as it began to unleash the horde within. She raised her hands and then brought them together, Singularity's Grasp forcing the whale's mouth shut, just as Anya detonated herself. Her fire spread quickly throughout the behemoth, killing whatever terrors it had been about to birth, and rupturing its body in countless flaming wounds. It fell like a tremendous flaming blimp and crushed the lesser gnosiphages beneath it.

Anya stood in the splattered wreckage of its corpse and let her lingering fire burn off the thing's blood and viscera as she glanced around. She'd managed to push back one advance, the horizon before her clear for the moment, and turned back to help Renn with the other incursions.

Renn was holding his own, at the moment, though not quite as dramatically as her. His clones, now numbering somewhere around seventy, had gathered into several small groups of three or four, and had proceeded to crush, snap, and dismember anything with raw telekinetic force that got close to them.

The device itself had also activated its self-defense features, and rings of aetheric energy surrounded it, launching glowing azure lances at anything that wasn't human for miles around. Anya also noticed that any alien within a mile or so of the device began to writhe and thrash around in a confused frenzy: the result of the psychic distortion field messing with their shared connections.

The swarm faltered for a moment, but then reinforcements appeared over the horizon again and rushed in. Worse, each incursion seemed larger than the last, until the entire area around the atmospheric bubble was a teeming mass of gnosiphages. What was worse, the more aliens that arrived, the less effect the psychic distortion field appeared to have on them. Their frenzied, chaotic thrashings mellowed to twitches and random spasms, and they were able to press closer.

Anya, Renn, and his clones were forced back toward the device, a shrinking circle of fiery and telekinetic death that contracted further with every second. The device increased its attack output, launching more aetheric missiles and lasers, its reactive metal body impaling any hostile that managed to get within a hundred feet.

But it was obvious which way the battle was going. More huge gnosiphages had appeared in the distance, lumbering across the land or floating through the air. They were slow, but it was only a matter of time before they arrived. And Anya had no doubt that more were behind them.

"I have some bad news," Renn said as several of his clones burst the heads off of a score of aliens.

"Is there any other kind?" Anya asked. She had just torched a swathe of enemies in front of her, one punch hammering through a dozen aliens, and the aftershock leveling several more.

"The other devices have been taken out. I think that's why they took so long to get to us. They spotted the devices, figured out what they were for, and then went hunting for the others before they decided to focus on us."

"Smart little bastards," Anya said.

"We may have to manually detonate the device."

"Gary showed me how. I'll do it, since I can give the explosion some extra boom, too."

"If we—look out!" Renn said and then he and some of his clones raised their hands and created a psychic dome before them, just as a barrage of green bolts of light shot down and deflected off of it.

A towering gnosiphage—an obelisk of obsidian flesh several stories tall that walked on spindly spider's legs, and was covered in huge eyes —approached, eyes glowing green as it prepared another assault.

Anya set off an explosion beneath her feet and rocketed at the obelisk alien's legs. She broke several of them off with echoing, brittle snaps, flung them at other nearby aliens as makeshift javelins, then soared up and around as the obelisk tottered and fell. Its many eyes focused on her, shooting at her with beams of poison light from its eyes. Several managed to impale her and eat at her skin, but none could stop her momentum. She slammed into the obelisk, cracked it open and exposed its wet insides, and then cooked it alive from the inside out.

The resulting explosion of golden fire bought her and Renn some breathing room as the gnosiphages regrouped. Anya flew back towards Renn, chugging a healing potion and using up one of her Shards of the Everstar. Her wounds closed, but her regeneration was slowing down already. And if Arvo was right (and he usually was), it would only get harder from here. Anya also gulped down one of his caloric paste things, and grimaced at the taste. It had a slightly bitter vegetable taste, and a thick, gummy texture. Like glue made from spinach and dirt.

Just as Anya was forcing herself to finish the last of the caloric paste, she noticed the legions of aliens had stopped.

They hadn't just stopped their inexorable advance and endless barrage, but stopped entirely: each one stood frozen, unnaturally still and unmoving.

"What the fuck is this?" Anya asked.

"Something to do with that, I assume," Renn replied, and pointed at a spot to Anya's left. The aliens had managed to intrude most of the way into the atmospheric bubble, despite the distortion field, and the closest one to Anya was a couple hundred feet away or so. It, and every alien from that point backwards—all the way to the distant horizon—stepped to one side or another, and formed a miles-long aisle.

A figure floated down the center of the pathway made by the motionless gnosiphages, moving at speed until it reached the end, and then stopped, hovering a few inches above the ground while still some distance away from Anya, Renn, and the device.

It was slightly taller than Anya, and covered in smooth gray skin, the shade and texture of a polished stone. Its body, from its bare feet to halfway up its chest, could have easily been mistaken for a tall, muscular human of indeterminate sex. It had the curved hips of a woman, and the broad shoulders and powerful arms of a man. However, there was nothing between its legs but a plane of featureless, gray skin, and its torso opened into a hollow, vase-like cavity just above the abdomen.

Thin flaps of its stoney skin, almost like lapels and a high-necked collar, curved around the opening where the neck and head should have been. Instead, a tangle of black vines—or veins, maybe—rose up out of the hollow chest cavity, and blossomed into some sort of red flower, its petals waving in a non-existent wind. Anya had seen that particular type of flower before in a shop, and been intrigued enough by it to ask the owner. It was a giant red lycoris, also known as a red spider lily.

Above the blossoming flower's blood red, arachnid-like petals, a sphere of perfect, complete darkness floated.

Anya was instantly reminded of what Arvo had said when he described touching the mind of the snake overseer weeks before, and when Esmeralda had felt the psychic presence of the centipede.

Not a passive absence of something, but an active presence of nothing.

As Anya stared at the black sphere, a thin white line appeared across its middle, then split and opened into twin rows of sharp, triangular teeth.

"What the fuck are you?" Anya whispered.

"The Herald of something greater. Better than you. Thieves. To come here? Foolish. You have taken from us, now we will take from you. But only what is ours. All of it. Ours. You have merely stolen. But we will consume. All of it. Ours," the thing said.

Anya recognized the voice from the snake, the centipede, and from Alpha. This thing had spoken through all of them. As she looked at how the entire gnosiphage swarm had frozen and allowed this creature's passage, she realized it *was* them. From the killer puppet in Brooklyn to Alien Alpha, to every single creature on this asteroid that wasn't her and Renn: this thing was all of them, to greater or lesser degrees.

"Fuck off," Anya said, and lunged at it. The thing grinned at her, the wide mouth in that black sphere stretching wider as it held up a hand. Her fist halted inches away from its chest, and her whole body behind it.

"You steal, but do not understand," the thing said. Its mouth opened wide, and a pale blue light shone from the back of it. It was similar to the blue light the other overseers had emitted, but also not. It was *more* somehow. More of something. Nothing good.

It pulled at Anya's gaze, forcing her to lock into it.

Anya had been waiting for a moment to try out her new skills, and figured this was it. Do or die. Anya focused, and unleashed her war form.

———

AFTER THINKING about Renn's offer the previous night, Anya thought at first that having a little clone army of herself that she could command would be cool. But after hearing Felix describe the skill, she learned that each of her clones would only be at a fraction of her power, and ditto for all her gear and enhancements. Renn had gotten around this weakness with hive mind and leveling the skill up a lot, and buying specific gear.

Anya couldn't do that.

No clone army for her.

But she really only wanted the clones to beat up on stuff with her, to multiply her power. After speaking with Felix for hours and going through the skills, she found two more that suited her.

Form duplication.

The skill was designed to duplicate the body of the user, to a lesser degree. It would create a semi-corporeal phantom, the solidity of which was determined by skill level, along with how far the user could project the duplicate, and how many of them they could create.

Felix had informed her that it was actually a weaker skill overall than Renn's ability. Anya had asked the AI some very specific questions, which he had answered, and then grinned right along with her as she told him what she wanted.

"Yeah, I think you could definitely do all of that with form duplication," Felix had said. "Do you want to confirm your skill choice?"

"Oh yeah," Anya had replied around a wide grin.

———

FIFTEEN POINTS in form duplication was enough to make two or three mostly solid versions of Anya that functioned at about a third of her total power, and could move within a few hundred yards.

But Anya had decided she didn't want full duplicates of herself.

She just wanted arms.

A shitload of arms.

And more Sun's Hearts.

And Singularity's Grasps.

Eight glowing, radiant arms blossomed from Anya's back and shoulders, four on each side. Each one enhanced by the Flesh of the Starforge, by the Light Dominion, and each pair with a phantom Sun's Heart at the bottom of their shoulders, fueling them.

"C'est quoi ce bordel?" Renn said behind her.

The Herald seemed rather taken aback by this development as well.

Then Anya punched it with all eight of her radiant arms—and both of her real ones—right in its weird, creepy mouth.

She'd loaded an explosive, gravity-condensed marble of shuddering fire and force and light inside the hand of each closed fist, and released that pent-up energy on impact. The resulting explosion was so immense that it blew Anya away from the Herald, and the Herald into space, and sent all the gnosiphages behind the Herald scattering like bowling pins. The first several rows of aliens were mostly incinerated on contact with the shockwave, while those behind them were crushed, or blown apart by the magnitude of the multiple blasts.

The rest of them had gone into some sort of turmoil when the Herald had been struck, mindlessly squirming around and flailing their assorted limbs.

Renn held onto the device, white coat fluttering around him as he was nearly blown away from the backsplash of Anya's attack. She turned to face him, bathing him in golden light. She couldn't see his face, but she'd have been willing to bet that usual sleepy expression of his was long gone.

"Hold them off as long as you can, then get clear," Anya said as she approached Renn and pressed a recessed switch on the side of the device. A smaller cylinder ejected itself, about as big as a beer keg. A glass cylinder rested in its center, and contained a trembling, blinding white ball of anti-matter.

"What are you—" Renn began.

"We don't have time. That thing's going to come back, the aliens are going to regroup, and we're going to lose. Unless I take this down the hole now, and set it off like Gary showed me. Got it?"

Renn continued to stare at her in silence for a heartbeat, then nodded his helmeted head.

"I understand. I will cover your back as long as I am able. Go. *Bonne chance.*"

Anya gripped the device's explosive central core, and then soared down the long tunnel it had made. She let out a breath as the opening shrank behind her and she sped, faster and faster, down the tunnel.

She drew on her Shard of the Everstar, draining it within seconds.

Her war form was formidable, but it taxed her. Duplicating her Sun's Heart and Singularity's Grasp didn't require as much energy as it might have without Light Dominion and energy focus, but it was still a lot.

The trade off was worth it, however: she could put out unreal amounts of damage for comparatively little investment... for a little while. Her form duplication skill was low, but since she was only focusing on parts of her form and not the whole thing, and since she was only creating them literally on top of herself, she got maximum value out of what she did have. Energy focus also helped to ensure that each of her duplicated Artifacts—Sun's Heart and Singularity's Grasp—operated at maximum efficiency despite being only a fraction as powerful as the originals.

It was Anya's first (and probably only) time using the move, but she knew the fallout would be steep. Like Renn's *Grande Armée*, she suspected she would crash hard. But that didn't really matter.

She just needed to make it another few minutes.

Something howled behind her, a nightmare chorus welling up from a thousand inhuman throats, baying for her blood.

"Come and get it!" she shouted over her shoulder, and she sped further down, powering her flight with her duplicated Artifacts and becoming a golden, radiant meteor within the asteroid itself. She would shatter it before it ever got close to her friends.

After another few moments, the branching tunnels narrowed, and Anya was forced to stop. She had no idea how deep into the asteroid she was. Miles and miles. It was pitch black, but for the light Anya herself emitted.

And the howling was closer.

Anya opened a series of latches, flicked a pair of switches. Gary had labeled them all, just for her, nice and easy to read in case she had to be the one to throw the switch. The final activation button was behind a small metal panel that Anya lifted. The big red button would release the antimatter within, and activate the device's final function.

But Anya did not look down at the big red button, nor up as the sounds of howls and mad slavering grew ever-closer. Gary had written something on the underside of the panel in thick, dark letters.

PROUD OF YOU.

Anya laughed, starting to cry as she did, then wiped at her eyes.

"Could've told me before I left, you old fart," she said, and pressed the button. The antimatter trembled within the cylinder as it began to crack its housing.

The Herald appeared at the edge of Anya's light, along with the horde behind it. Anya stood in front of the device. She only had to wait a few more seconds.

"Come on!" she roared.

The Herald fired a dark beam of energy at her, slicing two of her radiant arms away. Anya blasted the aliens that closed to melee range, incinerating them and using the close confines of the tunnel to her advantage. She filled the narrow space with furious golden flames, walls of crushing gravity, and the unrelenting hail of her fists as she destroyed the gnosiphage army that had been stupid enough to fight her down here.

She closed distance with the Herald, even as it flipped the space around in the tunnel, sending her and several of the other aliens tumbling and slamming into walls. It opened its mouth once more, the somehow hungry blue light within glowing brighter. Something deep in Anya's guts told her that was nothing she wanted a part of, and used all of her radiant hands to grab the void of nothing at the top of the Herald, and force its mouth shut.

Something pierced her then.

Something cold.

Anya looked down, and saw that the Herald had crafted a sort of dagger out of the same blackness as its circular head, and stabbed her with it. Through her Regalia of St. Llothec, through her sacred orichalcum chestplate, through her flesh of the Starforge, her ribs, and finally through both of her hearts.

"Ours," the Herald said as Anya's grip on its head weakened, and withdrew the dagger.

Anya slumped backward, her radiant arms flickering, dimming.

What you have now is a battery, but a Sun's Heart is a doorway, the bird had said.

"No," Anya said as blood welled up out of her mouth. "Mine."

She moved all her arms—radiant as well as flesh and blood— toward her chest. Something beat there, strong, primal. Not just her heart, or her Sun's Heart. Was it a beating? Or a knocking? She couldn't tell. It was insistent, whatever it was. Her fingers touched something near her hearts. It was warm, comforting, but there was fury behind it too.

Behind her, the device beeped, and the antimatter burst free from its casing.

Within her, Anya opened the doorway.

Before her, the Herald and the nightmare tide of gnosiphages howled.

There was light, and heat, and inexorable force.

And then there was nothing at all.

38

ary sat in his armchair in the hub, at the center of his factory, miles below the surface of Antarctica. On a normal day, the hub would have been filled with floating screens showing input-output ratios, power readings, security feeds, and more. A flood of data coursed through the hub at any given second: from the factories around it, to the oceans around the frozen continent, to news feeds across the planet, to the mining droids out in deep space.

On a normal day.

Not today.

Only one screen floated in front of Gary, and the information it gave was sparse. Four words.

FINAL DEVICE PROTOCOL ACTIVATED

Gary was currently able to process flows of information that would have been impossible for a normal human, and even most other hosts. But those four words had drawn his focus for a while now.

Final device protocol activated.

It had worked, at least in some capacity. The delay between whatever events happened deep in space, and the time it took that information to reach Earth was measured in hours. Gary should have been doing something else. There was plenty of work to be done—preparations to the outer and inner defensive lines to be made—and limited time to do it all in.

But he couldn't focus.

He couldn't think of anything else except those four words.

Final device protocol activated.

Maybe he hadn't protected the ship well enough.

Maybe he hadn't made the explosives in the device strong enough.

Maybe he had made them too strong.

Maybe.

Maybe.

Maybe.

The word repeated itself a thousand times against his skull, and new possible outcomes for every time it did. Most of them were bad. A few were good. However, Gary avoided hoping about the latter too much.

Hope was a dangerous thing. He'd learned how much it could sting when he'd been in Cambodia. Hoping all your buddies made it back from patrol. Hoping you didn't have to shoot at anybody. Hoping for sleep without nightmares.

Time and Mary becoming his wife had healed those wounds, but then her cancer had come. Gary had been stupid enough to hope again, to hope she would be okay and the doctors could help her, and it had stung him all the worse for it.

When the invasion had started, it felt like hope wasn't necessary. The Archive made it irrelevant. He could build the solution to any problem, given enough time. He just needed to stay focused, build his factory, and expand as needed.

Then Samaira had started to grow on him, and Pan, and the doc, and even those stinking bureaucrats at the DERD, Riley and MacDougal. They were still government toadies, but they weren't all bad.

And the kid.

Gary had a lot of things he wanted to say before she had taken off, but he had kept his mouth shut. He knew Anya didn't have much family to speak of, and he had even less.

Gary recalled a summer years ago, before Mary had gotten sick, before it became clear they'd never have children of their own.

Summer of '87. He and Mary had been sitting several rows behind home plate of Wrigley Field, cheering for the Cubbies like any good son and daughter of Chicago should.

"What if our kids aren't Cubs fans?" Mary had asked.

"We'll love 'em anyway. Unless they root for the Yankees," Gary had said and Mary had laughed at that. She'd had a good laugh: loud and assured, uncaring of who might be disturbed by her mirth.

"We'll just bring them here early. Cubs fans from birth."

"Never too young for baseball," he had said, and squeezed Mary's hand. The sky had been so blue, the grass so green; war and death and cancer, so distant.

But it hadn't worked out.

He'd hoped it would, but that had just been one more sting. After losing Mary, after losing their house, Gary thought he'd finally at last become immune to that particular optimistic toxin.

But Anya was a good kid.

She brought people together, like Mary.

And she could also tell somebody to go fuck themselves, like him.

He had never been the best with words. They felt awkward in his mouth, like he were suddenly gargling rocks.

Before Anya had left, he had been thinking about seeing if she wanted to go spend a day at Wrigley Field, once the weather had warmed and things had calmed down. An afternoon watching the Cubbies sounded pretty nice. Pan, Sam, Tori, and the doc could come. Maybe Riley too, if he didn't say a word about the Red Sox. The kid would probably eat every hot dog in the stadium.

That'd be okay.

That'd be pretty damn near perfect, honestly.

But for now, all he had was the screen in front of him, and its useless, maddening words.

And hope.

———

GARY HAD FINALLY FORCED himself into one of his labs after another hour of waiting and driving himself crazy. The news from around the world was chaotic, following the announcements from several world governments about the asteroid. Riots had broken out almost everywhere, but things had become eerily calm in the last few days as the planet held its breath. It only reminded Gary of his own anxiety, and he switched the news feeds off. He was still distracted, still gnawing away at the maybes and what-ifs, but he needed to at least try and do something.

Their first line of defense was a series of large mobile artillery arrays that floated about a hundred thousand miles past the moon's orbit. Those were the big guns, and Gary and Vastukar had managed to make five of them. What they lacked in the diverse capabilities of the devices they had sent with Anya and Renn, they made up for in raw firepower. Aetheric conversion cells had been loaded into each array, and they would pull in aetheric current from space when they got the signal from Earth. After that, they'd fire aether-reinforced anti-matter warheads at whatever targets Gary and Vastukar selected, or anything big enough to be considered a threat if they needed to rely on automated systems.

The secondary line of defense was a swarm of millions of drones that would deploy in a vast ring between Earth and the moon. Vastukar had programmed the drones with the gnosiphage signals, and they would hone in when they detected it, up to a distance of several thousand miles. When they picked up on a signal, they'd fly toward it and release a seismic charge strong enough to shatter stone. It would certainly kill aliens, and at the very least, weaken the integrity of any asteroid chunks they still rode on.

Thanks to the all-in efforts of pretty much every country on the planet, Gary and Vastukar had a massive influx of raw materials to work with. This meant that they could repurpose their mining droids for their penultimate line of asteroid defense.

Vastukar's overloaded mining laser—the one that had pierced Alien Alpha's belly and allowed Gary's antimatter missile into its guts —had been a one-shot. That wouldn't work against the asteroid fragments.

Gary had helped Vastukar redesign his mining laser to channel more energy without overloading, and Vastukar had shown him how the droids could be more mobile. The makeshift attack droids would target the chunks, prioritizing the largest first, and then on downward to anything that was too big to burn up in the atmosphere on its own.

If there was anything left of the asteroid after that, America and every other country that had nuclear warheads was firing them into the sky. Gary would do the same with his remaining anti-matter bombs, of which there were still a few.

After that, It would be down to the gnosiphages themselves, however many survived and made it to Earth. The hosts would hunt them down and crush every last one, assuming they weren't vastly outnumbered.

After three defensive lines of apocalyptic firepower, they shouldn't be.

But it was still an awful lot of gnosiphages.

All of this was assuming the asteroid had suffered at least some damage. To avoid any impact whatsoever, Gary and Vastukar estimated the asteroid needed to be down to at least 40% integrity. Anything higher than that, and they'd be in trouble. Anything higher than 80%, and Earth might not make it.

Vastukar said he had an ace up his sleeve, but refused to reveal what it was unless the asteroid approached the secondary defensive perimeter at 80% integrity or higher. He'd hinted that New Bengaluru —and maybe much of India—would be lost as a result, but the planet and humanity would survive.

Gary had been more up-front with his weapon of last resort: hijacking every power grid on the planet and overclocking his factory to power a blast of energy from a makeshift cannon. He had the plans, and if the asteroid was above their optimal threshold by the time it reached the secondary defensive perimeter, he'd have just enough time to build it and fire one shot.

A significant chunk of Antarctica would be melted, the whole planet would lose power for an indeterminate amount of time, and a lot of people would suffer. His factory would be a smoking ruin as well. But there was a good chance the asteroid would fracture and split, and the planet would carry on, eventually.

Not an ideal scenario, but better than absolute extinction.

Gary busied himself with studying the defensive perimeters and making adjustments on the display screens as needed. The drones in the secondary perimeter could have better placement. The artillery arrays in the first perimeter could have their targeting algorithms adjusted. He could probably adjust factory output to squeeze out a few hundred more mining and attack droids if he diverted power for a few hours to—

A flashing light on a console across the lab caught his eye.

Updates had arrived from space.

"Show me," he said. A screen appeared in front of him, and displayed what was left of the asteroid. The asteroid had a shattered look to it, and it was obvious pieces were missing, but most of it was still held together. Though as Gary continued to stare, it became obvious that it was by unnatural means.

ASTEROID MASS: 65%

ASTEROID INTEGRITY: 35%

ENERGY ANOMALY DETECTED: SPIKING MAGNETIC AND GRAVITATIONAL FLUCTUATIONS.

GNOSIPHAGE POPULATION: 242,094 UNIQUE SIGNALS DETECTED

HUMAN LIFE SIGNS DETECTED: 0

The asteroid was broken to hell, and cracks in its surface ran the length of the shattered remains. The devices had worked. It should have been in at least a hundred smaller fragments, but most of it was still clinging together.

"Bastards," Gary muttered. His gaze strayed to the "Human life signs," readout and he clenched his fists.

It didn't mean anything bad. Their ship could have been blown behind the asteroid. Or temporarily disabled and floated off in space. If the asteroid were between Earth and the ship, it could be interfering with the scans. After all, Anya and Renn weren't supposed to stay with the asteroid, they were supposed to get the hell away and come back ASAP.

Gary's ear beeped, and a communication window from the Archive opened in front of him. Vastukar looked back at him from in his own lab, several white-clad technicians and silvery drones in the background.

"Seen the latest?" Gary asked.

"Of course," Vastukar said. "What do you think?"

"That energy anomaly, whatever the hell it is, is holding the thing together. Barely."

"But still together. The integrity rating does not appear to be accounting for the magnetic and gravitational power holding it. We can't be certain how stable it actually is."

"Still better than what we were dealing with yesterday. And it doesn't change the plan. It'll be in range of the first perimeter artillery in another day or so. Thirty hours, tops," Gary said as he checked the clock nearby.

"I will check in when we have a better estimate," Vastukar said, paused, then added, "I'm sorry we don't have news about Anya and Renn."

Gary shrugged.

"Let me know if you need anything else," he said, then shut the communication window, and returned to work.

———

DESPITE GARY'S PERSISTENT HOPE, the drones monitoring the asteroid's progress failed to deliver any news of human life. All updates were solely about the asteroid itself. However, the news there was an improvement.

Progress reports came in regularly, and over the course of the day, it was clear that the asteroid was degrading. Its mass and integrity dropped a little every hour or so. By the next morning, it was down to 52% mass and 29% integrity. Whatever force was holding it together was faltering.

It would still obliterate all life on Earth if it hit, in its current state, but that was looking less and less likely by the minute. The defensive perimeters would—probably—be more than a match for it.

Gary had thrown himself into his work over the last twenty-four hours, tweaking and fiddling with everything he could, from the planetary defense systems to the food replicator in the dining area.

Pan had broken the latter.

He, Arvo, and Samaira had shown up at the lab earlier. They'd brought Riley, Tori, and MacDougal with them. Normally Gary wouldn't have been thrilled to see MacDougal, and considered telling her to take a hike, but he had bigger concerns.

Besides, she was there representing not just America, but the rest of the United Planetary Response Cooperative. So, basically the entire planet, minus the New Allied Territories.

Gary had told them all to wait in the dining hall until he had updates to report, and left it at that. At least, up until Pan broke the replicator by trying to make it produce ants.

"You said it makes any food! Ants are food!" Pan insisted as Gary sat in front of the disassembled replicator, trying to clean out the mess.

"Ants are also alive. You gotta be specific," Gary grumbled.

"Why would I be the ocean?"

"Specific. Not Pacific."

"Words are stupid sometimes."

Gary sighed. "If I want food, I don't order a cow. I order a steak. Or a hamburger. Or just beef. It's not your fault, little guy. I just didn't account for non-human dietary requirements."

"That's okay," Pan said and patted Gary on the shoulder.

"Pan?" Tori asked from across the hall. "Let Gary work for a bit. Come talk to me?"

"What about?"

"Uh, what kinds of rock are the most fun to dig through?"

"Oh! Okay!"

Gary shook his head and grumbled to himself, then glanced up when Samaira came over, Chandrali purring in her arms.

"This is sweet of you and all, but we don't need this particular replicator right now if you're busy," she said.

"Might as well. Nothing else to do," Gary said, and smirked when Samaira raised her eyebrows at him. "I'm serious. All defensive construction has been completed, automated, or is on-hold until we get a significant update. I'm just spinning my wheels, otherwise."

"Have you slept recently, Gary?"

He grunted.

"I'll take that as a no," she said.

"Have you?"

"Not really. Not much before, and less since you told me about… about when the device was activated. Still no news on that front?"

"You'd be the first one I'd tell if there was. No sign of her, Renn, or the ship."

Samaira took a deep breath.

"Can I help with this thing any?" she asked and looked at the complex innards of the replicator.

"Maybe. You know much about carbon-paste conversion trays?"

"I do not."

"Well then hand me those wire clippers with the blue handles, and talk to me about something that doesn't involve aliens or asteroids while I finish up here."

Samaira gave him a smile, passed him the clippers, and began to tell him about recipes he should include in the repaired replicator.

Gary had just finished the replicator, including a few recipes for ant matter (what Samaira called "ant-y matter," to the groans of everyone assembled, save for Pan, who didn't get it), when a notification chimed over the dining hall's speakers, followed by an automated voice.

"Attention: asteroid approaching outer range of primary defensive perimeter artillery," the voice said.

"Aliens!" Pan quailed, and hid behind Tori.

"It's okay, buddy. They won't be here for a couple more days. Right?" she asked and looked at Gary.

"At their current rate of speed, yeah," he replied.

"What about Anya?" Pan asked.

Nobody answered for a while, until Samaira spoke up.

"She'll be here."

"Sam," Gary whispered, but stopped himself before he said anything else. What the hell was he going to say? Don't lie? Don't get your hopes up? She was young, and cared for Anya in a way he could never. If it had been Mary up there, and some old fool told him to tone it down, he'd sock them in the mouth.

Samaira turned to look at him and said, just loud enough so only Gary could make it out, "She'll be here."

His smile didn't quite reach his eyes, and he looked away as he began to clean up his tools and head back for the hub.

MacDougal and Riley followed him. The director's mouth thinned into a tight crease as she stared out at the factory as they sped by. Gary caught her eye and the two studied each other in silence, Riley between them.

"So, how about them Red Sox?" he said, and both Gary and MacDougal glared at him. "Yeesh, tough crowd."

"There's a world ending threat on our doorstep," MacDougal said and looked from Riley to back out at the factory. "So for now, I won't push. But we're gonna need to talk about all of this once we get a breather."

"If this is about Hanover wanting lasers and anti-matter bombs—" Gary started before MacDougal shook her head.

"Hanover can go to hell," MacDougal said, and Riley and Gary both blinked at her in surprise. "But he's not wrong to be worried about a man at the bottom of the world with a factory that makes killer robots and anti-matter bombs."

She paused for a moment, then continued, "You know, I haven't always been the director of the DERD or the FBI. It took me a long time to get where I'm at, and during that time, you know what I learned?"

"Do tell," Gary said.

"I learned that it's real easy for people with power to lose perspective. Their intentions might be good, their goals may be noble, but the more power somebody gets, the more their view of things starts to shift.

"You, Nowicki, Vastukar, all of you, have more power than anybody else on this rock. Power enough to change the way the world works forever. If you're smart, that should make you nervous. And I think it does, which is why you moved down here to the ass-end of nowhere."

Gary didn't respond.

"If we survive the next week, we need to talk. All I'm saying."

"And you'll want what in return? More goodies for the DERD?"

"The same thing I told Nowicki I wanted from her: a chance. I know you've been through the wringer, Hendricks. But if we all just go off on our own, nothing's going to change. It's just gonna be new people running the same show, doing the same shit."

Gary grunted.

"The kid seems to think you're all right. Once things settle down... we'll talk. Only 'cause you said Hanover can go to hell, though."

MacDougal's posture relaxed a fraction, and her lips twitched in what might have been a smile.

"Happy to hear it," she said as the tram pulled to a stop. She turned to Riley and muttered, "You heard none of that."

"Hey, I mentioned the Red Sox, and then Hendricks gave me the hairy eyeball for the rest of the ride," Riley said.

"You got a real career in politics, Riley," Gary said as he led the others off the tram.

"Thank you."

"Not a compliment."

Gary entered the hub and sat in his recliner, MacDougal and Riley flanking him. As soon as he was settled, a thousand holographic screens sprang to life around him. All of the screens showed different views of the asteroid, space, and five different satellites.

The satellites each consisted of a wide circular platform that had something like a gigantic snail-shell sticking up out of the middle. A long, slender stick that could only be the main cannon extended from the shell, its significant length bristling with thorn-like antennae.

It was all constructed of silvery metal and what appeared to be glass, but was actually artificially constructed diamond panes. Glowing blue power lines extended from the back of the central shell, and conduits and lights along the whole satellite began to flash and pulse with energy.

"Those the big guns?" MacDougal asked.

"Yup. Each one's about the size of cargo freighter. Looks like the asteroid'll be in firing range in another six minutes," Gary replied. "At the current rate of speed, each platform will have time to fire two to three shots each, before the asteroid passes."

"And then what?" Riley asked. "Shoot it from behind?"

"No. Neither me or Vastukar wanted those things pointed at Earth. Any chance at missing a shot or something else happening was unacceptable to both of us. Once the asteroid gets close enough, they'll start to converge on its location, then self-destruct. Assuming the aliens don't blow them up first."

"That's a relief. But you could just make something like this again, couldn't you?" MacDougal said.

"By myself? Yeah. Not as good, but yes. These things had me, Vastukar, Samaira, that mecha pilot from Brazil, and a bunch of lab techs working on it. Not easy to recreate."

MacDougal let out a sigh, but said nothing. The hub was quiet as the minutes ticked by, and then the largest screen switched to focus on one of the satellites.

"Firing the first volley," Gary said. The satellite on the main screen began to glow even brighter, and bright blue lines of energy appeared to be sucked into the end of the protruding cannon. A ball of light appeared at the tip, then rapidly expanded as something fired outward in a brilliant, lethal flash. Rockets along the sides of the platform fired to stabilize it, and the humming energy running along its surface dimmed.

Silence filled the hub for several seconds before Riley asked, "Well? Did it hit?"

"Target's still several thousand miles away. Gotta give it a minute," Gary replied.

The other satellites fired within seconds of the first. After what felt like a small eternity but was only about eighty seconds, the image on the main screen switched to show the asteroid. The view was from far away, but much closer than the satellites. The asteroid filled about half the screen, fragmented and unstable. A hair-thin, glowing blue line appeared on the edge of the screen, then struck the side of the asteroid. There was another flash of light, and then a bluish-white sphere of radiance blossomed on one side of the asteroid, and was soon joined by four others.

"Direct hits," Gary said and his shoulders relaxed a fraction. The light from the explosions faded, and he allowed himself a grin.

"Holy shit! That's good, right! Is that good?" Riley asked.

A third of the asteroid was just gone. It was like something had taken giant, cartoonish bites out of it. What remained wasn't even in a single piece. The force that had been holding it together had weakened even further, and now the asteroid was a collection of random chunks barely maintaining a basic formation around each other.

"Looks damn good to me," MacDougal replied.

"Recharging, preparing second volley," Gary said, and felt that old, familiar swell of hope somewhere between his heart and his stomach. They might be able to settle this now. If they could get off two more shots, plus the self-destruct operation, that could wipe the asteroid out.

A screen appeared, flashing a message in bold red letters.

INCOMING PROJECTILE

"Shit," Gary said and began tapping on a nearby display. One of the artillery satellites had detected an approaching mass and was using its repositioning rockets to avoid it. But whatever was hurtling forward curved along its trajectory, tracking it.

A fragment of the asteroid sped towards the satellite with unnatural speed, and intercepted it as it tried to move. There was no sound, but Gary could almost feel the vibrations of the smaller meteor crashing into the satellite. The cameras showed a shockwave of bright energy, shrapnel, and ore as the cannon exploded.

Gary's ear beeped.

"Vastukar," he said as the other host appeared in a screen beside him.

"One down," Vastukar said. "Did you see what did it?"

"My guess would be the big fucking rock."

"On the back of it. Some kind of gnosiphage had modified itself to act as an organic propulsion and guidance system."

"They can do that?" Riley asked.

"If they have enough time, they can shift themselves into whatever they need. Judging by the size of the meteor that hit the weapons platform, I'd say it was one of the bigger aliens. Possibly Alpha-sized," Vastukar said. "The only good news is that it vaporized itself in the process."

"More incoming," Gary grumbled. "I'm prioritizing a second

volley. They'll overheat, probably explode afterwards, but I don't think we'll get a second shot otherwise."

"Agreed," Vastukar responded. "I'll take platforms one and three. You handle four and five."

"On it," Gary said as a swarm of new holographic screens appeared around him and he began tapping on all of them with inhuman alacrity.

Another screen appeared above the others.

INCOMING PROJECTILE

"Firing platform five," Gary said and pressed a final button. The cannon on the main screen unleashed another blast, the glowing conduit lines bursting and the platform exploding as it did. Another alien-propelled meteor streaked forward, and was obliterated by the blast.

"Firing platform three," Vastukar said, and another screen showed a similar result.

"Firing pl—dammit!" Gary snapped as platform four was destroyed, followed a moment later by the single remaining cannon.

"All weapons platforms destroyed," Vastukar said.

"Shit," Gary scowled and thumped his fist against the arm of his chair.

"Less than ideal. But still, progress. Look," Vastukar said, and the main screen of the hub switched again to focus on the asteroid. They'd managed to fire another pair of shots, and the damage—while not as extensive as Gary would have liked—was significant.

20% mass and 19% integrity. The camera drones Gary had focusing on the asteroid zoomed in. It was an uneven clump of what looked like loose rocks now. There were occasional flashes of something like lightning that crackled between the disparate segments, and drew them together.

"Is that still big enough to wipe out all life on Earth?" MacDougal asked.

"Oh yeah. Still about 400 miles across. But at that integrity? Pieces of it are already falling off," Gary said.

"We still have the secondary and tertiary defensive perimeters," Vastukar said. "This isn't over."

"No. Not yet," Gary said and allowed himself to relax a fraction. At the current mass and integrity, they wouldn't need to fire their weapons of last resort. The artillery platforms had done their job.

But that was only because the devices with Anya and Renn had done most of the heavy work already. If the devices hadn't gone off, the artilleries would've done little more than scratch the damn thing's surface.

They had a real chance of stopping it now. Not just of mitigating damage, but maybe—if they were lucky—avoiding it entirely.

You did good, kid, Gary thought. *We can do the rest. Just please, please come back.*

39

Pan did not entirely understand what was going on.

This was nothing new for him.

Well, it was still relatively new, given that he had only been sapient since earlier that year. However, once he had gotten used to understanding some things, he also became accustomed to not understanding most things, and felt this was an improvement from not understanding anything.

Before, Pan had only understood digging, ants, and curling in a ball if he was scared. Now he understood things like New York City, and ant farms, and the DERD, and pants, and the Earth Dominion, and more every day.

Best of all, he understood friends.

Worst of all, he understood fear.

Friends were great. When he thought of Anya, or Samaira, Brody, Ursula, Riley, Gary, Tori, and others, he was happy. Happiness was something that was still new to him, and he hoped it never got boring. It was a warm sensation in his tummy, and it made him want to stand up and hug somebody.

Fear was not so great. Fear was pretty terrible, actually. It made his tummy tight, and it made him want to curl into a ball and hide, to run, to do anything he had to to get away from that feeling.

Fear had been some shapeless, muffled feeling before the Archive: his basic animal brain telling him to hide and not move. But since the Archive had come, the feeling had become sharper. Before, it had only been an insistent tapping; now it could cut. Sometimes it felt like it would cut right through him.

Pan had only ever been able to help in fights so far because his skills let him hide. He burrowed into the earth, and let his golems do the really scary stuff. That was easy. But it sounded like with all the aliens coming, he might not be able to just hide anymore.

Gary had said that the ass-tur-oid (big rock) had been mostly destroyed. Sometime later, he came back and said that the second defensive perimeter (Or parameter? Pear eater? Words were silly) had been breached.

"Its integrity has stabilized as a result of the magnetic and gravitational forces pulling the pieces back together, but its mass has continued to erode significantly. Whatever's holding it together is slowly failing," Gary said in the dining area. He sat at a table with Pan, Samaira and Chandrali, MacDougal, and Tori. Pan didn't understand all of Gary's words, but he got the impression that the big rock was less big than it had been before.

"And how's the secondary perimeter affecting it?" MacDougal asked.

"Too soon to say, but initial contact reports are showing some promise. The seismic disruptors are breaking off larger and larger chunks the more the asteroid passes through the defensive line. Any stray meteorites that have broken away have been cracked to gravel."

"That's good, right? Good stuff?" Pan asked.

"Very good stuff," Samaira said and patted him on the back. Her cat sat in her lap, making that happy rumbling noise. Samaira called it "purring." Pan had tried it when he had been happy, but he'd just coughed up an ant. However, that meant he got to eat an ant again, and he'd been even happier.

"No aliens?" he asked. The humans all looked at each other with some expressions Pan couldn't quite understand. Words were hard, but sometimes humans said things with their faces without even speaking, and that was even harder. People being happy, angry, or sad was easy to see. Anything other than that, and Pan got confused.

"There's probably going to be some aliens that make it through. And they're probably going to be tough," Gary said.

"Tougher than Alpha?"

"Maybe. We're scanning for any big ones, and prioritizing them as targets before they get to Earth. But some may make it anyway. Also… they're probably going to come here, and to New Bengaluru."

"Here?" Pan squealed. "Why?"

"The aliens are pretty smart. They likely know about Gary's factory, and that it's a threat to them. Same for New Bengaluru. It's why they attacked it back in February. They're what we would call priority targets," MacDougal said.

"We should leave!" Pan said and tugged on Samaira's sleeve. She smiled at him, but it didn't look happy.

"We can't. If too many aliens make it to Earth, we'll need Gary's factory and Vastukar's facilities to help us track them down and get rid of them. There's still a lot more aliens than there are hosts like us," she said.

"Don't worry too much, little guy. This place is as safe as it can be. I got lots of surprises the aliens won't like," Gary said. "Plus, some friends will be stopping by later tomorrow."

"Okay," Pan said and twiddled his claws together as he sat back down. Friends sounded nice, and Gary and Samaira were both smart. He hoped the friends Gary mentioned included Anya. She'd had to leave for reasons he didn't really get, but he didn't want to ask Gary and the others about her. Whenever he did, they got sad.

"I'm going to the hub to keep an eye on things," Gary said as he stood up. MacDougal went with him, but Tori, Samaira, and Chandrali stayed behind.

"What if all the aliens make it through?" he asked.

"We'll figure it out," Samaira said.

"And we'll make sure to keep you safe," Tori added. Pan nodded, but that was another thing he'd understood since he'd gotten the

Archive. You could be afraid for other people, too. And in a lot of ways, that was much worse.

———

THE LAST NEWS Pan heard about the asteroid before bed was that it had cleared the secondary defensive line, but was badly damaged. Much smaller. Less aliens to worry about.

But it was still coming, still a problem. Maybe it could still kill a lot of people. Even if the asteroid went away for good, the aliens could still survive and get to Earth again.

All the worrying throughout the day had given Pan a headache, and he went to bed early that night. He didn't want to think about aliens, or asteroids, or how many people were in danger. Especially not Anya.

He just wanted to sleep, and rest, and maybe he could just sleep through the whole thing. That would be really nice.

No sooner had Pan closed his eyes and drifted away, than he opened them again and saw he was somewhere else. It was a huge cavern, filled with all sorts of rocks, glowing crystals, glittering minerals, and even funny mushrooms that glowed just like the crystals. Tunnels stretched away in different directions, so far that they faded away with the distance of it.

It was cozy, being in this cavern. The air was warm and thick, like a soft blanket. Sometimes the cavern rumbled, but it wasn't scary. It made Pan think of Chandrali purring. A happy sound.

Pan had been here a couple times before, always in his sleep.

The Earth Dominion.

"HELLO, PEBBLE," a voice boomed from all around Pan. A section of the ground rose up beside him and formed itself into a creature. Though Pan had never seen one in-person before, his English skill told him that this thing before him was a turtle. This particular turtle had a shell made of gray stone, and a tree sprouted from the top of it. Its head and legs were made of pale green stone, and its eyes were sparkling emeralds.

The last time Pan had been here, it had been small, only about half as big as Pan himself. But it had grown since then, and now loomed over Pan.

"Hello, turtle! You got bigger!"

"YUP. THE VOLCANO WAS FUN. AND YOU DID IT, EVEN THOUGH YOU WERE SCARED," the turtle replied. Even though Pan saw the turtle's mouth moving, the voice—a little slow and ponderous —seemed to echo from the walls themselves.

"I wasn't too scared since Anya was there. And it wasn't really fighting. Mostly just pushing dirt and stuff around."

"I THINK MAYBE YOU WON'T HAVE IT SO EASY, IN THE NEXT FIGHT."

"Yeah," Pan said and looked down at his clawed toes. "I'm really worried."

"WHAT ABOUT?"

"That my friends will get hurt. That I'll get hurt. That the aliens will win."

"AND SO? WHAT'LL YOU DO?"

Pan shook his head.

"I wanna help, but it—it's scary! Before, I could just hide and let my golems and Anya and the others do everything. Even with the volcano, I just had to dig! But now Gary and Sam and other people say there might be a bunch of aliens. Lots! So many that I might have to really fight. And I don't know if I can."

"WHAT'S WORSE? FEAR OF FIGHTING? OR FEAR OF LEAVING GARY? SAM? ANYA?"

"I don't want to fight… but I don't want to leave the others more."

"GOOD. EARTH DOESN'T RUN. STAY. PROTECT. DON'T LET THE MONSTERS MOVE YOU. I'LL BE THERE WHEN THE FIGHTING STARTS."

"Thank you. You're a good turtle."

"AND YOU'RE A GOOD PEBBLE. NOW REST HERE, TONIGHT. AND BE READY."

Pan curled up beside the turtle as it settled over him, the branches of its tree swaying above. He closed his eyes and decided that while he might be afraid, he was done hiding.

———

4% mass and 10% integrity.

"We're going to make it," Samaira said as she stood in a large assembly room next to Gary. The room was little else but a big empty cube of space that some droids had set up tables and chairs in at the last minute.

The latest defensive perimeter had been breached last night, while Samaira had been asleep. It had mostly been small chunks of debris ahead of the main asteroid that set off the alarms, plus a few scout aliens.

Samaira had joined Gary in the hub, then moved to the larger assembly room as others awoke and came to see what the commotion was. Hours had passed, but the main asteroid—or what remained of it —had finally reached the outer edge of the defensive perimeter, and the briefing room buzzed with hushed conversations.

Quite a few people had journeyed to Gary's lab during the night, once it was clear that it was going to be a primary target for the aliens, along with New Bengaluru. A few tiny, stray meteors had advanced ahead of the main asteroid, all of them falling near Antarctica or India. The atmosphere and Gary and vastukar's automated defenses had taken care of them, and it erased any doubt as to where the aliens would focus their efforts.

Mona and Harrison had come in her gothic chariot, the former looking pale and wan, her cyan hair less vibrant, and with dark circles under her eyes. Jiro and Esmeralda had arrived with Brody and Cooper in their flying convertible, followed by a number of DERD agents and other armed forces serving under the flag of the United Planetary Response Cooperative.

Everyone had assembled in the large briefing room, staring at holographic screens that lined the walls. The screens showed swarms of aliens countering the seismic disruptor drones from the second perimeter, but sacrificing themselves in waves to do so. Whatever was controlling the asteroid had also sent smaller chunks of it out as decoys, drawing the attention of the drones and allowing the main mass somewhat safer passage.

"Don't break out the champagne just yet," Gary said and looked at Samaira. "For some comparison, the asteroid is still about eighty miles across. A meteor that's 200 feet would cause an air burst that would be like a nuclear bomb. At ten miles across, it'd still be a potential humanity-killer. So, yeah, we've made some progress, but we ain't outta the woods."

Another alarm blared as the asteroid came into range of the third perimeter: Gary and Vastukar's upgraded, repurposed mining laser squads.

"Should MacDougal be here for this?" Samaira asked as the screens showed the mining drones moving into position. She looked around the busy assembly room, but didn't see her or Riley.

"She's talking to Hanover. Takes quite a bit of doing to organize firing every nuclear weapon in America's arsenal, and they're finalizing stuff now. So's everybody else with nukes, apparently."

Samaira took a deep breath and held Chandrali against her chest. The cat sensed her agitation and anxiety, and allowed herself to be held more tightly than she otherwise preferred.

"If this doesn't work?" Samaira asked.

"I've got anti-matter bombs in reserve. Vastukar says he's got some kind of solar array that can be redirected toward the asteroid. We'll know if we need those in about ten minutes," Gary said just as the first mining drones intercepted the asteroid.

Samaira, along with everybody else in the room, watched as beams of orange energy blasted out of the drones and struck the asteroid at its weakest points. The rock glowed in places, breaking away in disintegrating chunks of smoldering ore and stone. The drones were quick, moving with erratic speed as they avoided projectile attacks from the aliens and chunks of the asteroid itself.

A group of about thirty drones managed to carve a huge segment out of the asteroid and then blow it to pieces. A beam of dark energy shot up from the surface of the asteroid itself, and turned the drones into scrap an instant later.

Another screen drew her attention as a large squad of drones overheated a segment of the asteroid, and another massive chunk blew apart.

"Hot damn!" Gary said, his tight fist thumping the arm of his chair, a fierce smile spreading across his face. The percentage of the asteroid's mass dropped.

2% mass and 7% integrity.

Another lance of dark energy destroyed the drones, and a swarming horde of aliens defended against the next laser strike. There was a brief back-and-forth of orange drone lasers and alien projectiles, and then the asteroid broke apart. The force holding the fragmented pieces of the giant rock together finally faded, and the asteroid drifted away into countless smaller pieces.

The cheers that went out through the assembly room were almost deafening. DERD agents gripped each other in hugs, Brody and Cooper clinked enormous beer steins they had produced from... somewhere, and lit a pair of joints. Pan and Tori cheered together, along with Arvo, and even Mona managed something like a smile, despite her exhausted and haggard look.

Samaira squealed and clutched at Gary, Chandrali yowling in protest as she was smooshed between them. Gary patted Samaira on the arm, laughing as he did.

"Take that you rotten bastards," he said.

0.48% mass.

The measurement of integrity had been for the large asteroid chunk that had been held together, but was now in pieces. It had gone down to 0%, and vanished.

"Looks like the remaining pieces are all heavily damaged, but still intact. Barely. It's enough. We'll get 'em," he said.

However, the asteroid's shattering happened just as the last of the mining drones were obliterated. The aliens had separated onto the drifting fragments, hordes of them on each one. Gary's cameras only showed them at a distance where they looked like ants on stones, but it was obvious they still numbered in the thousands.

"How many left?" Samaira asked when she had calmed somewhat. The room around her was still a boisterous cacophony of jubilation. Gary glanced at an open Archive communication window.

"Vastukar says about ten thousand. Maybe a few hundred of those are around Alpha-sized."

"With the exception of the big ones, that's fewer than the initial invasion numbers. Those asteroid chunks, are they going to be a problem?"

"The biggest is less than half a mile. We'll see how the conventional nukes and my last few anti-matter bombs do. Probably pretty good, based on how cracked these last bits look," Gary said and tapped a few buttons on another screen. "Whatever survives, it's going to hit in about two hours. When was the last time you ate something?"

"Last night," Samaira replied. "I'm not exactly hungry."

"No, but your body needs food. Go to the dining hall and ask the replicator for a calorie pill. It'll help. I'll announce any updates when they happen. Go on, Sam. I'm gonna tell these folks to calm down and get ready for the fight that's still heading right for us."

Samaira sighed, then leaned over and kissed the top of Gary's head.

"Whatever happens, we'd never have made it this far with you. Thank you, Gary."

"Same goes. Now scoot. I still got work to do." Gary cleared his throat as he turned away, clearly flustered. Samaira and Chandrali left the assembly room together and made for the nearest dining area.

She was a little surprised to find Mona in the dining hall, facing a corner, staring at her Archive just as she entered. Her hand was gliding over her main status screen, not as if she were updating her stats and skills but as if she were… *caressing* her Archive.

MONA DE ROZARIO: LEVEL 50 GENERAL OF THE UMBRAL HORDE

First Class: Necromancer

Second Class: Shadow Strider

Statistics

- Awareness-39 (+8 from gear)
- Dexterity-21 (+8 from gear)
- Fortitude-34 (+12 from gear)
- Intelligence-35 (+10 from gear)
- Strength-9

- Willpower-48 (+17 from gear)

Skills

- Necromancy-71 (+12 from Artifact)(+15 from gear)
- Hive Mind-5
- Battlefield Tactics-35 (+17 from gear)
- Undead Affinity-45 (+8 from gear)
- Shadow Dominion-47 (+8 from Artifact)(+12 from gear)
- Life Drain-40 (+8 from gear)
- Touch of the Grave-35 (+8 from gear)

"Mona?" Samaira asked, and the other woman closed her Archive screen at once, and spun around with a sweep of her black and purple cape.

"Bloody rude to sneak up on people, don'tcha think?" Mona snapped.

"I'm sorry. I didn't mean to. I just figured I should eat something before things get busy."

Samaira set Chandrali down on the edge of a nearby table, patted her head, then activated the nearest replicator and told it to give her a calorie pill. A plain, beige pill appeared within seconds, alongside a glass of water. Samaira took them both.

"Pretty pathetic for a last meal," Mona said as she leaned against the far wall, next to another food replicator.

"Who says it's my last? I dunno if you saw but things are looking pretty good," Samaira replied.

"That's usually how they look right before they turn to shit, darling." Mona had the replicator produce a glass of red wine for her, then sat at a nearby table and looked into the dark liquid.

"It's going to be okay," Samaira said. Mona clicked her tongue at her and didn't look up from her wine. "I mean it. I know you must be worried about Renn. I'm worried about Anya too. But—"

"But what?" Mona snapped and her gauntleted hand tightened on the wine glass. The metal claws of the armor scratched across the smooth surface, leaving white lines behind. "But have faith? But we have to do our best? But there are other people depending on us? Fucking absolute pap. Even if we win today, will it matter to you if your girl doesn't come back? When the world's cheering our victory, will you be thinking how many people you saved, or will you be wondering how your lover died, alone and adrift out there?"

Samaira swallowed, having to force the movement as her throat had tightened.

"I've tried not to think about that too much. But it's been impossible not to," she admitted. "But even if Anya is... dead, yes, of course it will matter to me if we win. It's the entire planet. Billions of other people. I'll mourn Anya, but I'm not so selfish as to think that just because I might be sad, that those people don't matter."

Mona looked at her from behind the drooping shroud of her hair.

"You've never lost somebody, have you? Not somebody really important. A best friend, a lover," she said, paused, then added, "A child."

"No. I've been lucky."

"There's no bringing them back, you know. Believe me, I've tried," Mona said and a wet chuckle slid out of her. It was a mirthless, exhausted sound. She gestured down at where the folds of her cape pooled around her feet. Skeletal faces lurked in the shadows there, along with the glint of tiny eyes, like coins catching moonlight.

Samaira looked between Mona and the skeletal figures lurking in her shadows. Realization turned to horror and she took a step away.

"Is that—?"

"Somebody I knew? No. These little ones are only bone, shadow, and the necromantic energy that animates them. The one I tried to bring back..." Mona's voice softened, and despite continuing to look at Samaira, her gaze shifted to somewhere else. Somewhere beyond the quiet and otherwise empty dining hall. "They're resting. As the dead should."

Samaira didn't know how to reply to that. Mona sipped her wine and the two women regarded each other in silence for a long moment before she finally spoke again.

"I'll fight those bastards when they come here, no worries. If Renn is alive, then I'll fight to live long enough to see him again. And if he's dead, then I'll fight for revenge, and to ensure his death was not in vain. But there won't be any celebrating for me afterward. I've seen a bit too much of death for my liking, and I'm sick of the living rubbing their happiness in my face," Mona downed the rest of her wine in a gulp, then stood and left the room with a flap of her cape and a chorus of agitated whispers from the horde within it.

A bump at Samaira's ankle made her squeak with surprise. Chandrali arched against the side of her leg, purring and rubbing her head against Samaira's boot. She picked her cat up, and cradled her against her chest.

"C'mon Chandrali," Samaira said after she took a deep, shuddering breath. "We still have work to do."

40

The alert came about ninety minutes later.

The entire nuclear salvo of the planet—some 12,000 warheads and change—combined with Gary's anti-matter bombs and some sort of solar weapon from Vastukar, had mostly pulverized the remnants of the asteroid to powder. The remaining pieces were small enough to burn up in the atmosphere, would splash down harmlessly in the ocean, or would only cause minimal damage on impact.

Except for two.

Two chunks of the asteroid had split, defying the behavior of regular space rocks and acting more like guided missiles as they shot toward New Bengaluru and Antarctica. They were tiny in comparison to what had come before, only several hundred yards across, but still big enough to cause problems.

They were also swarming with aliens.

Samaira stood on a wide elevator platform with Chandrali in her tiger form, Pan, Brody, Cooper, Mona, and about two hundred agents of the DERD and the UPRC. Gary had seen fit to give the regular people advanced weaponry, just this once. The agents all shouldered chrome rifles with glowing tubes of plasma, or heavy cannons with multiple barrels and magnetic rails. Riley was among them, though Samaira almost didn't recognize him until he lifted the armored visor on his helmet.

"You ready for this?" he asked as the elevator platform let out a warning noise, and then began to ride up the wide concrete shaft.

"Not really. But I'm used to my weapons at least. Have you had time to train with that?" Samaira said and locked down at Riley's rifle.

"Yeah. Hendricks showed us this stuff yesterday. He apparently modeled most of its functionality after existing weapons, so it's pretty easy to use for anybody with any kind of basic marksmanship training. Got a few hours on a test range with it. It'll have to do."

"Are you gonna try and smuggle that out of here?" Samaira asked with a smirk.

"Hell no. Hendricks told us they'd melt if they leave Antarctica. I dunno if he was kidding, but I'm sure he's got some way of making sure nobody gets outta here with his toys."

"We're sure these things will work?" one of the other DERD agents asked. Brody laughed and patted the man on the back almost hard enough to knock him over.

"Yeah, they'll work fine. These alien cunts ain't that tough. Just hit 'em or bite 'em enough and they'll go down. Works for me anyways!" Brody said.

"What about the other hosts?" another agent asked.

"Jiro, Esmeralda, Harrison, and Dr. Immonen are with the bulk of the DERD and UPRC forces. They're about ten miles away, near the other side of the factory. We're hoping the aliens land in the middle of us and we can surround them, but we didn't want to offer a single tempting target of all of our forces," Riley said.

"Plus plenty of those killer robots, right?" Cooper asked, a faint tremor in his voice.

"Right," Riley confirmed.

"Don't worry. If you die, I will make good use of you," Mona said and tapped Cooper on the chest, then winked at him.

"I'll pass on that one," Cooper said with a nervous chuckle.

"Listen up folks," Gary's voice echoed from the speakers around the elevator platform. "I've got my defensive turrets up and firing.

They've locked onto the asteroid chunk right above us. The aliens look like they're projecting some kind of protective barrier, but it's faltering. Should punch through it soon enough. If we don't, you may feel some, uh, mild tremors following impact."

"Gonna get shook around like shit in an outhouse during an earthquake, is what he means," Cooper said.

"What I mean is that you'll be safe, but the aliens are going to land —one way or another—before the elevator reaches the top. Dunno how many of the freaks are gonna survive, but be ready. Stay behind my bots, let them take the hits, and get anybody wounded back into the elevator and use the medical gel and aid kits on the walls."

"Thanks Hendricks," Riley said.

"Try to make us look good out there," MacDougal added over the speaker.

"Director? Shouldn't you be in a bunker or something?"

"Agent Riley: I'm here representing the DERD, America, and the UPRC as a whole. I'm not going to sit out the invasion in a bunker. Bad enough I'm down here with Hendricks."

"Just be careful, ma'am," Riley said.

"Same goes."

"Maybe we should all consider staying in the heavily armored factory?" Cooper asked.

"Sounds fucking boring," Brody replied.

"And dangerous. They get in here, it's over. I've got some light internal defenses, but nothing compared to what's outside. With my defenses, the hosts, the DERD, and UPRC, we wipe the bastards out before they even get close. Stay near my bots and defensive structures and you'll be fine," Gary said, then added, "And don't try and steal my guns. Good luck."

The line clicked off.

"You okay, Pan?" Samaira asked and knelt beside him. The pangolin nodded at her, his expression set, steady.

"Earth doesn't run," he said.

"What?"

"Something my turtle told me."

"Oooookay," Samaira replied.

"You and me, eh little buddy? First we teach these fuckers a few things, then we head home, and get proper fuckin' wasted," Brody said as he took out a joint and lit it, the smoke billowing out of his mouth and blowhole. Smoke also started to emerge from the sides of Cooper's robotic helmet, and he laughed as he pointed finger guns at Pan.

"Fucking wasted," Pan repeated, and returned the finger guns as best his claws would allow.

"Mm. We'll see," Samaira said.

"Attention: incoming projectile detected. Please brace for impact," an automated voice intoned.

"Looks like they couldn't get the whole thing," Riley muttered, and grabbed a nearby rail. Everybody else followed his example, except for Brody who stood in the center idly scratching his butt, and Mona, who hovered a few inches above the elevator platform itself.

There was a muffled boom from far above them, and then a series of shakes that made the elevator squeal and the lights flicker.

That was all.

Everybody was silent as the elevator stabilized and resumed its speedy ascent. The agents double-checked their weapons, and the hosts readied theirs. Mona's scythe appeared in her hands just as Samaira materialized her bow. Brody's form thickened, bulging with muscle and blubber, and took on a faint sheen of polished stone. Cooper's robotic suit beeped and clicked as its integrated weaponry came online, and Pan's armored scales clicked against one another as he shook himself.

The elevator stopped with a heavy bang in front of a pair of enormous, armored doors. With a click, a hiss, and a thud, the doors opened and revealed the frigid, eternal twilight of Antarctica. The ice field stretched away to distant white mountains, and flurries of snow whistled past the opening.

Squat metal towers had risen up out of the snow at regular intervals, each with a set of four huge barrels emerging from their tops. They fired shrieking rounds of glowing ammunition into the distance, at targets Samaira couldn't see. The towers were each roughly as big as a house, and the sound of all of them—perhaps a hundred or more—

firing at once rattled the air itself. There was an equal number, or more, of Guardians and combat droids, rushing away from launch tubes and other elevators, and towards the horizon.

A towering plume of snow and debris rose up in a massive cloud over the landscape in the distance, dominating the otherwise dark sky with its pale intrusion. Whatever had been left of the asteroid had been large enough to create a small mushroom cloud upon landing. Dark shapes emerged from the base of the cloud, lurching, loping, slithering, and lunging forward.

"Let's fucking go!" Brody called out and barreled ahead, his bulk making the ice crack beneath his feet. Samaira mounted Chandrali and sped after him, bow at the ready. A dozen blue crystals hung from the sash at her side, all of them constructs she'd been working on for the past several days.

Cooper rocketed overhead, his mechanical suit blasting loud rock music, and the DERD and UPRC agents charged beneath him, shouting battle cries as they did.

A rumble behind them made Samaira glance over her shoulder, and her eyes widened as the skeleton of some sort of dinosaur—something with a very long neck that stretched up at least four stories, and four thick, trunk-like legs—burst out of the ice below. Its eyes glowed with unearthly light, and a honking wail emitted from a throat covered in rotting skin.

Mona's usual horde had become a literal army that rose up alongside the dinosaur skeleton. An entire legion of undead centurions, archers, mages, berserkers, cavalry, and inhuman beasts of bone and sinew clawed their way from shadow and earth and ice. Mona sat astride the top of the dinosaur's neck, pointed forward with her scythe, and her army advanced with stomping, inevitable momentum.

"Pan?" Samaira called out, having lost sight of the pangolin during the rise of Mona's army.

Another rumble from the ground drew her attention, and she laughed with surprise.

A golem, easily the same height as Mona's dinosaur if not taller, assembled itself from the black stone beneath the ice. It looked like a cross between a human and a pangolin, its back hunched and covered in scales, its hands tipped with claws. Pan himself was set in the middle of the giant golem, right where its heart would be. He had also summoned his own group of smaller golems: creatures of stone, shale, and crystal. While not nearly as expansive as Mona's army, they looked more than adequate for whatever was coming.

Chandrali soared into the air, and she ran level with Pan toward the onrushing aliens.

A gargantuan cube the size of a castle emerged from the cloud of debris. It was covered in armored black scales and twitching eyeballs. It stomped forward on elephantine legs, and emitted a resonant honking noise as it charged forward. Samaira and the others continued their advance until the mass of Mona's undead army met the front line of the gnosiphages.

The DERD agents took up positions at the rear of Mona's army, unleashing bright beams of laser fire and superheated plasma. Towering skeletons in plate armor subdued some of the larger aliens, and the DERD agents blasted them to bits. Riley stood at the head of the agents, calling out targets, and organizing any wounded getting taken off the field. Gary's Guardians and droids fanned out, circling around the gnosiphages and pummeling them from every side with every manner of weapon.

Brody chomped through any hostile in range, literally eating a few, his body changing as he did, and turning the aliens' own powers back against them. Cooper soared overhead, his mechanical armor launching tiny missiles, thin lasers, and powerful concussive blasts that scattered the gnosiphages if they started to gang up on anybody.

Pan's golems acted as defense for the humans and other hosts, intercepting anything that came close. Pan himself closed on the lumbering cube beside Mona and her dinosaur, both of them slamming into its side in an effort to knock it over. The cube groaned, stumbled, but stayed upright. Several of the eyes focused on Mona, and beams of energy shot out toward her.

Pan stood in the way, and his colossal golem raised its huge arms, tanking the shots. Chunks of black stone were sliced and shattered away, but the golem remained standing. Mona's dinosaur reared its long neck around Pan's colossus, unhinged its bony jaw, and breathed a jet of whitish-green flames over the cube.

Samaira did what she did best: adapted to what was around her. If a DERD agent had been injured, she healed them; if a gnosiphage was giving somebody trouble, she shot it; if their flank needed defense, she created a field or dropped a protective rune.

She took several of her crystal constructs, threw them down onto the snow, and they burst outward into a variety of forms. A wall made of crystalline blue bricks appeared around the DERD agents, healing the wounded and shielding everyone behind it, while small exploding darts shot out at any enemy in front of it. A tall, slender sapphire appeared over the battlefield and deflected enemy projectiles harmlessly away into the air, and turned more than a few back against the aliens. A pair of aetheric turrets materialized at the gnosiphages' flanks, hammering them not with aetheric arrows, but sets of pre-assigned runes Samaira had crafted. A gnosiphage would get shot, and a glowing rune of weakness, blindness, paralysis, or worse appeared on its side.

The snow itself became a weapon under Samaira's control of the Water Dominion. She heard phantom music in the distance, and felt the pull of invisible tides on her as she caused the snow to condense into deadly, aetheric-infused spears and snares. Her own arrows were a constant hail on the forces below as Chandrali flew above. Anything foolish enough to attack her directly was swatted aside by the powerful tiger, or slashed to ribbons.

"Weird one coming up!" Cooper said from her side, and pointed. A lone gnosiphage had emerged from the distant debris, flying past the giant cube battling Mona and Pan and over the battlefield, ignoring the combatants below as it went.

It had the basic size and shape of a person, but with pale gray stony flesh, a hollow chest cavity, and a large, spidery red flower blossoming where its head should be. A strange circular black dot floated above the flower, bisected by a toothy rictus. The flower appeared wilted, dying, and the black circle was dripping splotches of inky darkness that vanished when they hit the snow.

"I got ya, ya weird motherfu—" Cooper said as he moved to intercept the gnosiphage. The grinning maw turned toward Cooper, and spat out a crackling bolt of dark energy. Cooper's head burst, along with most of the top of his chest. The crackling energy skittered over the rest of his body, making it twitch as it fell to the ground.

"Coop! *Cooper!*" Brody roared from below, smashing through a crowd of aliens to rush to his friend's side.

"No you don't!" Samaira said, took one of her crystal constructs from her sash, nocked it into her bow with an aetheric arrow around it, and fired. The arrow hit the creature dead-center, and a crystalline cage formed around its body, then shattered as it burst free. It turned the black, leaking orb to face her, and hissed.

"Thief. Weakling," it spat, and flew straight at her. Crushing force surrounded Samaira as it neared, and she had a moment to think that this might be it before Chandrali threw her aside. The gnosiphage made a slashing motion with its arm, and sliced Chandrali in half from nose-to-tail. Samaira screamed as she turned and saw her beloved cat fall into two separate, bloody pieces onto the ice below, and the alien sped onward and away.

It ignored Mona's army, the DERD agents, Gary's Guardians, and flew straight down the nearest elevator shaft. There was an explosion as it destroyed the first level of armor within the shaft, and then it was gone.

It was going for Gary, or maybe just the factory in general.

"Coop! Coop!" Brody wailed over the dead man. Samaira fought back tears as she looked at Chandrali's remains, stroked the cat's side once, then grabbed Brody by the shoulder.

"It's going for Gary, probably the hub," she said. "If it gets to him and shuts his robots and defenses down, we're in trouble. Are you with me?"

Brody looked up at her, his broad features slack with shock for a moment before they hardened.

"Yeah. Let's go run that cunt down," he said. Samaira handed him another of her crystal constructs, and it expanded into something like a long, slender saddle with handles near the front.

"Keep up," she said, gave one last sad look to Chandrali, then expanded her bow into its flying shape, and flew down the ruined elevator. They sped past melted and warped armor plating, further and further down into the earth.

Whatever the flower gnosiphage was, it wasn't normal. It didn't look, act, or feel like the others. It had sounded a bit like the centipede overseer, and Samaira recognized the telltale blue light, but that was it. The aether actually appeared to be repelled by it, and she had never even suspected something like that was possible.

She and Brody emerged out the bottom of the elevator shaft, through the last of Gary's external armored doors that had been reduced to glowing metallic puddles. The nearby tram entrance had been broken through, and they soared through it and followed the trail of destruction.

Automated turrets, security droids, Guardians, and more had all been reduced to heaps of trash and sparking electronics. A terrible, roaring howl echoed through the tunnel ahead of Samaira as the gnosiphage continued its advance.

She and Brody finally emerged into the central tram terminal, what Anya had dubbed Gary's Union Station. A trio of Guardians, with heavier armor and weapons than the usual models, stood between the flower gnosiphage and Gary and MacDougal. Gary was outfitted in heavy mechanical armor, and surrounded by a shimmering forcefield.

Samaira unleashed her last crystalline construct as soon as she burst into the station: a sphere of glowing blue water that floated before her, and materialized pressurized jets of aether-enhanced water. The pressure from the jets was intense enough to slice through metal.

The gnosiphage turned as Samaira's construct shot it, digging a furrow in its gray stone flesh. Wherever the water hit, it blossomed into clusters of aether-ice that pulled on the strength of whatever it was attached to. The gnosiphage lashed out at the water sphere, but when it approached, the sphere manifested a vortex around it, like one of Anya's gravity wells, and held it in place while it blasted it again and again.

The Guardians fired upon the gnosiphage while Gary retreated toward another tram with MacDougal. The salvo from the robots was relentless and deafening, a hail of lasers and magnetically accelerated tungsten rounds, battering the flower gnosiphage into the ground.

Samaira pelted it with arrows along with her sphere, and Brody chucked his aetheric flying saddle at it, then found an opening in the assault and began chewing on the alien's leg.

The gnosiphage let out a resounding bellow, and a flash of glacial blue light and crackling bolts of dark energy blossomed from its mouth and flashed across the whole of the chamber. The Guardians were thrown back, chunks of them shattering, and half of Brody's side was blasted away in a spray of blood and blubber. Samaira's water sphere splashed to the ground, while Samaira herself was thrown across the station and into the far wall with a crack.

Gary and MacDougal were tossed through the air, and both skidded to a stop across the tiled floor. MacDougal cried out as a stray bolt of energy shot through her chest, and she collapsed against the wall.

"Sam! Check on Brody!" Gary shouted as he checked on MacDougal. Samaira was dizzy from the impact, but unhurt. Brody, however, was bleeding profusely from a huge wound in his side. She knelt beside him, using all of her aetheric foci to heal him. She wasn't nearly as good at this as Arvo, but she could do it. Brody's wound sealed, but did not regrow, leaving him with a sort of chunk missing from his torso.

"Gotta get that fucker," Brody rasped and forced himself up. Samaira didn't bother to tell him to rest. He was right. The flower gnosiphage had destroyed two of the advanced Guardians by crushing them into cubes, and had sliced the third in half. The last Guardian's upper torso crawled toward the alien, gripping it around the waist with its electrified gauntlet and shocking it before it too was crushed by an unseen force.

Gary stood over MacDougal in the distance. She was surrounded by a pool of blood, and still. She was dead.

"Up! Get up!" Samaira tugged on Brody as the gnosiphage turned on Gary, and raised its hand towards him. Its body was covered in bloodless gashes, cracks, and missing large sections. Its flower had almost entirely wilted, the red petals fallen and scattered on the floor. Its "head," for lack of a better word for the circle of blackness, was dripping pieces of itself in thick globules, and most of its teeth were missing.

"This one Heralds something greater. This one may fall, but so shall you," the creature said, and a dark, crackling energy materialized at the finger it pointed at Gary. He raised the arms of his mechanical armor, his forcefield intensifying as he tapped at some control on his gauntlet.

One of the high-speed trams smashed through the station and plowed into the alien just as it released its deadly attack. It wailed as several cars of heavy metal smeared it across the floor of the station, then slammed it against the wall.

Samaira used the aether to place a glowing rune of strength on Brody's back while Gary opened fire with a series of shoulder-mounted laser cannons, and a huge plasma gun that extended from his arm. Brody roared, lifted up the tram car, and smashed it into the Herald once, twice, and was knocked aside by a sweep of its arm. It blasted Gary, who took the hit on his forcefield, and was then blown back toward the hub by the force. Pieces of his armor broke away, and his forcefield flickered and died.

Samaira charged the aether around her into a powerful arrow, and fired it from her bow. The alien roared as it struck its side, then flung itself at Samaira, snatched her bow, and shattered it.

Samaira grit her teeth and pulled on every speck of the aether and her Ichor of the Ocean. An elegant blue lance appeared in her hands, and she rammed it through the Herald's mouth as it charged at her. It shrieked in pain and surprise, then grabbed her by the neck and began to squeeze.

Her vision darkened along the sides, her healing crystals struggling to keep her alive.

A golden light filled the tram station behind the Herald, and a resounding voice called out.

"Get away from my girlfriend you fucking bastard!"

Anya, glowing and radiant, exploded into the station, and descended on the Herald.

41

The Flame Dominion.

Comforting, warm, endless. It surrounded Anya, soothed her.

"Huh. So I did come here after I died," she said.

"You're not dead! Isn't that great news?" a voice replied, and Anya assumed it was the bird, but it didn't sound the same.

Felix appeared beside her and looked around, their rose-head unfurling its petals as they did. Their expression went from wonder to confusion as they stared at Anya.

"What the hell are you doing here?" Anya asked the AI.

"Where's here?" Felix said.

"Oh, hey, you made it," the bird said as it appeared in a flash of sparks and glowing feathers. It had changed again.

It now resembled something like a griffin, with even larger wings, and a quadrupedal body of something between a lion and crane: feline and avian; graceful, but muscled. Its head was still mostly eagle-like, though the beak was a bit longer and more hooked, and the frill of feathers around its head had a distinct leonine look to it.

"Is this what you were talking about?" Felix asked. "The Flame Dominion?"

"Yeah. How is this... what's going on?" Anya said.

"You're here," the bird said. "All of you. Not just your mind, but your body, too. That means the Archive is here with you, and your little AI pal."

"Whoa," Anya said, and brought up her Archive. It appeared in front of her, like always.

Except, not quite.

ANYA NOWICKI: LEVEL 50 COSMIC WARDEN
First Class: Phoenix Monk
Second Class: Ascendant Skirmisher
Statistics

- Awareness-10
- Dexterity-37 (+15 from gear)
- Fortitude-73 (+26 from gear)
- Intelligence-18
- Strength-43 (+10 from gear)
- Willpower-10

Skills

- Flame Dominion-[ERROR: SKILL VALUE NOT RECOGNIZED] [ERROR: ARTIFACT PARAMETERS NOT RECOGNIZED][ERROR: GEAR SCORE NOT APPLICABLE]
- Kinetic Dispersal-26 (+16 from gear)
- Combat Cognition-23
- Regeneration-47 (+25 from gear)
- Xhama Thul-26 (+6 from gear)
- Gravity Dominion-31 (+8 from Artifact) (+14 from gear)
- Energy Focus- 21 (+16 from gear)
- Flesh of the Starforge-20 (+14 from gear)
- Light Dominion-35 (+8 from Artifact)(+16 from gear)

- Zero-G Combat-10
- Sure Footing-10
- Form Duplication-15

"Huh. That's new," she said.

"There is a lot going on in the Archive right now. I'm getting a bit of information overload. That's kind of neat!" Felix said.

"That's what happens when you try to quantify infinity, or divide by zero, or whatever the hell your little power calculator is trying to do," the griffin said.

"What happened?" Anya asked. "I was setting off the bomb and then, it was like there was all this power inside me, trying to get out."

"You opened the doorway, little ember. At least a little bit. A crack, just for a second. It was enough for you to unleash some of the Flame Dominion in its purest form, and escape the blast yourself. Think of turning a sock inside out. You switched your position in regular space with a fragment of the Flame Dominion for an instant. Almost killed yourself in the process, too."

"So I did it? The asteroid's gone?"

"Seeing as how we're all in here, and the asteroid's out there, I have no idea. What about you, little one?"

"Also no idea! It's nice having something in common though!" Felix said.

"Am I stuck here now? Because I should really get back out there," Anya said.

"You'd likely die immediately. Give the blast waves a minute or two to calm down. Also, you haven't noticed since you're here and this place is sustaining you for the moment and repairing the damage done to your body, but it is gonna hurt like a motherfucker when you go back out there. The shock of it alone might kill you."

"I just used the Flame Dominion like always. I guess I used it a lot more than normal, but I should be fine. Right?"

"Little ember, you did not use the Flame Dominion 'like always.' You're still stuck using that knock-off Sun's Heart, but for a second there, you forced it into being something like the genuine article. You basically used your body to prop open a dimensional gateway. You're lucky you weren't blown to bits."

"Is that why my Archive is showing the Flame Dominion as all goofed up?"

"I don't know how that damn toy works," the griffin said.

"The Archive measures skill level based on complex formulas. It collates data from the numerous beings, cultures, and information databases it's scanned, and uses that to approximate a baseline average, then adds the relevant amount to increase it a 'level,' which is determined by further data analysis," Felix said.

"Sounds like nerd shit," the griffin yawned.

"Shush," Anya snapped, then turned to Felix. "Go on."

"If a skill level goes beyond all available data, it extrapolates further skill levels based on previous known quantities. So if the maximum skill level ever recorded was only a 30 for a given skill, but a host wanted to raise that skill to 31, the Archive would create a new model using existing models as the jumping off point."

"So it's making shit up," the griffin said.

"The Archive can't make anything up on its own, but it can build off existing information. So I guess, kinda, yeah! But this, what Anya just did, it's confused the dataset. It doesn't have a prior model for what she's done, so now the whole thing is out of whack. It's attempting to readjust, right now. But since we're, uh, in another dimension, it can't connect to the Engineer's primary Archive."

"I broke it?" Anya asked.

"Just for minute! Or two. Maybe," Felix said and then shrugged their tiny shoulders.

"Told you it was a cheap knock-off," the griffin added and began preening itself.

"Yeah, you have. A lot. And since I have to wait here for a bit, why don't you tell me how to get a real Sun's Heart? Like, what's it even made out of?"

"Haven't you figured that out yet? It's made out of you. You are the blacksmith and your heart—physical and spiritual—is the iron. You've started the forging process already. Whether you finish it, and risk melting your own body and soul in the process, is up to you.

Keep your knock-off. Or risk the fires of the forge. Up to you, little ember."

"Why now? I've been pushing myself since day one in pretty much every single fight. How come now's the time my knock-off starts acting like the real thing?"

"You had more on the line. Not just you, or your friends, or a town, or city, but all of it. But really, if I had to guess, I would say it was that thing that stabbed you."

Anya thought of the Herald, and the wicked looking black knife it had shoved through her hearts.

"Me getting stabbed with a knife let me open a gate in my chest to another dimension?"

"No, you getting stabbed with a shard of another Dominion allowed you to do that. It attacked you, your hearts, physically, pierced through to here, and you felt this place—really felt it—for the first time."

Anya touched her sternum, and thought of the heavy beating. Or the knocking.

"Whatever that thing was, I felt it too. And I know what a Dominion feels like," the griffin said.

Anya squinted at the griffin in confusion. Her mind began to wonder what the hell Dominion the strange creature possessed.

"The Shadow Dominion?" she asked. The griffin shook its head again.

"Shadow is just the absence of light. A passive absence. It's entropy. Just part of the universe. That thing, whatever it is, isn't something I've encountered before. You've stumbled across it once, though, in the Archive."

"The redacted Dominion!" Felix said.

"That thing has the Whatever Dominion?" Anya asked and the griffin shrugged its wings.

"It's my guess. Never seen it before."

"Isn't the Flame Dominion some kind of primeval force of creation? Billions of years old, cosmic, and so on?"

"Yup."

"And you don't know what this thing is?"

"Nope. But like I said: I know a Dominion. The part of the Flame Dominion that isn't you is the part that knows how to make a Sun's Heart, how the other Dominions behave and feel, instinctively. The eight primeval Dominions are all a part of the regular flow of the universe. This ninth Dominion exists outside of them. If I had to pick a single word to sum it up?"

Anya thought of the Herald's mouth: a singular maw floating in tangible nothingness, a glacial light that seemed to suck everything back into it.

"Hunger," Anya said, and the griffin nodded.

"Not just hunger, but that's a decent enough word for now. But assuming it survived your attack and the device exploding, don't hold back when you fight it. Speaking of, I think it's time you were on your way. Places to go, interdimensional horrors to fight."

"Will I have to forge a real Sun's Heart to beat that thing?" Anya asked.

"It's a process, and one you've already started. But it's not gonna happen overnight. Use what you have for now, and that includes all the bonds you've forged. It might be enough. Now go on. And don't let the door hit you on the way out."

"Thank you."

"I'm serious. The energy required to physically get in and out of here could blow you to pieces."

"Oh, right."

"Bye, bird-thing!" Felix said.

"Don't call me that," the griffin said, and then gave Anya a nudge with its head. She raised her hand to her sternum, felt the beat of her hearts, the knocking, that rush of energy, and pulled.

A flash.

A shudder of reality.

Space.

Cold.

A moment of terrible, body-quaking pain.

Sleep.

———

I FEEL LIKE SHIT, Anya thought.

That was her first thought, even before the one that she was awake.

Not dying was a mistake, she thought as wave after wave of pain and nausea flooded through her. She coughed, and a spasm of agony went through her, making her cry out.

"Awake at last?" a familiar, French-accented voice asked. Anya cracked an eyelid open, that single movement making her wince again.

Renn stood over her, helmet off, allowing Anya to see an undeniably smug grin on his face.

"Fuck you," was all Anya managed to croak out. The words clawed their way out of her ragged throat, past cracked and swollen lips.

"Mm. My feelings are the same. However, I don't know why you're upset. I saved your life. God knows it would have been easy enough to leave you out there."

Anya glanced beyond Renn for the first time, and saw that she was in her room on the ship, stretched out in bed. An empty IV bag was nearby, the remains of a red liquid still inside. Probably a healing potion. A tube ran from the bag to her arm, and Anya scowled as she saw it.

Renn really had saved her.

"Thanks," she rasped.

"You're welcome. Maybe. It's been a few hours since I retrieved you. You were rather banged up when I found you. Missing an arm, a leg, several fingers, and quite a bit of skin. I've already given you two of the healing potions Dr. Immonen set aside, but his medical notes say no more than that for you in a day, or your regeneration skill will start to reject it."

Anya looked down at herself. Her arms and legs were all there, but had that pinkish, sunburned look to them, the same as when she'd lost her arm fighting Alpha. Her regalia was missing in places as well, but her Rune of the Mender would grow it all back with enough time.

Time.

"The asteroid?" Anya asked and started to sit up, then clutched at her chest as more pain swept through her. Her Sun's Heart felt strange. The warm, cozy glow of it now spiked into something else. It was only for a second, but it was a sharp, stabbing pain that radiated out from her center, then vanished just as quickly.

"The asteroid is in pieces. But that thing, Mssr. Smiley-Face, I think it still lives and is holding most of those pieces together. It's continuing towards Earth. We are a few hours behind it, delayed while I picked you up and made sure you would live. Some debris from the explosion also partially damaged an engine, which took some time for the ship's automated systems to repair, but that is all. We should be able to catch up to it by the time it reaches Earth. Maybe."

"Damn," Anya sighed and leaned back into her pillows.

"Rest. The food replicator is at hand, and from what I know of your powers, your calorie requirements are great. Eat as soon as you are able, and sleep the rest of the time. I suspect we will have more fighting in our very near future," Renn said, then turned to leave.

"Wait," Anya said, and Renn paused at her door, his hand on the frame. "I really can't thank you enough. I know I didn't follow your plan, but…"

"But now the asteroid will reach Earth, and people may die," Renn said, and his grip on the door frame tightened. "If you had the opportunity to choose differently, would you?"

"No."

"Well, at least you're honest."

"Not letting anybody in my head," Anya rasped. "But I owe you. I'll help, when I can."

Renn glared at her, then turned away.

"Rest. I will take us home. If it's still there."

The door hissed shut behind him, and Anya was left alone in silence.

———

SHE SLEPT for the next few days, except if she was awake, and then she was eating. It was a cycle of base needs that blurred together, and left no room for anything else. Her fear, guilt, anxiety, anger, all of it was pushed to the back of her mind and reduced to white noise.

She slept until she was starving, and then she ate until she was exhausted.

Repeat.

She did start to feel better in increments, then more and more as the days passed. The sharp, stabbing pain that had flared around her Sun's Heart popped up now and again, but the pain settled into discomfort, then mild irritation, and then it too faded into the back. There was also a mark on her chest, where the Herald had stabbed her. It was a black ugly splotch over her sternum, but as the pain faded, so too did the mark.

"We're almost out of the replication paste," Renn said to her on the morning of the third day. "Gary gave us enough for weeks, as an emergency, but you've devoured almost all of it."

"And Doc's calorie stuff."

"I do not mind so much that you had that. It did not sound very appealing."

"Yeah, it tasted like shit."

"I'm glad you ate it, then. We should be arriving at the moon within a few hours. And Earth, not long after. I've not been able to make contact with the others via the Archive, or the ship's radio. I'm assuming that is because the gnosiphages are in our way and blocking us. At least, I'm hoping that is the cause. The only other reason they are not responding would be if they are no longer there."

"They're there. Some busted-ass rock isn't going to stop them."

"A bit reductive, but I hope you're right. How're you feeling?"

"Like I wanna get outta this bed and kick an alien in its ass."

"*Bon*. We have two days worth of food left. Think you can make it another few hours?"

"Har har. I need a snack, but yeah, I'm mostly good to go."

"Then I'll be in the cockpit if you need me," Renn finished, and left. Anya settled on a comparatively light meal of a gallon of ramen with extra pork belly, a whole turkey, a supreme pizza, and a giant salmon salad. She polished it off with a few gallons of water and a pitcher of soda. At the end of it, she emitted a belch loud enough to echo throughout the ship.

It was answered by an exasperated sigh and a string of irritable French from the cockpit.

Anya spent the rest of the flight pacing the hallways, and trying to reach Earth via the ship's radio and her Archive.

No luck.

However, once they reached the moon's orbit, the ship was able to give them up-to-date scans.

Anya almost melted with relief as a hologram of Earth appeared above the projection table, blue and green and intact. The asteroid existed only as scattered fragments, which were quickly disappearing in flashes of light as whatever defenses Gary, Vastukar, and the assorted Earth governments had set up took them down.

"Dieu merci," Renn said as he entered the communications room.

"Looks like they got it cleaned up," Anya said, grinning wide.

"Not quite. Here and here," Renn said and pointed at two areas on the holographic globe that had red warning lights flashing over them: New Bengaluru and the center of Antarctica.

"Shit," Anya said. "How'd they know to go there?"

"New Bengaluru they have already tried to attack once, and failed. As for Gary's factory? Maybe some ability to detect energy readings, or finding some sign of it earlier. He hasn't made too many efforts to keep its location entirely hidden since it's been up and running."

A glowing white dot and a cluster of smaller red ones appeared at the center of Antarctica, and Anya's mouth stretched into a fierce grin.

"Well, I know where I'm going," she said.

"Likewise. I'll take care of the autopilot," Renn said, and left. Anya gave one last glance at the hologram of Earth, and the glowing white dot at its base.

"Round two, asshole."

————

Anya stood in the launching bay, her hand next to the big red button that would manually open the rear hatch of the ship. An alarm sounded and lights began to flash as Renn's voice spoke over the loud-speaker.

"We're entering the upper atmosphere now," he said. "I know this is a stupid question, but you're sure you want to do this?"

"I need to recharge my Shards of the Everstar, and I want to give these bastards a taste of their own medicine. I'm sure."

"There's a meteorite that fits your specifications that we're closing in on. According to the ship's computer, it'll breach the exosphere and hit the ground in under a minute. We'll pass right next to it in about fifteen seconds."

"Perfect. See you when you land," Anya said, and then hit the button. The air was sucked out of the launching bay instantly, and Anya didn't bother to fight against it. She whooshed out in a rush as she activated one of the temporary atmospheric bubbles Gary had made for them.

Earth lay below her, and Anya couldn't help but pause for a single heartbeat at the view. She hadn't gotten a good look at it when they'd launched. The white mass of Antarctica stretched below her, surrounded by indigo oceans. Above it, the green tips of South America and Africa, along with the wide stretch of Australia and the islands of New Zealand. Flashes of light burst in the upper atmosphere, and countless glowing orange motes flared and then died out as the fragments of the asteroid disintegrated within it.

Anya spotted her ride not too far away: an asteroid chunk hurtling toward Earth at unbelievable speed. It was big, but microscopic compared to what she and Renn had shattered with the devices. She just needed something big enough to survive atmospheric entry, and this one would do fine.

Anya flew to it, intercepting it just as it passed and grunting as she dug into it with Singularity's Grasp. It was on a course for the icy continent below, though not its center. Anya used the Gravity Dominion to steer it, her Starforged skin to protect herself, and her grin grew as fire and heat blossomed around the chunk of iron and stone.

She used the incredible heat of atmospheric entry to help her charge up her Shards of the Everstar, crushing the rock beneath her hands as she held on while her impromptu vehicle shuddered and quaked. Chunks of it broke away and were incinerated, and flames licked at the sides of Anya's face, swirling in her hair and her gleaming Crown of the Firmament.

A resounding boom echoed around her as she and the now-reduced meteor burst through the atmosphere, and into the pale blue sky below. Anya laughed, and let out a mad whoop of joy as she continued to ride the meteor, tearing a flaming trail across the heavens towards Gary's factory.

It wasn't hard to find from the air. Explosions and pillars of smoke could be seen from miles up. The shape of a towering alien became clearer as Anya drew closer. It was a walking cube of glossy black armor as large as a castle, striding across the ice-covered wastes on elephantine legs that cracked the ground with each step. Energy beams emitted from eyes across its otherwise flat, featureless surface, and a whole army of Gary's Guardians had been reduced to scrap around it, while smaller human figures fled from its advance.

A huge golem lay sprawled across the snow and ice to one side, and some kind of zombiefied dinosaur was making to rush the alien cube.

Anya's meteor had been reduced to something about the size of a car. But at its current rate of speed, it would hit with a force several times greater than its size might indicate. Plus, she was going to give it a little nudge.

She stood atop the meteor, arms folded across her chest, eyes and Crown alight. She yanked on the gravity around her and the meteor, bending it to her will, and diverting the chunk of flaming rock from its downward coarse and into the side of the huge cube alien. She gave it an explosive kick for good measure as she dismounted, and watched with savage delight as the piece of the asteroid intended for Earth slammed into the alien and partially vaporized it.

One moment it was a lumbering juggernaut of extraterrestrial death and destruction, and the next, most of its body had been converted into organic mist. A deafening explosion rocked the air, and waves of force radiated from where the meteor had struck, obliterating itself as soon at it hit. The elephantine legs continued to march forward for several steps, then collapsed, twitched, and went still.

Anya landed with a heavy thud, and a flash of flames and light. Dozens of smaller aliens around the cube had been crushed beneath it, splattered by their nearness to the impact point, or maimed and were now crawling away. Surviving Guardian mechs, and people in DERD enhanced armor and wielding sleek guns closed on the downed aliens, finishing them off without mercy.

Anya glanced up at the zombie dinosaur, and saw Mona riding atop it.

"Renn's on his way!" Anya shouted as loud as she could across the ice field. Mona was too distant for Anya to see clearly, but she could make out the other woman giving her a wave, and then scanning the sky as her and the giant, skeletal sauropod charged away to go kill more aliens.

"Anya!" a tiny voice said, and a familiar rotund figure emerged from the ruins of the black stone colossus.

"Pan!" Anya cried out and flew towards him, sweeping him into a hug.

"Anya!" Pan cried again and curled against her as she embraced him. Her joy at seeing the pangolin almost made her forget why she had rushed down.

"Pan, I'm happy to see you, but was there—" Anya started to say, and then her gaze stopped on something near the fallen stone giant.

A human figure in mechanical, robot armor, half his torso missing.

Cooper.

And beyond him, something else.

A white tiger in silver armor, unmoving but for the wind ruffling her snowy fur.

Something had sliced Chandrali in half from nose to tail.

"Anya! There was a thing! Really scary! More scary than anything! It killed Chandrali and Cooper, and then it blew a hole in the elevator!" Pan said and pointed at a distant smoking structure. "Samaira chased after it with Brody! I think it's going after Gary!"

"Stay up here, stay close to Mona. I'm going after it."

"Are you gonna kill it?"

"Fuck yeah I am."

"Good."

Anya gave Pan a quick pat on his back, and then flew forward, into the crater, past layers of molten stone and slagged armor plating. Anya didn't know how quickly the Herald had taken to blast past Gary's defenses, but she prayed it had been long enough to keep everybody alive.

She reached the bottom of the elevator shaft with a thud, and continued to hurry along the path of obvious destruction. Security bots lay in pieces along the wide hallways, along with the remains of pop-up turrets and other automated defenses. Anya sped onward, through destroyed tram tunnels and sections of damaged factories, until she finally began to hear the sounds of conflict echoing towards her. It sounded like it was coming from Gary's Union Station, or maybe even the hub itself.

She exited from the ruined tram tunnel and flew into the recreation of Chicago's Union Station to find chaos. The Herald was there, along with Gary, Samaira, and Brody.

Gary was near the back of the vaulted central tram station, retreating into the hub. He was wearing some kind of damaged mechanical suit with a single arm cannon he fired as he limped away. Samaira and Brody were both wounded. Brody had a chunk missing out of his side where something had almost cut him in half, while Samaira sported numerous cuts and slashes across her body, and the healing affects of the aether weren't enough to repair them. Her bow had also been broken, shattered into alabaster shards across the floor.

The Herald was missing large chunks of its stony body, and the dense, depthless void at its top appeared to be leaking, losing its circular shape. Its red flower was gone, and the rictus of its mouth was missing teeth, while the cold blue light in its throat had dimmed to a weak flicker.

Slumped against the far wall, a gaping hole in her chest, was MacDougal. She wasn't moving, and her body emitted no heat.

The Herald turned on Samaira as she materialized a wicked lance of aetheric crystal in her hand and impaled the alien directly through its mouth from behind. It turned on her, mouth agape to consume her as she fell backward.

Anya summoned all of the energy from her Sun's Heart, Crown of the Firmament, Singularity's grasp, and shot out of the tram tunnel so quickly and with such overwhelming force that the entire station shook around her. Her radiant, muscled arms of light blossomed from her back and shoulders as she collided with the gnosiphage seconds before it could attack Samaira.

"Get away from my girlfriend, you fucking bastard!" Anya said, and then the arsenal of glowing fists at her sides descended on the alien in an avalanche of burning force. The alien collapsed under the assault with a screech. It was weak, much weaker than when she had faced it on the asteroid. Days spent holding that giant rock together, then getting pounded by Gary and Vastukar's defenses, plus whatever Samaira and Brody had done to the thing, made its body crack and shatter under her relentless barrage.

But whatever power the alien had, it wasn't gone yet. It screeched in fury, pain, and refusal, and gripped the sides of Anya's head with a strength and desperation she hadn't expected. She struggled against the alien's grip, bashed and pounded on its arms and body with her glowing fists, but it was stuck to her. The creature's dark hole was losing shape by the second, like a deflating ball of nothingness, its teeth dropping to the floor. It leaned its toothy maw forward, opening it wide to reveal the last glimmers of that baleful blue light within.

"Join us. Be with us. There. In the Dominion of the Abyss," it rasped at her, and Anya felt the awful illumination from the back of that empty void pulling her into it. Not just her body, but *her*: everything that was Anya. Her thoughts became loose, scrambled, a panicked, horrified mass of confusion as she felt herself being extracted.

As they did, the blue light solidified into a color that wasn't blue at all. It was some color Anya had never seen before. It stung her to look at it, scratched at the front of her brain like a ragged and diseased claw. The stinging sensation turned to a burn; not of fire or acid, but the growing and relentless burn of hunger.

Greedy, demanding, fathomless hunger.

All of Anya's thoughts, memories, and she suspected her very soul, were being pulled toward the shattered mouth of the gnosiphage, and the eternal well of impossible color in the back of its throat. Like the true Sun's Heart, this thing was a doorway to somewhere else, somewhere that would consume her utterly.

Then Anya snapped back into herself as the world came rushing back and the mouth drew away.

Brody had begun pulling on the alien's hand, his huge arms straining, actually starting to break the Herald's arm off at the shoulder. Powerful cables had wrapped around the gnosiphage's frail-looking body, connected to what remained of Gary's armored suit and whirring with strain as he pulled back along with Brody. Aetheric chains materialized around Anya, and they tightened around her as Samaira tried her best to get her away from the alien.

Whatever force the abyssal light had that was pulling on Anya stretched between her face and the alien's mouth. It was visible as a cold shimmer in the air between the two of them, flickered, and vanished. There was a crack of sound, and then Anya and the mouth gnosiphage flew apart from each other, along with Brody, Samaira, and Gary. Brody and Gary snapped the Herald's arm off with a resounding crack, like a mountain breaking in half.

The others groaned from the impact of hitting the ground or being thrown against the wall. Anya could feel her energy draining away as she maintained her war form. She sprang to her feet, just as the mouth gnosiphage floated upward.

"The Abyss… waits…" it rasped. The light in its mouth flickered once, twice, and then died. The alien did not die with it. Instead it used its one remaining arm to withdraw something from the black hole of its head before it could finish collapsing in on itself. It was a familiar dagger, a simple curved blade of emptiness that had a solidity the head no longer possessed.

"All is ours. All will be—"

"Shut the fuck up," Anya said. She leaped straight at it, kicked her foot through the creature's torso, blocked its weak attack with the black blade with one of her glowing arms, and then proceeded to beat the ever loving shit out of the thing. She tore off its last arm, crushing it as she did.

The immediate beatdown that followed was inelegant, brutish, and quicker than the alien deserved. When Anya had turned the alien into little else but a collection of unrecognizable body parts and dust, she used her array of arms and the Singularity's Grasp within each to create a powerful gravitational field in the center of all of them, and compressed the alien into something the size of a tangerine. She focused again and crushed the tangerine into a marble.

The alien's brittle, weakened body collapsed with the sound of somebody stepping on a box full of crackers. Anya let the pale ball of dead alien fall to the floor just as her golden arms faded, and she collapsed with a sigh.

"Thank you," a tired voice said beside her. Brody looked up at her, his body battered and bloody from the fight, one of his eyes missing, along with most of his teeth. A pale blue rune on his back faded into a shimmer of aetheric sparks. "Fucker got Coop."

"I'm sorry I wasn't here sooner," Anya said to him, and he only nodded, and closed his remaining eye. Anya thought he might be dead, but his heartbeat was regular, and she realized he had just passed out. He'd used the absolute last of his strength to help save her.

"Anya!" Samaira cried out as she latched onto her.

"Kid!" Gary said as he extricated himself from his mechanical armor, and limped to her side.

"God damn, it's good to see you two," Anya said, and sniffled, trying not to cry with relief. She wiped at her eyes, then her gaze fell upon MacDougal's cold form. "MacDougal. Fuck. What happened?"

"The bastard with the mouth came off an asteroid chunk with a shitload of aliens. Left the main force topside, and came straight down here, like it knew exactly what it was doing. Cut through the factory's armor and defenses like they were cheap plastic. I threw everything I had at it, but it was too strong. Too quick. Sam and Brody showed up while I was trying to get MacDougal and myself the hell outta the way. She took a hit, went down. We fought it for a while, then you came," Gary said as he looked at MacDougal. He left Anya's side, knelt beside the older woman's body, and closed her eyes, then covered her with his jacket.

"Cooper. And Chandrali," Anya said. Samaira's hands tightened on Anya's regalia and she sniffled.

"That thing," she said and nodded at the pale marble in the center of the crater Anya had made, "got them too. Brody and I came right after it while… Oh my god. Pan! Is he…?"

"He's fine. A little rattled. Mona and Riley are alive too, and Renn. So are most of the DERD and UPRC agents I saw up there," Anya said. Samaira let out a relieved sigh as she leaned back into Anya.

"We've still got a helluva mess to sort out. Dead to mourn," Gary said as he came back to Anya's side, reached up, and grasped her by the shoulder. "But right now, I'm just glad to see you again. Welcome home, kid."

Anya pulled Gary in for a hug with Samaira. The three of them stood in the ruins of the tram station, and held each other.

42

enn came whooshing down the tunnel a few moments later. Anya, Samaira, and Gary extricated themselves from their group hug as he and his clones (one of them holding Mona like an exhausted, desperate bride), arrived in the Tram station. The clones spread out over the interior of the station as Anya informed him that the Herald was very much dead.

"And probably all his little gnosiphage puppets," she said.

"Not quite, I'm afraid," Renn said. "The surface is still teeming with aliens, but they are behaving erratically. Some of them have begun attacking each other, while others are just running in circles. I came down here to see if something had happened... which I suppose it did."

Renn looked at the crater in the station floor, and the pale marble at its center. Some of his clones stood at the edges of the crater and regarded it curiously.

Anya had sort of hoped that all of the remaining gnosiphages would just fall over dead when the Herald had been killed. It had been the one controlling them all, using them like tools. It would be just like the movies where the Dark Lord, or Alien Mothership, or whatever, got blown up and all the little bad guys fell over. Everybody would cheer, then go home, and that'd be it.

Except not.

"Clean-up crew, then," Anya said and popped her neck to the side.

"You good enough to keep fighting?" Gary asked her.

"I'll charge up with an Evershard and be good enough. To fight another Herald? Hell no. But a handful of aliens suffering their version of the blue screen of death? Yeah, I got this. Gonna sleep for a week afterwards, though."

"All right. Sam, c'mon. We gotta get you and Brody to medical. You've both been beat to hell."

Samaira was reluctant to let go of Anya at first, but did after giving her one last hug, a smile, then hobbled after Gary and a small squad of medical droids carrying Brody. Another group of droids had emerged to gently pick up MacDougal and carry her after Gary.

"All right. Let's go finish these bastards off," Anya said. Without another word, she, Renn and his clones, and Mona flew back to the surface to wipe out what remained of the alien menace.

————

THERE WERE STILL about two thousand aliens scattered across the planet, and Anya wasn't going to be able to rest until all of them had been killed. The good news was that since the Herald had been turned into a sphere of dust (and currently in a high-pressure, shielded specimen tube surrounded by layers of forcefield, armor, and security cannons deep underground in Gary's labs), Felix and the other AIs could now approximate the gnosiphages locations. Vastukar's alien tracking system was more precise, and he updated all available hosts and militaries of their whereabouts.

Earth's conventional military forces took down hundreds, but the overwhelming majority were felled by hosts. Anya and Pan took down several dozen on their own while Samaira, Brody, and other hosts recuperated. The various hosts of the NAT came out in force, escorted by Asmund, Zixin, and Ursula, and cleared almost the entirety of Asia and Europe. The remainder were cleaned up by the other hosts on

Anya's contact list, Gary's Guardians, and the smattering of unknown, independent hosts who still existed in hiding around the globe.

Anya caught sight of a few of the independent hosts, but they vanished or darted away from her before she could even attempt to approach them. The scrambled signals the Engineers had put into place weeks before to hide the hosts from the gnosiphages also kept Anya from locating them. She didn't chase. She was tired, and the aliens took priority.

It took two days to wipe them all out.

Anya ate and slept between fights in the Shadow Ray with Pan, but it all caught up to her in the end. By night of the second day, she was entirely wiped, and collapsed onto a bed Gary had left for her in the living quarters of his factory, while Pan rested on the floor nearby. Anya's hand hung over the side of her mattress, and Pan reached up to hold her fingers with his claw as they fell asleep.

———

THE FACTORY itself had been somewhat repaired, but the damage was more extensive than it first appeared. Gary still had the majority of it running as usual all through the final invasion and clean-up, and by the time Anya awoke on the third day post-invasion, all it needed was some cosmetic polish.

When she stirred from her much-needed sleep, she saw Samaira beside her, snoozing quietly. She was in her normal clothes—a long dark dress and a white blouse—her glasses folded on the bedside table. Some of her hair had fallen in front of her face, and Anya reached over to tuck it behind her ear. Samaira stirred, then blinked her eyes open.

"Hey," Anya said.

"Hey," Samaira replied, and embraced her. Anya held her for a while, then eased back.

"How're you feeling?"

"Better. Arvo healed me up, had me rest for a day, and then I've been helping Gary upgrade some of his defenses. Some very light aether work. Nothing serious. You?"

"A helluva lot better now," Anya said and caressed Samaira's hair. "Is Pan still here?"

"I saw him out in the hallway earlier, talking with Ursula over the Archive," she said, then paused before she asked, "What happened out there?"

Anya took a deep breath, and recounted everything after her launch from New Bengaluru. Samaira's eyes widened when she got to the part about Renn asking her to take the hive mind skill. But she stayed silent until Anya had finished.

"That manipulative little asshole!" she said. "I can't believe Renn!"

"He didn't sound wrong, though. And part of me wonders if I had taken it, MacDougal might be alive, and Cooper, and Chandrali. And a whole bunch of DERD and UPRC agents, plus however many civilians were killed or injured."

"Esmi said that psionics can let you feel—or at least know—what another person is feeling. Renn knew you were worried about me, and Gary, and everybody, and he tried to turn that against you. No. Fuck him," Samaira said and Anya smiled a little at the venom in her voice. "He wanted to use you. Mona has the same skill. I saw it on her Archive. She acted like somebody going through withdrawal most of the time while Renn was away. Him doing something like that to you… it makes me sick."

Anya raised her eyebrows at the revelation that Mona had taken the skill, and her guilt over not taking Renn's offer subsided a little.

"Even if you had done it, you don't know if you would've obliterated the asteroid out there. And if his plan had worked and he was right, then he'd just come back to Earth with you under his thumb. Don't feel bad about wanting to stay who you are," Samaira said. "You risked everything for everybody. And you came back."

"Thanks, Sam," Anya said, and Samaira kissed her forehead. They spoke for a while longer, about what Samaira had been up to, about Anya going into the Flame Dominion, until they decided it was time to get up and go back out into the world. There would be time to be alone later.

They both left for the hub, where Gary was in his chair, a donut and a cup of coffee on the little table beside him. Riley was with him, his own coffee in one hand, donut in the other, the latter of which he waved as Anya and Samaira entered.

"Morning! Welcome back to Earth, thanks for saving the entire planet, etcetera, etcetera," he said.

"Knock it off," Anya said and smirked.

"You're gonna have to build up a tolerance for people fawning all over you. All of the hosts will. It's gonna be 24/7 hero worship for you people for a while. And I gotta tell you: Hanover is mighty pleased. Wants to throw you an honest-to-God ticker-tape parade in Manhattan, give you some medals, the whole shebang."

"That sounds exhausting."

"It could be fun," Samaira said. "Gary? You gonna come?"

"Maybe. Do I have to talk to Hanover, or can I just hang around?" he asked.

"Actually, since you renounced your citizenship, you're not included," Riley said and winced. "Not my call."

"None of us would be here without Gary!" Anya said. "Tell Hanover if Gary isn't invited, I'm not going."

"Me either," Samaira added.

"Ladies, really, it's fine. Riley's right: I told Hanover to piss off, and it's you two that worked with the DERD from the word go. I've been a stubborn old bastard this whole time."

"No way. You're coming with," Anya said.

"If Riley can work it out, then fine. But don't push on my account."

Riley sighed and said, "This is the sorta thing MacDougal coulda sorted out in her sleep."

Silence fell over the hub as everybody looked out into the repaired tram station outside where the director had fallen.

"Has she already been buried?" Anya asked.

"No. Tomorrow. News hasn't hit the public yet, either. Hanover's gonna announce it after the funeral. Got some posthumous awards for her lined up."

"I'd like to be there for that, if I may," Gary said. "I owe the director a couple of apologies."

"I'll arrange it when I speak to Hanover about the parade."

"Thank you, Riley."

"So, how's the rest of the world faring?" Anya asked.

"Vastukar's sent drones to anywhere hit by asteroid chunks. Nothing too serious, but between that and the aliens, some places still got nailed pretty hard. Nothing they won't bounce back from, but still, a mess. I've sent my Guardians and droids to help as well. We're getting things sorted between the two of us," Gary replied.

"Still no word?" Riley asked and looked between Samaira and Gary. Anya arched an eyebrow at them.

"The Engineers," Samaira said. "We talked about it a little while you were resting. We thought maybe they couldn't contact us after Alpha because the asteroid was closing in, blocking all communications or something. But it's been days now, and no response. No Level-ups or RAC or anything for the fighting we've done."

"Yeah, you're right. I should be rolling in RAC after all the aliens I killed out in space, plus the Herald. The Engineers really need to pull their heads out of their asses. Geez, I can't believe I forgot about them," Anya said.

"And me!" a voice cried out from behind them, and Anya turned just in time to see Tori rushing at her.

"Tori!" Anya said and swept her friend up in a hug.

"Don't you hug me! I'm mad at you! I was hiding in a bunker while you were up here kicking the shit outta that Herald thing, and then you took off before I could come out to say hello! Then you collapse into bed as soon as you're back, and now you're saying hi to *Riley*, of all people, before coming to find me?"

"No offense taken, I guess," Riley muttered, and Gary coughed in a poor attempt to conceal a laugh.

"I'm sorry, Tori. I was just… it was crazy. I was so caught up with everything, and I didn't know you were at the factory, and—"

"It's fine, I guess," Tori said and hugged her back. "You get a pass since you helped save the world."

"Thanks, Tori."

"So, no big payday from the Engineers, huh? Still waiting on that flying scooter and RAC store shopping trip."

"I'm still broke, apparently, right Felix?"

"Pretty much!" the AI said. Anya squinted at them, and they looked back at her. "Something the matter?"

"Your head. It's a rose," Anya said.

"Yes! It's always been like that!"

"You okay, Anya?" Tori asked.

"I'm fine, just realizing… that thing, the Herald. It had a flower for a head too, sorta. I never really questioned it with the AIs, just figured it was some sort of cutesy gimmick but, now I'm starting to wonder."

"You're right. Boo, any insight?" Samaira asked, and her blue AI appeared.

"No, sorry. My head's technically a type of tree, so I don't know if that helps or if I'm causing trouble," the AI said. Samaira rolled her eyes and dismissed it.

"I don't have any data on the Herald either. Just that it was a gnosiphage, though one with a unique signal. And before you ask, no, there was no datastream from the Herald. It just sort of went poof when you crushed it," Felix said.

"No messages from the Engineers, no datastream from the Herald," Anya muttered. "I thought the quiet might be nice, but… not so much."

"Yeah, normally I'd say no news is good news, but not this time. Makes me think anything could be coming down the pipe," Gary said.

"I'll leave you to your hypothesizing or whatever. I've gotta get back to DC, start working with Hanover and some others about who's gonna step up for the DERD. And not me, before any of you even suggest it."

"I wasn't going to," Gary said.

"Yeah, you don't seem the type," Tori added.

"I think you'd be better than most," Anya said.

"Me too," Samaira said.

"Well, thanks for the support regardless. Except for Gary and Tori. I'll mention you coming up for the funeral, though, Gary. See the rest of you soon enough," Riley said, and then left for one of the hangars.

"Is there anything that needs to be done?" Anya asked after he had left.

"Yeah. You could park it somewhere and relax for a few minutes.

Dunno what's going on with the Engineers or what, but for now, clear skies. Take a breather, kid. You earned it."

"We should get ready for the parade, now that Gary's coming," Samaira said.

"Who said I was coming?"

"Oh, stop. You know Riley's going to get Hanover to agree, and we know you'll come because we want you there with us."

"Tch. All right, fine, I'll go. If it doesn't cause any problems."

"C'mon," Samaira said and tugged on Anya's arm.

"Pretty sure Gary converted some of the recreation rooms into noraebangs, if you feel like it later," Tori said.

"Gimme a minute with Gare. I'll catch up," Anya said, and the other two women left them alone in the hub.

"What's up, kiddo?" Gary asked. Anya paused as she looked down at him, then leaned over and hugged him.

"I saw what you wrote, on the bomb," she said. Gary stiffened a little inside her arms, then relaxed.

"Wanted to tell you earlier, but just… I dunno. But I meant it."

"I know. Proud of you, too."

Gary blinked at her, then cleared his throat.

"Should get back to work," he said.

"Not too hard. Old farts like you should take it easy."

"Nah," he said, then looked up as Anya exited the hub. "Hey, kid?"

"Yeah?"

"After the funeral, the parade, whatever political showboating has to happen… well, it's spring. Baseball season. Maybe me, you, some others, we catch a game at Wrigley Field?"

"I'd like that," Anya said, and smiled.

"Yeah. Me too. Go on, then. We'll chat later," Gary said, and returned to the work of cleaning up after an alien invasion.

FROM EARTH #9

From *Rutherford International News Network*:

ALIEN INVASION DEFEATED! EARTH VICTORIOUS!

Since mid-January, the world has been through more collective turmoil, change, and upheaval than perhaps at any other single moment in history. The discovery of extraterrestrial life, the threat that life posed, the appearance of supernatural forces wielded by otherwise ordinary people, the attacks on world leaders—as well as entire towns and cities—that have resulted in catastrophic destruction, and then, the looming threat of planetary extinction, have taxed world governments and their people to the breaking point.

But, as many world leaders announced recently, they have not broken. Now, perhaps the worst is behind us.

Secretary General Al-Balawai of the United Nations released a statement yesterday that confirmed the defeat of the invading alien forces that arrived earlier this year.

"This was all of us," Al-Balawai said during the most recent meeting of the United Nations. "Not one, or a few, but all. If any nation on this planet had not contributed, we would not be able to claim victory today. And as we celebrate a world saved, a world changed, I hope we remember what incredible things we can do as one united whole. As we put our defeated external enemy behind us, I pray we can likewise leave our internal divisions behind as well."

Many countries are declaring a national holiday to celebrate Earth's victory, and celebrations in several major cities are already underway.

―――――

From *The New York Times*:

PRESIDENT RECOGNIZES HEROES OF THE INVASION DURING VICTORY PARADE IN NEW YORK

At the end of a ticker-tape parade held in New York's famous "Canyon of Heroes," President Hanover, along with Mayor Bell, presented several awards and honors to the agents of the Department of Extraterrestrial Research and Defense. Each received a newly authorized Medal of Honor for the DERD, and is the fourth variation after those awarded to the members of the Navy, Army, and Air Force. Director Suzanne MacDougal also received a medal posthumously, following her sacrifice during the Battle of Antarctica.

The agents were also presented with the key to the city by Mayor Bell, and told that a statue of them would be erected in Central Park. A statue of Director MacDougal will also be erected outside Federal Plaza, where the former head of the FBI worked diligently for many years.

"Today, we celebrate determination in the face of despair, courage in spite of fear, and victory against all odds. We celebrate the heroes of the DERD: those that stand with us here today, and those that laid down their lives. Today we celebrate the future that lies before us, and we celebrate America," President Hanover said to a jubilant crowd.

Other DERD agents were recognized for their service, chief among them Agent Christian Riley, also formerly of the FBI, where he served with MacDougal. Following the ceremony, Agent Riley fielded questions along with the President from the press.

"I hear a lot of folks asking what the DERD's for, now that the aliens are gone. Well, while I can't get into details, I can say that following the invasion, the DERD will have its work cut out for it," Agent Riley said. "We've won, but that doesn't mean we're alone in the galaxy. Quite the opposite. We'll have more statements in the future, but for now the DERD's focus will be to make certain Earth will always be ready to defend itself in the future We're going to remain as one integral part of the UPRC, and continue to share resources, intel, and whatever else might be necessary to protect our home."

When asked if he would be taking over as director of the DERD, even in a temporary capacity, Riley laughed.

"I'm honored, but I don't think I belong in the hot seat. MacDougal, she was one of a kind. Whoever takes over is gonna have some mighty big shoes to fill."

———

From the public chatlogs of *World of GuildCraft*, an MMORPG:

Arbiter Dane: Anybody wanna do the Netherworld Dungeon raid now that we're not all gonna die

ZerkerZach: That's what you're gonna do in the wake of the world almost getting plastered?

Arbiter Dane: Hell yeah dude. Feeling lucky. Might have good loot rolls.

Orka_Thragskull: Dane, do you ever do anything else but play this game?

Arbiter Dane: When the asteroid was coming I spent most of my time watching hentai and getting high

ValkyrieOfLight: I spent it with family.

Arbiter Dane: Yeah I can't watch hentai with my family

ValkyrieOfLight: We didn't watch hentai!

BartyMcBly: Seriously tho Dane, do you do anything else besides raid and act like a perv on public chat? You didn't wanna embrace life or anything?

Arbiter Dane: You all are on here too! Why aren't you out partying or something?

Orka_Thragskull: I just need to decompress after all the craziness. Something normal. Kill ten boars for their pelts, craft some gear, grind out a few skills.

ValkyrieOfLight: I wanted to see if my friend from across country was on, how they're doing

ZerkerZach: I'm with Orka. Just want to do something normal.

Arbiter Dane: Me too! So let's go raid! The past days have just been everybody freaking out and getting ready to die. This is me embracing life! Doing normal, everyday shit, not living like I could get smooshed by a giant space rock any second and sobbing with my family. One of the best things about life is taking it for granted!

ValkyrieOfLight: I dunno if that's nice or sad

BartyMcBly: Makes sense in a weird kinda way. I dunno if I wanna spend my life on here, but it's not bad to just relax and enjoy simple things either

Arbiter Dane: That's what I'm saying! Now let's go raid some shit!

43

The world became one giant, endless celebration after the last alien died. Photos from New York, Toronto, Hong Kong, New Bengaluru, Seoul, Cape Town, Rio, Sydney, Tokyo, and more showed jubilant crowds throwing off the fear, anxiety, and uncertainty of the last few months. People who had been afraid to go outside now flooded the streets in dancing, cheering throngs.

The invasion was over, and Earth had won. That it had coincided with the coming of spring was a happy coincidence.

Paris was in the midst of its own celebrations, as President Bisset awarded Renn the Légion d'honneur on the steps of the Musée d'Orsay. Press from all over the world assembled to witness the award ceremony, and the streets of Paris were crowded with its citizens. Mona was there in a dark gown that complimented her figure, her own medal—the Victoria Cross—gleaming from the sash it was pinned to. Renn himself wore a more formal version of his usual attire, and kept his helmet on.

When he accepted the award from Bisset, the crowd erupted into cheers, and everything after that was a blur of handshakes, speeches, photos, parades, and more. When it was finished, Renn and Mona retired to an elegant townhouse within the 7th arrondissement, not far from the Grand Palais Éphémère, that Bisset had gifted to Renn as the first of many such rewards.

He and Mona showered together, made love, and lay in bed afterward, bodies entwined. Mona clutched a slender pipe in one hand, smoking something from the RAC store called abat leaf. It was some kind of relaxant and anti-depressant, and Mona usually smoked it a few times a week. The Archive said it was also used in divining rituals, and mystics on some alien worlds used the red-hued smoke to prognosticate possible outcomes, like reading tea leaves.

Renn watched the clouds swirl idly above the two of them, but could make out nothing in their shapes that might tell him what the future held.

"Are you better now?" Renn asked.

"With you? Always," she said.

"I felt our connection break shortly after take-off. A few minutes."

"Vastukar said you were a few thousand miles away pretty quickly. About a minute to get through the atmosphere, and then you started accelerating. Something like that."

"Good to know. I'm in no hurry to do that again."

"Me either. I missed you so much. It all started to come back, about a day after you had gone. I thought I was going to lose myself again."

"Shh. It's fine now," Renn said and caressed her bright, cyan hair. He thought back to how he had found her, during those first few days. The signal his AI had picked up, coupled with the psychic flare that had been her overwhelming grief, had led him right to her.

She had been in a graveyard, crouching over a small headstone. The ground had been disturbed, and she had been holding something tiny, unnatural, and writhing; sobbing over it in the rain.

Renn had helped her bury the dead thing she had tried to bring back, the thing that had been Mona's daughter—but never could be again—and then told her he could help. He could share whatever pain she was feeling, and make it go away.

She only needed to do one thing.

And she had done it.

Anya had not.

Renn had felt her anger when they had spoken of their parents on the ship. It was an emotion and association he was very familiar with. Or rather, one he had been familiar with before he had become Renn, back when he had been Gabriel DuClaire, and murdered his parents.

There had been something behind Anya's anger when she spoke of her mother, something she had buried. But Renn had felt it, even so.

Guilt.

A deep wound of it in her mind, and he had tried to press on that when they had been alone, after communications with Earth had stopped. But she was too stubborn, too selfish, and too unempathetic.

He wondered if he had made the right choice saving her. When her Archive signal had vanished, he thought her dead, and good riddance. But then it had reappeared, as if from nowhere. The ship's autopilot detected her life signs, and began flying toward her.

His hand had strayed toward the manual controls, but Gary would know if he left her. He would be able to find out by accessing the ship's logs, maybe. Something else.

He had no doubt that if she had joined with him, he could have erased her guilt, her anger, as he had done for Mona and her well of grief. Likewise, he knew they would have obliterated the asteroid, saved more lives. And best of all, they would have been stronger together; enough to convince others to join them.

But maybe she could still help his cause. Serve as an example of the selfish, unbridled chaos that people were capable of. She'd had a chance to truly save the world, and turned away.

Renn looked across the room at a table where he and Mona had thrown their clothes and items. The beacon from the attack on the centipede was still there, switched off. Renn had given it to Mona to hide in the depths of her cloak after the battle, then made sure Esmeralda had been exhausted and far enough away to not detect his lie when he had said the beacon had been destroyed in the fight.

The creature still alive inside of it might prove useful, someday. It wasn't Renn's first choice, but the possibility of truly uniting mankind as one—of unlocking all of those cages and freeing everybody from lifetimes of isolation—that was worth anything. Its ability to control a person directly had been removed, but Renn had sensed some latent potential there when he had activated it. It had other uses, besides, and if it died, Mona could always reanimate it.

Next to the beacon was a short dagger made of a darkness so complete that it looked more like a knife-shaped hole in reality. One of Renn's clones had picked it up off the floor of Gary's tram station, following the death of the Herald. Anya and the others had been too tired and relieved to find each other alive to notice him taking it.

"Promise you'll never leave me like that again," Mona said to him. Her voice was becoming distant with sleep, and Renn took her pipe from her and set it aside as she cuddled closer. He felt her heartbeat against his side, in perfect time with his own.

"I promise. Sleep now, mon chou. We have much work ahead of us," Renn replied, and held her close as the world celebrated outside.

———

THERE WAS A CRACK LIKE A GUNSHOT, and a pale white sphere launched itself into the flawless blue sky over Chicago. The crowd around Wrigley Field cheered as the batter for the Cubs shot off for first base, the baseball arcing overhead and going for the fences.

It had been a couple of weeks since MacDougal's funeral, the parade, the endless barrage of press conferences, and all the clean-up. Restoration projects were ongoing all over the world, but the worst of the damage was behind them. Things had almost started to feel normal, and Gary had taken the opportunity to make good on his invitation to catch a game with Anya, Samaira, Pan, Tori, Arvo, and Riley.

"I think I like this more than cricket," Samaira said. "It's a lot less complicated. My dad tried to get me to watch a few games with him, but I never knew what was going on."

"You mean to tell me you've lived in Chicago your whole life and never once been to a baseball game?" Gary asked.

"Nope."

"Downright shameful," he grumbled as he shook his head. He wore an old Cubs jersey, its once vibrant blues and reds faded from time and use. Everybody else had Cubs jerseys as well, though theirs were brand new.

"I never went to a game in New York," Anya said. She had a small cart beside her, filled with hot dogs, brisket sandwiches, French fries, some kind of spiraling fried potatoes on skewers, and pitchers of beer. They were seated along the third base line, behind the Cubs' dugout.

"Yeah but you guys are stuck with the Yankees and the Mets," Gary scoffed. "The Mets, all right, maybe. But the Yankees?"

"What is so bad about the Yankees? Aren't they one of the more famous teams?" Arvo asked. Gary frowned at him.

"You don't get it, Doc," he said.

Anya laughed and Riley shook his head.

"Gary's too set in his ways. If you're ever up by Boston, we can catch the Red Sox," he said. Gary scoffed again.

"Maybe," he replied.

"If the player guys don't want to get touched by the ball, why don't they just dig under the ground?" Pan asked as he watched one of the runners avoid getting tagged.

"Against the rules," Anya said.

"Are there any human games that have digging?"

"I don't think so."

"Actually, the Archive has volleyball, and 'digging,' is a type of move," Felix said from above Anya's shoulder. "But it's not the sort of digging you're thinking of. Sorry."

"Maybe you could make up a sport for actual digging," Anya said.

"Oh! Good idea! I could get Brody and Ursula to help."

"How is Brody, by the way? Been a few days since I heard from him."

"Physically he's still fine. I checked in on him last week," Arvo said.

"He's with Ursula in the NAT right now," Pan replied. "I talked with him last night. He sounds better. Still kinda sad, though."

"The Aussies aren't too happy with him leaving, I can tell you that much," Riley said, and was drowned out by a loud groan from the crowd as the next batter hit a foul ball. It soared up and over the bleachers, toward a converging crowd of people with their hands in the air. A little girl in an oversized jersey and an equally oversized catcher's mitt stood on the fringes of the crowd, desperately reaching for it as well.

Anya pointed her finger at the ball, and gave it a small gravitational nudge. It swerved to one side and plopped into the kid's mitt, and her face beamed with surprise and delight as she stared at it like some holy relic. Samaira turned to face Anya as she noticed the ball's sudden swerve, smiled at her, then hugged her arm.

"Any word on MacDougal's replacement yet?" Anya asked.

"Not yet. Hanover's going to personally select them, though. For whatever that's worth," Riley continued. "I know your deal was with MacDougal, God rest her, but look: if anybody gives you shit, including Hanover, give me a chance to smooth things over. I don't have MacDougal's silver tongue, but I'm not totally useless."

"Don't sell yourself short, Riley. I'll stick to my agreement with MacDougal. You and she deserve that much, at least," Anya said.

"It's not certain, but right now it sounds like they want you, Sam, Pan, and Esmi to act as temporary ambassadors to the NAT, post-invasion."

"I could do that."

"I would get to visit Ursula more?" Pan asked.

"Probably. I doubt the motivations are entirely altruistic on Hanover's part, but it sounds like a done deal, if you want the job," Riley said.

"I do," Anya said, and her Sun's Heart warmed a few degrees.

"Me too! I can't wait to get a chance to explore New Bengaluru. I spent the whole trip in a lab during my last visit," Samaira said.

"Me also!" Pan said.

"What about me?" Tori asked.

"You're still just an accountant, officially. Unofficially, that aether stuff you can do… well, MacDougal let it slide, and told me to keep my mouth shut, so that's what I'll do," Riley said, and Tori grinned at him.

"You're the best."

"Just don't make me regret it."

"What about you, Arvo?" Anya asked.

"After some paperwork and discussions, it's been decided I would be of better use with the United Planetary Response Cooperative. Still working with the DERD, but under the Finnish government and the UPRC, instead of America," Arvo said. "It makes sense, though I'll miss seeing you all so regularly."

"You'll still come visit though, right?"

"Of course! And you can come visit me in Finland whenever you like."

"Enough work talk. You folks're spoiling the game," Gary said, though he smirked as he did. "We've got a beautiful day, good company, and the Cubbies are kicking ass. Couldn't ask for more."

Anya looked at Gary over Samaira's head and smiled at him, which he returned. Pan asked him and Riley some question about why the Cubs were the "good team," and both men began to exuberantly argue over him. Tori and Arvo were busy discussing what sorts of food were good in Finland, a conversation which resulted in Tori making a variety of skeptical faces, the doctor laughing as she did.

Anya sighed with contentment.

The sky was so blue, the grass so green; war and death and killer aliens, so distant.

Her hand entwined with Samaira's as they leaned back in their seats to watch the game, and bask in the company of their friends.

FROM SPACE #3

From the message logs of Luorian Security Force Special Operatives (Translated from Luorian Basic):

Operative 1: Primary squad reporting in. Levels one through ten secured.

Operative 6: Secondary squad reporting in. Levels eleven through twenty secured.

Operative 11: Tertiary squad reporting in. Levels twenty-one through twenty-six secured.

Operative 1: Central Command, confirm: Enclave secured.

Central Command: Engineers' Enclave has been secured, confirmed.

Defense Minister Feuxellian: Are the Engineers detained? Specifically the Prime and the Grands.

Central Command: Squads to confirm.

Operative 1: We have the Prime Engineer, 183 Elders, and 509 Initiates accounted for. Fifteen fatalities from the Initiates.

Operative 6: We have secured four of the Grand Engineers. We've also detained 215 Elders and 435 Initiates. No fatalities.

Operative 11: Five Grand Engineers are in our custody, along with 107 Elders and 720 Initiates. Two fatalities from the Initiates.

Central Command: Confirmed.

Defense Minister Feuxellian: Operatives from Primary and Tertiary squads will report to the accountability court to review fatalities. Otherwise, good work. Sounds like you got them all. What about the Archive?

Operative 1: The Prime claimed to have deleted everything. We're scanning their databases now and it seems like they're telling the truth. Nothing here, yet.

Defense Minister Feuxellian: Dammit! Get the Prime and all nine of the Grands to an interrogation site. I want Class 1-1 psionics on location by the time they arrive. And don't let Qohara tell you they're not warranted. If she gives you any resistance, contact the Prime Minister directly.

Central Command: At once, Defense Minister.

Operative 6: Central, can you confirm the current life scans of the Enclave minus operatives, the life signs immediately prior to our breaching the Enclave, as well as life scans received from the Intelligence Ministry one hour, and one day before?

Defense Minister Feuxellian: Something the matter?

Operative 6: Apologies, Defense Minister. Going over the numbers from the intel reports. Possibly a mistake on my part.

Defense Minister Feuxellian: Carry on. Central?

Central Command: 2,181 life signs prior to breach. 2,164 life signs post-breach, which accounts for the seventeen total fatalities and does not include operative life signs. There were 2,181 life signs one hour before breach. Yesterday there were… ah. Intelligence reports indicate there were 2,183 life signs aboard the Enclave one day prior.

Defense Minister Feuxellian: Two? Two of them? All this preparation and hunting and spying and two of the gods' cursed Engineers escaped?

Operative 1: The intel reports state there's only a total of 2,182 Engineers. Somebody else was here, then left with one Engineer.

Operative 6: They must have known we were coming. Dumped the Archive backups, and sent the pair off. How'd they know?

Defense Minister Feuxellian: It's all those blasted comm spikes Qohara kept sending! They were sloppy, and the Engineers caught most of them. They knew we were closing in so they sent off whoever and whatever they could. Probably the best Engineer they had, minus the Prime and Grands. They knew we'd spot them missing right away.

Damn. Damn! So close, after all this time, and now it's all gone down the drain because of two blasted—

Operative 1: Defense Minister, There's some data left behind. Looks like a broadcast of some kind from yesterday. Encoded.

Defense Minister Feuxellian: Better than nothing. Send it to my personal receiver and the Prime Minister's. And tell Qohara to get off her tail and get me those psionics!

Central Command: At once, Defense Minister. All squads: begin transport of prisoners to containment ships. Commence final data sweeps, and place charges for demolition.

Operative 1: Confirmed. All squads, move out!

———————

From a recovered transmission from the Engineer's Enclave (Translated from Luorian Basic):

Grand Engineer Black-3: Archive back-ups have been removed by 97%. We predict they will be eliminated entirely by the time the Luorian Security Forces arrive. Are you sure this is wise, Mr. Prospector?

Mr. Prospector: Of course not! My goodness, this could all end so terribly for everyone. But nothing's certain, Black. Sometimes you just have to roll the dice. Like we did with Earth. That turned out pretty well, didn't it?

Grand Engineer Black-3: Against our projections, yes. However, you are the dice-roller, Mr. Prospector. We have tried to adhere to our guiding principles and avoid our passions and intuitions since our... mistake. But maybe that was just another error. We regret that we must once again ask you to save us, to save others, from our decisions.

Mr. Prospector: Nobody makes a "mistake," that big by themselves, Black. I'm just paying my own penance. And his.

Grand Engineer Black-3: And you are certain you did not want to take one of the more experienced Elders with you?

Mr. Prospector: I've found they tend to lose familiarity with the Archive once they ascend to an oversight position. No, this little Initiate suits me fine.

Initiate Engineer Red-507: Th-this one is humbled by your confidence, M-Mr. Prospector!

Grand Engineer Black-3: That one has a number of errors on record.

Mr. Prospector: As do we all. Perfect is the enemy of good, Black. That's something I learned they say on Earth, recently. I rather like it. Something about eggs breaking and a kind of breakfast food as well.

Grand Engineer Black-3: I do not entirely agree with this course of action, but the Prime Engineer has spoken, and you have served us faithfully for many years. If our projections were wrong before, then perhaps they can be wrong again.

Initiate Engineer Red-507: This one will return for you and the others, Grand Engineer! This one is certain!

Mr. Prospector: An admirable spirit, but first we need to get away from all this Luorian-controlled space, and find somewhere to reestablish the Archive communications and full functionality with Earth. Traveling with the last one makes me more than a bit paranoid.

Grand Engineer Black-3: Though I do not put much weight in it: good luck to you both.

Mr. Prospector: Farewell, Black. We'll meet again. Prepare for subspace entry, Initiate. I'll check on our food and water.

Initiate Engineer Red-507: Food and water?

Mr. Prospector: Did you not stock the ship before launch?

Initiate Engineer Red-507: Oh. Oops.

––––––

From a letter sent to Prime Minister Axun, from the Cosmic Wardens (Translated from Luorian Basic)

To His Esteemed Prime Minister, Artran Axun:

I've received your report regarding the situation. Any race using the Archive to defeat a lesser Herald of the gnosiphages is of concern to the Wardens. That it is Earth is even more serious. However, as much as I would like to, I cannot devote the forces required for such a situation.

The Vet-Har Empire has fully invaded the Tuhd system, and several planets have already fallen. Word is that the Emperor himself has taken to spearheading the attack within Tuhd. I do not suspect you wish me to remove the Wardens I have stationed there until that situation is resolved.

The gnosiphage splinter swarms we discussed recently are merging, and may contain an ascended Herald, as well as a potential rift. If this is the case, I will need to be on the front lines myself, along with some of our strongest Wardens.

The star in the Gelwyn system is going nova, and while the Luorian Galactic Union may not care about frontier settlements, the Wardens give their assistance to all, if the cause is just. Settlers there require rescue, and the Wardens overseeing the operation will not be of assistance until they have been properly evacuated. Similar such events across the galaxy and smaller gnosiphage swarms demand our attention.

However, I gave you my word, and the word of the Wardens is sacred. I am taking three Warden Errants from patrolling the sectors that are being harried by the Henahkten Marauders. Your security teams should be enough to handle some pirates on their own, for a while.

Though the Warden Errants are new to our order, they maintain the dignity, virtue, and courage demanded of us all. They will secure Earth until your own forces are in a better position to respond, or I can send further assistance.

At this time, that is the best myself, and the Warden Council, are able and willing to do. We hope it will be enough.

Justice and Virtue,

Warden Commander Soqloa

ACKNOWLEDGMENTS

As before, while writing may be done in solitude initially, it's the efforts of many people that bring that writing together into a published book. I was not, and am never alone in my work, and I have a lot of wonderful people and groups to thank.

First, foremost, and forever: my wife and family. You were there from the start, and you've never left. Thank you.

Enzo Fernandez, artist extraordinaire: You did it again, you wonderful, outstanding man. You can see more of Enzo's amazing work by following him on Twitter @pkblitz.

Scott and Noelle: still champs, still amazing.

My patrons, particularly Dustin: thank you for being patient and supportive, and giving me your kind words I won't lie: the money is very nice, too.

To the members of my Discord, but most especially StrayHero, jjffjhjf, and the rest of the Typo Hunters: thank you for sweeping up after my boneheadedness when it comes to squashing errors. By the way, you, Fellow Reader, reading this: if you find an error or mistake or whatever: swing by the Discord (linked in the "Stay in Touch" section ahead) and let me know and I'll fix it. Obviously I try and catch as many as I can, but I'm only human.

There are a lot of really delightful reader and author communities out there that I owe a successful Book 1 launch to, but chief among them are the ProgressionFantasy and LitRPG subreddits and the wonderful mods and posters, as well as a couple of author guilds I owe for the laughs, advice, and camaraderie. Also, big shoutout to the imgur community for getting me to Most Viral that time in January. Made my month!

And I now have the delight of thanking the fine people at Podium Audio, who reached out after Book 1's launch with an offer to turn this weird little series into some excellent audiobooks. To all the fine people at Podium, thank you, and to Stephanie Savannah, the narrator, thank you for bringing my story to life with your amazing talent.

Finally, but so vitally, thank you, Fellow Reader. If you're still here after two books, I hope to see you in the third. Time is fleeting, stories are many, and it means more than I can say that you chose to spend your time with me and with this story. If I'm lucky, I'll see you next time.

Take care of yourself, and each other.

———

All the Best,
    Justin "JayAck" Ackerknecht

LITRPG

LitRPG Group

To learn more about LitRPG, talk to authors including myself, and just have an awesome time, please join the LitRPG Group.

FACEBOOK GROUPS

Facebook Groups for LitRPG, Gamelit, Progression Fantasy, and more

———

A lot of these groups help authors like me, and readers like you find other great books in the growing LitRPG/Gamelit/Progression Fantasy genre. If you liked this book, there's a very good chance you'll like some other books that are frequently talked about in these groups. Also, they're generally full of nice people who post funny memes.

Gamelit Society
LitRPG Books
LitRPG Forum
LitRPG Releases
Fantasy Nation
Science Fiction and Fantasy Book Fans

STAY IN TOUCH

If you'd like to get updates about anything I'm working on (including the sequels to this very story) you can find me on-line at www.jjackerknecht.com and sign up for my newsletter there (assuming I've gotten it up and running).

If you have business or other inquiries, you can e-mail me at jayack@jjackerknecht.com

Previews of upcoming work, including advanced chapters of my current projects, are at https://www.patreon.com/jayack which is also a great way to support me between releases if you're so inclined.

On Twitter, I'm likely retweeting cool artwork very talented artists have done along with absurd shitposts if you'd like to follow me at https://twitter.com/jjackerknecht or just search for @jjackerknecht.

There's also a Discord that you can come by to chat at https://discord.gg/un2wVMf

Hope to see you there!

ABOUT THE AUTHOR

Hello there! I know these are usually done in third-person or something, but that feels weird to write about myself like that.

First, I've been writing since before I properly knew the alphabet. I'd get my parents to write for me while I dictated. Once I was able to, I spent most of my waking moments drawing and writing stories of my own, or inhaling the stories of others through books, comics, video games, and later anime and manga.

I was born in Arizona, raised in California, and then moved back to Arizona for college. I definitely preferred California. Post-college, I moved to South Korea, where I spent about a decade living between the cities of Ulsan, Suwon, and Seogwipo. I'm currently living next to several large, pastoral sheep fields in the UK.

I've had a lot of jobs over my life: a snake handler, a janitor, a bus-boy, an accountant, a cashier, a car-washer, an associate professor, and a few others. Presently, I'm working as a writer. Hopefully this'll be a permanent gig, as it's my favorite one by far, and I've been doing it for free for years anyway. Fingers crossed it works out!

www.ingramcontent.com/pod-product-compliance
Lightning Source LLC
Chambersburg PA
CBHW061505020726
47502CB00006B/1944